Compiled & Edited by
Ben Thomas & D Kershaw

Also available from Black Hare Press

BHP WRITERS' GROUP SPECIAL EDITIONS

STORMING AREA 51
EERIE CHRISTMAS
BAD ROMANCE
TWENTY TWENTY
SCHOOL'S IN

OTHER VOLUMES

DEEP SPACE
WHAT IF?
KEY TO THE KINGDOM
BEYOND THE REALM
DEEP SEA
WETWARE DRABBLES
WETWARE
BANNED DRABBLES
BANNED

AUTHOR LED PROJECTS

PASSENGER 13
QUIETUS 13
ZERO HOUR 2113

DARK MOMENTS

YEAR ONE
YEAR TWO

DARK DRABBLES

WORLDS
ANGELS
MONSTERS
BEYOND
UNRAVEL
APOCALYPSE
LOVE
HATE
OCEANS
ANCIENTS

SEVEN DEADLY SINS

PRIDE
LUST
SLOTH
ENVY
GREED
GLUTTONY
WRATH

Twitter: @BlackHarePress
Facebook: BlackHarePress
Website: www.BlackHarePress.com

Table of Contents

NIGHTMARES MADE FLESH

by Sam M. Phillips

Holistic haven of a heavy soul, shuddering into life as the levels rise to rinse us free of the fallout of doubt; double bass kicks craving my attention, bent around a tube, tuberculosis lungs and halitosis breath, death metal rattle to awaken the kraken.

"You ready yet?" asks Jones, and I shrug, look down at my feet, reach over, twiddle thoughtfully with the screws like I know what I'm doing. I give a few test taps, raps of raven call which fall on loose feet. I nod and the world wakes up.

Crash falling as the stalling strum of guitars bars off the

rest of existence, all consciousness focused around the locus of vibrating membranes.

It is the echo call of the wild in the depths of the earth, bubbling up through a metal band, clinging to your throat and tearing out your jugular.

I don't know if you could call us "good" but there is something there. Something beyond fear, yet invoking the primal, and I feel like getting laid tonight, so I push myself hard into my drum kit, thrash my body, and transform into the were-beast I know I can become when the full moon sound echoes deep in my heart.

Elation at the destruction of all modes of being, I'm seeing red and I don't care if I drop dead the next moment. Hex and torment, foment and terror, an error in our DNA…

In the end, I just want to play.

***

"That was crazy! You're a madman," she says, and I nod, smile, and let her rev me up. I could talk it up myself, but she's doing a pretty good job.

"Thanks," I say, pretend to look around, not be so interested in her.

"That's your first gig? It was wild!"

"Umm, yeah."

The lights in the place are hot and heavy, casting long shadows. We're playing out the back of a tattoo parlour, some type of art exhibition, and the displays dot the yard leading to the stage at the back. Farther forward is the glass wall of the back of the store, framed by brick walls covered in freshly painted murals. Riots of colour and me, still sober, wanting to get fucked up.

I see the person I'm looking for—the store owner.

"Hey, excuse me for a moment," I think I say, but I hear an echo bouncing off the walls, my voice saying, "Can you fuck off a minute?"

Walking over to the tall German bastard, I slap a palm and fist bump.

"Hey, Kroner, what's going on?" I ask, nodding at his big bag of tricks.

He nods his stupid cowboy hat, kicks his snake leather boots in the sand. "Yeah, yeah! Come on, try it, fucking Pez dispenser, man!"

I take the pill, and it *is* shaped like a Pez.

"What the fuck is this shit?" I ask, but nicely, grateful for what I hope is drugs, not just bloody candy.

"Eccy, bruz, dripped in acid. You're going far out, man. Look at this art!"

His eyes are like UFOs, flying saucers escaping out of the atmosphere. I see my reflection in their heavy depths and want in. Black pools to reveal the memories, crushing comedowns to balance the euphoria. For a moment, I shudder in fear and nearly drop the pill.

"Take it!" he says, throwing another one in his mouth, and I do.

Of course nothing happens.

"See you in a while, if you're still on the planet!"

"Yeah, yeah."

I'm already walking.

***

The colours are swirling in a euphoria that tips me upside down into a pit of hell. The demons are coming out of the walls and then turning into "error statements" where my consciousness cannot seem to fathom what they are. It's like my mind is censoring itself, and I stumble across the yard, the whole earth tipping beneath my feet.

For a while, there I lie on the giant ball which is the globe of the world we live on, and I fear I might slide off, so I fight it, try to balance, and for a time, I manage it.

Then she comes back and breaks the spell. I suppose it was always going to happen.

"You okay, man?" she asks, hair growing out of her face like green, green grass.

I sit up, or am dragged up.

"You're beautiful," I say, and I mean it, her face popping like a bubble, then growing back, the colours dancing in my mind.

"Oh, thanks!" she says and beams, and for a moment she looks like a wolf, ready to eat me, and I tremble with fear.

She sees me shake and laughs. "Oh, man, you need to sit down. Come on, let's go inside."

Then she's hugging me and it feels good, even as I feel her tap into my life force, suck me dry.

My eyeballs shudder in their sockets.'

***

Brogan is designing something, and I know he's into occult shit. I look over his shoulder, and I try to get something from it, from the shapes he's conjuring, and I guess I'm down for whatever tonight.

"I'm getting this tattooed on the back of my neck," he says, pointing at the magical symbol. I see it writhing like a snake, changing and living. I can hear it whisper to me, or scream, and I back off a step.

"I should get a tattoo," I say, and begin shaking with anxiety-induced adrenaline.

"What are you going to get?" he asks.

"Well, I don't know."

"Just get anything, man, it's punk rock!"

"We're in a metal band…"

"That's what I said, it's fucking punk rock!"

"Okay, can I get this?" I point at the symbol he's drawn.

"Hell, yeah, man, blood brothers. Brand for life!"

"Brand?"

"Band for life, brother!"

"I don't want to be banned for life; I like this shop."

"Shut the fuck up and sit in the chair."

***

The guy tattooing me is called the Mechanic, and I'm terrified of him. People say he "fixes things," and I believe them. He's carving the symbol into my wrist with his angry, burring needle gun, a swarm of killer bees filling my ears with the threat that I'm the one, I'm the one stinging myself and that I'm full of hate.

"Why do I hate myself?" he asks, but he says it in my voice, with his lips moving, and I'm paralysed, wondering which of us actually said it.

"I don't know, maybe I asked for it, but it was just stupid, you know."

This time I'm sure it's him, but the echo inside my mind makes me unsure. Now he's talking about scars, something about stabbing, an argument, and it all cycling back around again, turning into a demon licking my ear, telling me sweet nothings which I'll never forget, or perhaps never knew.

I shake my head and try to forget the demon speech echoing up through the buzz of the needle darting in and out of my skin like a possessed humming bird.

"You sure you want to be putting that shit into me?" I ask, and I'm relieved to feel my voice leaving my own body.

"What shit is that?"

"Oh, all your issues, with that stabbing… I feel it infecting my arm."

He laughs. "Did I tell you about the cut-off extension cord I keep in my trunk?"

"No…"

"So, this fucking guy owes me money, and I see him on the street, buying a taco… 'Fuck this', I say to myself. 'If he's got taco money, he can fucking pay me.'"

I black out for a second, dragged into the infinite abyss of the black ink. Time seems to swirl and distort, but when I come back, I realise it must be half an hour later—he's finishing the tattoo—but it's like no time has passed in the story.

"And so I throw him in the fucking trunk of my car with

the extension cord, let him see it, and he freaks out, pisses in my fucking car!"

I look at the tattoo; it's like a hot brand he's marked me with.

"I got him in my garage," he continues. "Plug that baby in to a power point, whip the cunt with it till he spills."

"Spills what?"

"His guts."

"You cut him open?"

"No, that was my uncle." He lifts his white wife beater. "Here, here, here." He points at the knife wounds in his gut. They are like giant white maggots writhing through his pallid flesh. I look up at his face, and it's a mask of pain reflected as anger. I shudder.

"So, the guy gave you the money?"

The Mechanic sits, sprays soapy water on the fresh tattoo, and wipes it down. "Fucked if I know."

***

Worms are crawling beneath my skin, and I look at the tattoo, thinking it's alive. It's certainly moving, changing shape, meaning God one moment, Satan the next, and I'm in the middle, trying to be human, feeling my breath rising and falling too heavily, and time, always time flowing away.

It's the acid. It never lets you be in the moment; you're always reaching for the next moment, and the next.

"That's deep," says the girl, and I turn to her. I didn't realise she was there. We're hugging.

"Did I say something?" I say, and she just looks into space like she's deaf.

Rather than puzzle this shit out, I take her by the hand and walk out to the ocean. There's some commotion going on down in the dark of the beach, yelling and splashing. I ignore it and take her face in my hands. She has tattoos on her face…faces within faces…screaming…

We kiss.

***

I am enmeshed. I am a demon. I have four arms, four legs, two sets of genitals, and breasts. I have a goat's head and I'm horny.

I stand under a streetlight, swallowing myself like an endless, curled snake.

It is pleasurable; it is horror. It is nighttime, and I feel alone, even as I become one with her.

I wish I never got this stupid tattoo. I feel it spinning its strands of fate. Lines within lines become a concrete image and dissolve into abstract symbolism.

Who are you to haunt me? Who are you to speak?

We pull apart.

"You're pretty special, you know that?" she says to me, hugging me.

I want to pull away from her, her skin burning like acid.

***

The band gathers at the girl's house for a party. Her housemate Jessie is chasing me around, trying to tackle me into the dirt. I sidestep her, let her fall on her face. She gets up, all dirty, and has stories about it. Someone hoses her down with the garden hose. She strips off naked and says her grandma used to do this to her when she was younger. It gets oddly sexual as she dances in a circle in the water's spray.

She's messed up.

We all are.

***

"There's some weed for you, do you want a drink?" the girl asks me, and I nod. She brings me a beer as I'm packing a pipe. I get rip, snorted, stoned off the back of the ecstasy and acid, and it pings both back up, but with a mellower edge now as we sit around and shoot the shit about the gig and the future.

I guess everyone wants to be a rock star. Jones has even gone on a trip to get some cocaine—shire shit, which is basically diesel baked to a powder in an oven.

Oh well, we don't all get to actually *be* rock stars.

But for now, with a girl on my arm and drugs in my blood, I feel okay, a reasonable approximation of important, or being on the verge of important.

The dark of night closes in like a veil, and I shiver, as Jessie's body glistens wet in the full moon, transforming into a beast and then disappearing into the inky blackness.

What has swallowed her up?

No one ever mentions her again, and I wonder if she was ever real. I get to thinking that her grandma was a witch and simply ate her.

It's less sad than the stories Jessie tells. No one's grandma is that fucked up.

I look at the tattoo and try to count the legs, the genitals. They are getting fewer, at least. I look at my watch.

It is nearly midnight.

***

The cocaine—or at least an approximation of it—has arrived.

I'm shaking like a leaf. I don't really need more drugs, but I don't want to look like a pussy in front of *her*. You can feel the sexual tension, but it's become soft with too many drugs already, and I wonder when it's going to pick us up and dump us breathless on some rocky beach of desolation.

Sex has a comedown too, but I'm more afraid of this diesel fuel.

Jones is talking about the drugs on the glass countertop as he cuts it into lines. He sees me shaking.

"I get it, you're nervous. Get used to it, my friend, we're going to the top!"

He snorts a line, gives the girl the rolled up note. I'm next, and I barely cough the bitter tang down the back of my throat. The Mechanic has his, and we all jump up and down to the metal music blaring on the stereo. It's the demo track of our band.

I feel like a god for a lifetime or ten minutes.

Then I need a pipe and sit down. Even rock stars get tired of themselves.

***

Mirrors aren't your friends. Mirrors make your face stretch like that of a werewolf, your nose growing long and hairy. You can see all the pores on your skin and suddenly you're a zombie. You open your mouth; there are the fangs of a vampire.

The acid is experiencing a revival, and I'm getting the good old terrors.

***

"When you get tired, my room is just through there." She points. "So just crash out whenever you want and I'll join you when I'm ready." She smiles, and her flesh feels soft, like a vat of jelly I sink my arms into up to the elbows.

She goes back to doing more drugs and drinking straight from the goon sack. I've seen my bandmates do the whole all-nighter on the goon sack. It's a vicious hangover the next day. Coupled with the diesel comedown, I'm wondering when, if ever, we're going to have the good sex her body has been promising all night.

***

The Mechanic is telling a story and it's fucked up.

"So, she's in the fucking ocean, screaming 'I don't want to live anymore', and I'm trying to drag her back in, and I can't fucking swim, and she knows it. I'm like, 'Don't do this to me'. I'm on the tips of my toes, trying to grip the sand, holding onto her with just my fingers, and the waves are buffeting us. ”

We're all staring at him in a drug stupor.

"And this fucking *thing* comes up and pulls her out to sea…so, yeah. She's dead."

He does another line.

So *that's* the commotion I heard down on the beach earlier.

Maybe he murdered his wife tonight.

***

The sun comes up, and it's not a welcome addition to the party. It shines like a mighty demon of hate and anguish.

We still drink and do drugs, but everything is slowing down. I haven't crashed yet, but it is only in a superhuman effort to stay awake long enough to actually get laid while the drugs are still in effect. No one wants to be woken up to comedown self-hate sex.

***

I can't outlast her, not like this; I need some food, or sugar, or something. Jones is going to the service station.

"You want anything?" he asks. I look at the girl, at the

Mechanic; they're talking about something, smiling.

"Yeah, but I'll come, I need some orange juice; I'm starting to feel the fear."

"Tell me about it," says Jones, his eyes shining like glass, beard ragged, last smoke dangling from cracked lips.

***

We return and walk up the side of the house. The world outside is a terror I cannot even begin to describe, but orange juice is a treasure to cure all ills.

In the backyard, we find Brogan transformed into a bizarre beast, but he's curled up in the dog's bed, so he's not doing us any harm. He has half a goon sack as a pillow and growls contentedly.

There's no sign of anyone else. We pack a pipe because that's the priority and take the necessary drags to feel human.

Jones settles in to enjoy his cigarettes and a few more pipes while I search for the girl. I can't find her anywhere, so I figure she's gone to bed.

Finally, it's time for sex and I feel a flood of relief wash the burning tang of the quaking comedown from my blood.

I go back and have a couple of quick pipes, the weed

hot and heavy in my throat, fuelling thoughts of flesh. The burning spreads through my body and lights up my dick.

"See you on the other side," I say to Jones, but he's off in a haze, staring into the distance like some quaked out Vietnam vet. I try not to look at him for too long or I'll catch the fear.

In through the house to the girl's door, I pause outside, run my fingers through my hair, and take a deep breath.

I knock.

Nothing happens.

She must be asleep already. I curse myself for leaving. I open the door.

The Mechanic briefly looks up from behind the girl, his face a distorted, bestial mask.

For a second I'm confused; I don't know what I'm looking at.

"What do you think you're doing?" the girl asks.

She's naked, her breast swinging as the Mechanic does his thing, ignoring me.

"I…I thought…"

I shake my head as if trying to clear an illusion. The two of them blend into one being, a demon, reflecting back all my self-hate and mocking me with its animal lust. I back out of the room and close the door. Convinced the demon will come for me, too, I quickly go outside and pack a pipe, desperate to escape.

I claw at the tattoo on my arm, frantic to remove the mark the beast has carved into my flesh.

BLACK HARE PRESS

SAM M. PHILLIPS is the co-founder of Zombie Pirate Publishing, producing short story anthologies and helping emerging writers. His own work has appeared in dozens of anthologies and magazines such as Full Metal Horror and World War Four. He recently published his debut novella, SCIENCE FICTION DOUBLE FEATURE: Phosphorus & Into The Eye.

He lives in northern New South Wales, Australia, and enjoys reading, walking, and playing drums in the death metal band Decryptus. He is also a prolific poet and his poetry can be read on his blog.

Bibliography

FLASH FICTION ADDICTION: 101 Short Short Stories, Zombie Pirate Publishing, 2019

FULL METAL HORROR 2: A Bloodstained Anthology, Zombie Pirate Publishing, 2019

FULL METAL HORROR: A Monstrous Anthology, Zombie Pirate Publishing, 2018

PHUKET TATTOO: Crazy Tales of Far Away Places, Zombie Pirate Publishing, 2018

Relationship Add Vice: A Thrilling Mashup of Romance and Crime, Zombie Pirate Publishing, 2017

SCIENCE FICTION DOUBLE FEATURE: Phosphorus & Into The Eye, Zombie Pirate Publishing, 2019

The Collapsar Directive: A Science Fiction Anthology, Zombie Pirate Publishing, 2017

WITCHES VS WIZARDS: A Fantasy Anthology, Zombie Pirate Publishing, 2018

WORLD WAR FOUR: A Science Fiction Anthology, Zombie Pirate Publishing, 2019

Connect
Blog: bigconfusingwords.wordpress.com

BODY ELECTRIC

by Tim Mendees

"Listen!" Ned hissed, eyes wide and dilated, as the sound undulated and skipped. "Hear it?"

Steve took a long drag on the tarry-black stub of a pungent reefer burning his bottom lip. "Nah, man," he replied, dropping the dog end into an empty beer can. The cinder sizzled and died as he shook the dregs from side to side.

"Damn," Ned grumbled, lifting the needle and replacing it in the desired groove. "Now, pay attention, man," he instructed his stoned compadre. As he began to wind the turntable backwards, a jumble of sounds made his red eyes burn with feverish excitement. "There! Heard it?"

Steve grinned widely. "Yeah, man!" he drawled, sounding like an inebriated buffalo. "He said 'Hell Sausage!'"

Ned spat warm super-strength lager over the lurid picture of the Devil cavorting with a lady in leather on the album sleeve. "Nah! You twat!" he bellowed beneath chokes and splutters. "He said 'Hail Satan!' Why in the name of the devil's balls would he say 'Hell Sausage'?"

"Dunno," Steve mused, blinking his bloodshot eyes. "Maybe he's talking about the devil's knob or something."

Ned huffed and rolled his eyes. "This isn't getting us anywhere." He put the needle back at the start of the LP and set it going. Harsh, speed metal guitars burst from the tatty cabinet speakers. Ned cracked open another beer and started to head bang enthusiastically. His stringy black hair whipped the glossy magazine posters of naked girls on big motorbikes that adorned his wall with a sharp *thwap!* Steve grunted in approval and grabbed a can. After a couple of gulps, he joined Ned in a frenzy of air guitar.

It often went like this. After reading about the heavy metal band Judas Priest being put on trial in America, they had become obsessed with backmasking. It was alleged that Judas Priest incited a suicide pact through hiding the phrase "Do It" in one of their songs. Of course, it was thrown out of court after the singer demonstrated that you could decipher any old crap from playing songs backwards, including the phrase "I asked her for a peppermint, she said she would get one."

Nevertheless, Ned and Steve were convinced that somewhere amongst their stacks of scratchy metal albums lurked the key to satanic power—a message from the Devil himself. In their addled minds, this was their fast track to wealth, fame, and most importantly, chicks.

As the nineties dawned, ushering in a sea change in music, they had found themselves becoming swiftly unfashionable. Grunge and industrial rock had started to filter in from the States, and it looked to many that metal was dead. Not on Ned and Steve's watch! They saw themselves as crusaders, the last bastion of NWOBHM—the Devil's house band.

The second track started in a squeal of fret masturbation. This was one of the slower ones. Though, that was like saying that formula three was slow compared to formula one; it still galloped along at a million miles per hour. It was Ned's turn to do rolling duties, and he plonked himself down on a beanbag with a copy of Anton LaVey's *Satanic Bible* containing his spliff paraphernalia in his lap. Steve continued to rock out, showering the carpet in sweat and beer.

As the track progressed, it inevitably hit the point

where they had been trying the backmasking. The heavy high-fidelity cartridge had gouged a deep scratch in the vinyl and skipped harshly when it hit.

"Bollocks!" Steve boomed and kicked the desk under the record player. "That's another record knackered. We need to find a better way of doing this, man." He righted the needle and the song played on. He plopped down on another beanbag opposite Ned.

Ned paused in his task for a second. He was currently engrossed in sticking Rizla papers together to form a large sheet—he intended to produce the stoners equivalent of origami: the Camberwell Carrot. "I had a thought about that, man. Dan down at Cove Records has a tape for me. It's supposed to be the one. The real deal."

"Wow, man!" Steve beamed. "What is it?"

"Some crazy industrial metal band from Massachusetts. They all disappeared after recording the album. Dan reckons that they live in Lucifer's palace."

"Whoa! Hell?" Steve rubbed his wiry ginger beard.

"Nah, the casino in Vegas. Imagine the chicks, man. Swimming pools. Poker tables. Rock n' roll, man."

"Yeah! Bang on, man!" Steve raised the devil's horn sign and banged his head…then stopped and looked at Ned quizzically. "Tape?"

"Yeah."

"How are we gonna play a tape backwards? It's not like a turntable, man. You can't just drag it with your finger."

"I know that, you donkey, and I came up with a solution." He carefully picked apart a Marlboro and sprinkled the dry tobacco along a stiff crease he had made in his masterpiece. "We could go down the studio, man. Use the desk. You can run it backwards on that."

"Awesome!" Steve grinned and flashed the horns again. "Hey, we could take our gear and have a jam."

Ned nodded in quiet resignation. They hadn't played together since their drummer, Lee, the traitor, had cut his hair and got himself a job in accountancy. Steve wanted to find a new drummer and start over; Ned wanted to get Lee back. It was a common argument that Ned was far too stoned and drunk to have right then. He thought for a second, maybe a good jam session would do him good. "I'll get the tape tomorrow and see if Dan has any acid. You talk to Stan at the studio. He still owes me for a sleeve of fags I brought him back from holiday; tell him if he lets us have it for the night, I'll call it quits."

Steve nodded in approval. The track changed again. It was back to warp speed. Steve rose unsteadily and resumed his frantic moshing. Ned finished rolling his monster joint and sparked it into life. A dopey grin spread across his stubbly face as the smoke filled his lungs. Tomorrow was going to be awesome!

***

Steve's day had dragged. The more he had stared at the clock, the slower it had seemed to go. Every tawdry household item that he ran through the barcode scanner was met with contempt. Every customer greeted with a surly expression. Soon, when he and Ned manage to contact the Devil and cut a deal, the checkout at Kwiksave would be a distant memory. A blip on an otherwise glorious existence. And these people… They would bow before him.

Stan had readily agreed to let them have the studio for the night. It wasn't booked in any case, and it got him off the hook for a fiver that he didn't have, so everyone's a winner. Steve had gone around to Stan's basement flat on his lunch break, then popped to the shop to stock up on cigarettes and rolling papers. All that remained was to make it through the final turgid hours of his shift, then use his staff discount on a crate of Special Brew.

Ned's day hadn't made it off the starting blocks. He worked as a window cleaner, and due to the beer sloshing around in his system, he had made it halfway up the ladder, then had to stop and vomit in his bucket. Deciding that it wasn't happening, he slunk back home and hit the mattress for a few sweaty, churning hours.

Finally rousing himself mid-afternoon, Ned had headed into town and made a beeline for his own personal Mecca—Cove Records. Frantic thrash metal riffs and a dense cloud of cigarette smoke greeted him as he stepped through the shop's hallowed portal. Dan sat behind the desk wiping an old Sabbath record with an ether-soaked rag.

"Hey, man!" Ned hollered above the din. "How's it going?"

It took Dan a moment to register that he had been addressed. Something of a casualty, Dan had owned the small but well-stocked shop since the mid-seventies and had dropped more acid than Timothy Leary. "Ahh," he drawled. "Hey, Ned. What's shakin'?"

"We got the studio tonight." Ned grinned. "Gonna call on the big guy. Got the tape?"

"Tape?" Dan brushed a ratty dreadlock out of his eyes, blinked twice… Then, "Ahh, yeah. Right here." He held out a cassette for Ned. "That's going to be a collector's item. They are burnin' all the copies of it over in America."

"Wow!" Ned was impressed. Ritual burnings of albums were akin to a badge of honour in his view. "It must be the real deal then."

"Yeah, people have gone mad listenin' to it and

everything."

"How much you want for it, man?"

"Fiver." Dan held out his grubby palm.

"Deal." Ned rummaged in the pocket of his patch-adorned denim cut-off jacket. "You got any tabs, man?"

Dan grinned. "Of course."

Ned passed him a ten-pound note. "Hit me up, baby!"

Once the deal was done and the sheet of blotting paper was tucked into his wallet, Ned left the shop clutching the tape like it was a holy relic. The artwork was bleak, just a series of interlocking iridescent spheres on a plain black background. His lips moved as he mouthed the title of the album, *All in One and One in All*. It gave him a chill. The band's name was similarly full of evil portent: Opener of the Way. Ned could feel it in his water, *this* was the one—the musical key to unlocking the gates of Hell.

***

Ned was on his hands and knees when Steve crashed through the studio door, a crate of beer under one arm and his bass guitar slung over his opposing shoulder.

"Ned, man, what you doin'?"

Ned was in the process of painting a large pentagram on the floor using a large decorator's brush dipped in a viscous red liquid.

Steve's eyes widened. "Is that blood, man?"

"Nah, man." Ned shook his head in frustration. "It's Dulux. The butcher had already turned all the pig blood into black puddings."

Next to the tub of claret paint was a shopping bag stuffed full with tealights and a large box of cooks' matches. "Candles?" Steve asked.

"Yeah, the hardware shop had run out of anything bigger than tealights. If we put a bunch of them around the place, it should make His Satanic Majesty feel at home."

Steve shrugged and opened a can. Ned did a crab-like pincer gesture with his right hand. Steve knew what he needed and passed him a beer. After all, painting a ten-foot pentagram is thirsty work. Steve picked up the bag of small candles and started to place them around Ned's *art* in a perfect circle. "Isn't Stan going to be pissed that you painted the floor, man?" he asked.

"Nah. Stan's well up for it. Said it would add to the ambience. He gave me the brush." Ned made a final couple of brush strokes. "There. Now, let's get smashed."

The next few hours passed in a blur of booze and marijuana. Ned and Steve rocked out to the tape, blasted through the studio speakers forwards. Neither man had given much thought to embracing Industrial music before… But now, Steve especially had started to romance the idea of foregoing a drummer altogether in favour of a drum machine, sampler, and Atari ST. As Ned pointed out, you only have to kick a computer once to make it do what you want, unlike most drummers. They wouldn't be the last stalwarts of heavy metal to fully embrace emerging technology.

Ned was excited about playing for the first time in a very long time. He sat on an amplifier battering his Fender Stratocaster copy into oblivion along with the pulverising beats and "donkey with a sore throat" vocals. They had decided to wait until midnight to perform the ritual. At the allotted time of half-past ten, they would drop the acid. This meant that they would be peaking at just about midnight. Then they would don their instruments, flip the tape, and say a big hello to Beelzebub.

***

The satisfying pop and hum of the amplifiers kicking into life sent a warm fuzzy feeling down Steve's extremities, his battered, second-hand Yamaha bass feeling powerful in his clammy hands. Ned stood across from him, fiddling with the tone dial on his six-string. After what seemed like forever, the one-note intro, originally the outro, fired into pneumatic beats, and the LCD of Ned's black plastic watch flicked to a line of zeros.

What was so genius about the choice of a straight four-four beat was that it worked just as well backwards as it did forwards. The samples used by the band had been manipulated in such a way that they sounded like they were meant to be played in this manner. Steve marvelled at the talent that went into making a tape that sounded great in both directions. He also wondered where he could get hold of whatever drugs the mysterious band from Kingsport, Massachusetts, had obviously been on.

The frantic guitars had melted into the background somehow, dulling and levelling into a monotonous rumble. Ned's eyes rolled in ecstasy as he struck a crunching G chord. Steve's body shook as the brutal strike resonated in his guts. Without thinking, he started to pummel the E string, hammering his fingers on the third and fifth frets. Looking down at his hands, he was amazed to see his fingers move with a fluid rapidity that he had never possessed before. Raising his head, he gazed, enraptured, at Ned.

Ned's eyes blazed as he thrashed at his guitar. The notes chugged and riffed, washing over his skin like heavy rain. The beat was propulsive, relentless, urging his fingers faster and faster. Steve watched, agog, as he tipped his head back and opened his mouth wide, almost bisecting his face.

At that moment, the reverse of the guttural vocals kicked in. Where before they had been an incomprehensible bellow of syllables, now they seemed to make more sense, in a very strange way. What assaulted Steve's senses *was* language, but not any language he recognised. The effects of the reverse punctuated the speech with new apostrophes and hyphens, lending an unearthly aspect to the rhetoric. Sentences were repeated and repeated. It was a mantra. A ritual.

The candles flickered as a cold draft sent chills down the back of Steve's neck. Ned's mouth was moving with the chant, slack and drooling. His eyes registered no reality; his mind was drifting beyond. Fear started to prickle at the back of Steve's neck. The pineal gland, once dormant, was becoming wide awake and pulsing.

A strangled cry burst from Ned's throat and twined itself around the demonic structure of the music. His arms let go of his instrument and shot out in a cruciform. Steve couldn't believe his senses; the staccato riff he was playing continued to be audible, as though it had now become part of the hellish tape.

Steve wanted to stop, but his fingers wouldn't let him. They continued their worm-like dance up and down the neck of his bass. This was going too far. He didn't want to

go to Hell—not really. It was just fantasy, something they told themselves to get them through every tedious, soul-crushing day. A reason to do drugs and drink beer. He didn't actually want to meet the Devil.

Dimly at first, a rent in reality started to brutally slash the air in the centre of the pentagram. In a rush of foetid air, it split open like an angry wound. Steve shook in terror as small, wispy tendrils gripped the edges of the rift and dragged it wider. With a hiss of steam, the first of a plethora of evilly glowing iridescent bubbles forced itself into our world. Steve cried in alarm, the sharp noise becoming part of the driving cacophony.

Candlelight, and whatever luminescence the god-like entity produced, projected hellish shadows on the studio walls. They moved like a puppet theatre, showing Steve horrors unimaginable. He wanted to shut his eyes, but found himself compelled to watch the world consume itself in fire and madness.

Sparks showered from the amplifiers as the music rose in pitch and ferocity. The pile of cables that ran through a wall conduit and into the sound booth started to writhe and squirm. The pointed metal of the jack leads tasted the air. Hunting. Searching for fresh meat. The globular mass of the thing from outside continued to build in the centre of the room. Two cables snaked across the room and, with savage accuracy, flew and embedded themselves in Ned's upturned wrists. His eyes burned with electricity and fire before melting away to hollow sockets.

This savage horror was enough to break Steve's trance. He called for his friend and tried to ditch his guitar. The bass had other ideas. All four strings snapped and reared back. Agony racked his body as they dug themselves into his arm, burrowing deeper and deeper. He roared in pain as he undid the strap and launched the instrument across the room and into one of the amps. The strings ripped from his arms, taking skin and flesh with them.

Another plume of sparks burst from the equipment. Steve held his arm tight against his chest and turned to Ned. The final strands of Steve's sanity were harshly severed as he watched helplessly as his friend burst into flames. The worst thing about the sight was the expression of terrified rapture on his blistering features.

Finally able to move his feet, Steve bolted for the door. An arc of electricity halted his flight. He was trapped with the formless horror that was materialising in the pentagram. In lieu of anything useful to do, he began to throw beer cans at the creature. Unsurprisingly, they did little more than irritate the abomination. And all the while, the music droned on.

Steve knew he was dead. He could taste oblivion. In a

final act of rebellion, he picked up a microphone stand and charged towards the fuse box. His life was extinguished as he drove the metal into the circuits. Everything popped and tripped as he took the current into his body.

Steve's final thought was of the dawning realisation that the music had finally stopped and the rift sealed in an instant. The unearthly deity had been banished.

***

Stan surveyed the wreckage of his recording studio. This was the first time he had been allowed inside since the tragic deaths of Ned and Steve. In the interim, police, fire officers, and skilled electricians had scoured the property to find the cause of the accident. In the end, it was put down to a pair of known drug users "freaking out" and accidentally electrocuting themselves amid a spate of rock star destruction. They were sure that had there been a TV, then it would have gone out of the nearest window. The tragedy was officially put down to bad acid.

Taking in the massive pentagram on the floor, Stan mused to himself that it did indeed add to the ambience of the room. Looking on the positive side, the repairs wouldn't cost that much in the grand scheme of things. And, let's face it, if the story of musicians dying in the studio during a strange ritual didn't bring the metalheads flocking to use his facilities, then nothing would.

Stepping into the booth, Stan smiled at the undamaged desk. Sitting on the side was an open cassette box. Stan picked it up and ejected the evil tape from the desk. Once the tape was safely back in its case, Stan tapped it against his open palm, then placed it in the inside pocket of his leather jacket. Stan smiled. The guys had said it was pretty rare. He could probably flog it for a few quid…

TIM MENDEES is a horror writer from Macclesfield in the North-West of England that specialises in cosmic horror and weird fiction. He has recently had stories appear in over twenty publications and has had many more stories accepted for forthcoming projects. He has two novellas, Miracle Growth (Black Hare Press) and Burning Reflection (Mannison Press), coming soon.

Tim is also a goth DJ, crustacean and octopus enthusiast, and the presenter of a popular web series of live video readings of his material. He currently lives in Brighton & Hove with his pet crab, Gerald, and an army of stuffed cephalopods.

Bibliography

A Monster Told Me Bedtime Stories, Soteira Press, 2020
Death and Butterflies, Suicide House Publishing, 2019
Colp: Black and Grey, Gypsum Sound Tales, 2020
Ghastly Gastronomy, Madness Heart Press, 2020
Gruesome Games, Thurston Howl Publications, 2020
Horror For Hire: First & Second Shift, Emerald Bay Books, 2020
It Calls From The Forest, Eerie River Publishing, 2020
Little Boy Lost, Mannison Press, 2020
Lockdown Horror #2, Black Hare Press, 2020
Scary Snippets: Sibling Edition, Nocturnal Sirens Publishing, 2020
Solitude, DBND Publishing, 2020
Twenty Twenty, Black Hare Press, 2020
UnLeashed, Emerald Bay books, 2020

Connect
Website: timmendeeswriter.wordpress.com
Facebook: @GoatInTheMachine
Amazon: viewauthor.at/tim_mendees

HERE COMES MY GIRL

by Trisha McKee

Jordan focused on tuning his guitar. "Yeah, just…we like to start on time, okay? Can you try to not be an hour late?"

Sederick and Finley paused, shooting each other "oh shit" looks. But they continued on with their tasks and never added to the conversation.

After a long moment where the tension was louder than any words could be, Sunny threw her head back and laughed. Grabbing the microphone, she waved away Jordan's words. "What's the band called, Jordan?" When he shook his head and sighed, she repeated, "What's the band called? Because I may be adjusting…I mean, re-adjusting to everything…but I thought the band's name was Sunny Storms. Right?"

Jordan lowered his guitar and stared at her. "Right."

She blew him a kiss. "Then all you need to do is play that guitar and look pretty. Got it?" She led them into the first song, her voice flawless, her pace aggressive. If there was any doubt that she could jump in and pick up where the band had left off six months ago, this banished it.

After they finished the set, Sunny dropped the microphone and stomped off the stage, giving the band members the finger as she walked away.

For the next several minutes, the guys worked at breaking down the equipment, as if nothing was amiss. But then Sederick sighed. "Is it really all that different? She's always been…a bitch."

"It is different. And you know it," Jordan snapped.

Trey, their manager, trotted towards them, his finger pointed. "Hey. No, we don't talk about it. Got it. That is Sunny. Back from a retreat to get over exhaustion. Anything else leaks out and this is over, got it. We're over, and I don't think any of us can survive that."

Jordan finished packing up his equipment and drove straight home, not hanging out with the band members, his friends, like he usually did. He feared nothing would ever be the same. But he had to admit, Trey was right. None of them were willing to give up the money, the lavish lifestyle this band afforded them. Any changes, any leaks of changes would ruin them. And no matter how heartbroken Jordan was, he was not ready to give up the lifestyle.

As a child, he had grown up in severe poverty with a drug-addicted mother and an overwhelmed father. But he had always known he was meant for greater things. He was not academically inclined. He was not athletic. In fact, he was skinny and pale, his black hair and electric blue eyes getting endless attention from the girls.

Then his neighbour taught him to play the guitar. And he understood what he was meant for, how he would get out of that dirt-road town, away from parents who had never wanted to have a kid, away from a school that did not know what to do with a quiet boy that barely managed to get Cs. He was meant for the stage.

Jordan had met Finley his first week in Los Angeles. They became roommates with three other guys in a two-bedroom, roach-infested apartment, paying the rent by working two to three jobs each.

Finley was a drummer and had already had the good fortune of being in a band that played at bars and local events, making some money, enough for a taste of that life, that thrill. He and Jordan formed a band with a few other guys, but it never took off. Jordan had a decent voice, but it was not enough to make people stop and listen.

Sederick joined them a year later, his bass-playing skills known through the circles. He told Finley and Jordan about his ex-girlfriend, who could play guitar and had the voice of an angel. He insisted she was crazy, but she was professional. He just had to convince her to join their band.

The first time Jordan saw Sunny, he knew his life was going to change. Tall, tan, and wild, wavy blonde hair, she had a way of commanding the entire room's attention before she ever sang a note. But when the notes did fall from her full lips…Jordan realised they would be going somewhere quickly. Preferably to the top.

Now, five years later, they were at the top of the charts. They were in demand, sold-out tours, and crazy fans. They had more money than they knew what to do with. The finest hotels, mansions, sports cars, and people running around fetching them anything they requested. People telling them yes, insisting they were right even when they were wrong, following them to ensure they did not go a minute without having every whim satisfied.

Five years later, and as Jordan walked into his ten-bedroom mansion, he realised things could change overnight. You could lose the one thing that made you see what was truly important. A golf course in the backyard? A bowling alley in the lower level? He did not even like bowling.

"Hey, honey. I was wondering when you'd make it home."

He set his guitar case down in the foyer and sighed, facing Sunny. "You only had a ten-minute head start. You knew I had to stay and break down equipment."

Sunny grinned, those famous green eyes sparkling. "I ordered in. You hungry?"

And he knew he could not do this. At least not yet. Slowly, he shook his head. "I…I'm going to go take a drive."

"I'd rather you not. It's my first night back."

"It's your first night. Let's not pretend with each other."

Sunny straightened, those eyes flashing. "I am sure you've been prepped on what to say and how to act. So this isn't about pretending. It is what it is. Got it? We need to do this."

Something in him snapped. Maybe it was months of stifling his mourning. Maybe it was the unknown. Maybe it was being forced to accept a situation that made no sense, that seemed to go against everything Sunny was. He leaned forward and jabbed his finger in the air to punctuate every word. "No. We need to keep playing music. This, home. I don't need to do shit!"

Her body trembled as her stare intensified. Jordan was unable to look away, ice-cold sensations crawling up and down his spine, his skin puckering in goose bumps. Suddenly, there was an explosion of shattering glass behind him and turning, Jordan saw the vase had broken.

"Do you remember," Sunny asked calmly, "the night you took me out to that park in the middle of the night? You told me you wanted to talk to me before things got crazy. It was right before we signed the record deal. You told me you'd always love me. I told you that you were full of shit, but you just calmly insisted this was love. It would not vanish, it would not lessen. It was pure and intense love. For me." She laughed, a hard, bitter noise that sounded as if it scraped her throat on the way up. "And I could not even imagine. I mean, me. The girl that grew up in foster homes. That scared guys away with my brashness. Me. Beautiful, kind Jordan loved me."

He stared at her, his mouth hanging open for a few moments before he managed, "How…how do you know about that night?" His mind raced as he tried to remember if Sunny had kept a diary, a journal, something that detailed her days, but he knew she was not good at reading and writing. Her focus was on performing, her talent was in creating obsessions and tangling heartstrings.

Sunny laughed. "There's a lot you don't know, so if you want to do what's good for you, don't cross me. Don't ruin this. I've gone through too much to lose it all because of your precious heart. Now, again, do you want some dinner? I worked hard at calling the order in." Again, she laughed.

But Jordan was lightheaded, grief washing over him as if this were the first day, the moments after hearing the news… "I can't stay here. No."

He was careful to wear sunglasses despite the late hour, and he had his hood up. He did not want a chance of being recognised as he escaped to the one good thing left in his life. But as he tried to run to the other part of his life, he could not help but remember the day he married Sunny.

The day had been a flurry of activity, panic as helicopters circled the area in hopes of pictures to leak to the tabloids. But Jordan remembered little of it except the moment Sunny started to walk down the aisle towards him. Her hair had been magically tamed into an up-twist, her makeup soft, and her dress a dream of white lace and chiffon. And he no longer cared if pictures were leaked or if their reputations would change by being married. He only wanted to share this life with her.

"How is she?" Rachel asked as soon as she opened the door.

"Rested."

Because not even Rachel knew. Sweet, petite Rachel that was carving her own path with a lesser known band. Her rock group had released a top-ten hit two years ago and then seemed to fall back into oblivion. But she kept a sweet outlook on life, enjoying the small crumb of fame that song afforded her. She was humble. Slightly shy. She was everything Sunny was not. Everything Sunny never was.

It was an intoxicating change. Jordan was able to confide his fears and dreams to Rachel with no worries of being scoffed at. No matter how close he got to Sunny, there was always that wall, that block to getting close enough. She was guarded with everyone, including him.

But Rachel was open and sincere. Refreshing. Even her looks were more subtle with dark blonde hair, long and silky and straight, and deep blue eyes he could get lost in.

And while Jordan felt he could confide everything about his soul to her, he could never tell her about this. She would be horrified. He could not risk any word getting out. And he felt fake, not truly there because a large part of his life was now shrouded in mystery. In lies.

And yet he could not stay away. He needed Rachel's embrace. The normalcy. The humdrum of her life and routine.

Jordan had settled into Rachel's bed, into her hungry

arms, when she asked, "How is she really?"

It was a subject he wanted to avoid, to escape, but he realised in doing that, he would only attract suspicion. "She's not herself. It was a pretty bad breakdown."

Rachel twisted and wiggled until she was facing him, those eyes huge as they implored him for the right answer. "Was it because…of us?"

"Rachel. Please."

"I mean, I knew from the beginning that it could never be—I get it. You're not only married to her, but the band… That's a lot to give up."

Jordan shifted away from her, hating what that symbolised, how it changed the light in her eyes. "I love her. I don't want to downplay that."

"And this? What's this?"

He left her house without giving her the comfort of answers. He left without baring his soul. It was the one luxury he could never afford, and therefore, he would never be fully whole.

Instead of returning home, Jordan escaped to the one place he could speak freely. The one man who understood his turmoil. His manager, Trey, who appeared to be expecting his visit.

"Give it one year, Jordan," he advised, pouring him a shot. "One year and you can leave without tearing the band apart. If you leave now, you'll just look like an ass. I mean, come on. Your wife comes out after six months of suffering from exhaustion, which everyone knows means emotional breakdown, and there are already rumours that you chasing other women led to that… You leave now and your career is over. The band's life is over."

Jordan let the alcohol warm his throat before responding. "What happened, Trey? How did that girl that merely resembled Sunny become Sunny?"

Trey pressed his palms against Jordan's shoulders so that he sat down, and then he leaned forward to stare into his eyes. "You don't want to mess around with that stuff. It's better that you don't know all of it. But that is Sunny. With…some extra voodoo added in. Tread lightly."

"Tread lightly? I want my wife back. And if I can't have her, I want to grieve. I want to be able to grieve openly. I want to move on with my life."

"You want to move on? Give it one year and buddy, you can walk right out the door. Walk out on Sunny. Walk out on the band, if that's what you think you need to do. But one year."

Jordan lifted his head to return Trey's stare. "This is so wrong. She knows things about me and Sunny that…how does she know?"

"This isn't a simple process of pushing a lookalike into

place. That would never work. There's more to it. Darker powers at work. That's why I'm telling you to be careful."

It seemed Jordan had more questions than answers by the time he left Trey's. He hoped Sunny would be asleep when he arrived home, but she was lounging in the living room, clad in silk pyjamas with a glass of wine dangling from her manicured fingers, as if this had always been her life. As if she had been there for the past five years, adjusting to the glamour. As if she had not been a simple farm girl with an eerie resemblance to a rock star that happened to be pushed into this life at the last minute.

"Where were you, love?" she sneered, slowly rising to her feet.

"Out."

"For hours? You had your phone shut off. This doesn't look good, you know. My first night home."

Jordan raked his fingers through his thick hair. "Sunny. I need to adjust. This…it's a lot. For you. For me."

"The best way to adjust is to just jump right in." She moved with intention, setting down the wine glass and then swaying her hips as she made her way to him. Her fingers danced down his chest as she gazed up at him. "Do you remember that night, Jordan?"

He knew. Dammit, he knew what she meant, but he swallowed and stated evenly, "What night, Sunny? We have years of nights to reflect upon.”

“The night, Jordan. Don’t play dumb. The night that set this all into motion. The night that has haunted you every single day for the past six months. Remember it?”

He licked his lips. “Of course I do.”

“So you remember why I drove out into that storm, racing over 100 miles per hour. You know why I lost control of the car and drove straight into the tree. Instant. It was instantly over. I lost control because I couldn’t see past my tears, couldn’t drive straight when I was shaking with sobs—”

“STOP IT! You don’t know! You weren’t there! She was! Sunny wrecked.”

There was a loud boom, and he jumped as the barstools flew across the room. She laughed. “Be careful. I lose control.”

“What do you want from me?”

“I want an answer. Do you remember why I drove that night? Why I was beyond hysterical?”

He nodded. No one else knew. Only he and Sunny. And Rachel.

“I found out about your affair. You were the one to convince me all those years ago that we could make it work. That you loved me beyond this world, beyond human error. And yet, you were sneaking around with a low-rate musician. A hack. I took us to the top. Me! And I let you in. I would have been satisfied with a simple affair, but you promised me the world. And your actions drove me into that tree six months ago. You created this situation. And you learned nothing! Because you were with her tonight!"

A lamp flew past his head, and he ducked. This time there was no laughter. He straightened and looked at her, seeing the red eyes, the glowing skin, and he knew this was not a situation he could control. This was out of his hands.

"Sunny, I'm sorry. I needed to talk to her."

"Bullshit! You just don't learn. You killed Sunny! Your lies, your betrayal. You killed her. And I'm here giving you another chance. At fame, at wealth. At love. I'll be damned if you just throw it away." Her eyes glowed even brighter, and he felt himself being pushed back by a force he could not fight. "You are trying to throw me away."

"No. I just need time to adjust. But you're right."

"You're going to ruin all the plans. My work. I gave up my life to come here. For you. Just like Sunny gave up her independence to fall in love with you. And you still want to run around. Do you even have a soul?"

"I do. I'm sorry." By now, he was pinned against the wall, helpless as he watched her hair fly around her glowing face. There was little resemblance now to the Sunny he knew. Ironic, considering this was not the Sunny he knew.

"Things are going to change. You're not going to make a fool out of me anymore. Got it? Now I'm telling you, I ordered in. Dinner is in the kitchen. Are you ready to sit down with me and eat?"

"I am. Yes, of course."

"Are you ready to be the husband you should have been all along?"

"Yes."

She smiled, and he felt that force dissipate. Her eyes were back to that sparkling emerald, her face tan and youthful as she tilted her head. "Good. I've missed you, Jordan. By the way, I have some new songs I want to run by you. The creativity…it's just flowing!"

As they sat down to eat, Jordan's phone lit up. He glanced down and saw Rachel's number flashing.

"Go ahead. Answer it," Sunny urged with a soft smile. "It's okay."

He stood and moved to the edge of the kitchen, ready to tell Rachel it was over. But when he answered, Rachel's bandmate Paul was sputtering words, speaking nonsense until Jordan barked at him to slow down.

"She's gone."

"What do you mean gone?"

"Dead. She's…There was a freak accident. She came to practice early, and when we got here… We found her…some stage equipment collapsed. She's…she's gone. I'm sorry. I knew you'd want to know."

Jordan hung up and stood there, shock icing his insides, his throat coated with bile that was trying to force its way up. Slowly, he turned and watched as Sunny chewed her food with a calm smile.

"Well, honey, I don't think she'll be a problem anymore," she stated as if talking about the weather. "I mean, her band wasn't really all that good, so they won't be searching for any lookalikes to replace her. Sit down. Your food's getting cold."

There was nothing to do but sit and finish his food.

BLACK HARE PRESS

TRISHA McKEE writes romance, horror, sci-fi, and anything that pops into her mind. She started publishing her work in April of 2019, and in less than a year, her work has been featured in over 33 publications. She has earned the Story of the Month award, and her short story Where We Meet was nominated for the Best of the Net 2019 anthology. When she is not writing or talking about writing, she is fishing, dreaming, spending precious time with her handsome hubby and beautiful daughter, attending murder mystery games with her dearest friends, and hanging out with her bulldogs.

Bibliography
Already Paid For, Thirteen Press, 2020
Class Pet, Fantasy Short Stories, 2020
Evening Flea Market, Night to Dawn Magazine, 2020
Full Moon Date Night, Horror Magazine, 2020
Golden Boy, Black Hare Press, 2019
How to Break an Alien's Spirit, The Oddville Press, 2019
Late Fees, Sincyr Publishing, 2020
Lost to the Sea, Black Hare Press, 2020
Road Trip Buddy, ParABnormal Magazine, 2020
Screams and Shots, Youthful Imagination, 2020
Take That Chance, Breaking Rules Publishing, 2020
The Next Room, Breaking Rules Publishing, 2020
Where We Meet, Crab Fat Magazine, 2019

Connect
Website: trishamckee.com
Amazon: amazon.com/author/trishamckee
Twitter: @wordromancer

TRANSMISSION

by Antonia Rachel Ward

"Sid! What the fuck are you doing?"

Nigel's voice drifts into my consciousness, gritty black sparks exploding on a sea of liquid gold.

"Sid? For fuck's sake, it's time for your set. You're half an hour late already. The crowd are getting pissed off out there."

As I'm yanked upright, I open my eyes to see Nigel's face swimming in front of mine. His skin oozes like molten clay. His eyes are empty black holes, and when he speaks again, his mouth yawns open so wide that I'm afraid his head might fall off. I resist the urge to grab hold of it, to make sure it stays on his neck.

"Bloody hell, Sid." Nigel sounds like red—red ribbon

being sliced into tiny pieces.

"Wotter doin', Nige?" I put my hands to my face. My skin comes off in clumps beneath my fingers. "Fuck."

I turn my hands over, look at them, but there's nothing to see. No clumps. That's a relief.

"You have a show to play, Sid."

"Time's it?"

"Half ten. No, quarter to eleven. Why the fuck are you out here?"

"Out?" I look up from Nigel's face. Behind him is only darkness. And an orange light, floating behind him. Must be God.

No. A streetlight. It's a streetlight. I put my hands on the ground. Rough. Pavement. And it's cold. Really fucking cold. It's all coming back to me now.

I start shivering, and then I can't stop. It's like my whole body's rejecting itself. I think I'm going to be sick. I *am* being fucking sick. On my hands and knees, retching so hard I'm sure I'm going to cough up my actual guts. Nigel waits for me to finish, then crouches down beside me, and hands me a cup of water.

"What did you take?" he asks, as I slump against the wall and drink a few cautious sips.

"I didn't," I say, and the effort almost sets me off again. I take a deep breath before I carry on. "I swear, I didn't take a thing. I just really needed some air, so I came outside, and…"

"And?"

"And…I dunno. It was like my brain exploded. Blinding lights everywhere. Next thing I remember is you waking me up."

I've known Nigel since we were kids, and I know when he doesn't believe a word I'm saying. He looks at me with his head on one side, arms folded. At least he doesn't look as though he's melting anymore. He seems to have solidified into his usual twatty self. In his V-neck jumper and skinny tie, he could be my old geography teacher, except he's only twenty-three. The man that style forgot. He's even got the beginnings of a comb-over going on.

"D'you think you can still play?" he asks me.

I drag myself to my feet, crawling my hands up the wall. The abrasive brick surface sends a few sparks through my fingers, the last dying embers of the fireworks that shot through my body when…when *whatever it was* happened. Nigel might not believe me, but I know for a fact that I didn't take anything.

So what the hell is going on?

There's no time to think about it. The moment he's satisfied that I'm not going to keel over, Nigel drags me back past the overflowing bin bags and crates of empty beer bottles that surround the back door of the club. Inside is a narrow, grotty corridor, beige walls covered with the scrawled signatures of all the bands who've played here before.

"I need a fag," I mutter, patting the pockets of my jeans. Spotting a door, I stumble through it to find myself facing a wall of urinals. Above them is a row of mirrors, and for a moment I lean in, gawping at my own face, pale and waxy. My eyeliner is smudged, and my back-combed black hair flatter than I usually like, but, what the fuck, right? Looks kind of ok, actually.

I fumble with a roll-up while Nigel bounces on his toes behind me, wound tight with impatience.

"Hurry the fuck up, Sid."

"I can't go on stage without a fag." But once I've got one in my mouth, and I've had a drag to calm the shrill buzzing in my veins, I take pity on the poor sod and lead the way out of the toilets, through to the backstage area where the rest of the guys are waiting.

A draped black curtain is all that separates us from the babble of the club's crowd. They've been waiting a while, and they're getting impatient. Shouting turns to chanting as I pick up my guitar and make a clumsy attempt to tune it. By the time the sound of smashing bottles reaches my ears, Nigel is physically forcing me through the curtain, and the

next thing I know I'm in the heat of the spotlight, surrounded by a wall of incomprehensible noise.

I stumble up to the mic, manage a first chord on my guitar, and then, out of nowhere, the performer in me kicks in. As he always does. I know the words, the motions. They come to me like second nature, like being possessed. And, as I play, the formless roar from the crowd rises higher and higher.

The lights are glaring, sharp points firing into my eyes. The music descends into tuneless chaos; the notes, like black pinpricks dancing in the air around me, pierce my skin. My bones are on fire. *Shit*. It's happening again.

You belong to us.

The voice is no more than a whisper, expressionless and flat, but it rings out with perfect clarity beneath the cacophony, like a radio transmission beamed straight into my brain.

I stumble. The guitar strings slip beneath my fingers. Somewhere in the back of my mind, I'm aware of Nigel yelling my name. My view of the crowd freezes; colours inverted like the negative of a film. Their faces are still, mouths gaping, eyes like empty sockets.

You belong to us.

"What are you?" I try to shout, but no sound comes out. I am immobile. Numb. The buzz of the transmission rises to a deafening screech. White light sears across my vision. The edges of the film curl, crinkle, and burn to nothing.

***

I'm bobbing on a cloud, drifting on the breeze. But there's something covering my face. When I reach up, my hands float in front of me like balloons—a mask.

"Don't." A voice washes over me in a sea of turquoise. "The oxygen will help you wake up."

That's definitely not Nigel. I cast my gaze around, and the formless chunks of beige and mint green around me resolve themselves into something vaguely familiar. A hospital? Hovering near my side is a shape in white—a nurse, young, dark-haired, with hazel eyes. Perhaps things are already looking up. After a few moments, during which she glances at her little upside-down watch, she lifts the mask from my face.

"How are you feeling?"

"Like a fuckin'…sorry…like a…" My tongue feels as slippery as an eel in my mouth. "Cigarette. I feel as if my brain was stubbed out like a cigarette."

"Sidney…" She looks at me kindly. I attempt what I hope is a dazzling smile, although I'm aware that I probably look like shit.

"Sid," I say. "Sid Rockwell."

"Yes." The nurse bites her lip, as if trying not to laugh. "Yes, I know who you are." As I open my mouth to speak, she adds, "Your name is on the admission form."

Of course it fucking is. Stupid of me to think she might actually have heard of Atrocity Exhibition. I mean, we do ok, but it's not like we're being played on Radio One or anything. Not yet, anyway. Nigel says he's working on it, but then Nigel says a lot of shit.

"I'm Lisa." She wraps a thick cuff around my bicep. "I'm just going to take your blood pressure, ok?"

"Lisa… How long was I out?"

She pauses, her fingers resting on the cuff. "About an hour. Can you remember what you took?"

"I didn't take anything!" That comes out sharper than I'd intended, and I smile sheepishly. "Sorry. But I told Nigel this already. My manager, I mean."

"No drugs?" Lisa raises her eyebrows.

"No drugs. I swear."

"We've already sent a blood sample off to the lab, so…"

"So you'll find out I'm telling the truth," I reply, trying not to sound as irritable as I feel. Fact is, I'm shaken, and I can't get that voice out of my mind. "But what else it could've been?"

Lisa gives me a sympathetic-yet-exasperated look that she probably reserves for her most troublesome patients. "One thing at a time," she says, patting the blood pressure cuff as it tightens around my arm. "We'll get those blood results first, and the consultant will take a look at them in the morning. Until then, you're best off trying to get a bit of sleep."

Fuck that. I watch Lisa in silence as she finishes her observations and bids me good night. Once she's gone, I swing my legs out of bed and stand up. I feel pretty steady, so that's good. Finding my clothes folded on a nearby chair, I discard the hospital gown they've forced me into and get dressed.

Out in the corridor, a row of plastic chairs sits empty. There's no sign of Nigel, or any of the guys. I guess it must be well past midnight by now. Perhaps they've gone back to the hotel. I might as well go for a smoke.

I make my way down the corridor, following the exit signs. It's like a fucking maze, this place. Turn left here, turn right there, through those double doors. The whole way round I see only two people: a night janitor pushing a trolley and an old man lying across one of the rows of chairs, snoring. There're no windows here—I must be close to the heart of the building—but the night is palpable in the sour taste of the air. I can feel it in the tingle that runs down the back of my neck when I turn yet another corner into yet another empty corridor. Am I going around in circles?

Above me, the strip lamps burn with a sick white glow, giving off a rising hum that becomes increasingly shrill with every step I take. The steady pound of my footsteps joins the squeak of my boots on the linoleum floor to create a disjointed rhythm. My breath, short and sharp, is the melody. Another corner. Another corridor. These signs can't be right.

Sidney.

"It's Sid," I mutter reflexively, turning to look over my shoulder.

Nobody there.

Sidney. You belong to us.

No. No, this isn't happening. I up my pace, turn yet another corner, and suddenly, to my immense relief, the front door is right ahead of me. I burst out into the cold night air, watching my hot breath steam into crystals that glow, shatter, and break apart. There's an ambulance unloading a few feet away. The blinking of its blue lights is mesmerising.

We need you.

"Like fuck you do," I snap. One of the paramedics gives me a puzzled look. His face snaps from blue to white.

Blue to white. Blue to white.

You have been chosen. You are receptive.

I wrench my gaze away and stumble in the opposite direction, out across the road and into the car park. It's fucking freezing out here. I pull my pack of tobacco from my jeans pocket and try to make myself a roll-up as I walk, but my fingers are cold and clumsy.

Sidney. You will comply.

The whisper is pin-sharp, a bolt of pure white against the blurred background of my thoughts. If it were a real transmission, it would have the kind of audio fidelity our producers can only dream of. But it's not. It's in my head. My half-rolled fag slips from my fingers.

You belong to us.

No! No! I can't do this. Get out of me. Get out of my brain.

"Sid?"

"Get away from me! Leave me alone!"

A hand comes to rest on my arm. I look down at it, trace a line from the slender fingers, over a wrist, to an arm covered in grey mohair. It's Lisa. She's thrown a big coat over her nurse's uniform.

"What are you doing out here?" she asks me. "You should be resting."

"I…"

"Let me take you back inside."

Her touch is a lifeline, drawing me back to reality. My racing heart begins to slow. I look into her face and nod.

***

"He's in no fit state to play." Pete, our bass player, jabs his cigarette in Nigel's direction. It's late afternoon, and the night's show is rapidly approaching.

"This is the biggest gig we've ever had," Nigel points out from his seat in the corner of my hotel room. I can almost see him adding up the lost takings in his head. The cost of the ticket refunds. The cancellation fee to the venue.

"Yeah? And if Sid bombs out like he did last night?"

"I'm right here," I say, sitting up in bed. I spent the rest of the night in the hospital, and when they discharged me in the morning, I came back to the hotel and slept some more. Right up until Nigel barged in, wanting to know if I was awake and ready to get down to City Hall.

"And what do *you* think, Sid?" Nigel's voice is clipped. "D'you reckon you can make it through the night without…"

"Without what?" I say. "Cracking up?"

I catch his eye, hold his gaze, and wait. I'm looking forward to hearing what he's going to say, now that the blood tests have proven I was telling the truth. I never took anything.

"I just want to know if you can get through the show."

"Because that's what matters, isn't it?" I mutter, looking up at the ceiling. "Just get up on the fucking stage, Sid. Nobody cares if you feel like shit, as long as the money's rolling in."

"Well, if you don't think you can do it, mate, that's your decision." Nigel's not impressed. Well, fuck him.

"Lisa said I'm supposed to rest."

"Who the fuck is Lisa?" Pete says.

I lift my head. "The nurse. You know, the one who found me out in the hospital car park?"

Nigel and Pete exchange glances.

"That was me, you muppet," Pete replies. "I found you in the car park."

"Bollocks. It was Lisa." But even as I speak, cold tendrils of doubt creep over me. It *was* Lisa. Wasn't it?

"Wouldn't we be better off postponing?" Pete says. "Last night was a fucking disaster, and…"

"You're allowed to admit you're worried about me," I say. "I promise I won't take it the wrong way."

The joke sinks like a stone. He's not worried about me. He's worried about the band's reputation. That rankles. Nobody has worked harder to make this band a success than

I have. The thought of getting up on stage again, facing those blinking lights, makes my skin creep like I'm being overrun by thousands of tiny insects. There's a buzzing at the back of my brain that tells me this is a bad idea. But I'm not going to let this band go down and be blamed for it.

"I'll keep my shit together," I say. "It'll be fine."

I wish I could feel as confident as I sound.

***

As we wait for the support act to come off stage, Nigel watches me like a hawk, pouncing on anybody who tries to give me booze or—God help them—drugs. I'm strictly teetotal tonight. Not that I even *want* to take anything. I feel like I'm walking a tightrope over an abyss. Any slip, any tiny imbalance, could send me spiralling back into the endless blackhole beneath me. The thought of hearing that voice again makes me shudder. Mind-altering substances are the last thing I need.

The preparations for the show go on around me. Guitars being tuned. Roadies coming and going, lugging heavy amps. The drummer, lounging on a moth-eaten old sofa trading, banter with our small handful of groupies. I might as well be watching it all from behind a pane of frosted glass. If anybody notices that I haven't moved or spoken for an hour, they don't say anything. Eventually, Nigel hands me my guitar, and I follow the others on stage.

Newcastle City Hall. Our biggest gig ever. Fucking Blondie played here last week. Nigel's invited radio execs. Music journalists. The place is crammed full of rowdy punks and kids in Atrocity Exhibition t-shirts. The air is thick with the stink of stale sweat and beer. A scream meets us as we step out of the wings. An electric energy crackles around the room, right up to the high ceiling. This should be the moment the adrenaline kicks in. But it doesn't.

I stare out at the audience, and they gape back at me, full of anticipation. I feel like an empty shell, but I have to do something. So I go through the same motions I always do—even that bit that Nigel hates where I kick in the amp— like I'm wading through treacle. Every flash of the overhead lights rings out a resounding clack in my brain.

And then I hear it.

Sidney.

No.

I look out at the crowd. As one, they stop dancing and turn their blank faces in my direction. When they speak, it is in perfect unison, in that horrible whisper.

Sidney, absorb us.

This isn't happening. If I can ignore it for long enough, perhaps it will all go away. I keep playing, one chord after another, but the music twists, spiralling into discordant flares of colour. Jade green and violent orange. The crowd advances on me, one synchronous step at a time.

In desperation, I pull the strap of the guitar over my head and hurl it at them. It disappears into the mass, devoured. The others in the band are still playing like nothing's happened, but the bodies in the front row are clambering up onto the stage.

I back away.

Sidney.

They're moving faster now, piling up on each other, the people at the back climbing over those in front, like a surging tidal wave.

Absorb us. Take our darkness.

I turn to run, but my bandmates are behind me. Glassy-eyed. Staring. Somehow the music's still playing without them. Even Nigel's there, blocking my way out.

A black fog floods my veins. My limbs grow weak. I can't think clearly. I need to get out.

The crowd continues to advance, tearing at each other in their haste to get to me. Clutching fingers pull at hair, claw at skin, gouge into eye sockets. And finally, crawling, the first of them reaches my feet. Before it can drag me into the swarm, I bolt, forcing my way through the outstretched arms of my bandmates, off the stage, and down the corridor, until I burst out of the back door and into the night.

***

We require a vessel.

I've no idea how long I've been walking, stumbling blindly on numb legs as the city streets flow past me like snapshot scenes in a movie. Pinpricks of cold needle at my bare arms, sharp and opalescent. Orange street lamps spit flame above me. I wade through a throng of drunken Saturday night revellers, their bodies pulsating with heat, mouths shrieking sharp pink sparks.

A girl gets up in my face, howling, her skin sliding off her bones. A spark catches on her hair, and its ends start to blacken and smoulder. I push past her only to find myself on the road. A car bears down on me, headlamps radiating pools of acid. As it swerves, the horn blares, a single, violent shock of pure white.

The bridge looms ahead, and beneath it, the dark river. The black silence of the water sings to me. Relief. Oblivion.

You must accept us, Sidney. Absorb us. We need you.

I understand what it wants, now. What they all wanted. A vessel for their darkness. Someone to soak up all their fury, all their loathing. That's what I became, the moment I stepped on stage. I've already taken all I can. My flesh is peeling off me in shreds. Their cancer is eating me from the inside.

"Sid!"

I turn slowly, drawn by the familiar sound. Turquoise. It's Lisa, standing on the other side of the street. She smiles, waves. From a million miles away.

For a moment, I feel the pull of her warmth, but only for a moment.

Sidney. You belong to us.

I can't stop. I must keep walking. The bridge beckons me, its steel arch pulsating with a blinding green glow. Why the voice needs me there, I don't know, but that's where I must end up. Bathed in the radiant light, with the abyss opening out below me.

Transmission ends.

BLACK HARE PRESS

ANTONIA RACHEL WARD writes mostly supernatural and psychological horror stories, drawing on interests as diverse as rock music and 18th Century Gothic literature. She also enjoys the occasional foray into poetry.

Her work has been published in Black Hare Press and Friday Flash Fiction.

Bibliography
OCEANS, Black Hare Press (2020)

POWERSLAVE

by Beth W. Patterson

"Here, let me get that for you," I insisted. Watching the petite woman with shockingly blood-red hair and tattoo sleeves carrying the massive speaker, or whatever it was, went against my ethical code. I was a fucking gentleman, after all.

She gave me a tight smile, amber eyes locking with mine. "No thanks, I've got it." I recognised her as Amitra, the guitarist and lead singer of Noise Lesion. I'd heard that they were playing at this club tonight, but wasn't expecting to see them hauling gear hours before the show.

"Miss, leave the heavy lifting to a guy like me." I reached down and grabbed the handle.

"Dude, I said I've *got it*!" she snapped. Her grip on the

handle was stronger than I expected. "Leave my amp the fuck alone!" she snarled. We played tug of war for a few seconds before I let go.

"What you need is a roadie," I chided her.

"What we need are a lot of things," she growled, "but tell that to a record label on a budget. So we carry our own gear, and we're the ones who know how to do it."

Little bitch couldn't even accept a nice gesture. She must have been one of those feminist man-hating sluts. I waited until she set down her burden to open the door to the loading entrance, then I dashed forward and grabbed the handle of the amp, pushing past her.

"Hey! You can't just barge into the musician's entrance, and what part of 'leave my amp the fuck alone' didn't you understand?" her voice snapped after me.

Shit, that fucker was heavy, but I wasn't about to let that on. She should have been grateful, for there was no way in hell she had had an easier time of lifting it than I did. I ploughed down the narrow hall to the backstage area. To prove my superior strength, I hoisted it onto the stage and slammed it down with all my might as if it were no more than a suitcase. There! That would show everyone what brute force was. I heard a small tinkle inside the amp.

"You asshole! That's my vintage Ampeg amp. It has glass tubes inside, and I'm pretty sure you just broke one.

Plus, you never set an amp down on its fucking face!" She was already on the stage, although I never saw her jump. Setting her amp upright, I saw that my prowess had dented the faceplate and torn the grill.

"Sir, come with us," said a deep voice behind me. I turned to see a swarthy man with an earpiece, his thin shirt stretching over his muscles. His short-cropped hair was too shaggy for him to be a security guard out of uniform, but something about him made me freeze.

The zip tie binding my wrists behind my back was a very bad sign.

***

"Why am I in the tour bus?" I demanded. "I thought only groupies got to go here. First, I'm not allowed backstage, next thing you know, I'm in an exclusive…"

My captor hit a button on the wall. The swank-looking bar swivelled around, showing that it was a clever veneer for a hidden compartment.

My blood ran cold. My nose was assaulted first with the stench of sweat, piss, and other odours I couldn't identify, and I gagged in spite of myself. Inside was a primitive engine, with dozens of people packed like sardines—mostly men, but a few women as well—shackled to a series of cranks lining every section of the wall and down the middle row. The chamber resembled a boiler room packed with a tightly interlocked network of gears and pistons.

The muscular man's level gaze made whatever I was about to say next die on my tongue. "You will answer to me from now on," he informed me. "I am Nashala. When I'm not keeping the rest of the band safe from assholes like you, I'm also the bass player. This is what becomes of the punters who fuck with our musicians."

I heard a jingle of metal and he shackled my legs to a narrow metal seat and my wrists to a crank handle caked with someone's dried blood. "After the show, we'll see how much you really want to help this band with your brute strength."

***

While waiting to see what would happen next, I sat in the darkness, trying to make sense of it all. I could hear the muffled roar of Noise Lesion tearing it up inside the club, all thunder and lightning and screaming of crowds.

Bleeding-heart pussies typically felt sorry for victims of human trafficking: women, children, and immigrants. But it turned out that many people could turn a blind eye on the matter if the cargo comprised mere douchebags, as Noise Lesion called us. Most of these forced labourers had been traded from band to band, bought and sold like used gear.

The other prisoners regaled me with their own crimes. One poor bastard had tried to physically pick up Amitra while she was signing merchandise after a show. The rest had been trades from other acts. Another man had refused to stop emitting two-fingered, ear-splitting whistles during a small acoustic concert that the act had tried to tape for a live recording. At a large club, a woman had jumped behind the soundboard and tried to make her boyfriend louder in the mix, not knowing what the knobs and faders were for, blowing out the entire sound system. Some old curmudgeon, who looked like he wasn't going to last much longer, had thrown a dart at an Irish singer in a pub for refusing to sing "Danny Boy," embedding the object three inches into the singer's leg. The young woman chained to the crank next to me complained that all she had wanted to do was get onstage at a festival with a funk band, sing a song, and play her tambourine. She'd slipped past the security guards and had even grabbed the microphone before they hauled her off. This had actually been her sixth offense of trying to join in on concerts. She couldn't understand why musicians were so *mean* about not letting fans join in. Did they think they were better than anyone else?

The stories were interrupted by an imperious male voice. "It's time to put your talents to work, everyone! Grab your handles!" A towering man, long ponytail bound in a series of bands like a biker, lurched to the front of the engine room. His white teeth glinted through his shaggy beard, a smile that almost put me at ease until I realised that the rictus was at our expense. "I'm Trog," he announced, "and not only am I the drummer, I'm also your hortator!" He flipped a bass drum in front of him and grabbed two mallets.

"That's the guy who makes us crank in time to the beats, when we need to speed up or slow down together," mumbled the old man. I hadn't known that, but I might have seen something like that in the movie *Ben Hur*. I sneered at the geezer as if this were common knowledge.

A mighty boom made me jump. Then another and another, and I realised we were supposed to turn our gears in time to the drumbeats. We were essentially slaves on a galley ship, but instead of oars, we were making the engine of the tour bus run with our assigned crank handles.

Trog grinned as he pounded out a steady beat like a sadistic bunny in a battery advertisement, his eyes glowing in the dark. "If you damage our equipment or harm one of us," he drawled, "the least you can do is help us save money on fuel. So come on. We have to make it to Phoenix by morning."

"Don't you need to save your energy for the next show?" I blurted out.

He smirked. "You're about to find out that we're no ordinary band. And that neither are a lot of touring acts out there."

I grabbed my crank and cursed. It was clearly welded in place, or so I thought until it budged an inch, and then another. As collective manpower began to gain momentum, it got easier, but my arms were shot with pain after ten minutes. I wasn't sure I'd make it through the night.

"Oh yeah, and there's another reason we're called Noise Lesion!" cackled Amitra's voice from the other side of the veneer. "If you don't pull your weight, everyone suffers!" A series of speakers embedded in the walls I hadn't even noticed burst to life with ear-splitting feedback shrieks. We pushed harder and harder, and the noise began to abate somewhat, although I saw blood trickling from the ears of several prisoners.

The members of this band were nothing short of killers.

***

Sometimes when the bus would stop for the band to get food or stretch their legs, I'd get a glimpse of the other prisoners. The woman next to me complained the most, but she had pretty blonde ringlets, sweat-dampened and greasy as they had become.

"What's your name, sugar?" I whispered to her when Trog wasn't around.

"Morla," she sniffled.

"I'm Fred Verdin," I told her, "and if I get us out of here, what say we stick together and form a partnership? You can sing and play your little tambourine as much as you want to. I'll be your roadie and your manager, and I can carry shit the way these motherfuckers could never appreciate."

We were caught somewhere in time, but had no idea how much had passed. The crew slept in fits and starts, never knowing when we would be woken again. Sometimes our fare had just enough protein in it to keep us strong, but we mostly had red M&Ms to fill our empty bellies.

Sometimes I'd slide my arms just far enough ahead of me that I could reach Morla's fingers with my own. She could turn her body to let me see the tops of her tits from the neckline of her little sundress. The edges of those pink-brown nipples were like teasing little sunrises, and perhaps the only thing that gave me motivation to stay alive.

Oh hell yeah, when we got out of here, we were going to make a fresh start. She could sing to her heart's content, and I'd haul her gear, like a real man.

***

"It appears that you lovebirds are thinking of escaping," said Nashala one day when the bus had pulled to a halt and we were given our food rations and toilet privileges. All of Noise Lesion had assembled to study us impassively, as if assessing a car for a tune-up.

"I'd almost wonder if you read our minds," I slurred, "but I guess you can do all that esoteric shit when you worship Satan or something." I was too delirious to be sure if I was mouthing off or kissing up.

All three members broke into peals of laughter. For the first time, I could see the true nature of their teeth: needle sharp and too numerous for a human skull to contain. Then, in the blink of an eye, the glamour returned: mirthful, normal-looking smiles all around.

"Satan? *Satan?* Isn't that *cute*?" chortled Amitra. "Cupcake, you'd better hope you never find out what elder gods we are aligned with. Go on, keep thinking that we worship that cuddly tragic figure." Nashala nearly lost his beverage out of his nose, sending twin jets of steam from his nostrils.

I wondered if I could break these chains by sheer force of adrenaline. I'd heard of people lifting cars in a moment of panic for total strangers, so my chances of breaking a simple chain to get laid by someone I already sort of knew wasn't that outlandish. But my body was so exhausted and my mind addled by irregular sleep and lack of light, I had my doubts.

The snick of a key in the locks didn't register in my brain immediately. For the first time in forever, nothing was binding me. The pins and needles of blood rushing back to my wrists burned like a motherfucker, but I was going to *live*!

"You mean that's it?" Morla breathed. "We're just free to go?"

"We have fresh cargo," said Trog. "We received three young guys who wouldn't stop screaming requests for Free Bird at a chamber music concert, and we need to make room. That weak old man is just going to disappear, and let's just say that he's not as lucky as you are—fuck that guy! So go. We're even going to give you a complimentary microphone for your good behaviour in prison. The rest is up to you."

"One more thing!" hissed Amitra. "Don't forget that the name Noise Lesion is a palindrome. That means it's spelled the same way forward and backward. You can backpedal all you want, but you'll end right up at the beginning if you never learn."

As the door to the tour bus opened, we stumbled down the stairs and collapsed onto the pavement, our legs weak from disuse. The sunlight seared our eyes even though the worst of the setting sun had already passed. I glanced at my newly freed companion, grimy and exhausted as we both swayed to our feet. Neither of us had stood upright in weeks—or had it been months?—and now we clung to one another for support. I noticed a faint glow on the side of Morla's neck, just under her jaw. It was barely noticeable, like a venue's admission stamp under black light. It almost resembled an eye of Horus. I felt a tingling sensation like a mild shock in the same spot and didn't doubt that I'd been similarly marked. I'd have to get used to it.

We might be reunited with the normal world, but we would never forget that we had each been a powerslave.

***

The showers at the closest cheap motel were more luxurious than I'd imagined possible. Noise Lesion had even given us a small stipend. It took us two days of sleeping and ordering takeout before we were even feeling strong enough to screw.

Within walking distance, we eventually found a thrift store. We might not have had the means to buy new clothes, but at least we could throw away the ones on our backs tainted with blood and sweat and nightmares. We also found a drug store for toiletries and even a hair salon in a dodgy-looking strip mall. Once Morla had some fresh threads, a haircut, and some makeup, I swear she looked like a fucking goddess to me.

"Now is when we get to make our new start!" she chirped. "Let's go to a karaoke bar!" It was already a little late, but we were giddy with our freedom. I looked up the biggest bar that had karaoke that night and splurged on a taxi so that my little piece of ass didn't have to get sweaty from walking.

***

The joint was packed, and we had to wait an hour and a half for our turn. But she'd made a good song choice with "I Will Survive." Because survive was what we had done indeed.

It was two minutes to midnight by the time they called her name, and for the first time since our enslavement, I was actually excited. I watched her stand with confidence, moving her hips and gyrating to the music. Her beautiful mouth opened, and the whole room breathed in the discovery...

...that this was quite possibly the most tone-deaf bitch to ever desecrate a stage. I'd heard cats fuck with better intonation than that. And the rest of the audience knew it too, and nobody was holding back on booing and even threats.

The spot on my neck began to burn, and I saw Morla's matching mark glow noticeably brighter. Was it a warning, or was it causing the outrageous backlash from the other patrons? The burning turned into a searing pain, and I clapped my hand to my neck, astonished that the skin still felt smooth and unscathed.

The song wasn't even halfway over when someone rushed the stage and grabbed her microphone… *Just like she had done,* I reflected. I threw myself between Morla and her aggressor and saw that the crowd was becoming so irate that the people were storming the stage. We had to run to the hills, or at least get the fuck out of the bar and back to our hotel immediately.

I hoisted Morla over my shoulder and ran for the door, and that's when I threw out my fucking back. The security guard had to carry her bag for me, even though I insisted that I had it.

***

Neither of us slept a wink that night. I was desperate. I didn't want it all to end like this.

We noticed that Noise Lesion was playing only fifty

miles away. The last thing we wanted to do was see them ever again, but perhaps we could find out what had gone wrong. So we packed our bags and caught the next Greyhound bus and waited outside the club until the last patron had left. I was afraid I'd wet myself when we approached them as they were tearing down, but I licked my lips and hailed my flame-haired nemesis.

"Look, I fucked up," I admitted to Amitra. "I really thought we had a shot at the real thing, with Morla being a singer and me being her roadie and manager."

"As you've already figured out, we're not an ordinary band," she replied with a voice that held no warmth, but no grudge—just that of a mortal woman who had just sung and played a high-energy concert and didn't have time for the likes of us. "We can give you a taste of what being a working musician is really like. If you want to try giving it another shot, we might be able to fix that princess' little tin ear."

I trusted neither the favour nor the forgiveness, but my ego took the wheel. "We've learned our lessons, and we're ready to pay our dues," I said, hoping that I meant it. "We appreciate your gift."

She doubled over in laughter at that. It was kind of a shame that it was the first time I'd seen her do it without those fearsome teeth. She'd have been a lot prettier if she smiled more.

"Oh, don't worry," Amitra said. "It's not a gift. Everything has its price. But I'm not going to hit you with some oogity-boogity bugfuck curse. You'll just be getting a taste of what working musicians go through."

That didn't sound too bad at all.

Amitra cupped her hands over Morla's ears and whispered an incantation. A hot, dry breeze blew around our legs. The mortal woman whimpered slightly but stayed standing. Amitra's eyes closed, head tilted back in pleasure as my girlfriend's body began to spasm convulsively.

Oh yeah, she wants it, all right, I told myself, trying to distract myself from thinking that I could have done something to alleviate Morla's agony if I hadn't been so chickenshit. Amitra finally turned on her heel and walked away as if she'd just delivered a mild rebuttal to a heckler, and Morla collapsed to the pavement like a sack of bones.

I had to wait with my girl in the adjacent alleyway for several hours until she came to. After all, I couldn't take an unconscious woman into a hotel or onto a bus. That fucking hashtag movement was ruining everything in my life.

***

Two nights later, she sang her heart out, and some

people even clapped. Nearly everyone in the audience was talking or engrossed in their cell phones, but I was bursting with pride sitting at a front row table of Pompino's Pizza. My baby was gonna be a star, and I would be earning some serious dough.

After closing time, we stood there gazing triumphantly at the empty restaurant, the karaoke machine already unplugged, waiting around to get paid. When I finally approached the manager, he looked surprised. "Paid? I never agreed to pay you. You got free pizza and beer all night! Plus, it's great exposure." He lunged towards us with the push broom. "Come on, I've gotta get this joint cleaned up." The bristles scraped at Morla's slender ankle and she squeaked. We tried to make as dignified a retreat as possible for two people who had done a gig at a pizza joint, not got paid, and then chased out of the establishment with a goddamned broom.

I draped my arm around her shoulders as we made our way to the taxi stand and tried to inject her with some false cheer. "So, what do you think, girl?" I tried. "Next week we take some nice headshots of you, I make some business cards, and now we even have something to put on our resumé. It was your first real gig!"

She sat down on the kerb, face buried in her hands. "No, it wasn't. We're not professionals. We got *exposure*.

How are we going to make a living on that?"

***

As the kids may or may not still say, we "did a thing," if only for a little while. We hired a local guitar player to record some tracks and sequence a drum machine and did a short run of some CDs. Neither of us wrote original music, but she could sing the hell out of those covers. We were supposed to pay licencing, but I said fuck that shit. I was sure all those songwriters were already pretty rich. We made it work for a little while in coffeehouses, open mic nights, and busking on the street.

When we kicked it up a notch, it started to get real. We found a string of dive bars, and I put an official tour together. But it wasn't anything like the big shots got to do. There were guys in the audience screaming at Morla to show her tits while she was singing, club owners short-changing us, and so-called radio promoters taking our money and our CDs and then disappearing off the radar. It became a life of driving for hours on end every day, defending Morla, and crashing exhausted in cheap motels. The days turned into months, and we had no mailing address, so creditors began to call my cell phone.

Morla and I fought after almost every show. She may

have been the star, but I was the trooper. My nose had been broken twice in fights with guys who couldn't keep their hands off of her. I blamed her for the harassment, encouraging those men with her slutty little moves during her act, and she fed me some bullshit lines about stage presence and selling product. What was she supposed to do, she said, just stand there like a bump on a log? That little bitch suddenly thought she was the expert on being a singer.

I could have wasted years with this bullshit dream, but we finally knew that if we didn't hang it up, it would kill our relationship. Not that I really wanted to spend the rest of my days with Morla, but because there was no one else who would understand what we'd both endured. We had to stick together, simply because we didn't have any better options. We kept how we met a secret so as not to risk being thrown in jail or the loony bin. The evil that men do couldn't have been worse than the tour bus galley, but neither of us wanted to be trapped again.

After a while, we threw away all the remaining music business cards and started our own company, making and selling homemade jam, soap, and candles. We worked the circuit at the local farmer's markets and food co-ops. Morla found a little trailer thirty miles out of the last town we'd played, so we bought it and moved in. We fixed up our home with some windsocks and political flags, just to let the neighbours know who was boss in this town. I suppose having developed a fear of the dark was natural, so we draped our walls in cheap Christmas lights, and we let them twinkle year-round.

But now every time someone drives past our house blaring a metal song from a car, our hearts nearly burst out of our ribcages. The only music we can stomach now is easy listening. I'm not sure if that's the result of a psychological aftereffect of our shared trauma or some supernatural shit, in spite of Noise Lesion telling us that they weren't going to curse us with anything worse than a musician's life. The band had let us go, but how the fuck can I be sure they were telling the truth? It has me constantly on edge.

We're going to enjoy our little down-home lifestyle for as long as we can. We bake pies, we fuck, and we binge watch monster truck shows, all just to pass the time uneasily. If Noise Lesion ever comes back for us, we know where the fake red M&Ms are hidden. There's one for each of us, and I hear that the effect is just like falling asleep before anything can take our souls.

For the first time in years, my slave mark is tingling again. For all I know, they could find us tonight.

BETH W. PATTERSON writes urban fantasy, horror, bizarro, and subgenres such as circuspunk.

She was a full-time musician for over two decades before diving into the world of writing, often incorporating her stranger-than-fiction performer's perspective into her stories. She is the author of the books Mongrels and Misfits and The Wild Harmonic, and a contributor to over forty anthologies. Patterson appears on over a hundred and ninety recordings (including seven solo albums of her own), has played in nineteen countries, and never sleeps.

Bibliography
Across the Universe, Fantastic Books, 2019
All Dark Places 2, Dragon Soul Press, 2020
Baker Street Irregulars, Diversion Books, 2017
Dark Corners: Night Chills Volume 2, Iron Clad Press, 2016
Fable, Iron Faerie Publishing, 2019
Forest of Fear, Blood Song Books, 2019
Heroika: Dragon Eaters, Perseid Press, 2015
Monsters, Black Hare Press, 2019
Poets in Hell, Perseid Press, 2014
Release the Virgins, Fantastic Books, 2018
Sha'Daa: Inked, Moondream Press, 2016
The Binge-Watching Cure, Claren Books, 2018

Connect
Website: bethpattersonmusic.com
Facebook: @bethodist
Amazon: amazon.com/author/bethwpatterson
Goodreads: bethwpatterson
Twitter: @BethPatterson5

FROM HER TO ETERNITY

by David Green

I gaze into my dressing room mirror. My raven hair falls to my shoulders; ice-blue eyes stand out against my pale, porcelain skin. It's funny; the stories say I should see nothing staring back, but my reflection does. I'm beautiful. Achingly so, the artistry of my face has increased since Katherine sank her teeth into my neck.

Sometimes, when I close my eyes, the sensation of her fangs piercing my skin lingers. I raise my fingers to where she punctured me, but the wound has long since healed. Katherine. My creator and the reason for this eternal blessing and curse. I long to see her again, to feel her neck beneath my hands as I throttle the life from her. It would not kill her, I know that. It wouldn't stop me from trying. Then, the thrill of her lips pressing against mine once more, lighting a fire in my cold blood. I hate Katherine as much as I desire her.

Often, I wonder why she did this to me. How many others are out there? Did she turn countless more, leaving them without an explanation of what to do next?

We met at a bar. Normally, I'd have a steady flow of fans approaching me for selfies or autographs, but not that night. It was like she'd staked her claim on me, and everyone else knew it. The morning after she turned me, I woke in my hotel room alone. Blood covered the bedsheets. Somehow, I could smell that it was my own. I'd staggered to the bathroom, the sight of two puncture holes in my neck jogging my memories of the evening with Katherine. I dressed quickly; my band Lovecraft's Pussy had booked the week in a recording studio. I looked at my cell phone to find many missed calls and messages, the texts increasing in their fury as their count increased. I'd missed the previous day's session completely. All because of Katherine.

Hurrying into daylight, I jammed sunglasses on my face. The morning wasn't too bright, but the sun burned at my eyes and caused my head to pound.

"The fuck have you been, man?" Zak yelled as I

entered the studio. He was behind the glass, laying down a guitar track for one of the new songs on our album. The sound engineer and the other guys in the band avoided looking at me. I could tell how pissed they were, but something else told me the depths of their emotions—like a whisper in my ear, granting my insight into their souls. I hadn't focused on the music lately. Drugs, alcohol, and women had distracted me. I'd become addicted to fame, and they resented it.

"Sorry," I mumbled, "met a girl. Lost track of time."

"Fuck sake, Nick, a whole day wasted!" Zak shouted, throwing his guitar down in frustration. He was from England like the rest of us, born in Liverpool, hometown of The Beatles. We'd all upped sticks to America after our first album went big. Zak thought of himself as the McCartney of the group, composing most of the music and arrangements. I wrote the lyrics. We argued a lot.

"Sorry," I said again, not feeling myself. Usually we'd get right into it, throw a few things, each quit the band before making up and getting down to record. This time was different. I was *aware*, could tangibly feel how I'd let everyone down.

"Right," Zak replied quietly. "Nick, are you all right?"

"Yeah," I said. "Haven't eaten yet, came straight here when I woke up."

Zak exited the booth and moved in front of me.

"You gonna take those sunglasses off, mate," he asked, before turning and winking at the lads, "or are you going all Bono on us now you're famous?"

"Think I'll leave them on," I replied, showing him a grin I didn't feel to ease any weirdness between us. "I'm cool enough to wear them indoors."

"Right," he said again. "Just need your vocals for that track, so we can move on. You sure you're up for it?"

"Yeah," I said, pushing by him into the booth. "I'll leave the jacket on too. Fucking freezing in here."

It wasn't, but the high collar hid the bite marks on my neck. I picked up the headphones and prepared to sing. We'd attempted vocals for this one a few times, but I just wasn't feeling the track and aborted. Another reason to piss the lads off, calling me a diva. Raising a thumb, the music flooded into my ears.

That majestic sound moved me. I'd never heard a melody like it, even though I'd attempted vox for the same piece for four hours two days previously. Whatever Katherine had done to me had awakened a new appreciation in the texture and depth of the piece, the music somehow taking on a life of its own.

My cue arrived, and I sang. The words didn't come from my stomach, but from my soul. Weeping as I sang, connecting with each syllable. After what felt like years, the song ended. Before I opened my eyes, I knew what I'd done was perfect.

The lads behind the glass were silent, Zak a little paler than before. Dave, our drummer, dropped the sticks he always twiddled in his hands.

"Want me to do another one?" I asked.

Zak coughed. "No," he said, "I think that'll do, mate."

The recording went on for the rest of the day and long into the night. The sounds created intoxicated me. I even suggested ideas to Zak who, annoyed at first, appreciated my input as the session wore on. At one point, the lads stopped to order food in. I had no interest, despite not recalling when I ate last. Something else stirred my hunger. The string on Ben's bass guitar snapped, gouging into his finger. It happens to musicians, it's unavoidable. I smelled his blood as soon as it left his body. Its metallic aroma causing me to salivate. Looking away, I tried to distract myself. I picked at the pizza I'd barely touched, but it did nothing to fill the gnawing desire growing inside me. Ben patched his finger up, sealing the blood away, and restrung his guitar. I watched him, like a hawk tracking a mouse on a forest floor.

"Hey," Zak said, leaning in close. "You ok, mate? You're sweating."

My fingers came back wet after I wiped them across my brow, the scent of blood still thick in my nostrils.

"Think this girl spiked my drink or something," I muttered, resisting the urge to lick my lips. Instead, I ran my tongue across my teeth. The K-9s felt sharper.

"Why don't you head off?" Zak replied, patting my bicep. I looked down at it and could see the pulse in his wrist twitch. "Fuck, you deserve an early finish. Those vocals, man…"

He stared off into the recording booth, his eyes misty.

"All right," I said. "See you tomorrow?"

"Yeah. Mate, we made art today. Did you feel it?"

I nodded to him as I lurched to my feet and left the studio. Night had fallen. I removed my sunglasses, but the colours seemed as vivid and distinct as daytime. More so, I put them back on and hurried to the hotel, panic rising. Entering the lobby, I ran up the stairs to my room. I always made a habit of leaving the "Do Not Disturb" sign on my door, and that morning had been no exception.

The key card didn't work the first two times, but the mechanical click came on the third attempt. I burst into the room, the flavour of my blood in the air. It still stained the bedsheets, and my body craved the nourishment it offered. I fell to my knees and crawled over to the sheets, taking them in my hands.

Holding them to my face, I inhaled deeply. The scent didn't inflame me like Ben's did. I stuck out my tongue and licked my blood. The iron taste flooded my mouth, then bile from my stomach raced to meet it. Vomit erupted onto the floor, my abdomen cramping in response. Crawling to the room's phone, I pulled it from the table and cradled it as I lay on the ground. Somehow, I dialled a number.

"Room service," a pleasantly professional American voice said.

"Can I get a chicken sandwich and a bottle of red wine?" I croaked. "Room 237."

"Yes, sir," came the response, "it will be with you in ten minutes."

Pulling myself together, I acted quickly. The sheets I rolled up and wiped at the mess on the floor, then dumped them in the bathtub. I moved the bed, so it sat on top of the vomit stain. Next, I splashed myself with water. Black bags hung heavily beneath my eyes. I covered them again with my sunglasses and zipped my jacket a little higher, so it hid the teeth marks from sight.

The bell rang, followed by a brief knock and the sound of the door creaking open.

"Room service!" came a cry from a full and friendly female voice.

Taking one last look at myself in the mirror, I walked

from the bathroom. There she stood with a shy smile on her face, a covered plate in one hand and a bottle of red wine in the other. About twenty years old and cute. She gasped slightly when she saw me.

"Sorry," I said, moving a little closer. "Did I startle you?"

"No," she replied, her long eyelashes flashing along with her grin. "It's just I've never stood in a room with a celebrity before."

"How about drinking with one?" I took the plate from her and sat it down on a table, picking up two wine glasses instead and held them in my hand.

"I shouldn't," she said, biting her lip, "I'm on duty."

"I won't tell anyone," I whispered. My strength suddenly failed me, and I dropped the glasses. They shattered together on the floor.

"I'll get that," she cried, instinctively bending to clear away the shards and nicking her fingertip. Blood welled into a small, perfect bubble. My body almost surged towards it.

"Careful," I said, taking her hand by the wrist, "did it hurt?"

"No," she answered, looking at me with her big, brown eyes.

I felt her pulse race. Her scent filled me with desire. I

needed her. I glanced down at the blood trickling from her finger and down her palm.

"I don't even know your name," I muttered, glamoured by the crimson river.

"Melody," she breathed.

"Wonderful," I said, before kissing her finger. I sucked at the blood; it tasted sweet on my tongue. Melody moaned, and I felt her stand on her tiptoes in response.

Not able to resist any longer, I bared my fangs and bit down on her wrist. Her moan became a scream, first in shock then pain. She attempted to hit me with her other hand, but I expected it and moved quicker. Holding her arms wide, I sank my teeth deep into her exposed neck, tearing at the sinew and muscle. Her blood sprayed across my face and sent a thrill down my spine. I felt a moment of regret as I saw the light dim behind those beautiful eyes, but then my bloodlust chased those thoughts away and I settled down to feast.

***

That first kill happened over a year ago. I've lost count of how many I've fed upon since. I've grown detached from the band outside of recording and performing. They don't mind. We're creating better music than ever. We tour in all the big cities across America, and I only need to feed two or three times a week. Our travelling allows me the opportunity to select my prey without suspicion. I've learned not to use the hotel rooms I stay in. Disposing of a body is much easier in random places. I haven't killed for two days, and I feel the desire stirring inside. I must satisfy that hunger tonight.

There's a knock on the door. Zak pokes his head in. I don't turn around.

"Warm up acts done, mate," he says, "you ready?"

I nod at his reflection in the mirror, and he leaves. I have a dressing room to myself, preferring solitude. The lads often party after a gig. Drugs, drink, and sex. Things I have no interest in now. Pulling a plain white shirt over my head, I button it but leave the top four unfastened. It suits my black skinny jeans and raised heeled boots. I admire myself one more time. I am perfection.

Screams from the crowd become louder as I make my way towards the stage. The venue holds six thousand and is a sell-out. Joining Zak, Ben, and Dave in the wings, we wait for the right moment to walk on. The lights in the building switch off, plunging the room into darkness. That's our cue. The lads fist bump each other before heading for their marks and readying themselves to play. I'm not included in this ritual anymore. They know something changed within

me, but they see it as an utter devotion to my art. In a way it is. I'm in love with the music, the moods we create. Katherine's gift to me, if I can call it that, was deepening my passion for what I create. I exist to transmit our sound. And to that, I must feed.

Assuming our positions, I close my eyes, revelling in the barrage of emotions washing over me. Excitement, nervousness, rising frustration. Love. The crowd's smell is potent, a heady mix of sweat, perfume, alcohol, and aftershave. Everyone is waiting for me to begin, but I wait for the perfect moment. That exquisite juncture where the anticipation is about to explode into restlessness. It approaches as I count down from five, reaching one as the first whistle erupts from the crowd.

My voice in the microphone quiets the fans, and I feel the mood instantly switch to adoration. I sing a cappella, and such is the haunting quality of my voice, the crowd transcends attending a mere gig. Ben on bass kicks in, then Dave on the drums, and finally Zak. A flawless marriage of instrument and voice. The stage lights send out a faint green glow into the darkness, and the throng unleashes the breath they were holding as one when they finally see us. I reach out to them, my congregation, and they sway in step with the movement of my arm.

Someone catches my eye. In the centre of the crowd

stands a woman, with silver hair that flows to her waist. It's as if the mass of bodies have granted her space; she is curiously alone and now the object of my attention. Our eyes cross the distance and lock together. I see the green sparkling towards me, her full lips parted. Her chest heaves with each breath she takes, and I see the pulse in her neck vibrate. I perform just for her—as if I'm all that exists in her world. I mesmerise her. I've glamoured many men and women since Katherine and realise it when I see it. The way she affects me is something I haven't experienced. There is no doubt in my mind that we shall find each other before tonight is over.

Just like that, the gig's done. The electricity I feel from the crowd tells me how spectacular we were. I didn't notice. Somehow, the girl bewitched me too. I follow the boys to the backstage and with my head full of thoughts of the woman from the crowd, I almost enter their dressing room on Zak's heels.

"You coming in, Nick?" he asks, turning to look at me. He doesn't make eye contact anymore, he tells me I'm too intense.

I look beyond him into the room. Bottles of champagne litter, bouquets of flowers in front of the mirrors. Dave is already snorting a line of coke while Ben orders a stagehand to gather up any girls wanting to join the afterparty.

"No," I answer, my nose wrinkling at the smell of sweat seeping from him. Another thing I don't do anymore, my skin is permanently dry and cool. I'm not close enough to peer in their mirrors, but I know my appearance is as pristine as it was before the gig.

"Right," he mumbles. I sense his unease, it's always there when I'm around. "You were cracking tonight, mate. Best I've ever heard."

I nod and walk towards my dressing room. I'm not surprised at his comments; I sang for her.

Sitting in front of my mirror, I think about Katherine. The desire for her isn't as strong as it was two hours ago. The girl from the crowd cuts through my thoughts of the other woman. She stands there, beckoning me to find her. I leave without bothering to put on a jacket.

People will wait at the back entrances, they always do. It never occurs to them to loiter near the front of the buildings we play in. I head that way. There aren't many here. As ever, the rabble are eager to drink at a club or hang around an exit for the chance of an autograph. I push outside and in front of me is my silver-haired siren.

"Hello," I say, standing a few yards away. Feeling I need her permission to come closer.

"Hi," she replies, her voice chiming like crystal.

I take a step towards her. She doesn't move away.

"Who are you?"

"I'm Vanessa," she answers. "I heard you tonight."

"I know," I whisper, taking another step closer. Her scent reminds me of elderflowers, her skin pale but her lips so red I can already taste her blood. "I saw you."

Vanessa laughs. A rich, full sound that makes my hairs stand on end. The few passers-by stare at us. They recognise me but I don't react to them.

"You saw me?" she says, raising an eyebrow, "out of all those thousands?"

"How could I miss you?" I murmur, close enough now to take her hand if she didn't have them in the pockets of her black, fitted coat.

"I bet you say that to all the girls you meet after a gig."

I need to be with her. Is this how I make others feel? This desire inside me overrides every other sense. Except one. To feed. I see the vein in her neck throbbing, thick with her life source. Maybe this is the same reason Katherine didn't use me for nourishment. Perhaps she desired me as I crave Vanessa, so turned me instead. Not wanting to kill something so pure. I will do the same to Vanessa, but I won't leave her. I'll stay with her forever.

"Would you like to go for a walk?" I venture, pointing towards a darkened river close to where we stand.

"All right," she answers with a laugh, "though I should warn you, I don't put out on a first date."

"I wouldn't dream of it," I say. "I'm English. It's the land of gentlemen."

Our steps match as we walk in silence. It isn't awkward; it feels as if we've always been together. I glance towards her. She leans towards me unconsciously as we move. Inside her is an urge to be close to me, she isn't aware of it, but it's there. I focus my senses on her and hear her heartbeat speed up as I brush my elbow up against hers. Her feelings are a mix. Excitement, yes. Nerves. Fear, and why shouldn't she have that welling inside her? Famous musicians have earned reputations. There's something else too, a trickle she's trying to suppress, but it won't go away.

Hatred.

I'm puzzled by it. Is it for me or towards herself?

"You're distracted," Vanessa says. "Am I boring you already?"

"What? No," I answer, surprised she can read me so well. "I hoped I hadn't come on too strong, that's all."

She stops and reaches up to pat me on the cheek. Her hand is cold, just like mine.

"I know what I'm getting myself in for," she replies before walking again.

I hurry to catch up with her. She unnerves me in a way

I haven't experienced since I was human. Studying her from the corner of my eye, a thought pops into my head.

"Do you know someone called Katherine?" I ask, opening myself to her feelings. Perhaps she is more like me than I realised.

"No," she answers, a frown line appearing on her forehead. "Unless you mean my fourth-grade teacher—I think she's dead."

Her emotions are honest. She would remember my Katherine.

Trees are ahead of us on the riverbank and we pass into them. Vanessa stops and looks into the sky. The moon is large and white. She smiles up at it. I stand by her side and fight the urge to do what I need and want. The pull is almost too strong, but the moment is perfect, and I want to remember her this way. Even though I'll always be with her, she'll never be human again.

"Well," she says, turning towards me, "aren't you going to kiss me?"

I stoop and meet her lips. Her tongue pushes against mine, and her hands grab my hair. My body responds. I pull her waist into me, and she nips at my bottom lip. I do the same in return; she gasps and pulls away. Blood drips from a small cut, and I taste it on my tongue.

My fangs sharpen in response. The smell drives me

crazy and I feel dizzy, such is my need for it. The colours of the night become more vibrant. Vanessa's skin seems translucent; I can see the blood below the surface moving under it. She licks at the nick, an action that feeds my hunger and lust for her body at the same time.

"I'm sorry," I say, "got carried away."

"That's ok," Vanessa replies. "I wanted you to. I needed to make sure."

She moves in close again, her body pressing against mine, her eyes half closed.

"Sure of what?" I ask, leaning in to taste the blood dripping from her lower lip.

"That you wanted me," she whispers, kissing with force.

I respond, knowing it's only a matter of time before I cut my teeth against her perfect skin. I feel her fumbling to unfasten her coat and she pulls away; our lips still locked. Then pain. Shock. Disbelief.

Vanessa pushes me back, and I stare at her. There's an angry, victorious grin on her face. I feel the hatred I sensed from her before crashing into me. The pain assails me again, and I drop to one knee. I look down. Protruding from my chest is a stake, about the size of a forearm. It pierces my heart.

"Why?" I utter, blood spilling from my mouth.

"Hunting your kind is what I do," she says, kicking me on to my back. "I've watched you for some time, murdering your way across America."

She steps on the stake. I scream as it passes through my back and into the ground. I can't feel my fingers, so I lift my hand to my face. It is turning black and splintering away, ash drifting away into the night's air.

Vanessa spits on me. I reach for her, and she kicks my arm, causing it to disintegrate completely.

"Go to hell," she growls, pulling the stake from my chest. She aims it above my throat and slams it down. I feel it cut off my airway. I fade into oblivion, choking on my blood and fading into the forest floor; the hatred in Vanessa's beautiful green eyes the last image I see as my sight fails and I become nothing.

DAVID GREEN grew up reading sci-fi, fantasy and horror. Now, he writes it.

Spending his youth in Manchester, UK, David now lives in Galway, Ireland. New to publishing, despite harbouring ambitions since he could spell his name, David's first work appeared in 2020 and has featured in many Black Hare Press anthologies, with his own single-author novelette to come.

Bibliography

Ancients, Black Hare Press, 2020
D is for Demons, Red Cape Publishing, 2020
Drabbles of Dread, Macabre Ladies, 2020
F is for Fear, Red Cape Publishing, 2020
Fatal Faeries, Nocturnal Sirens, 2020
Harvest, Blood Song Books, 2020
Lockdown Horror #2, Black Hare Press, 2020
Lockdown Paranormal Romance #1, Black Hare Press, 2020
Nick Holleran: Dead Man Walking, Black Hare Press, 2020
Passenger 13, Black Hare Press, 2020
Quietus 13, Black Hare Press, 2020
Scary Snippets Family Edition, Black Hare Press, 2020
School's In, Black Hare Press, 2020
Wetware, Black Hare Press, 2020

Connect
Website: davidgreenwritercom.wordpress.com
Amazon: amazon.com/author/davidgreenirl
Twitter: @DavidGreenWrite
Facebook: @DavidGreenWriter

PIECE OF MY HEART

by Chris Bannor

Why didn't you tell me?

"You love picking at my memories. In all the years you've been attached to my soul, why would you leave that one alone?"

I don't touch memories of your mom or the bokor.

The pre-show was almost over, and the last thing Columbus wanted to think about was his father, or what he would do when he showed up. Edu wasn't being helpful either. The demon locked himself up tight as soon as he found out who Columbus's father was. Why the hell was he bringing it up now?

"Have you figured anything out yet?"

He needs a big sacrifice, which is why he's coming

after us during the concert. He's one of the most powerful creatures in all creation, without extra power. With these many people, he could turn Hell inside out.

"So, we can't let him take control, no matter what."

As much as I hate the idea of moving against the Prince, no. We can't. I made a deal with the bokor to get me out of Hell. I don't want to see the Earth overrun by the Devil's minions.

"So, all we have to do is keep you in control of this body. If we can stay together, he won't be able to do anything."

"Who are you talking to, Columbus?"

Columbus looked as his manager walked through the door. "Just myself, Davies," he said as the man took a seat on the couch beside him.

"The opening act is almost done. You ready?"

He wasn't but nothing would make him ready for this. "Let's get this done."

Davies left him, giving him the last few minutes to prepare alone. Columbus was never alone though, and as soon as he picked up the guitar, he wouldn't be in control either.

"We do this together this time," he said to the demon he'd grown up with. "We take the stage as one, Edu."

There's a first time for everything. To keep Hell from

freezing over seems like a good reason to give it a try.

Columbus picked up his guitar. As soon as the guitar strap slipped over his head and the guitar fell into place in his hands, his spirit fell back. It wasn't an out-of-body experience, but it was a loss of control. He couldn't see from within, but there was a sense of Edu rising over him, filling the space around him, and surrounding him until he couldn't escape.

Edu?

"Let's face your old man, Columbus."

It was his voice, but there was a different tone, a note to it that never failed to make him shiver. Edu was a demon through and through. This was possession, every time he touched an instrument, a cruel fate his mother had thrust on him as a kid. Now, he had to trust in the creature that held him captive as soon as he picked up an instrument.

We beat the Devil tonight, in Detroit.

Ann Arbor Motel

The sun glared across the bed, and he dropped his arm over grit-filled eyes. His head spun and nausea followed. He grabbed for the water bottle he knew would be on the bedside table and sat up slowly to take a drink.

"He could at least take the hangover with him when he's done."

On the bedside table were a couple of pills and a granola bar. He took the aspirin and downed half the water before he tore into the food. Then he turned his eyes to the room.

"Where the hell did we end up this time, Edu?"

He remembered the concert in Sandusky, remembered the fans and the drive to the upscale party afterwards. Then nothing. He rarely blacked out completely when the demon took over, but this wasn't the first time, wouldn't be the last either.

He swung his legs over the side of the bed and felt the threadbare carpet under his feet. The wallpaper was faded and peeled in places, and the drapes had burn marks from cigarettes. He didn't smell smoke, so it probably wasn't him this time. He opened the drawer of the table and rummaged around until he found the hotel's stationery.

He was in Ann Arbor, Michigan. H wasn't supposed to be in Michigan for another three days, of all the fucking places to wake up. He was an Ohio State boy, of course. Born and raised in Ohio with a name like Columbus, you had to be a Buckeye.

His cell phone rang, and he looked down at the floor to find his pants at the foot of the bed, thrown off casually in a long string of clothes that led from the door. There were no additional items, and he was glad enough of that. He

didn't want to deal with another awkward morning after a night he couldn't remember. He picked up the phone and didn't bother to look at the ID.

"Where the hell are you?" Davies screamed over the line.

"Don't yell."

"You left the party with Jack, but he came crawling back two hours ago without you. Do you know what time it is?"

"No clue. Davies, I just woke up in a strange motel room in Ann Arbor."

"What the hell are you doing so far from Sandusky? You know what, never mind. Give me the address and I'll send a car to you. Grab something to eat and clean up. You have another show tonight."

"Yeah, I know."

"Columbus, you can't keep doing this."

"Yeah." He dropped his head low and let out a shaky breath. "I know."

He gave Davies the address from the stationery, disconnected the phone call, and stared at it in his hands. "Did you hear that? We can't keep doing this."

I'll be good. Tonight.

Detroit Hotel

And he was. Edu performed their Sandusky concert and handed control back over so Columbus could do a PR interview where he did his damnedest to be the fun-loving, yet sweet-natured rock star they all loved. They finished the Ohio leg of their tour without incident and had three nights left in Michigan. He only went to parties his agent approved, and he kept a low profile when he did. He preferred his life that way—simple, uncomplicated. Some would even say boring. Some didn't have to keep a demon at bay.

"Columbus, baby?"

He looked up from the concierge's counter where he'd been flirting with the girl on duty, trying to get the name of a good Thai place for takeout. "Mom?"

He hadn't seen his mom in three years, not in person, but she looked as young and pretty as ever. Her face had damned her years ago, but it was her rotting soul that still tormented him.

"Mom, what are you doing here?"

"Columbus, I just wanted to see you again. Can we talk?"

He let out a tired sigh but put on his best smile for the girl behind the counter. "Maybe later," he said as he turned back to his mom. He walked closer and offered his arm to her. She smiled warmly and took it, but when he was close enough, smoke and whiskey filled his nostrils.

He avoided the rock star lifestyle, but she'd never given it up. Once a groupie, always a groupie, they said. She'd lived for years off the gifts and favours of a guitar player in her youth, and she never moved past it. That's why she'd been so desperate to see him become a great guitar player.

Five years back, she'd shacked up with some drummer in Vegas. The guy supposedly took good care of her. His father had graced her with an eternally youthful face and body, but years of hard living had taken a toll on her mind.

Columbus walked away from her the night she'd told him the truth and introduced him to his dad. He'd always thought her ramblings about angels and demons were crazy before, but that night everything changed.

Columbus grew up with the voice of Edu in his head, his own personal demon. When he was a child, it was his favourite playmate. When he got bullied and teased for talking to it, he grew to hate the demon. He'd mostly come to terms with hearing a demon in his head, but he never knew why. Not until that night. He'd just always thought he was as crazy as his mom.

Then his father showed up and his mother explained everything. He vaguely remembered the bokor, but when his father told him he'd said yes to the demon that would forever have possession of his soul, he understood. The Devil had seduced her in a guitar player's body, so she tried to make him the same: a famous rock star, with a soul bound to Hell.

His mother had asked him to make a pact with a demon to become a great musician. She knew that he'd never be free of the demon. She knew that it would possess him whenever he picked up an instrument and that it would forever share a space inside his body. She knew, and she'd asked her four-year-old child to do it, anyway.

He led her through the lobby, and they waited quietly as the elevator came. When they arrived at his room, she walked in and pulled the curtains open to check out the view from the top floor. It was a spectacular skyline at night.

"They put you up real good," his mom said as she took a seat.

"Coffee? Tea?" he asked.

"Nothing so plain," she said coyly.

"Water? Those are the only options you have here." He could see a flash of anger in her eyes, but he wasn't about to offer her alcohol. If she wanted to get drunk, she could do it on someone else's shoulder. He didn't want to listen to her breakdown again.

"Coffee."

The act of starting the coffee and the aroma of freshly ground beans helped settled his nerves. He didn't know what to do with her. She never came to see him unless she needed something, and even then, she usually she just begged over the phone. She looked clean, not too thin. She didn't look like the disaster he'd last seen. "So, what do you want, Mom?"

"Can't I just come to see my son?"

"Right." He nodded his head, knowingly. "What does the old man want?"

"Old man? Is that any way to talk about your father?"

Your father?

It was the worst time for the damn voice to wake and he tried to suppress it, but that never worked for long. Once Edu was awake, he heard everything.

"What does he want?"

"I haven't talked to your father in ages," she lied smoothly. He turned his back and poured a cup of black coffee and walked it to her. She smiled calmly at him as he handed it off, and that's when it hit him.

"What the fuck? What are you doing here?" he demanded.

"What?" Her eyes were comically wide.

But she was too well put together. Her nails were manicured. Her hair was perfectly tossed in the "looks too carefree not to have taken hours" sort of way. Her tee shirt was crisply ironed and the holes in her jeans were store-bought, not from too much wear.

"What are you doing in her body?"

His mom stood, and suddenly the room seemed to dim, and she grew bigger. There was a pressure in his lungs that made it difficult to breathe, and the sulphurs of hellfire filled the air.

What the hell is going on?

"Your 'old man' can't come to visit too?" The voice echoing strangely in the room, masked only slightly by the higher pitch of his mother's vocal cords.

"The last time I saw you—the only time I've ever actually met you—it was because you needed my blood for a ritual. You suppressed the demon inside me and tried to kill me."

Fucking Hell! This is your father?

Yes, he answered the screaming voice inside his head. *Now, will you shut the hell up?*

Your father is—

The Devil. Satan. Yeah, I got that.

"I need a throng of worshippers. Just a quick spell to cause some mayhem in the world. It won't take more than a night. Let me in and I can push that demon out of your body. Once I'm done, I'll let you go and you can live scot-free of all demons, forevermore."

Columbus scoffed, "Right. A throng of worshippers. So, you want to possess me before my gig tonight?"

"You do have a nice crowd lined up."

"And what do you want to do to them? Is it enough to have them worshipping the body you're in?"

"That's all just details. We can talk about that later. Nothing could be traced back to you, no matter what I do."

"No."

"Hear me out."

"No. Because even if I did, why would I believe you? You are the actual Father of Lies. The Tempter. The Beast."

Satan rolled his eyes, and Columbus wished he knew how to remove his father from his mother's body. She must have said yes at some point though, and once that happened, there was no way to rid the soul of a demon taint. He'd looked hard enough to remove his own.

"Isn't your mother more important than those other humans?"

"Look at her memories, bastard. She hasn't been my mom since she turned me into a demon carrier. She's just the first in a long, broken line of women I've met in my life. One life isn't worth whatever you plan on doing to my fans."

"They're not really your fans, are they? They belong

to your demon. What do you call him again?" His mother's smile was more vicious than he'd remembered it could be. "Edu?"

"Edu and I have a good thing worked out now. Leave us alone and we'll stay out of your way."

"You are my son. Did you think things could remain that easy for you?"

"I am one of how many illegitimate kids that you have? No one has ever taken an interest in me. And they aren't likely too."

"We'll see. In fact, we'll see tonight."

"What is that supposed to mean?"

His mother smiled, but then the facade crumpled, and he watched as the carefully cultured woman fell apart. Her wide blue eyes filled with tears, and her shoulders hunched forward. She brought shaking hands up to her face and sobbed.

This was the woman he'd left behind. The one who raised him. The one who asked him to sell his soul to a demon when he was too young to say no. The groupie who never stopped chasing the next man, the next hit, the next addiction.

"Mom, it's okay. He's gone now."

"I know," she sobbed. "Oh God, I know. How could he leave me again?"

Columbus, this is fucked.

I know, Edu.

No. Satan just sent you—us—a challenge. Whatever he's doing, he isn't giving up that easily.

Yeah. I guess we'd better be ready tonight then.

Detroit On Stage

The anticipation was worse than he'd expected. He waited in his own body, but they finished the first hour and a half of the concert and the show played on just as it always did. The Devil hadn't shown.

The audience was pumped up, and they screamed along with the lyrics. They headbanged to the drum solos and strummed the bass lines. They played air guitar along with Edu, and screamed their voices hoarse in the cool night air.

He didn't like the loss of control, so he usually drifted off into the sightless black of his soul, but tonight, he was constantly on guard. Every strange shout of the crowd, every time another performer missed a beat or made some unusual move, he was watching. Waiting. He was nearly twitching with the need for the old man to show.

When the opening chords of "Soulfire's Ballad" began, the crowd roared. It was their best-known hit and the song that had brought Columbus onto the map as a world-class guitar player and songwriter. He felt the surrounding air begin to twist and turn, felt the heavy dampness in the air. The winds screamed through the stadium, and the crowd shrieked even harder to be heard over it.

Fuck! Here it comes!

There was nothing for the audience to see, nothing for them to know that the Devil had arrived in Detroit, but between one stroke of the hand and the next fire poured through his veins and his lungs burned. Time stopped and acid dripped on his bones like they could erase the pact made between himself and Edu so long ago.

Hell no, Columbus screamed at the pressure inside his body. *I did not put up with his ass all these years to get a replacement just when we figured out how to live with this!*

His father pushed power through Columbus's veins, and a weaker demon would have buckled, but Edu was no weak thing. In fact, he was no Hell demon. As Satan pushed against the barriers that had bound Edu and Columbus together, Edu pulled his own power around him.

The acid of his bones turned to fire and pulsed, like waves of heat that singed everything they touched. His father screamed from it, but Edu and Columbus pushed, again and again, throwing the corrosion from their body and redoubling their efforts to seal their pact to bone.

The song crescendoed in the night air and the audience

screamed. The air pulsed around them once more, and this time Edu shrouded himself with the rest of his might and forced the Devil away from the body he was trying to steal from him.

The entire crowd fell to the ground as a gust of wind blew them down. The band was knocked around on the stage, and the set and stage stood only because of the dedication of the crew who had so meticulously bolted them in place. Columbus, alone, stood on the stage, looking down at the staggering, drunken masses.

How dare you! His father roared in his head. *You cannot cast me out!*

I did not let you in, bastard, Columbus answered. There was more to it than that, but the old man didn't need to know that secret. There were plenty of creatures in Hell that were called demons but were not.

Go try your hand at some other brat, Edu said. *This one is mine.*

They felt him leave, as suddenly as he had come, and then Columbus let his knees buckle and his eyes close. *Well, that was interesting.*

He came prepared to force a Hell demon out of your body. He did not come prepared for something older.

What are you? Really?

You don't remember? Edu asked.

He thought back to his many years with Edu in his head and remembered their first meeting. He remembered hiding under his covers at night, terrified of what he had done and the creature that followed him everywhere now. "What are you?" he'd asked Edu back then, afraid of the voice but too curious to curtail the question.

Shedu.

"Wha's a edu?"

Not edu. I am shedu.

"'Edu."

Even then he could feel the gentle affection of the beast in his head. *All right. Since you cannot say Shedu, you may call me Edu.*

"Shedu," Edu said. Though he used Columbus's voice, no other could hear him through the raging winds. "I am a shedu of Mesopotamia. I am the Storm Demon."

Columbus let out a laugh, tinged in hysterics, but it was freeing. He had fought, not just to keep his father from using him, but to keep Edu. For the first time since he said yes to the bokor as a child, he found peace with that decision.

CHRIS BANNOR is a speculative fiction writer who lives in Southern California. Chris learned her love of genre stories from her mother at an early age and has never veered far from that path. Her stories range from horror to science fiction, romance, and fantasy.

When Chris isn't writing, she enjoys movie marathons, binge-watching TV shows, musical theater, and road trips with her family. Otherwise, she is a general homebody who lives with her two teenagers, a cat, and a dog.

Bibliography

ANCIENTS, Black Hare Press, 2020
Clockwork Dragons, Zombie Pirates Publishing, 2020
Dark Solstice, EMerry Publishing, 2020
Drabbles of Dread, Macabre Ladies, 2020
Deep Sea, Black Hare Press, 2020
Forgotten Ones, Eerie River Press, 2020
Innovation, Queer Sci-fi, 2020
Lockdown Phantoms #2, Black Hare Press 2020
LOVE, Black Hare Press, 2020
Once, Iron Faerie Publishing, 2020
Scary Snippets: Sibling Edition, Nocturnal Sirens Publishing, 2020
Twenty Twenty, Black Hare Press, 2020

Connect

Website: www.chrisbannor.com
Facebook: @ChrisBannorAuthor
Twitter: @BannorChris
Instagram: @chrisbannor

THE MAN WHO SOLD THE WORLD

by Stephanie Scissom

Memories of my father were scattered, but warm. They didn't reconcile with the portrait the media painted of him—the sad, withdrawn rock star who'd taken his own life at the age of 27. In my memories, he was laughing. Happy.

We'd had our own sign language. Mom had known some of the signs, but not all. We'd held secret, silly conversations that invariably ended with him signing, "You're my favourite human." For sure, at six years old, he'd been mine.

He'd sung my bedtime stories instead of reading them; let me paint his nails and style his hair. We'd held dance parties in our pyjamas and eaten cookie dough straight from the tube.

Then one rainy November night, he'd stuck a needle in his arm, injecting nearly four times the lethal amount of heroin into his veins.

Everything had changed after that.

The house was so quiet and cold without him. My mother was never good at showing love, and sometimes I'd rebelled simply to make her react. I missed my father every day. The world had lost an artist, "the voice of a generation." I had lost so much more.

I was twenty-three when Magnum Enterprises broadcast their first resurrection—Walt Disney. The world reacted incredulously and violently. Some proclaimed it a hoax, while others thought it was the beginning of the apocalypse. Everything we knew—everything before and after—was changed. Another of Magnum's resurrections, a Greek billionaire, allowed himself to be subjected to a battery of public tests. The results were irrefutable. The technology existed that would defeat death, but the cost was unimaginable for most.

In two years, I would inherit my portion of an estate that was valued at nearly a billion dollars, and I did not hesitate to pledge it all to get him back. I met with the head of Magnum Enterprises, who told me more about what to expect, though little about how they could make it happen. To be honest, I didn't care how they did it.

He promised to return my father, complete with all his memories. He warned that, while any mental issues like depression and tendencies towards addiction would still be present because they are moderately to highly heritable, perhaps they could be combated with foreknowledge and adjustment of environmental factors. While not exactly a clean slate, he would have a chance. I was older now, stronger. Whatever demons he had to fight, I would fight alongside him. I had two major obstacles, however.

The first was my mother. I didn't dare tell her what I was planning, for I knew she would not approve. I always wondered about my parents' relationship—if she had ever loved him—but with her, it was hard to tell. She'd dated his former manager for the past seventeen years, but they maintained different households and never mentioned marriage.

My memory classified my parents' marriage as chaotic and angry—at least on her part. I remembered her yelling and raging until he retreated and hid. My mother said once that she'd grown weary of his addictions and his inability to grow up, but they'd tried to make it work because of me. Although she'd never say it, I always suspected his death had been somewhat of a relief to her, and I resented her for that. She was a person who liked certainties and stability, and he could provide neither of those things. She lived well and practically with the wealth he'd left behind and expected me to do the same. Money had never been a worry for me, but it had never been a prison either. I just wanted him back, and I didn't care if it left me penniless to do so.

The other problem was DNA. They needed a sample of DNA that was irrefutably and solely his—but after so many years, I had nothing. No hairbrush or toothbrush, and his body had been cremated and scattered. I asked my grandmother about his baby teeth or locks of hair, and she said they had been lost long ago.

Then it hit me. A few months before his suicide, he'd had his wisdom teeth removed. He had kept them, brought them home to me in an Altoids tin because he'd thought they looked weird and funny. We'd thrown them in a jar with my first baby teeth and forgotten them.

My mother kept my baby things in a trunk in her attic, and I snuck up there one day while she was grocery shopping to retrieve them. My hands shook when I poured them into my palm. Funny how those ugly, long-rooted teeth were the key to getting my heart's desire.

I still don't know how it worked. I brought them his teeth and his money the day after my twenty-fifth birthday, and three months later, just as he'd promised, Ezra Magnum called me.

"Katy," he asked. "Are you ready to see your father again?"

He met me at the airport in Denver, and we drove to a gated facility outside of Boulder. During the ride, he braced me for what was to come.

"Kolt is doing well," he assured me. "But as you can imagine, there's an adjustment period. He's trying to process the fact that he's been dead for nearly twenty years and that the world is different now. Time has moved on and he has to catch up. There's a lot of discombobulation. This is when we like to bring in the loved ones, because we feel that you—more than anyone—can help him adjust. You're invited to stay here with him, until his team feels he's ready for the outside. Then, you can take him home."

The facility was nice and well-staffed—looking more like an expensive apartment building than a lab or hospital. A smiling therapist met us at the door when Magnum rang the doorbell of apartment 405.

"Are you ready?" she asked and squeezed my hand. Her smile widened, and she said, "Wow, you look so much like him."

As we walked through the kitchen, she said, "He's

really quiet, and there's still a lot of confusion. I'm sure Dr Magnum told you to expect that. We will take it nice and slow."

I nodded, but I couldn't find words either. My heart slammed in my chest. Through an open doorway, I saw the back of his head. He sat unmoving on a couch, watching television.

"Would you like me to introduce you?" she asked.

I shook my head and walked into the living room, leaving them in the hallway.

He never moved as I approached. His eyes remained glued to the television while his hands lay folded and still in his lap.

His profile took my breath away—the long, blond hair and pale blue eyes. It was him, really him, though he looked so much smaller and frailer than I remembered. They'd dressed him in clothing he was comfortable in—faded jeans, grey t-shirt covered with a blue and black flannel, and Converse. He was the age he'd been when he'd died. It felt like a strange, beautiful dream.

My eyes filled with tears and I squeaked out, "Hi."

Slowly, he turned his head and looked at me. His eyes widened, and the colour drained from his face. He studied me for a long moment, then turned back to the television.

I stood there on shaky legs, unsure of what to do next. Then I saw his hand move. Just a slight movement, but one that meant something to me. He signed, "Scared."

I squeezed my eyes shut, feeling the tears escape down my cheek. We'd done those signs so much that it had become habitual. I still did the same thing he'd just done, reflexively. These doctors didn't know that. This was really my father—not a fake, not a clone.

I stepped in front of the TV and signed, "Me, too."

His breath expelled in a hiss, and he looked up at me with haunted eyes. "Kitkat?"

I couldn't speak, could barely stand. I signed, "Daddy."

He *launched* himself at me and seized me in his arms. I threw my arms around his neck and buried my face against his flannel shirt. His scent wrecked me—undefinable, long-forgotten, yet instantly recognisable and remembered.

I sobbed—ugly, heaving sobs—soaking his shirt with my tears. I was crying for all we had lost, and all that had just been returned to us.

My daddy was *alive*.

I'm not sure how long we stood there, clutching each other. He was crying as hard as I was, but he was smoothing my hair, trying to comfort me.

"Baby, it's okay," he whispered over and over. He pulled back just enough to rest his forehead against mine. "My God. Let me look at you."

He clutched my face in his hands and studied me like he was trying to memorise every detail. "You look just like me."

"I hear that all the time."

"I bet your mom hates that," he said with a smile. "Where is she?"

"She doesn't know," I admitted. "She doesn't know about any of this."

He blinked. "Oh."

Then he led me to the couch, and we sat, knee-to-knee, holding hands. I told him about my inheritance (he seemed staggered by the amount of it) and how I'd contacted Magnum Enterprises as soon as I'd seen that first broadcast.

"You were just six," he said softly. "You spent all that money, everything you had, just to get me back? Why?"

I signed, "You're my favourite human."

He huffed out a breath and gave me another fierce hug.

"You're mine, too. There were all these people around me, and they wanted all these things, and they were only happy with me when I gave them what they wanted. Not you. You were the first person in my whole life who really loved me. All you wanted was my time. And the only time I was really happy was when I was with you."

"Why did you leave me?"

The words burst out before I could stop them, horrifying me. I never meant to ask that, because the last thing I wanted to do was guilt him.

Instead of looking guilty, he looked confused.

"I don't remember—I can't remember what happened. They didn't tell me. How did I die?"

I looked back towards the kitchen, but Dr Magnum and the therapist were gone. I didn't know what to say, but I could not lie to him.

"You killed yourself. Heroin overdose, enough that they were sure it wasn't accidental."

He shook his head, slowly, then more emphatically. "No. No, that's not right. I never would've left you alone with her."

"With who?" I asked. "Mom?"

He wouldn't answer.

"Mom and Uncle Greg said you'd been depressed. There was a note…"

"Uncle Greg?" He frowned. "Do you mean Greg Warren?"

I hesitated, wishing Dr Magnum was in here. I felt like

I was handling this badly, and I didn't want to do anything to upset him, but he was going to find out soon enough.

"Yes," I said. "He and Mom…they're together now. Not married, but they've been dating for years."

The look on his face melted from astonishment to something else—realisation.

He took both my hands. His were shaking.

"Katy, this is not what I want to be talking about. I want to know everything about you, and your life. But…I need to know what happened. What you think happened. I don't know how your relationship with your mother is, or what you remember about our marriage—"

"I remember arguments. Her yelling, pounding on the bathroom door while you locked yourself inside. She told me that's where you'd go to get high."

His eyes narrowed, and his jaw clenched. I never remembered seeing him angry before, not even when she railed at him.

"She said I blamed her," I continued and gave a helpless shrug. "Maybe I did. Our relationship isn't yelling and fighting. It's distant. I'm very good at avoiding her and she's good at letting me."

He looked defeated. "I'm so sorry, Katy. I never wanted your life to be like that. I wanted you to have the best childhood any kid could ask for. I was changing things, making plans to get out. I was buying this little house in Alabama, on the Gulf of Mexico, because you used to love the ocean."

"Mother never told me that," I said.

"She didn't know. About the house, anyway. It wasn't going to be her home." He leaned back against the cushions. "The last time I saw Greg Warren, he was threatening to sue me. I was quitting the band. Quitting music. It didn't make me happy anymore. I hated the new album and didn't want to release it."

"*Euphoria*?" I asked. "It was released posthumously. It's sold over forty million copies worldwide."

Instead of looking proud, he grimaced. "I hated it. Commercial fluff. We'd become something I never wanted to be. I'd also told your mother I wanted a divorce. The only reason I was still there was you, but after Paris, I was done. And with the tapes, I had enough leverage to get custody." His eyes widened. "I need you to help me find someone. Liz Jessup. She was your mother's friend first, the lead singer of a band that opened for us that last tour. But she found out what happened, and she tried to help me. She can verify everything I'm about to tell you."

I pulled out my phone and googled the name. The first thing that appeared was a Wikipedia page. She was dead, only a week after my father's death. Also of heroin overdose.

"That is not true!" he said. "She wasn't using, either. Not for a long time—"

He looked like he was about to cry, so I said, "Paris. Are you talking about right before? They said that was the first time you tried to kill yourself."

"They told you that was a suicide attempt? Your mother drugged me. She said it was an accident. We'd been arguing and she put some of her pills in my whiskey. She said it was just to make me sleep, so that I'd calm down and stop packing. The next thing I knew, I woke up in the hospital. A maid had found me. I covered for your mother, but I never trusted her again. I had thought for a couple of weeks I was being followed, and my garage was broken into. I bought a gun, but she got that taken away from me."

"I think I remember that day. The police came."

He nodded. "You were crying. I was trying to get her to stop, and when she wouldn't, I just went in the bedroom and locked the door. She told the police I had a gun and was going to kill myself, but I never even touched it. And I wasn't high."

My blood ran cold. I knew my mother. She always thought two steps ahead, and it appeared she was trying to paint a very specific picture. Setting up the final scene.

My father wiped a hand down his face. "She and Liz were close. Allison told her some things, and then Liz started recording their conversations. She gave me the tapes, and I hid them in a tackle box in the crawlspace under the house. You said there was a note? Do you know what it said?"

"I can do better than that," I said, tapping on my phone. "Here."

His suicide note had been published online. He scanned it, his lips moving as he read. Then he looked at me. "This whole first part...I did write it, but it wasn't a suicide note. That was a note I wrote to the fans, explaining that I was quitting the music business. It had nothing to do with suicide. And this last part—the part about you and your mom—that's not my handwriting."

There had been some debate about his note online, with some wondering why he talked so much about music and so little about us. Also, the shaky, bigger handwriting at the bottom did look different, but that was attributed to him already being high when he wrote it.

"Katy, I need you to believe me. I was clean, and I did not kill myself. The day you were born, my whole world changed. I was a father. Holy shit, it was terrifying! Who was I to try to take care of anyone? I was barely taking care of myself in those days. The first time I held you, I felt like you were judging me, staring at me with those unblinking eyes. It was the first relationship in my entire life that had permanence. I had just married your mother, but, even then, I'm not sure either of us felt like it would last forever. People drifted in and out of my life; That's just the way it was. Even my parents. I'd never known my father. Truthfully, I'd never known my mother either, even though we'd lived in the same house until I left at fifteen. I wasn't going to let us be like that."

"We weren't," I whispered. "We aren't, even now."

"They had you bundled up, but your little hand escaped the blanket and I was trying to put it back when you grasped my finger. I knew right then that—no matter what I'd got wrong in my life—it wasn't going to be this. It wasn't going to be you. This was something I couldn't lose. I don't know what you've been told about me, but I swear this to you: I never used drugs after that day. Not once. When I told you that you were my favourite human, I meant it. From the day you were born, you were the only thing that mattered to me. You still are."

He was the only thing that mattered to me, too, and I was enraged at the ones who'd stolen so much from us. I could tell he was afraid—afraid of seeing her again, of confronting them. I didn't tell him I had no intention of letting him.

I spent the weekend there, then left him a note that Monday morning before he woke, saying I had to run a few errands and that I'd be back soon. I didn't tell him that my business was in Los Angeles.

I called my mother before I flew out, to make sure she'd be home. She told me she had an interview with a local talk show that morning, but she'd be home that afternoon. In all the excitement, I hadn't even realised today was the twentieth anniversary of my father's death. It seemed fitting, somehow.

I arrived at her place around noon. Before I went inside, I retrieved the tackle box from the crawlspace. It was right where he said it would be. The tiny recorder still held the tape, but the batteries were dead. I entered the house and rummaged through the kitchen drawer until I found a pair of AAAs.

The tape still played. I would've believed him even if it hadn't but hearing it with my own ears only strengthened my resolve. I put the recorder in my purse and lay on my mother's bed to watch a "Behind the Scenes" special about my father on MTV while I waited.

I was in some of the videos with him. In one of them, I was about three, sitting on my bed with him and strumming a toy guitar while he sang a song he'd written for me, "Katy Did."

My mother came in while it was playing. She glanced at the TV, laid her purse and phone on the nightstand, then brushed a kiss in the general direction of my ear before she said, "Have you eaten lunch?"

It infuriated me that she could look at him—look at *me*—without so much as a hint of remorse, but I didn't show it. "Not yet."

"I'm going to take a shower. Those studio lights made me sweat. When I get out, we'll order some Chinese."

"Greg's not coming over?" I asked.

"No, he's probably packing. He has a flight to Phoenix this evening."

I watched her grab some clothes from her dresser, thinking about what Dad had said about his own mother. How sad and telling that I felt so much more for a man that I hadn't seen in twenty years than I felt for the woman who'd been here my entire life.

She'd just shut the bathroom door behind her when her phone lit up. I guess she still had it on mute from the interview. As expected, it was Greg, wanting to know if she'd made it home yet and how the interview had gone. I decided to reply.

Yes. Do you ever get tired of the lies?

Immediately, he replied: *Have you been drinking?*

Does it ever bother you what we did?

He took a moment longer to respond this time: *We did what we had to do. Where is this coming from, Allison?*

Before I could reply, the phone showed an incoming call from Greg. I declined it, which he shouldn't perceive as particularly unusual. My mother detested talking on the phone. I texted: *I miss him.*

LOL! You HAVE been drinking. You hated him.

Katy wants to resurrect him.

The phone showed Greg is typing, then: *Good thing she doesn't have a DNA sample.*

I was playing with fire, hadn't thought this out, but I plunged on. *I think she knows what we did. She hates me.*

She knows nothing. Wth, Allison?

I just want to tell her the truth. Make her understand. It was for her, too.

Immediately, he texted: *Don't tell her anything. I'm coming over.*

In the next room, I heard the shower shut off. Hurriedly, I stuck Mom's phone under a pillow. Greg only lived a couple of blocks away. I didn't have much time.

She walked out of the bathroom, towelling her hair.

"I had Dad resurrected," I blurted.

I've never seen anyone turn so white. She froze, her hands still clutching the towel.

"I used his wisdom teeth."

She swayed and grabbed the doorframe.

I pretended to be distraught instead of angry. "He says you killed him and that he can prove it. He supposedly has tapes, made by some girl named Liz, that incriminate you."

She opened her mouth, but nothing came out.

"Mother, say it isn't true! He was so angry. He said he's coming here."

This wasn't how I'd planned it, but it fell into place perfectly. Downstairs, we heard a door slam and the beep-beep-beep as someone disengaged the alarm pad.

Mother panicked, scrambling for her phone. She dumped the contents of her purse on the floor and pawed through them.

Footsteps creaked on the stairs.

"Mama!" I hissed. "He's going to kill you! Where's your gun?"

She grabbed the gun from her nightstand and clicked off the safety. When Greg opened the door, she pumped two rounds into his chest.

She screamed when she realised what she'd done and dropped the gun before scrambling over to him and hitting her knees.

Blood gushed from his wounds, and she tried to press her hands over them. She never even looked at me when I walked up beside her and fired a bullet into her temple.

I might look just like my father, but I guess I was my mother's daughter as well. I didn't feel a thing as I cleaned my prints off the gun with her towel and placed it in her bloody hand. Then I wiped my prints off her phone and laid it with the contents of her overturned purse.

I took a bus halfway, then hailed a cab to take me to San Diego, where my house was and where I'd flown into. I'd left my phone on my kitchen counter in case anyone bothered to ping it. I sent a few work emails, chatted with a neighbour, then packed a bag, and headed back to Boulder. I was back in my father's apartment by six, bearing a sack full of his favourite fast food—double cheeseburgers from McDonald's.

They didn't find the bodies for two days. The police wrote it off exactly as I'd hoped—a remorseful widow and her lover arguing on the twentieth anniversary of her husband's death. Although I was sure they'd read the text messages on my mother's phone, they never addressed it with me. I caught my father looking at me a few times, mostly as we watched the news, but he didn't address it either.

On the day we left Boulder, we had new names, new appearances, and a new beginning. Because of our current age difference, we would live as brother and sister.

As far as the world was concerned, Kolt Jacobs was dead, and Katy Jacobs was a tragic afterthought.

"Let's get out of here," I said, pulling a baseball cap over his short, dark hair. "Alabama's waiting."

STEPHANIE SCISSOM writes paranormal romance, horror, thriller, erotica and anything else that catches her interest.

She's traditionally published four novels under the name Michelle Perry, with some shorter pieces listed below.

Bibliography

A CONTRACT OF WORDS, Scout Media, 2018
A FLASH OF WORDS, Scout Media, 2019
A MONSTER TOLD ME BEDTIME STORIES, Soteira Press, 2020
ANGELS, Black Hare Press, 2019
APOCALYPSE, Black Hare Press, 2019
BAD ROMANCE, Black Hare Press, 2019
BEYOND, Black Hare Press, 2019
DAUGHTERS OF DARKNESS, Blair Daniels, 2018
FOLKLORE, Zuma Press, 2019
FOREST OF FEAR, Blood Song Books, 2019
HARVEST 2ND EDITION, Blood Song Books, 2020
LOCKDOWN PARANORMAL 1 & 2, Black Hare Press 2020
LOCKDOWN SCI FI, Black Hare Press, 2020
LOUISIANA HORROR, Soteira Press, 2020
LOVE, Black Hare Press, 2020
LUST, Black Hare Press, 2020
PRIDE, Black Hare Press, 2020
Scary Snippets Campfire Edition, **Nocturnal Sirens Publishing**, 2020
Scary Snippets Family Edition, **Nocturnal Sirens Publishing**, 2020
Scary Snippets Halloween Edition, **Nocturnal Sirens Publishing**, 2019
SHATTERED VEIL, The Great Void Books, 2020
STORIES THAT SING, Havok Publishing, 2020
THE TRENCHCOAT CHRONICLES, Celestial Echo Press, 2020
TWISTED, Medusa Laugh Press, 2017
YEAR ONE, Black Hare Press, 2019

Connect

Twitter: @chell22_7
Facebook: @StephanieScissom2019

SAY YOU LOVE ME OR SAY GOODNIGHT

by J.W. Garrett

Conner's gaze drifted to the airport's display screen, as he watched his flight delay time increase again. This time from forty minutes to an hour. Several people around him shrugged and shook their heads in sympathy. Conner huffed out a breath in frustration. While he didn't have all the details nailed down just yet, it was still his vacation, and he didn't want to spend it stuck in an airport.

Someone seated nearby groaned as he stared at the departure screen, rolled his eyes, then shouldering his bags, took off at a run.

Conner plopped down in the vacated seat and dug into

his bag for the sandwich and chips he'd bought to eat during his now hour-long-and-counting wait. Before he finished unwrapping his lunch, someone's head slid across the chair back and collided with his shoulder. "What the hell?"

Diverted from his food and pissed now, Conner used his elbow to shove back against the growing weight, still not taking his eyes from the food in front of him. When that tactic didn't work, he gave up and turned his attention to the intruder. Long straight blonde hair splayed the length of his arm. Definitely not a dude… She was out; his shove hadn't been gentle.

Rewrapping his sandwich and stowing it once more, he leaned into her, trying to sway her weight in the other direction. No dice. Conner would need to stand and totally redirect her body in the other direction. God, were there any other seats? He tossed a glance around the immediate seating area. No. None… He was met with a few laughs—others just shook their heads. Hell, this wasn't his fault.

When he stood, the lady slammed into his seat, landing with a moan, her hand coming up to remove her hair from her face. Conner shook his head. "She lives."

Her brows furrowed in confusion before her green eyes widened, and she lifted herself back into her own space. An eerie sort of sadness registered in her eyes when she took in the snickering and silent laughter all around her.

She rearranged herself and scooted over. "I'm so sorry."

Conner stared back, captivated. How did she communicate so much through her eyes? Surely the depth of feeling there wasn't just because of this? And besides, sad or not, she was a knockout, more so now that he could see her curves without her bent over. "Hey, it's not that bad. No harm done. Don't let the idiots here bother you."

She smoothed her shirt and ran a hand through her hair. "It's just…well…I've been here all night. I haven't really slept in over twenty-four hours." She lifted her gorgeous green gaze to his again.

While he fumbled for his seat, Conner didn't break eye contact. "Sorry. No harm done."

"I'm Cecily Baker." She stretched out her arm. "My friends call me CeCe."

Already ranked as *friend* status—that sounded promising. "Conner, Conner Duncan. I'm a reporter, currently trying to find some downtime while exploring what Denver has to offer. If I ever make it there, that is."

CeCe flashed a smile, leaving behind a radiant glow in its wake.

Damn, now that's more like it.

"Me too." She beamed back at him. "That's where I'm going."

Could this piss of a day be turning up? "Yeah?"

"Yep," she said, popping the "*p*." "I've got gigs lined up for the next five nights, all in Colorado—the first two in Denver."

Conner pressed against her shoulder. "Are you in a band?"

"Well…" A shadow fell over her eyes.

Those eyes again…they told all.

"Not at the moment. But each job is a steppingstone, right?"

"Right." Conner nodded, wanting to encourage her to keep talking. "What do you play?"

"The electric guitar," she said, as the corners of her mouth eased up.

"That's hot." Only after she giggled, Conner realised he'd said that part out loud.

"Oh, don't worry. I get far worse comments than that. Yours was…nicer than most." She turned her head, scanning the long passageway full of travellers.

"Hungry?"

"Yeah." She brought her attention back to settle on his face.

"How about we share? I'm not that hungry. Just filling time till we board," he lied.

She tilted her head.

He could almost see her thoughts churning. Big

step…sharing food.

"Okay. If you're sure you don't mind. Whatcha got?"

"Turkey, bacon, and cheese." Conner's eyebrows arched upward, hopeful.

"Mmmm," she said, her lips vibrating.

Definitely needed to get her to do that again.

The next forty minutes flew by. They ate; she talked; he listened. Typically Conner wouldn't engage in small talk, especially at airports. He opted for his earbuds and laptop…always using every available minute following up on the next lead for a story—his favourite diversion. But time with her felt bigger, more significant than that.

The call came to board, and an inner panic seized him. He couldn't just let this connection go. He shouldered his bag and, going for a casual tone, lightly touched her arm. "Hey, I've got an idea."

She blinked those sparkling green eyes at him again, waiting for him to continue.

"For a story. A story about you and your week on the road." Her eyes widened, and taking that as a sign, he continued. "I'm certain I can get my editor's approval. Our music fans will eat this up." He jerked his head towards the line forming. "Maybe we can talk about it more during the flight." He held his breath. *Too pushy?* He'd know soon enough.

"But I'm nobody. No one would care."

This he could deal with. God, he hoped she could actually play. "Yeah, they will." He needed a quick listen before he formally requested to do a feature. Otherwise, he could get himself demoted or worse for not taking the time to properly vet the subject and content matter of a story. "I'm sure you have demoed your work, sent it to A&R reps at various recording studios, right?"

"Well, yeah, sure. In fact, one of them will be coming to hear me this week."

"See? This story could be the boost you need. Shoot me a link." As they walked down the ramp towards the plane, she handed over her phone, and Conner typed in his number. "I'll download it before we take off."

"Really?" CeCe stepped into her row, aisle ten; he was in twenty-one. "Wait. I wanna hear more. If you were serious, that is."

Yesss. "I'll see what I can do to change seats," he said, lingering in the centre aisle before continuing to his row. Hell… What exactly was he doing? He hadn't even pitched the idea to his editor, much less got approval for a lead story or approval for his expenses to follow her around for the next five days, gathering what he needed for a story. His boss might hate the idea…or more likely, just not give a damn. It would need to be one hell of a story.

And this was supposed to be his first vacation in three years.

Before he went over this cliff headfirst with no net, he tapped the link in the text CeCe had just sent. Catching a glimpse of her face before she sank into her seat, he winked, then dropped into his own until he had the information he needed. What had flashed across her face just now? Apprehension? Fear? Reading people was an essential skill for every reporter—a survival mechanism. That ability had got him more leads, helped determine the veracity of his sources, and steered him clear of danger more times than he could count. Where was it now?

Something felt off.

Clicking the link, he sighed. Well, damn, it wasn't her musical ability. "Miss, excuse me, I'm moving up to aisle ten. There's an open seat."

"Sure," the flight attendant said, flashing a practised smile. "We have a few vacant seats. Make yourself comfortable. Take off is in five minutes though, so you'll need to get settled quickly."

"You got it."

Conner manoeuvred his way back up the centre aisle, then scooted into row ten. "Looks like there's room, if you don't mind."

"Oh, did I pass?"

"What?"

"I assume that's what you were doing back there. Checking me out."

"Yeah," he chuckled. "You sure as hell did. Where did you learn to play like that?"

"Before I could walk, I had an instrument in my hand. Music is like…breathing to me and almost as essential."

Damn… "You mind if I record our conversation? I mean, not sure if I'll use any of it. But I'll need background on you. Adds depth to the piece."

"Sure, go ahead."

Conner pulled out his voice-activated recorder, housed in a flash drive. CeCe stared at the device. "Uh, yeah, these are pretty cool, huh? Lots of battery power, picks up everything, and I can play it back later, without sucking battery from my phone. We good to go?"

"Yeah."

"You'll see the story before it runs, when I get final approval."

CeCe grinned. "You haven't even asked yet, right?"

"No…But when my editor hears you play and what I have planned, he'll tell me to run with it. So…ready?"

CeCe jogged her head.

"Here we go. Just pressing record." Conner cleared his throat. "Why don't we start with when you learned to play.

You mentioned off-mike that you started at an early age."

"That's right. My parents were country music stars. My mom sang, and my dad played just about any instrument put in his hands. So, yes, from a very young age, I had music before I had words. In fact, I can't remember a time when music wasn't a part of my life. From morning till night, that's all there was, practising, writing songs, band practice until late. And of course, I went to sleep wherever my parents were playing for the night." Her mouth quirked up on one side. "I guess you could say music is my love language."

"But they were country musicians, you said, right?"

"That's right. And I learned to play guitar while listening to all their favourites—Willie Nelson, George Strait, Dolly Parton, Johnny Cash, to name a few. When I got older, I realised my interest was rock, and my parents weren't too happy about that. In fact, one night, after playing at the Ryman, they caught me jamming with a band—instead of where I was supposed to be, listening to their performance—they said I'd be on my own if I chose my own music over them."

"You weren't *not* choosing them though. It was about the music, from what I hear you saying."

She cocked her head. "They didn't see it that way."

"It must have been rough after that."

"Yeah, I left home two days later."

"How old were you then?"

"Sixteen."

"I'm sorry to hear that. Did you work it out with them later?"

CeCe hung her head. "Turn that thing off, will you?"

"Sure…done."

"Three days later they were dead. A murder suicide. Because of me. That's what the letter said." Tears seeped from her eyes and trickled slowly down her cheeks.

"God, CeCe. That was horrible, but that was their decision." Conner reached for her and squeezed her close. "That's not on you. No matter what they said."

"They made it clear in the letter what they thought about me—about my choices. Said they couldn't live with it."

"What parents would do that to their own child? I don't get it."

"The coroner's report stated they were both dying of various forms of cancer, completely eaten away with it apparently. They never even told me that they were sick. That night at the Ryman was their *last call*, so to speak. Their swan song. *And* was to be my formal introduction into their world. Which they did, touting their daughter as an up-and-coming music artist, but I wasn't even there to hear it.

My parents were understandably embarrassed to be stood up by their own daughter—and on stage no less. I screwed that up royally, rubbing their noses in it too by leaving. With all they were already suffering, it was just too much."

"I'm amazed at how well you've done. It's incredible really. You must have a very strong will."

Something flashed across her face, for only an instant.

So quickly that Conner thought he had imagined the smug, cocky grin before it disappeared. "CeCe, are you okay? We can finish this later if you'd like."

"No. I'm all right."

"Are you sure?" He gave her hand a squeeze.

"Yeah. At least it gets better from there."

"Did other family take you in?"

"Well, no. They kinda blamed me for everything as well. Nobody knew about their illnesses. *The brave front they'd put up for me*—so everyone said. Remember. I had just left home. I had been sleeping on a friend's couch and working my waitressing job. I kept it so I'd have money to eat, even though a social worker assigned my aunt as a formal guardian until I turned eighteen. She rarely came by and never gave me money or food. I used the little bit of money my parents left me to pay off the house. So I stayed there until I graduated high school, pursuing my own goals, going on the road when I could. That's pretty much it."

"How old are you now?"

"Twenty-three."

"Wow, what a backstory. You sure you're okay with me using all that?"

"Use whatever helps with the piece."

Conner blew out a breath. "Okay. Tomorrow is your first gig then, and you don't mind me tagging along? And you'll get me full access to the bands where you're playing, and I'll get a behind-the-scenes look?"

"Sure. I can do that. Parties and stuff, you mean?"

"That's part of it. Yeah. CeCe, I predict this will be a great collaboration."

She arched her eyebrows. "You ain't seen nothing yet."

***

After grabbing their luggage, the two shared an Uber ride to the Motel 6, where CeCe had already made reservations. *Motel 6?* It'd been a while, but he could handle anything for a couple days. When they'd landed, Conner had cancelled his reservation at the Ritz-Carlton. He rarely splurged. And he hardly ever took a vacation, but it wasn't to be this trip. Hopefully, the story here would pan out instead.

The steadily falling snow cast the budget hotel in a pleasing light, and as he crunched the snow under his boots on the way to his room, he could almost pretend that his room was more than just a desk, a chair, a TV, and a bed that he hoped had clean sheets. He knocked on CeCe's door, next to his, on the way to his room. No answer. He shrugged. *I'll catch up with her in the morning.*

Arranging his laptop on the bed and switching on the news, he settled on the bed and hit the speed dial for his editor.

He picked up on the first ring. "Talk to me, Conner. What's it about this story that's taken you away from your vacation three years in the making?"

"I've got a hunch that the world needs to hear her gritty Cinderella story…"

"Humph. How gritty exactly?"

***

Conner woke bleary-eyed, spending the better part of the previous night diving into CeCe's story. As long as the words flowed, fuelled by bad coffee, he kept writing. Breakfast and lunch came and went. No CeCe. Afternoon stretched to early evening when he finally got a text.

Sorry for the disappearing act. Needed some solo time

before tonight. The address is below, and your credentials will be at the bar. It's really just a hole-in-the-wall. So don't get your hopes up for anything special. We won't really get going until about 10:00 p.m. If you decide not to stay, I'll understand. No worries. See you later…or not. CeCe.

Hmmm. *No problem. Thanks for the address. I'll be there,* Conner responded.

***

A short drive later, Conner double-checked the address.

"This is the place," the Uber driver said.

"You sure?" Conner asked, eyeing the place again.

"Yep."

As Conner exited his ride, the door to the bar swung open, hovered for a two count as people exited, then drifted shut again, its exhale filling the street with the hard rock beat coming from the band playing inside. Conner handed over a ten for the cover charge, then made his way to the bar. "Rum and Coke," he murmured to the bartender, before turning around to face the growing crowd and sliding onto a barstool.

"Here ya go."

"Can you start a tab? Oh, and I'm Conner Duncan. Do

you have something for me?"

"Yeah. You're here with Shay, right?"

"Shay?"

"Yeah, the sexy guitar player up there."

"Uh. Right." *Shay?* Must be a stage name.

"Here. Put this around your neck. You can go backstage and meet the band, but not until they're done for the night at 2:00 a.m. Off-limits until then," the bartender said, his hand cutting through the air.

"All right. Got it. Thanks." Conner pulled out his flash drive, hit record, and sat at an empty table close to the bar. "Keep 'em coming," he yelled over his shoulder, lifting his drink to his mouth.

"You bet."

Two sets later, he hadn't left his seat but once to take a leak. The rest of the time he'd been transfixed, watching the perfection as she and her guitar became one. He'd caught her eye and smiled, but busy schmoozing with the crowd, she had shown him zero recognition.

The sparkle in her eyes from yesterday was gone, replaced by her hips shimmying to the beat of the music while men leered only a few feet from her. Conner got it. Lost in the motion of her, he felt the same way. Her connection with the music, screaming to get out of her, was nothing short of magical. Anyone with eyes could see it.

As the night unfolded, her story continued, taking shape in his head, and when the last set ended, he made his way backstage. "CeCe?"

"Nobody here by that name. Who are you?"

"Conner," he said, raising his badge. "Shay. I mean Shay."

"Ah. Yeah. Over there."

Conner's gaze took in the totality of the space. None of the band was fit for interviewing or comments. Empty bottles and cups littered the floor. Across the room, CeCe's eyes lifted to his, where she leaned over a table, snorting straight lines of white powder. She turned her gaze to a man next to her, who leaned down and joined in.

"CeCe, let's get you outta here."

"My name's Shay."

"All right. Whatever you say. Come on."

"See you guys tomorrow." She laughed. "Guess I gotta date."

Her body felt like a limp noodle as he dragged her outside.

"Hey, take it easy. What's the hurry?"

"I'm hoping the fresh air will sober you up some."

"You're kinda cute. What's your name?"

"Knock it off, CeCe."

"*Shay*. My name's Shay. But, for a price," she

whispered, "you can call me anything you want. I'll be her for you."

"Right. Get in the car."

A short, queasy ride later, Conner helped CeCe from their Uber ride.

"How about you take me to your room? You must be staying here. Huh? Whatda you say?"

"I'd say, you're wasted. You do coke after every performance? You can barely stand. You need to sleep, or you won't be in any condition to—"

CeCe crashed her lips against his, causing them both to stumble in the corridor leading to her room.

"Whoa there," he said, righting them both. "Not that this wouldn't be nice under different circumstances, but this isn't happening right now."

"*Nice? Nice!* I don't need you," she mumbled, the hatred from her gaze nailing him in place, throwing him off guard.

"Got that right," he said, swiping her key and pushing her inside. But the truth was, he wasn't sure how she made it from one gig to the next. Not if this was her normal routine. No telling what else she'd done besides coke before he'd got backstage. She'd been with the band for six to seven hours at that point. How did she live like this?

She plopped on the bed, and in the three seconds it took

him to slide off her shoes, CeCe had yanked her top over her head, somehow pulling him down on top of her in the process. They collided again in a tangle of arms and legs. CeCe tasted of whiskey and smoke. That, along with the faint aroma of shampoo and perfume, completely filled his senses. *Jesus*... He'd said he wouldn't do this, but God, he was only human.

***

Daylight plunged into the tiny dingy room, shattering the welcome cover of darkness. Conner blinked open one bleary eye, then another, startling when he bumped into CeCe, nestled beside him. He swung his legs over the side of the bed, groaning from the pounding inside his head. Coffee, he needed coffee. He tugged on his pants, grabbed his balled-up shirt, and made for the door.

A small moan sounded as CeCe lifted a hand to her head. When she raised her eyes to meet his, awareness dawned on her face, immediately followed by a scream.

Conner held up his hands. "Wait. Everything's okay," he murmured in soft tones, hoping to hell she wouldn't scream like that again.

"Oh, my God." She lifted the sheet, peered underneath, then clutched it to her chest. "What did we do?"

Conner's gaze drifted to the condom wrapper on the floor. Flashes of the passionate night they'd just spent together replayed before him in bits and pieces. "Exactly what you think we did, from what I remember."

"I barely know you," she whispered.

He stepped towards the bed. "CeCe—"

"Leave."

"I was just going to get us some coffee."

"Get. Out."

"If it matters…I think you're pretty great." Conner risked another glance in her direction. None of the sparkle in her eyes from last night showed in the dark pools that threatened to spill over at any second now. "I'll check on you later. Rest up."

True to his word, he texted several times over the next few hours, then called as well. No answer. In between, he hunched over this laptop, his fingers flying over the keys. The story—her story—all about the beautiful train wreck that was her life coming together on the page, tumbled from the keyboard. All the qualities painting her into future stardom were there: a tortured past, a stupendous talent, a rags-to-riches tale, and from what he'd witnessed, a balls-to-the-wall lifestyle that she thrived in, hanging so close to the edge that she just might fall off, but she'd do it in a damn hot blaze of glory.

When he didn't hear from her all afternoon, Conner asked for a key to check on her. And as he'd expected, she'd left on to the next venue, an outside one tonight, which he had learned last night at the bar. Her room smelled strongly of soap, and clothes lay in small piles, strewn around the room, as if she couldn't decide what to wear. He imagined her trying on each one, then discarding it for another, weighing the current pick critically, while staring through narrowed eyes in the mirror. He nodded, sizing up the options left behind. *A hard choice, indeed.*

Clearly CeCe liked her solitude, and with the intensity of her performances, he could understand why.

***

The weather tonight was mild for February, in the mid-forties, and the snow had melted, a front bringing in warmer, drier air. A crowd had already gathered when he arrived. After paying the cover, he asked if CeCe had left him a pass to get backstage. The man checked his clipboard and from under his papers, surprisingly produced a badge with Conner's name on it. Maybe she didn't hate him. Not really.

He bought a beer, making a mental note to drink much slower tonight, his aching head still reminding him of his overindulgence yesterday. The gathering grew, warming up the space, adding to the anticipation, stoking the energy rolling off the stage. Tonight could be it, CeCe's big break. At least one talent scout would be here to watch. Conner took a pull from his beer, emptied it, and bought another.

Tension and energy hummed through the sea of people gathered to watch as the opening act left the stage, and the crowd clapped and cheered, waiting for what came next.

The band took the stage to the roaring screams of the crowd. Two rows back, Conner locked gazes with CeCe, who gifted him with a wicked grin and winked. As he'd hoped, her mood had improved.

He scanned the crowd, taking a pulse. They moved and gyrated to the beat, enthralled with the music, the mild night, and the buzz from their drinks. He was the same, completely under the spell of the night and her. And she knew it. It dawned on him—she was playing him. But none of it mattered when he could watch her unfolding before him like this.

Mesmerised, Conner's gaze pinned CeCe's as she took centre stage for her solo. Strumming the guitar and rocking to the beat, her gaze connected to the audience, while she shimmied and flaunted the parts of her they couldn't have. But with her inner spirit on display—the hundreds here joined in freely.

The fans moved in time with the beat, drawn to CeCe like the sex goddess she portrayed. When she paused, throwing her head back, anticipating the next bar, the crowd clung to the last note, suspended, the silence palpable, as she made love to them through the chords she played.

Who was she? Not the scared teenager who'd been tortured by—and blamed for—her parents' deaths. Maybe the crowd couldn't name what made her special, but he could. Rarely seen and typically burned out quick, but when at its brightest, CeCe was nothing short of magical. Sex, music, emotion, glamour—they all fit together like a well-worn glove.

Perfection.

And she sold the goods with ease. When the last set ended, Conner flashed his badge and pushed his way backstage. A buzz still lingered from his fourth beer, but nothing like the haze of the previous night. CeCe caught his gaze—from the looks of it, about to join in the freebasing activity taking place. Conner tilted his head towards the corner, hoping she'd get outta here with him.

Her smile lit her face as she strutted towards him. "So, what did you think?"

"I thought you were fantastic. So did everyone else out there."

She nodded, then giggled. "I've got an appointment

next week in LA!"

"See! What did I tell you."

"This could be it, Conner… The real deal, my big break."

"I don't doubt it. I've been slaving away on your story all day. Now it just needs an ending."

CeCe cocked her head, grabbed Conner's shirt, and yanked him forward, covering his mouth with hers.

When they separated, his head spun.

The sparkle in her eyes was back. "Let's get outta here, go celebrate."

"So, all is forgiven? You didn't answer me all day."

"Huh? What do you mean?"

"I texted, called…"

"Oh…really?"

"Really." Conner scrutinised her. If he didn't know any better, he'd have sworn this act was for real.

"You want to go or not? I can always party here."

"Yeah, no," he said, taking a quick glance at the ongoing activities around them. "You're with me. Come on."

***

"Where to? Out on the town? Dinner? Drinks?"

She shrugged. "It's late. Let's pick up some booze and go back to the hotel."

He raised a brow. "Are you sure? We can do better than that."

"I'm completely sure."

They stumbled into her room; their actions like a rerun of last night. He poured wine into plastic cups, as she moulded her body to his, squeezing him from behind. "Take it easy," he said, twisting in her arms to give her a drink. "You don't want a repeat of last night."

"What was wrong with last night?" She narrowed her eyes at him over the rim of her cup. "You seemed to like it well enough at the time."

"Like it?" Conner cracked a grin. "Sure I did. But this morning you had a change of heart. Or don't you remember?"

"Oh. That. I'm going to let you in on a little secret."

"Okay," he said, studying her face for signs of panic or fear. "I'm game. What is it?"

"My name's Shay." She laughed. "You can't tell boring CeCe."

Conner took a step back. "What?"

"That's right. She's weak. When she runs and hides, I take over." Shay downed her drink and tipped her cup to Conner for a refill. "She can't handle this life. Never could."

Conner scrambled out of her arms, shaking his head. "What's going on? Are you playing games?"

Shay closed the distance between them and smiled with a coy bat of her lashes. "Now, now…you liked me well enough last night. I promise, you don't want CeCe in bed."

"You mean?"

"Yep, last night was all me." Shay dragged her tongue over his lips, and he shivered. "I thought so. It's *me* you want. Your eyes, your pounding heart, the way you hold your breath, waiting for my touch, all give you away without one word from you."

Conner put down his cup. "There's two of you…and when things get rough, you take over."

"There you go… Nothing gets past you…"

"Is that what happened when your parents died? You took over?"

"Who do you think handles shit when the going gets tough? That wimpy doormat? If I hadn't stepped in, CeCe never would never have survived, much less got her ass in gear."

Jesus…this is bad. "I'll be right back." Conner went in the small bathroom and hammered out a quick email on his phone, added a few sentences to his story, then attached the draft that he'd forwarded to his email earlier.

When he returned, Shay was sitting in the bed, her hands underneath her, her face a mask of innocence. "Ready now?"

"What do you say we go for a drive?"

"I'm not really feeling it. No. Hard pass." She stretched out her arm to the bedside lamp and flicked it off. "Come sit. I don't bite. Not much anyway."

His lips eased up. Well, that wasn't true. "Shay, can I talk to CeCe?" he asked, sliding in beside her.

"Maybe later. Tonight's not about her."

"Okay. Later then."

"Conner, tell me you love me. Now. Say you love me." For an instant, he glimpsed the steel blade hanging in the air before she plunged it into his neck. "I'm so sorry, baby," she cooed, stroking his hair. "You're a lot of fun. But you know my secret… No one knows my secret… And you want…her." Her lips caressed his ear. "You know, you're not my first kill, not by a long shot, but you're definitely the sweetest."

Conner shoved CeCe to the floor with the last of his draining energy. Tapping his phone awake, he pressed send on the email, smearing the screen red. His eyelids fluttered, then drooped shut, as he smashed into the wall and slid to the ground. One hell of a story here… *Fuck, I should have called 9-1-1 instead. I'd give anything to see the end…*

"Ce…Ce…"

"Shay," she whispered, joining him against the wall, the cool steel gliding along his skin.

BLACK HARE PRESS

J.W. GARRETT is a multi award-winning author. Her early love of fantasy began after reading The Hobbit for the very first time. She's been hooked ever since. She writes speculative fiction from the sunny beaches of Jacksonville, Florida, but she'll always love the mountains of Virginia where she was born. Her writings include novels, short stories and poetry. Since completing Remeon's Crusade, she's been hard at work on the next book in her Realms of Chaos series, releasing in 2021. When she's not hanging out with her characters, her favourite activities are reading, running and spending time with family.

Bibliography
Bad Romance, Black Hare Press, 2020
Banned, Black Hare Press, 2020
Blaze, Gleam, Portal, Clarendon House, 2019/2020
Burning Dreams, Fantasia Divinity, 2020
Hidden In the Arms of Time, J.W. Garrett, 2018
Jibbernocky, Black Hare Press, 2020
Lockdown Fantasy #1, PNR #1, Phantom #2, Sci-fi #2, BHP 2020
Love, Hate, Oceans, Ancients, Black Hare Press, 2020
Pride, Lust, Sloth, Black Hare Press, 2020
Quietus 13, Black Hare Press, 2020
Remeon's Crusade, BHC Press, 2020
Remeon's Destiny, BHC Press, 2018
Remeon's Quest, BHC Press, 2019
School's In, Black Hare Press, 2020
Storming Area 51, Black Hare Press, 2019
Twenty Twenty, Black Hare Press, 2020
Wetware, Black Hare Press, 2020
Worlds, Angels, Monsters, Beyond, Unravel, Apocalypse, BHP 2019

Connect
Website: jwgarrett.com
Twitter: @garrettjlw
Facebook: @JWGarrettWriter
Instagram: @jlwgarrett

WHO WANTS TO LIVE FOREVER

by Maxine Churchman

Saffya felt like crying. They had travelled through miles of bleak Bulgarian countryside with rarely a settlement in sight. The few people she had spotted from the coach looked dirt poor. She couldn't imagine huge crowds turning up here for a festival. How was this going to advance their career?

The others were making excited noises as they stood looking at the ugly grey edifice purporting to be their home for the next few weeks. It looked more like a prison—cold and hard in the dying light. She counted six rows of identical, small windows—all barred.

She shivered and looked at her phone screen. "Great! No signal."

Carly put an arm round her shoulder. "Come on, this is so exciting. This guy really loved our demos—and think of the money. We've never earned so much in such a short time before. It's like being paid to go on holiday."

Saffya looked up at the leaden skies and at the flat featureless fields, cut through by the one narrow road where the retreating coach was sending up a cloud of dust as it lumbered over potholes. Her idea of a holiday involved warm sun, golden sand, and beautiful scenery.

Carly was right about the money though; if the festival was a flop, they would still get paid, and she really needed the money. It would go some way to clearing her debts. Saffya lifted her chin; it was just a few weeks, and they would get plenty of time to practise. Perhaps she would feel better after a good night's rest. She just hoped they didn't end up in this bloke's harem.

She picked up her suitcase and followed the others up the stone steps to the entrance. A woman held the door open for them. She was tall and muscular with a square face and spiky blonde hair. As they approached, she smiled—or sneered—it was hard to determine which, unveiling uneven yellow teeth.

"Welcome! I am Tereza," she said. Her words were all

sharp corners and mangled vowels; she spat them out as though they tasted bad. "Follow; supper is in your rooms." She disappeared into the interior gloom, and they had to hurry to keep up.

Their rooms were on the second floor. Saffya's had three small windows overlooking the front of the house. Her door didn't lock, so she jammed a chair under the door handle, like she'd seen in movies, hoping it would prove effective.

She changed quickly in the chilly room and pulled back the bedcovers, revealing a large flat warming stone with an intricate carving on top. She sat on the edge of the bed, with the heavy stone on her lap, and pulled the lamp closer to inspect it. In the middle, on a raised dais, two figures were fighting. There was a skewed sense of proportion to the scene, with the fighters appearing to be much smaller than the onlookers surrounding them on three sides.

The faces were so detailed they looked real; she could almost imagine the cheers of the crowd and the grunts of the fighters as they traded blows. The warmth of the stone seeped into her, and she felt her eyelids droop; it had been a long day.

Tap, tap, tap…tap, tap, tap. A large black bird was pecking on her window. Its beak looked sharp and wicked.

It turned its head, and she saw her reflection in its beady eye. Tap, tap, tap. It pecked at the glass again, and she was horrified to see a small crack appear. Tap, tap, tap. The crack lengthened. She tried to get up, but a heavy weight on her stomach held her down. She waved her arms frantically, hoping to scare the bird off, but it just kept pecking until the glass smashed; great shards fell into the room, and the bird launched itself towards her. She screamed and covered her face with her arms, expecting to feel its sharp talons and beak.

She opened her eyes and found she was lying on the bed with the stone, now cold, resting on her stomach. She heaved it off, and it crashed to the floor. Shakily, she sat up and listened to see if she had disturbed anyone. Tap, tap, tap. She looked up at the window. It was intact; there was no bird. She must have been dreaming. The tapping continued and she traced it to a bulky radiator on the other side of the room. It was cold; perhaps there was air in the system. She was chilly and stiff, so she hurried back to bed and pulled the covers over her head, trying to ignore the annoying tapping.

She was woken by Tereza fussing around the room. The chair didn't work against intruders then. She groaned and turned over, waiting for Tereza to leave, before she got up and dressed.

Downstairs, the other girls were tucking into breakfast. Was she the only one who felt uneasy in this house?

"Good morning sleepy head," Carly said, and Pam dissolved into fits of giggles.

"Wow, you're all chirpy this morning?" she said, trying not to sound waspish.

"Just excited to meet our host," said Pam, her eyes sparkling. "He wants to meet us in the music room after breakfast."

Saffya grabbed some toast and sat watching the others while she ate. They were all animated and didn't seem to notice, or care, that she was a little out of sorts. Pam's blonde curls bounced and frothed as she laughed and speculated about their host and his eligibility. She was pretty in a baby doll sort of way, the type of girl who needs someone to spoil her. Carly was smiling as she watched Pam, like a proud mother watching her favourite child. Carly was the youngest of the four band members, but she mothered them all. Her makeup was already immaculate— bright red lipstick, thick eyebrows, and false eyelashes— and she had tied her luxuriant brown hair into an intricate plait that started just below her right ear and fell into her lap. Saffya ran her fingers through her own short afro hair; it defied gravity when it grew long.

Aisha smiled at her across the table. "Are you ok,

Saff?" She had a natural beauty—flawless olive skin and neat features.

Saffya lifted the corners of her mouth. "I'm fine. I just didn't sleep too well," she assured her.

After breakfast, Tereza led them to the music room. The excitement of the other girls started to rub off on her, and her stomach tingled with anticipation.

They unpacked their instruments and tuned up. They had just finished practising one of their own songs, "Forever Mine," when the door opened.

Atanas Popov, their host, was an impressive figure. Even though all the doors were oversized, he filled the doorway completely. She judged he must be seven feet tall, since the top of his head skimmed the frame as he entered. Everything about him was in proportion, from his barrel-like chest to his enormous feet and hands. His skin had the pale, youthful quality of someone used to indoor pursuits, and it contrasted starkly with his glossy black hair, bushy beard, and wild eyebrows.

He opened his arms wide and grinned, displaying straight white teeth. "Welcome to my humble abode." His English was good with a hint of an American accent. "I am honoured with your stay. Such talent. Such a beautiful song." He clasped his hands together and grinned so wide, his dark eyes became mere slits. "I hope you are feeling at home and very, very happy."

They all nodded and mumbled their thanks, but he didn't wait for them to speak.

"You have everything you need?" he asked, indicating their equipment. "If you need anything—anything at all—Tereza will see to it." He half turned, and they could see Tereza was standing in the doorway behind him, hidden by his bulk. "I won't keep you; I have much to do," he said. "So nice to meet you all at last." With a wave of one hand, he and Tereza were gone, closing the door behind them.

"Well that was short and sweet," said Aisha. "We all stood there like nodding donkeys in a hurricane."

Pam giggled. "He was rather intimidating, not at all what I imagined."

Aisha nodded. "So you won't be hurrying down the aisle with him anytime soon then?"

Pam's face turned a fetching shade of pink.

What would it be like to be caressed by those large hands? Saffya shuddered; was everything else in proportion?

Carly brought her back from her thoughts. "Come on, ladies. We were a little loose in the middle of that last practise." She glanced at Saffya. "Let's go again."

It was Saffya's fault. The others were always effortlessly slick, but her real talent was in writing lyrics.

Her brother couldn't believe anyone would want her to play in their band. "Where's your rhythm, my skinny blister?" he would tease her. She nodded at Carly, and they began practising again.

About midday, Tereza entered with a large plate of sandwiches and fresh drinks. They stopped to eat and discussed a few tweaks they could make.

Later, as the girls were laying down their instruments, Tereza entered. "I show you Mr Popov's collection. This way, please."

They followed her to the top of the house and through a large double door, carved with intricate scenes.

"This is Long Gallery," she told them. They stood next to her looking along an amazing room that ran the full length of the house. Sunlight was diffused through voiles, giving the interior a dim, shadowed look.

Between the windows, set into the wall, were large glass boxes that reminded Saffya of an aquarium, but there were no fish in these boxes, though each held a miniature scene.

"Mr Popov's grandfather was…Master Craftsman," Tereza told them. "This is first scene he make." She moved to the first box and pressed a button below the protective glass. Small lights illuminated the scene inside. Two boxers stood toe to toe, their chests bare, their fists raised.

Although the men were only about six inches high, every detail seemed to be perfect. The hair on their heads and chests looked real, and you could see the musculature in their legs as they stood braced, ready for action.

"It's so lifelike," Carly whispered.

Tereza smiled her sneer-smile and started turning a small handle next to the button. Stirring music played and the fighters became animated. They punched and jabbed, ducked and weaved. The movements were a little jerky and stiff, but their feet moved around the arena as if by magic. There were no visible signs of the mechanism that allowed the boxers to move.

It reminded Saffya of the warming stone. "How does it work?" she asked.

Tereza stopped turning the handle, and the boxers resumed their starting position again. "It is…family secret," she said. "Come."

She led them past some scenes to a tall box. This one had a switch and a button, no handle. Tereza clicked the switch to illuminate the scene. There was a hot-air balloon with a tiny man, no more than four inches high, in the basket. Everything was beautifully proportioned, and the features of the man were as lifelike as those of the boxers. This one had a backdrop of painted mountains.

"Father of Mr Popov," Tereza announced.

"So Mr Popov's father continued the family tradition," Pam said with a timid smile.

Tereza shook her head and laughed. It was a strange gruff noise, like she was trying to clear her throat. "No. This is tribute to father. He only interested in hot air balloons. One day, he go in balloon and disappear. Balloon and man, not seen again. Mr Popov make this tribute. First one without handle to turn." She pressed the button and the little man began to move around the basket, readying it for lift-off. He threw ballast bags out. They were attached to ropes, the other ends of which stayed in the basket. At last he lit a burner; it looked like a real flame. The balloon began to ascend slowly, towards the ceiling of the glass box, until they were looking at the bottom of the basket and all the ballast ropes were taut. Then the balloon started to descend with the burner extinguished. When the basket landed, the little man pulled in each of the ballast bags and stood waiting for his next adventure.

"Please. Enjoy other exhibits. They need time to…reset after performing, so please, one time only each. Dinner in one hour," she told them and left.

"Why do you think Atanas made him look so sad?" asked Pam. As the small man rested his hands on the rim of the basket, his head hung low.

Carly put a comforting arm around Pam and led her

away. "Don't upset yourself, Pammy. Let's have a look at some of the other ones, shall we?"

Saffya sighed; as beautiful as the dioramas were, they made her feel—uncomfortable—like a voyeur. She looked at the vaulted ceiling and all the other exhibits; it was like a freak show at a circus.

She caught up with the other girls, and they set more of the scenes in motion. Every small person was as unique as their setting. Most scenes involved one or two small people performing in some way. There were climbers, runners, a show jumper on a horse, and even a lion tamer. They all had an air of melancholy that marred the pleasure of their novelty.

Pam set a group of Morris dancers in motion.

"How do you think they are made to move?" asked Aisha, almost to herself, as they watched the group of dancers shake the tiny bells on their legs and sticks.

"It is our family secret." Atanas stood behind them; his booming voice made them all jump. For a big man, he could move quietly.

"Is there one missing?" Pam asked, pointing to a square plinth in the middle of the room.

"Ah, yes. My beautiful ballerina. My first attempt at a mobile version. She is on loan to a museum—in New York, no less. I hope they are treating her well. She will be home

again soon and I"—he spread his arms wide and paused—
"I will be famous."

Saffya could relate to that. They had often talked about how great it would be to have fans all around the world.

"Come and see my latest creation," he said. "It will be completed soon—with your help, of course." With a flourish, he removed a cloth covering another glass case to reveal an empty stage in front of a backdrop of the house. "It will be of your concert. Won't that be wonderful? You will live forever." There was a gleam in his eyes that made the hairs on Saffya's arms stand on end, but Carly squealed with delight.

Aisha hugged her. "Wow, that will be so brilliant. I can't wait to see it."

"Good, good. It is good you want it. To be immortalised." He looked at his watch. "We must hurry. Dinner is ready; Tereza will be cross if we are late."

Saffya took a last look around the room and felt an overwhelming sense of sadness, before Atanas led them down to the dining room.

Over dinner, Aisha and Carly could barely contain their excitement about the new diorama, smiling and laughing, bouncing on their chairs, and waving their arms about. They asked lots of questions about the scenes: how long he took to make them, what they were made of, and, of course, how they worked. While Atanas did not appear to avoid any of the questions, he didn't actually answer any. He was well skilled in the art of conversation and learned far more about all of them, than they did about him. What did they know? Very little—he was wealthy, lived in a large castle-like house, and made dioramas. It wasn't even clear what his relationship was with Tereza. Pam seemed a little subdued; perhaps she was having similar misgivings.

That night, Saffya was reluctant to go to bed. After dinner, Atanas and Tereza left them alone in the drawing room. Enthused by the prospect of being immortalised, Carly and Aisha dominated the conversation. They planned the costumes they would all wear for the concert, how they should style their hair and makeup, and in what order they'd play their songs. Atanas had chosen the song he wanted them to record for the diorama.

Pam's head had been nodding for the last few minutes. She yawned and stretched. "Let's go to bed. It's getting late and we have a recording to make tomorrow."

As they ascended the stairs, Saffya took Pam a little to one side. "Can I share with you tonight? My room's kind of creepy."

Pam squeezed her hand. "Sorry, Saff, I'm sharing with Carly. You could share with Aisha or take my room."

"You're not sharing with me," said Aisha. "You

snore."

"I do not snore." She looked at Pam, brows knit. "Do I?"

Pam shrugged and gave her a half smile. "Sorry, Saff. Will you be ok?"

She shouldn't have made a fuss. "Yeah, course. No worries."

In her room, she pushed and shoved until she had moved the heavy chest of drawers partway across the door. It would only open a couple of inches before banging into the unit; the noise should be enough to wake her.

She wasn't ready to sleep just yet, so she explored her room. Perhaps there was a secret passage; it wouldn't surprise her. She didn't find any passages, but she did find a notebook stuck to the back of one of the dresser drawers.

She climbed into bed, tossing the warming stone on the floor without glancing at the carving, and pulled the lamp closer so she could look at the book.

Stuck inside the first page was a newspaper article dated 19th July 2012, and the headline read "Morris Dancers Mysteriously Missing." According to the article, they had been on tour in Europe and were last seen, unexpectedly, crossing the border into Bulgaria.

On the next page was a handwritten list of dates with names; many were foreign sounding. She skipped over the next few pages containing maps and scribbled notes. The rest of the notebook was a kind of diary or journal; each entry was dated. The first entry was for seven months ago.

"Atanas Popov is a larger-than-life, jovial man and an attentive host. The sum he has promised me for writing and marketing his biography is eye watering, but I need to tread carefully: he is a powerful and dangerous man, and I am certain he is behind the disappearances."

She was startled by the sudden tapping of the radiator. She looked at her phone: 11 o'clock exactly.

She flicked through the journal, reading random notes, but the tapping got on her nerves with its monotony. She swapped her attention to the radiator—something about the tapping… That was it: "da da da, dit dit dit, da da da." It was Morse code for SOS. She tucked the notebook under her pillow and looked at the radiator pipework. Both ends disappeared into the floor and could go anywhere. She pinched her lip; if someone was imprisoned, where were they likely to be—in the attic—in the basement?

After a moment's hesitation, she picked up her phone and heaved the chest of drawers out of the way. Using her torch app to see, she tiptoed down the hallway, listening carefully as she passed each door. Nothing, not a sound. She headed down, towards the kitchen. If there was a cellar, it was most likely below the kitchen.

The farther from her room she got, the louder her heart seemed, until she feared she wouldn't be able to hear the source of the tapping—or if someone approached.

Large flagstones covered the kitchen floor, so it was easy to spot the wooden hatch in one corner. She pulled on the ring and hinged the door back onto the floor, being careful not to drop it. She shone her torch down the stone steps, but it only reached a little way down.

Faintly from below, she could hear the tapping. She couldn't go down the steps; she might get shut in. She listened to the tapping for a few moments. How must they feel locked in down there? "Be brave," she whispered and took a few steps down. When her eyes were level with the floor, she stopped and took a big calming breath before hurrying down the rest. The floor of the cellar was packed earth. Old furniture and other things were stacked against the walls.

On the far side was a door. A key hung from a hook next to it. She unlocked the door and pushed it open. The room was lit by a single bare bulb hanging from the ceiling. A dishevelled, skinny man looked up from a makeshift bed on the floor near a gas boiler. He was holding a spoon.

He jumped up. "Did you hear my banging? Do you speak English?" he spoke fast, posh.

Her heart was hammering. "Can we get out of here?

I'm feeling really claustrophobic." She turned to leave.

He pulled the door shut and grabbed her arm. "What about Atanas and Tereza?"

"Asleep, I hope." She tried to pull her arm from his grip, but he held fast. Panic closed her throat, she couldn't breathe.

"What are you doing at the castle? I take it you didn't come to save me?"

Blood rushed in her ears, and her knees buckled; she was going to suffocate.

He propelled her towards the stairs. Once she was moving again, her legs stopped shaking and she hurried up the steps, relieved to be out of the cellar and able to breathe once more.

"I found your notebook. I take it, it is yours?" she said as he replaced the hatch.

He nodded but held his finger to his lips, his eyes darting around the dark kitchen. They both heard the footsteps at the same time. Saffya dashed towards the sink and didn't see where the man went. The door opened, and the lights came on.

She squinted against the sudden glare and turned to see Tereza in the doorway. "Oh! You made me jump. I'm so sorry if I woke you."

"What you doing?"

"I came for a glass of water."

Tereza opened a cupboard over a work surface and handed her a glass. "You should ring. I bring anything you want."

"Oh, that's alright. I didn't want to disturb you in the middle of the night." She took the glass and quickly turned her back to Tereza, to hide how much she trembled. After drinking some water, she put the empty glass in the sink. "I'll leave the glass for you then, shall I?"

Tereza gave her a curt nod and held the door open for her. "I take you back."

Saffya resisted the urge to look for the man as she left the kitchen. They didn't speak on the way back to her room, and she was glad she had hidden the notebook in her bed. She thanked Tereza and closed her bedroom door in her face.

She was far too wired to sleep now. She thumped the mattress a few times. So many questions were buzzing round her head: Who was the man? Why was he locked up? What would he do now? Was she—and her friends—in danger? She stopped pacing and sat on the bed; yes, quite likely, but what could she do about it?

Something scratched at her door, and she jumped up to open it. The man pushed through, finger on lips, and she closed the door softly behind him. She started to manoeuvre the dresser across the door, and he helped her.

They sat on her bed, speaking in hushed tones.

"I'm Rory," he said. "Thank you. I know how terrified you were."

"I'm Saffya." Her face felt warm, and her heart was pounding. "I still am. What is this all about? Should we get out?" She felt panic rising again. "Where can we go? What…"

"Shhh. Breathe." He held her upper arms and looked into her eyes. She took a deep breath and swallowed hard, but it didn't stop the gnawing sensation in her stomach, or her trembling.

"You need to stay calm. We'll figure this out," he said slowly, while keeping eye contact. "Ok?"

She nodded and bit her lip. He looked to be about thirty. Under his long brown hair and beard, his skin was very pale and he had dark circles under his grey eyes. She tried to imagine what he would look like after a trip to the barbers.

"Are you here alone?" he asked her.

"No, there are four of us in our band." She felt tears prick her eyes. "He's going to make a diorama of us after the concert. We're recording a song for it tomorrow."

"When?"

"After breakfast. We'll probably practise a couple of

times before the take."

He lowered his gaze to the floor and ran his hands through his hair. "I think the people in the dioramas are real; Atanas miniaturises them somehow, but I don't know how yet. I do know it has something to do with music though, so you mustn't finish that recording tomorrow. I am going to search the house tonight, see if I can find out more. When Atanas is with you tomorrow, I will search his rooms. You must delay him for as long as possible and make sure he doesn't get the recording. Meet me here lunchtime." He stood up to leave.

"Wait! Won't you be missed?"

"No. Tereza brings me food once a day and Atanas only visits when I have finished a chapter of his biography. They won't miss me before tomorrow evening." He held her hands for a moment and she thought he was about to kiss her. "Don't tell the others; you all need to act as normally as possible." He squeezed her fingers. "I won't let him hurt you."

"Good luck," she whispered to the closed door after he had gone. She pushed the drawers across the door again, but knew she wouldn't sleep. She set her phone alarm for 6 am anyway and held it in her hand as she closed her eyes. How could she stop the recording tomorrow?

She was woken by her alarm. Her head ached, and her

eyes were sore. So much was at stake; she needed her wits about her.

Her stomach churned all through breakfast, so she just nibbled some toast. The girls were chatting and giggling, and she wanted to bang their heads together.

Aisha stroked her arm. "Another bad night, Saff?"

Saffya laid her head on Aisha's shoulder, and Aisha hugged her. "You can sleep with me tonight. You don't really snore."

Would they still have their freedom tonight? Not that they were particularly free now; where would they run to if they left the house—if they could leave the house? They were miles from anywhere in a foreign country. They couldn't even read the road signs. She clenched her fists and concentrated on the pain her nails made digging into her palms.

In the music room, they tuned their instruments and practised the song. While the others sought perfection, Saffya concentrated on how she could sabotage the recording without being obvious. She wished Atanas was here, so Rory could search his rooms, but at the same time, she dreaded his presence.

Atanas burst into the room, making Pam drop a drumstick. He threw his arms wide. "Ladies, ladies, you are in fine voice this morning. Tereza and I will set up the equipment while you practise." He beamed at them all.

Tereza wheeled a large box into the room, and she and Atanas worked together with well-rehearsed proficiency.

Atanas clapped his hands together and rubbed them enthusiastically. "We are ready to begin."

They took up their positions and waited for Atanas to give them a signal. Saffya caused as many delays as she could. She had a coughing fit, dropped the beat—several times in the same place—she even managed to break a string. That wasn't actually planned, but was very welcome. The girls were all getting frustrated, and Atanas was barely containing his anger. His eyes blazed, and his full lips were so compressed, they disappeared completely into his beard. She was running out of ideas and hoped she had given Rory enough time to find what he was looking for.

As a last resort, she burst into tears and collapsed to her knees. "I'm so sorry. I'm useless. I'm letting you all down." She blew her nose noisily and the girls rallied round her. "I have such cramps." She held her arms across her belly and lowered her eyes. "It's hard to concentrate. Perhaps I could lay down for a little while."

"Oh! Is it your time of the month?" Aisha whispered.

They all looked up at Atanas; the angry look fleetingly gave way to embarrassment, before he beamed his wide smile. "Of course. Tereza will prepare sandwiches and we will try again after lunch." He swept out of the room as though he had an important meeting, and Saffya relaxed a little.

Tereza glared at her, working her jaw like she was chewing a toffee. "I will bring your lunch to you. Get to bed." Her normally clipped tones were positively snappy.

Pam helped her to her feet. "Shall we come with you?"

"No, I'll be fine. I'm sorry I just feel so stupid." She felt terrible, if only she could explain.

Rory was not in her room when she returned. It was almost lunchtime; she paced up and down, willing Rory to arrive. The door opened and Tereza stood there with a tray. She stopped short and narrowed her eyes. "What you doing?"

Saffya stomped towards her before she could enter the room. "It helps with the cramps to keep moving." She took hold of the tray. "I'll rest once I've eaten." Tereza held on to the tray. Saffya watched as Tereza's neck and face grew red, but she was determined to keep her out.

Tereza let go of the tray and backed away.

Saffya put the sandwiches on the chest of drawers and closed the door. She was shaking. She went over to one of the windows and looked towards the distant hills, trying to calm her nerves.

The door partially open, and Rory stuck his head in.

He put his finger on his lips and entered, closing the door softly.

Relief flooded through her; her chest swelled with delight at the sight of him. She resisted the urge to run and hug him.

He threw some papers on the bed and pulled the chest of drawers in front of the door. "Oh! They look good. Do you mind?"

"I'm too stressed to eat. Have them all."

He stuffed one straight in his mouth and didn't seem to chew before swallowing. He wiped his sleeve across his mouth and brought the plate over to the bed.

"What have you found?" Saffya asked, indicating the papers.

"The answer, I hope. I don't understand all of it, but I think I understand enough to thwart their plan." He spread one of the papers out on the bed. It was covered in diagrams and symbols. It meant nothing to her. Rory started pointing at things and explaining about "vibrations" and "fields of stasis" it all sounded like gobble-de-gook, so she put a hand on his arm to stop him.

He turned to face her, his nose mere inches from her own. His long fringe had fallen over one eye, and she reached up to push it back. He took her hand and pressed her palm to his lips; he shut his eyes tight as though he was in pain or trying not to cry. A tingle ran all the way from her hand to her toes. Maybe it was the desperation of their situation, but she had never felt so drawn to a man before. She ached for him to pull her into his arms and kiss her, but she wasn't sure he felt the same way.

He let go of her hand and took a shaky breath. "Once he has your recording, he will calibrate his machine. When you play the song again, within the calibrated zone, the recording will resonate with the live song and you will be captured and miniaturised. The booths keep you in stasis, just allowing you to play out a moment of your life over and over again—forever."

"That's horrible. Is there a way to release the other performers?"

He shook his head. "I don't know; it would take a much smarter person than me to work out how to release them. We need to stop him doing it again."

"What are we going to do?" she asked.

"You need to go along with him. Record the song. I will alter his calibrations."

"Shouldn't we just get away and bring help?"

"We can't. I've tried." He gripped her arms. "Please, you must trust me. Record the song and let me do the rest. We need to know when he intends to complete the diorama. You may have to lock me up and let me out again."

"What! No. You can't go back down there." A cold sweat prickled her back.

"Unless Atanas decides to complete the process today, I must be in the cell when Tereza comes to feed me later." He drew her into his arms and hugged her. "You can do this," he murmured into her ear.

She felt light-headed. It felt so good—his body pressed against hers. All too soon, he released her. "Go back and make the recording. See if you can find out when the final process is likely to be, although don't let on you know what is going to happen. Atanas will probably suggest a dress rehearsal and complete it then. He will want you dressed the part."

"I thought he would do it during the concert. That is still a couple of weeks away."

"That must have been an excuse to get you here. There won't be a concert."

She didn't want to leave him, but the sooner they got the recording done, the sooner they could get this over with. Hopefully, he wouldn't have to go back to the cellar.

As she approached the music room, she could hear the babble of girls' voices. They went silent when she entered.

Carly got up and gave her a hug. "How are you feeling?"

"I'm ok now. I'm sorry; I let the pressure get to me."

They picked up their instruments and ran through the number. Everything went well and just as they finished, Atanas and Tereza entered. Saffya pretended not to notice Tereza staring at her with narrowed eyes and pinched lips.

Atanas took up a position behind the recording equipment. "Good. Good. Let's record while you are in such good form."

They played the song twice more, and Atanas said he was satisfied.

"How are the ticket sales for the concert going?" Saffya asked. He looked startled, but soon recovered.

"Very well indeed," he said. "In fact, it would be good to make a short promotional video. Get your costumes on and I will record it now. Can you be ready in an hour and a half?"

Saffya felt sick. This was it. Atanas would go and calibrate the machine. At least she wouldn't have to lock Rory up and make it through another fraught night.

Carly, as usual, took command. "Bring your outfits to my room, we'll get ready together."

They hurried up to their rooms, giggling and chatting like they were about to get ready to go partying. Her door only opened an inch or two before it was stopped by the dresser.

Aisha called to her, "Is everything alright, Saff?"

"Yes, no problem. I'll see you in a minute." The door was pulled open from inside, and she almost fell in.

"Well?" Rory asked.

"We have an hour and a half to get ready. I am so scared. I think I might be sick."

***

He watched her leave and closed his eyes, trying to commit her beauty to memory: her dark skin, smooth and silky under his fingertips; her brown eyes, clear and trusting; her full shapely lips, soft and sweet. He hoped he wouldn't let her down. He only half understood the techniques Atanas was employing, and he hoped the calculations he had made to alter the calibrations would work the way he expected. Only time would tell. Four lives depended on him. Five if he included his own.

The main controls and equipment were in Atanas's suite on the fifth floor. He hoped he would be out of range of the new field of scope he intended to create once Atanas left to miniaturise the girls.

Atanas would need to be able to watch and talk to the girls as he recorded them, but he would want to be outside the calibrated area: the dais in the music room. The plan was to reverse the field so the girls would be safe and everything outside the dais would be captured. The problem was, he wasn't quite sure what that would do. Would the field be strong enough to disable Tereza and Atanas? What else would be shrunk? Would it be strong enough to reach him, or so strong it took in the whole house and crushed the girls? He was sweating and shivering. He looked over the calculations again and tweaked a setting he thought was the field strength. He wiped his palms down his trousers and cleared away the papers, putting his calculations in his back pocket. He made his way to Atanas's suite and hid himself outside in the corridor to watch for him to leave. He would need to make all his adjustments quickly before the process began.

***

The girls had decided on their black jumpsuits with colourful platform boots, capes, and headdresses. These were their most flamboyant costumes, and Saffya would have preferred something more practical, considering they may need to make an escape or fight for their lives. Rory had not said what his plan was, and she wished she had asked more questions. She was putting a lot of faith in a man she had only known for a few hours; yet she had feelings for him and was worried for his safety.

Everyone but Saffya seemed excited; she felt drained and alone. If only she could tell the others what was happening, share the burden, but they would think she was being neurotic.

Her legs were weak as they made their way downstairs. She was shaking so much; she wasn't sure she would be able to play.

Atanas and Tereza were already in the music room, setting up lights and checking readings. The girls fidgeted quietly in the doorway while they waited.

"Come in. We are ready," Atanas said.

They took their positions. Atanas moved each of them slightly and tweaked the lights before joining Tereza by the recording equipment.

He pointed a fat sausage finger at them. "Whenever you are ready."

Saffya looked at her friends with their huge grins and shining eyes. She wanted to cry and hug them all. Pam tapped the drum to count them in, and they began the song. Atanas was concentrating on the panel in front of him. About five bars into the song, the room seemed to shimmer—like the ground above a hot road in summer. The girls were still smiling and performing. Atanas was frowning; his hands danced across the switches. Then everything happened fast; he pounded the panel with his fists, bellowing as if in pain. Tereza moved towards him, hand outstretched. Then they, and the panel, were gone. So were the chairs and table. Large cracks appeared in the walls. Pictures crashed to the floor and disappeared. The whole house seemed to be groaning around them. The girls stopped playing and looked at each other. Carly started forward.

Saffya yelled, "Stop! Stay where you are."

"What's happening?" asked Aisha. "Where did they go?"

Everything went quiet. Dust fell from the ceiling.

Saffya dropped her guitar. "I think we should get out of here."

She ran for the door; something crunched under her foot. She'd trodden on the shrunken panel, just missing Atanas and Tereza, who were lying still, just four inches tall. She picked them up. They were soft and warm, and she nearly dropped them again. Aisha was trying to open the door, but it was misshapen. She put a foot on the wall and tugged on the handle. Something heavy fell against the door on the other side and she let go. There was another blow and one of the panels splintered. The girls stood back and watched as the panel gave way.

At last, Rory's face appeared at the hole; he looked tired and grey, but Saffya was relieved to see him.

His voice was strained. "Stand back, stay close to the wall. The ceiling may be unsafe."

When the hole was large enough, they climbed out.

Rory sat with his back to the wall; a fire axe discarded by his side. The front of his shirt was red and shiny with blood.

Saffya rushed to him, and he smiled weakly up at her.

"What happened? How badly are you hurt?" There was so much blood.

"Just a flesh wound. The control panel fought back." His laugh turned into a cough and his head fell forward.

"Rory!" Saffya lifted his chin.

"What the fuck is going on, Saff?" Aisha asked. Saffya had forgotten the others. She wanted to scream at them. Selfish, vain, stupid girls. Couldn't they see Rory needed help?

"He's hurt. Find a first aid kit." There was no time for explanations. "Now!" she yelled when no one moved.

She was satisfied to see them scamper away, muttering to each other.

Rory squeezed her hand, his grip weak. "I'll be alright—after a little rest."

She carefully lifted his jumper. There was a deep gash, several inches long. She took off her cloak and ripped a section off. Balling it up, she pressed it hard against his

wound. Rory winced and banged his head against the wall.

"You need an ambulance. Is there a phone in the house we can use?" She didn't even know what number she needed to dial or how to talk to anyone who answered.

"On their way," he whispered through gritted teeth.

"What about these?" She showed him the little dolls of Atanas and Tereza.

"Secure…journal…papers." He closed his eyes and his head rolled to one side.

"Rory, stay with me." She shook his shoulder gently. Aisha and Carly returned with a first aid pack.

"See what you can find in there to stem his bleeding— and keep him awake," she commanded, tripping over her words.

She ran to her room to put the notebook and papers in her suitcase, along with Atanas and Tereza. She needed to get back to Rory. How long before the ambulance arrived?

She heard the wailing of sirens as she raced back downstairs. The girls were fussing round him. Carly was holding a pad against his stomach and it was already soaked through. He looked terrible.

She sat next to him and stroked his face; it was cool and sweaty. "Someone open the door."

Heavy boots raced across the floor; foreign words assaulted her ears. She was pulled away from Rory and handcuffed before she could protest. As she was dragged outside with the other girls, she passed a couple of people with a medical bag on a stretcher going the other way.

"Please help him," she begged them.

In the back of a police car, she watched the entrance, frantic to see Rory brought out. Just as the car pulled away, the medics emerged carrying the stretcher. Rory was covered in a sheet—including his face.

She let the tears stream down her face unhindered. She thought about the two tiny bodies in her suitcase and imagined crushing them—feeling their bones break. She closed her eyes, easing her pain with thoughts of their suffering.

***

Two years later, Saffya felt good as she held the book in her hands. She had split from the band after Bulgaria and gone home to Mum. Using notes from Rory's journal, she had written a novel—*The Demon Puppeteer*—under the pen name Rory Forsaff. It was only loosely based on Atanas, and she had changed his name, hardly the biography he'd desired.

She turned the book over. Atanas and Tereza stared back at her—two tiny figures in a jar. Her eyes flicked up to the actual jar on the shelf.

"How do you like it?" she asked them, holding the book up for them to see.

BLACK HARE PRESS

MAXINE CHURCHMAN writes dark fantasy, paranormal romance, and anything else that catches her interest. Mainly short stories but also poetry, and she is currently working on her first novel.

Her shorter dark pieces can be found in several Black Hare Press anthologies, and other styles of flash fiction can be found online at cafelit.com and at Enchanted Conversation. Her poetry has been published by Stormy Island Publishing and Clarendon house.

Bibliography
APOCALYPSE, Black Hare Press, 2019
GREED, Black Hare Press, 2020
HATE, Black Hare Press, 2020
LOVE, Black Hare Press, 2019
LUST, Black Hare Press, 2020
OCEANS, Black Hare Press, 2020
POETICA, Clarendon House, 2019
PRIDE, Black Hare Press, 2020
SEA GLASS HEARTS, Stormy Island Publishing, 2019
SLOTH, Black Hare Press, 2020
UNRAVEL, Black Hare Press, 2019

Connect
Website: cccmaxine.blogspot.com
Amazon: amazon.co.uk/-/e/B07WVF4GBF
Twitter: @ChurchmanMaxine
Facebook: @ChurchmanMaxine

WHORE

by Zoey Xolton

Jareth, the lead singer of Triple6, stands abruptly from the grungy cigarette-burned couch in the converted garage studio, kicking his prized electric guitar across the room as he does so. It clatters across the floor with an ungodly sound.

"Fuck, Jay!" says Sebastian. "We can't afford to keep fuckin' replacing our gear! We haven't landed a gig in a month. Just calm your tits, will you?"

"Yeah, for fuck's sake, have a bucket and chill," agrees Wallace—their drummer—letting out a lungful of sweet smoke.

"You got something to fuckin' add, Muz?" accuses Jareth, his bloodshot eyes finding their bass player by the dented drinks fridge.

Murray casually grabs another beer before turning to face the band's front man. "Nah, mate. You're good. I know how it is. I fuckin' feel you. All this small-town shit? I've had enough of it, too. We need to take our music to the next level."

Jareth grins, pulling a durry from the breast pocket of his worn leather jacket. "I knew I could rely on you," he says, lighting up. "Any ideas?"

"Fuckin' ay, I have. I'm an ideas man. Don't know how far you lot are willing to take it, though…?"

"For a shot at the big time? Fuckin' anythin', ya fuckin' numpty," says Wallace as if it were a given.

"Yeah, what's so fuckin' hardcore that you'd think we wouldn't be up for it, anyway?" asks Sebastian, flicking his long dirty blond hair out of his face.

"Well," says Murray, side-saddling the back of the couch. "It involves Heather, one of my pretty blades, and a little bit of black magic."

"Aw, fuck, man! Not Heather. Come on! She's our most loyal girl, and a good root, to boot," argues Sebastian.

The whole band laughs, raising their drinks.

"Fuckin' ay," Jareth says. "We've all been there, but we can always get more groupies, Seb."

Sebastian takes another drag of his spliff. "Too right, I suppose. She's just fuckin' hot is all I'm sayin'. Bit of a waste."

"But she's a sweet thing, isn't she?" Wallace chimes in. "She parties hard, doesn't mind being shared around, but she's never done anything *real* bad, you know?"

"Which is why she'll make the perfect sacrifice, Wally," interrupts Murray. "She'd follow along, wouldn't see it coming. Fuckin' Lucifer would be glad to have her."

Jareth grins from ear to ear, the sick smile contorting his animated face. "I'm down."

Wallace slams his shot glass on the rubbish-littered table, scattering guitar picks and rollie papers. "Same here."

"Seb?" prompts Murray, fingering the mouth of his beer absently. "You down?"

Their lead guitarist scoffs. "What's to say this shit will actually work? I don't fuckin' fancy spending the next twenty behind bars for murder."

"You fuckin' pretty boy. You know all the greats are in league! That won't be an issue. My sister will perform the rites. She's solid with Satan."

"Li'l Cass?" asks Sebastian, eyebrow raised.

"Li'l Cass," Murray confirms.

"And what does she want out of this, for helping us?"

"She wants in, of course."

"She *can* sing," says Jareth, dropping his spent durry on the cement floor before squashing it out with his steel caps.

"She's improv'd with us before. I can't believe I didn't think of it sooner. She'd add a nice bit of sex appeal—a pretty little goth vixen in the group. She could do accompaniment or back-up vocals."

Murray tosses his bottle into the metal bin by the fridge—the metal clangs, and the sound of shattering glass bothers no one. "Exactly. Sex sells!"

"So, Seb? You really in, or you want out before this thing goes mother fuckin' nuclear?" asks Jareth, as all eyes fall upon their very own real-life Skid Row doppelganger.

Sebastian makes a face. "Fuck you, cunts!" he says, sitting back. "I'm fuckin' offended. I just wanted all the deets. Of course, I'm bloody in! You pricks fuckin' need me, anyway."

His blood brothers slap him on the back, mussing up his long beachy locks.

"Fuck, yeah," says Jareth. "Alright. All in. Let's do this shit!"

***

Cassandra sits in the back of the ute with Heather as the band blaze up in the cabin. The 4x4 rocks chaotically as they navigate the off-road trail, leaving a cloud of red dust in their wake. The stars above burn like white hot jewels in an ink-black sky as the Shopping Trolley constellation swirls by.

"It's fucking pretty tonight, right?" asks Heather, craning her neck back to admire the starscape.

"Yeah it is."

Murray leans out the left rear window. "You girls good out there? Not too fuckin' scary for you, is it?" he yells.

Cassandra reaches for the joint as her older brother passes it to her and rolls her eyes. "We're all good," she calls back, taking a long draw. She holds her breath as she passes it on to Heather, before exhaling into the brisk night air. She watches the smoke whorl and vanish, like a phantom in the night.

Heather bum-sucks the spliff, and Cassandra scrunches up her nose in disgust. *Fucking amateur.*

"So, what are we doing out here, anyway?" Heather asks. "The boyos didn't say much, just that it was a surprise."

Cassandra tucks a lock of bright purple hair behind her ear. "We're going to do some magic," she says matter-of-factly. "It's Friday the thirteenth *and* a full moon. We're going to make sure this band makes history."

Heather's eyes narrow as she takes measure of her fellow goth. "Really? We came all the way out here to do some kind of crazy fuckin' black magic in the bush?"

Cassandra leans over to steal the spliff back. "Not just any old black magic, Blondie. Tonight is all about *sex* magic."

Heather's face lights up, her cheeks flaring pink as her glazed eyes shine. "Sex magic? Fuck yeah," she says. "That's what I'm talking about! I fuckin' love the occult, and witchcraft, and all that shit! Fucking epic." Biting her lip, she adjusts her assets and fluffs her platinum bleached hair.

Cassandra's smile is veiled as she waggles her silver-clad fingers that bear distinct occult tattoo designs. "You're preachin' to the choir, sister."

***

The ute skids across the gravel to a halt and Jareth kills the engine. Each of the four doors fling out, a leather-clad musician slides out from each, stretching in the darkness after the two-hour-long drive.

"Nice," says Murray, inspecting the clearing by the light of the roof-mounted flood lights. "No one's gonna disturb us here."

"Not a chance," responds Jareth.

"Alright," says Cassandra, jumping from the back of the tray. "I want rum, and I want it now. Let's party!"

"Watch yourself, li'l sis," teases Murray. "You never know what could happen out here, in the middle of nowhere. What these deviants will get up to," he says, gesturing to the others.

"We're not fuckin' pussies are we, Cassie?" announces Heather, as she swipes the bottle of Kraken from Murray's hand. "Us girls will get this party started. Feel free to play catch up." She winks.

The band makes eye contact as Heather flounces across the clearing, necking the bottle as she goes. Cassandra glances over her shoulder and smiles back. "Soon," she mouths and stalks to catch up with the bottle thief.

"So, what now, Muz?" asks Sebastian, leaning against the 4x4.

"We wait for Heather to get fuckin' good and wasted, and then we get on with the ritual," answers Murray, twirling his ripple-edged sacrificial dagger.

"Where'd you get that from?" asks Jareth, eyebrow rising.

"Where do you think? Stole it from Cass fuckin' years ago."

"And where'd she get a hold of something like that? She's only eighteen this year."

Murray shrugs. "I have no fuckin' idea. That kid's been off the fuckin' charts since she was barely able to talk. I swear she's the real deal. I've seen some pretty fucked up shit that I can't explain happen around her."

Jareth grins. "That's good enough for me, mate. Before

long, Wollongong will be a fuckin' memory and we'll be headlining in the fuckin' USA with the best of them! Bongs with Black Sabbath before they kick the bucket, meet the Hollywood Vampires!"

"Fuck yeah!" Sebastian and Wallace echo.

Jareth sits on a large tree stump, finishing his beer. "You give the roofie to Cass, Muz?"

"Back at home," he confirms, rolling a new joint. "She'll let us know when it's time."

"You cunts are mental, you know that? None of you want a last stab at Blondie before she's fuckin shish kebab?" asks Sebastian.

The band laughs, rolling their eyes at the pretty boy's predictability.

"Be our guest, mate. She should have some fun before she meets the devil," says Jareth.

"Too fuckin' right she should. It's the least I can do for poor Blondie. I am a gentleman, after all. Last rites seem fitting."

Jareth, Murray, and Wallace watch as Sebastian puts on his best swagger and joins the girls.

***

Heather's breath comes slow and shallow as Sebastian

traces kisses along her neck, nibbling her ear as he rakes his fingers through her waist-length locks.

"I want you," he whispers. "Do you want me, Heather?" he asks, fingers trailing down her chest, deftly unbuttoning her dress.

Heather moans, as her eyes close. "Yes," she sighs, dragging out the *s* like a snake's hiss.

Guiding her against a tree at the edge of the clearing, he pushes her hands above her head. He holds her wrists firmly as Jareth suddenly appears at his side, armed with cable ties and silver duct tape.

"Kinky," Heather rasps as she recognises Jareth through her drug-induced haze.

The lead singer just winks as he pulls the black plastic ties tight, before wrapping the silver tape over the top and around the tree several times, hard enough to support her body weight.

"Have at it, mate. We'll get on with it when you're done," he says, clapping Sebastian over the shoulder. He leaves Sebastian to his fun and joins the others for more drinks.

***

"She's good to go, totally lights out," says Sebastian,

231

zipping up his fly, gesturing back at Heather—head fallen forward—still securely taped to the tree.

Murray stands, twirling his blade. "Go time, ladies."

Cassandra rolls her eyes, snatching the ritual tool mid-spin. "I believe this is mine, douche," she says, shouldering her brother playfully.

"I'll let you borrow it back." He winks.

"Alright, boys. Each of you grab a candle," she says, pointing at the bag by the ute, "and follow me. I'm going to assume you all have lighters." Crossing the clearing, gravel crunches under foot, and the young witch gets to work. She lays down her *Book of Shadows*—open to the correct page—and pours a circle of salt that encloses Heather and the tree, then draws a pentagram within it. Placing a silver dish by the unconscious twenty-year-old, she pulls the ceremonial dagger from her boot and directs each of the band members to take a position at an annex of the pentacle—Heather at its utmost point.

Approaching their human sacrifice, she pulls Heather's dress wide across her breasts and draws a series of runes from her clavicle to her belly in black chemi pen.

"No matter what happens, don't move. If you break the circle, the ritual won't work."

Triple6 nod in acknowledgement.

"Place your candle in front of you and light it. And I

mean it, no matter what you see, do not move," she stresses. "Or becoming a group of murderers will be the least of our problems, got it?"

"You got it, sis," says Murray, saluting her with a mock flourish.

"Okay. Are we committed? If you cunts puss out…" Cassandra is met by a circle of deadpan expressions, and she has her answer. "Alright then, raise your arms and do as I say." Raising her arms above her head, an athame clutched in her right hand, she raises her voice to the night sky. "I call upon the Darkness, and the powers of Hell and Earth. Hear us, oh Great Satan! We offer the blood of an innocent unto you, so that you may look upon us with favour and honour our request!"

Taking a deep breath, the young witch steps over her *Book of Shadows* and stands before the unconscious groupie. Grabbing a fistful of Heather's hair from the scalp with her free hand, she reefs her head back, exposing her pale neck. Before she can second-guess herself, she slices the blonde's throat, deep and fast—from ear to ear—in one fluid motion. Heather's body jerks and twitches but shows no conscious reaction.

Blood sprays instantly from her carotid artery and external jugular veins; the pressure release showers Cassandra in warm, thick red. Without flinching, she lets

Heather's head fall unceremoniously forward and retrieves the silver dish, holding it beneath the gaping wound. The dish fills quickly and she approaches each of the men in turn. Sebastian flinches when the dish finally reaches him, but he drinks, buoyed on by his mates' stony-faced display of determination to make history—to be more than just another backyard metal band.

Cassandra takes her place at the centre of the pentacle and empties the remainder of the dish down her throat before dropping it at her feet. She raises her arms once more. "Hear us, Dark Lord, we beseech thee to appear before us. We would make a pact with you, bound by honour, fear, and blood!" Her voice rings out in the darkness, but the night is otherwise silent, save for the song of cicadas, and the odd rustle of small marsupials and rodents in the fallen leaf litter.

"Did it work?" asks Murray.

"Shut up!" Cassandra commands.

Moments later, Wallace gasps, clutching at his throat. Cassandra watches as Triple6 moan in unison, then her own throat burns, as if on fire. *Heather's blood!* A spark of flaming orange catches her attention, and she watches in morbid fascination as the runes inscribed upon Heather's flesh begin to glow and burn; the odour of seared skin fills the circle. One by one, they fall to their knees, struggling for breath, eyes wild.

A sudden gust of hot air extinguishes all five candles, and a tangible darkness swirls within the circle of salt.

"What the fuck!?" Jareth chokes as the candles re-ignite and the darkness clears, revealing the most devastatingly handsome man he's ever laid eyes upon. Silver-blue eyes like burning stars bore into his soul, and a voice like silk and distant thunder fills his mind.

You desire fame and fortune, like so many before you... it whispers. *This is a wish I can grant...for a price.*

Long black hair, much like his own, spills over his dark form, and at his side—without question—the single most breath-taking woman he's ever seen. Raven hair falls to her backside, scarcely covering her modesty. Stormy violet eyes regard him with curiosity as a wry smile spreads upon her luscious lips.

Hello handsome, she says to his mind. Her voice is like seduction incarnate, and he feels he would fall if he weren't already upon his knees.

"Greetings, my children. You may rise."

Slowly but surely Jareth, Murray, Sebastian, Wallace, and Cassandra are able to rise.

"Lucifer, my Lord," utters Cassandra reverently.

Lucifer reaches out, placing a finger beneath her chin, raising it until their eyes meet. "Fear me, but love me, my beauty," he commands. Her instinct is to bow her head, to seek comfort in subservience, but he does not allow it. "What is it that you desire?" he asks, his voice causing a soul-deep shiver.

"We—" her voice trembles. Though she has called upon him before, each time is as terrifying, as awe-inspiring as the last. The beauty and splendour of the Dark Lord never grows old. "For the blood paid, we would ask for worldwide popularity, for more wealth than we know what to do with, and immortality, so that we might enjoy it, always."

"I can give you what you ask," Lucifer began. "But the price is more than the life of one innocent," he says, gesturing to Heather's drained corpse. "The blood paid was merely the cost of an audience. I do believe, back in the garage, it was said that you'd do anything for a shot at the 'big time', no?"

Cassandra's eyes widen and she glances back at the band, apprehension written as clear as day upon her features. "What would you ask of us in return then, my Lord?" she says carefully.

Lucifer tilts his head to the left and the beautiful woman waiting at his side. "I do not believe that Lilith, my queen, is in need of an introduction?"

"Hell's Whore," murmurs Jareth with breathless

admiration.

"Hello dearies." She grins, swaying her hips and biting her lip suggestively.

"My dark love desires to play Earth-side for a time, and what my love wants, my love gets," says Lucifer.

Cassandra licks her lips—a nervous gesture.

"The price I ask is this: I want you, Cassandra, to join me in Hell. You are young and full of rebellion. There is a dark fire in you, one I have fostered and fanned from afar since your infancy. Come with me, become my thirteenth priestess, and I will tutor you in the ways of the Occult. Join me, and you will command dark magic beyond your wildest dreams. Be mine, little witch, and I can give you more than this world has to offer."

Cassandra swoons, her breathing hard and shallow.

"You want to take my little sister to Hell?" says Murray. "To fucking Hell?"

Lucifer smiles, side-eyeing the bass player. "You will join her in time, Murray, be assured of that. She will come to no harm by my hand," he promises. "It would not make sense to damage such a precious asset," he drawls.

"And what about us, then?" says Jareth, speaking for the band. "If you're taking her, do we get what we're asking for?"

"You're bold and arrogant, just like me… I admire that

about you, Jareth. You know what you want, and the gift of song and music is dear to me; it is my calling, and so yes, I will grant you all that you have asked—though there is a caveat, or two."

"Which are?" asks Sebastian, surprising his friends.

Lucifer leers wickedly at the beach-blond, before placing a kiss on Lilith's cheek. "Lilith will be joining you in your musical endeavours. She has quite the siren song and will take on the role which you had originally intended for my Cassandra. She will be—how did you put it?—the sex appeal. Your vixen, and your muse."

"I'll be adopting this one's flesh," purrs Lilith, extending a slender finger in Heather's direction. I will look like her but will be so much more than she ever was. The pitiful mortals will not be able to resist my allure. Together, we will conquer, and you shall be the gods of men you so desire to be, and I will have my fun."

"There is one other small detail," says Lucifer. "I require a sacrifice—an innocent, once a year—on All Hallows' Eve, or our deal is null and void. The blood pays for your ongoing immortality. Do you think you can manage that?"

Jareth looks to his bandmates, and each in turns nods their consent. "We agree to your terms," he announces.

Lucifer inclines his head, acknowledging them, before

turning his attention to Cassandra once more. "Will you join me, little witch?" he asks, his voice dripping with temptation and promise.

Cassandra tucks an errant lock of purple hair behind her ear before meeting his electrifying gaze. "I will," she answers, finding her courage. "I was meant for you, I think I've always known it…and I cannot ignore my fate."

"None of us can, my precious," he purrs. "Now, say your farewells and we'll be on our way."

"Muz," says Cassandra with a curt nod.

"What do I tell mum and dad, li'l Cass? You still live at home…"

"No need to worry about that," says Lucifer.

Not a heartbeat later, Cassandra cries out as two deep cuts—from wrist to elbow—manifest up both of her inner arms, marring her pale tattooed skin. Looking to Lucifer, then back to her brother, she grimaces as her blood begins to flow, unhindered. "Suicide," she says simply. "Tell them I got drunk and killed myself."

"Lilith, my love?" says Lucifer. "Time to take possession of your new flesh."

Lilith winks at the band. "Untie me and we can have a little play before we get on with making history." Lilith blinks out of existence, it seems—vanishing before their very eyes.

The band jumps, a string of obscenities filling the night as Heather gasps, raising her head, a lurid smile upon her purple lips. "We haven't got all night, boys," she quips.

Cassandra sways on her feet, her life now a congealing pool at her feet.

"Our deal is struck," concludes the Fallen Angel. "It is done." He reaches out for Cassandra's hand. Just as she takes it, her body collapses upon the pentacle of salt—Lucifer is gone and so is her soul.

"Fuck me," says Sebastian, releasing a breath he didn't realise he'd been holding.

Heather drinks him in from head to toe with hungry eyes as Jareth cuts her bonds. "Sounds good to me, pretty boy," she says.

Triple6 breathe a collective sigh of relief as they wander, awestruck, back to the ute.

"It's over," says Jareth, running a hand through his hair. "We did it. From here on out, we're fuckin' stars. I can't believe it… America, here we come!"

"Thank fuck for that," says Murray as he casually pulls a spliff from his pocket. Behind them, by the tree, Heather tackles Sebastian to the gravel, mounting him like a wild animal in heat as she feverishly unbuckles his jeans.

The group's bass player clears his throat, pointedly averting his eyes. "Anyone got a light?"

Jareth and Wallace roll their eyes, both producing matching black lighters engraved with '666.'

241

BLACK HARE PRESS

ZOEY XOLTON is an Australian Speculative Fiction Author. She likes to daydream, and write stories about the beautiful and improbable, the dark and fantastical, as well as the adventurous and utterly romantic!

Whether it's fairy tales, fantasy, horror, paranormal romance, urban fantasy, or science-fiction…she dabbles in it.
Zoey has featured in over 100 anthologies to date, and is currently working on progressively longer stories.
She prays you enjoy, and fall in love with the deliciously tempting tales, and the characters that she brings into the world. Writing is Zoey's guilty pleasure…perhaps reading her work will become one of yours?

Bibliography
Bad Romance, Black Hare Press, 2020
Banned, Black Hare Press, 2020
Blood & Silk, Black Hare Press, 2020
Curses & Cauldrons, Blood Song Books, 2019
Dark Drabbles Series, Black Hare Press, 2019 - 2020
Darkly Ever After, Blood Song Books, 2020
Deep Sea, Black Hare Press, 2020
Eerie Christmas, Black Hare Press, 2019
Falling for Shifters, Dangerous Words Publishing, 2020
Forest of Fear 1 & 2, Blood Song Books, 2019 - 2020
Key to the Kingdom, Black Hare Press, 2020
Midsummer Night Shifts, Dangerous Words Publishing, 2020
Of Fables & Fae, Pauline Creeden Anthologies, 2020
Seven Deadly Sins Series, Black Hare Press, 2020
Storming Area 51, Black Hare Press, 2019
Twenty Twenty, Black Hare Press, 2020
What If?, Black Hare Press, 2019

Connect
Website: zoeyxolton.com
Amazon: amazon.com/author/zoeyxolton

THE NIGHT CREEPER

by Robin Braid

The bus pulled away at speed, kicking up a cloud of dust at Luke's back as he looked up at the house at the end of the street. This was his intended destination—the home of the Night Creeper.

The house looked modern and well kept, not quite the sinister gothic dwelling he was half expecting, and the surrounding neighbourhood was deathly quiet. He passed through an archway sculpted from knotted thorn branches and headed up the driveway. A dark purple van was parked outside, a goggle-eyed skull hanging from the rear-view mirror grinning maniacally, and a few feet beyond, steps at the side of the house lead down to a basement door. Luke adjusted the strap on the case slung across his shoulder and carefully descended.

With a knock on the door, he took a slight step back, and a few seconds later, it slowly eased open with a loud creak, unveiling the darkness within. "Night Creeper?" he said.

A hooded figure, face obscured, appeared in the doorway and beckoned to Luke with a long pale finger. "Come," he said.

No sooner had they entered when a loud crash rang out, echoing around the room. "Jesus Christ," the figure said, throwing the hood off. "Gubby, you idiot."

In the dim light of a lone candle, Luke saw a rotund guy in a black t-shirt by the left-hand wall. A wild explosion of twisted curls atop his head as he wobbled on a drum stool, one hand flailing hopelessly in the direction of the fallen cymbal. "Too dark, Jase," said Gubby.

Jase grumbled under his breath as he removed his cloak and threw it into a corner, then stomped around the room to turn on a couple of table lamps. Their weak orange glow partially illuminated the main body of the basement. He ran a hand through his spiked black hair as he turned to Luke. "Welcome to our lair," he said, "What was your name again?"

"Luke."

"Great. I'm Jase."

"Jase the bass," said Gubby.

"And this is Gubby, our drummer."

"And driver. You saw my awesome van outside, Luke?"

Luke smiled and nodded.

"So, Luke. You can play, huh?" said Jase.

"Yeah, I like to think so."

"You've played in bands before?"

"Yeah, one or two. Didn't work out though."

"Creative differences?"

"That's usually the case. And hooking up with the wrong guys in the first place, I guess."

"What do you mean?"

"Oh, you know. Guys that like to play at being rock stars without actually creating anything."

"You're ambitious then, that's good." Jase gestured towards a battered old amp sitting on a stack of magazines. "Okay, let's hear you," he said.

Luke laid his case on the ground and popped it open. The guitar inside was sleek and white. "Nice bit of kit," said Jase. "Might have to do something about the colour though, we're into black."

As Luke unwound his lead in preparation to plug in, Gubby grinned at him. "Melt our faces, man," he said.

***

"One more time, one more time." Gubby's hands lashed out at speed, clattering his sticks across the drums in a frenzy.

Hunched over their guitars, Luke and Jase were knocking out a stock heavy riff, beads of sweat forming on their brows. Luke struck a high note and held it, a signifier that they'd gone on long enough and it was time to draw things to a close. The other guys took the hint and the jam ground to an uneven halt. Jase laid his bass down and scurried behind the drum kit to exchange whispers with Gubby behind cupped hands. When Jase finally turned to address Luke, he gave him a thumbs up. "You're good, man, it feels good, yeah? What do you say?"

"Yeah, I think we could give things a go."

Gubby stood up from his stool. "Welcome to Night Creeper, the hardest rocking trio in the goddamn universe."

Luke wiped a forearm across his damp brow. "Thanks guys, I think it'll be fun."

Gubby reached across his drum kit to offer Luke a high-five. "Alright, cool. We should tell him now though, right, Jase?"

"I was getting to that," said Jase.

Luke lifted his strap over his head and carefully leant the guitar against the wall. "Tell me what? Are you auditioning anyone else?" he said.

"No, no auditions. But we do have a third party we haven't introduced you to yet."

"Or two," said Gubby.

"Okay," said Luke. "What's with all the secrecy?"

"You read our ad," said Jase. "We're not like other bands. It's probably best if we just show you though. I think you can handle it."

Jase led the way deeper into the basement, past piles of discarded furniture and decaying cardboard boxes overflowing with reams of paper, to where the fingers of light strained to reach. In the gloom at the back of the room, a large square of chipboard sat, elevated a couple of feet off the ground. "Is this where you eat?" said Luke.

Jase gripped one edge of the board with both hands. "Gubby, grab it," he said.

They tilted the board upwards and let it fall against the far wall, exposing a circular hole in the floor with a two-foot-high stone wall around its perimeter. Luke edged closer and attempted to peer into its darkness. "What is it? A well?" he said.

Jase smiled. "Maybe it started out that way, but it's something much more now." He threw an arm around Luke's shoulder. "It's a gateway....to hell."

Luke snorted. "Is it really?" he said.

"Well, it's damn sure not a stairway to heaven."

"Okay, looks cool, I guess, but what's the point of it?"

Jase pointed down into the pit. "Listen," he said.

As though on cue, from somewhere deep in the hole, a high, wavering sound floated up to them—an eerie, echoing female voice, a siren's call across worlds. "What the hell?" said Luke.

"Exactly." Jase smiled.

Gubby fell to his knees by the edge of the pit. "Fairchild," he said.

Jase knelt next to Gubby and tugged on Luke's arm to encourage him to do the same. "Let her song in," he whispered.

In a silent row, they knelt as the song of the enchantress filled their minds with sounds and visions borne out of the darkness, the mystical, and the mundane. Visions that folded themselves over and over to be reborn anew. Voices and faces. Fire and thunder. Beauty and decay. And throughout, doom and destruction skated around the edges of all they knew and all they could ever know. The limitations of mankind, every experience and emotion, encircled by the serpents that came before and the fallen angels who would herald the inevitable end.

Time seemed to stop and accelerate all at once, and almost without knowing, the three returned to their instruments. They stood facing each other in a triangle, and

Jase thumbed a steady pulse on the bottom string of his battered bass. "Lyrics will come later. We do the music first, that's where the real enchantment lies," he said.

Luke started to play with hands that felt strange and new. A grinding, sludgy riff snaked around and around as Gubby began to pound out a marching rhythm.

"Keep this groove going," said Jase. "Feel the power. Don't let it slip."

The hypnotic cacophony of sound swelled. The walls trembled as a swirling blanket of dust crept up around their ankles and cobwebs danced in high corners.

***

The clock on the wall had been long since past midnight by the time the bewitchment that held them began to ease. How long they had played and how much they had repeated, they could not say. Jase was the first to speak. "Now you know what makes this place special, Luke. What makes us special."

Luke held his throbbing hands in front of his face. His fingertips were bleeding. "That was unreal. What just happened?" he said.

"You heard the voice of Fairchild, the demonic songstress. She is the one who shows us the way. We have been blessed with the assistance of a power not of this Earth. Don't you see?"

Luke removed his guitar and dropped it to the floor. "I don't understand," he said.

"Let us return to the pit," said Jase. "Perhaps Berbell will help things become a little clearer for you."

Luke wiped his fingers on the front of his t-shirt. "Berbell? Another demon?"

"He's many things."

"He's our manager," said Gubby, rising from his stool.

Jase shot Gubby a glare over his shoulder. "Of sorts."

The three made their way back to the hole. It looked much the same as before, but now a faint red glow emanated from somewhere deep down. Jase squatted and placed his hands on the stone perimeter. "Great Berbell," he said. "Come forth and bless us once again with your unholy wisdom."

A sound like dripping water reverberated within the pit, but no voice could be heard. "What now?" said Gubby.

Jase raised a hand and made to speak, but a sonorous voice from the pit stopped him short. "I hear the earth creak in the wind. A galleon of the damned," it said.

"Great Berbell, we have done as you asked. Our numbers have swelled. May I introduce you to Luke, a believer and a guitar player worthy of deliverance. He's ready to join us as a disciple of the Dark Lord we were all born to serve," said Jase.

"This pleases me, gentlemen," said Berbell. "I heard your composition. We are satisfied with the progress being made, but we believe more can be done."

"More? You mean we need another? A fourth member?"

"I speak of refining your skill. The song has a power, but it can be so much more."

"Whatever we have to do, so be it, wise one."

Luke pulled at Jase's sleeve and gestured with his head to step away. "One second, Master Berbell," said Jase.

Once they were a few feet from the hole, Jase frowned at Luke. "What is it? I thought you were cool with this?"

"Call me crazy but I have a few questions," said Luke. "How do you know whoever is down there can be trusted for one?"

"You felt the power of Fairchild's song, you know it's something not of this Earth. We'd be fools not to tap into that."

Gubby had appeared at Jase's shoulder. "They're going to help us become awesome, Luke. Don't you want that?" he said.

"Sell your soul in exchange for talent? Like an old-time bluesman? Is that what this is all about?"

The voice of Berbell piped up from the pit. "Gentlemen, my time is valuable."

"Look, this basement is our crossroads. You can go up or down," said Jase. "But up only leads to mediocrity. I want greatness. I want to go down there. Really feel it. Stand toe to toe with the dark one and embrace all that he can give me. I'll be legendary."

"You literally want to be in hell?" said Luke.

"Better to be somewhere than nowhere, right Gubby?"

"Um—"

The voice of Berbell cut him off—it was louder this time. "Gentlemen, I sense a disturbance in your ranks."

"Just an impromptu band meeting, sir. Ironing out a few kinks," said Jase.

"Perhaps a little display shall allay any fears regarding our authenticity," said Berbell.

A rumble came from somewhere deep in the pit, and the red glow below began to rise, up and up, to the surface. The light burst forth in a blinding pillar and struck the basement ceiling with an almighty crack, causing Jase, Gubby, and Luke to be thrown backwards, crashing into boxes as they instinctively raised their hands to shield their eyes. The thundering shaft of red light contracted to a writhing rope, then expanded into a kaleidoscopic ball of a million colours. Shapes were thrown forth on its surface, then retreated, writhing and shifting, till the undeniable features of a face began to form. A smooth, pointed chin and sharp, protruding cheekbones. Thin strands of broken light seemed to drift across the face before hanging loose in a frame of long flowing hair. Two pinpricks of blackness punched through the rainbow of colour and stretched out to form a pair of empty eyes, endless in their depth.

Over the sound of the rumbling earth, the booming voice of Berbell, "Behold the face of the Fairchild."

Jase got to his feet, and peering through his fingers, slowly walked towards the pit. "She's beautiful."

On hands and knees, Gubby crawled after him, entranced by the vision. "Wow, oh wow," he said.

"Breathe it in, gentlemen, you are the chosen few," said Berbell. "Great rewards await you."

Jase raised both arms into the air as a sudden gust rushed out of the pit, scattering paper and dust around the room. "What do you say, Luke? Are you in?"

Propped up on one elbow, squinting in the face of the debris caught in the swirling wind, Luke's fingers twitched. The echo of Fairchild's song throbbed in his ears. "I'm in," he said.

***

Guitar squealed, bass roared, and the rapid pummelling of the drums brought the jam to a crescendo. The deep voice of Berbell, an axe slashing through the basement's musty air, called out, "Excellent. I believe you are ready to take the final step."

"This is it," said Jase. "The keys to the kingdom."

"Approach the pit, gentlemen, and bring your instruments."

The three walked in single file back through the junk pile to the edge of the hole, Jase and Luke brandishing their guitars and Gubby clutching his drumsticks.

"Drummer boy, present your sticks to me. Quickly," said Berbell.

Jase gave him a nudge. "Reach down in there, Gubby."

"I'm not sure I—"

"Do it now, this is what we've been waiting for."

"Present them to me, and they shall be blessed," said Berbell. "Your musicianship shall be unsurpassable."

Once more, Gubby knelt by the edge of the pit. With a drumstick in each hand, he leant against the stone wall and slowly lowered his arms over the edge, into the darkness. "Bless me, Great Berbell," he said.

There was the sound of something heavy cutting through the air at speed, and the colour swiftly drained from Gubby. His eyes, wide and confused, stared at Jase from a pallid mask of a face. A foul-smelling breeze exhaled from the pit and the sleeves of Gubby's t-shirt flapped gently where his arms had been. His body slowly rocked on the edge of the pit wall, his belly pressed down against it, then his feet went up in the air, and his body slid into the hole, sinking down into the sea of darkness.

"Berbell," Jase cried. "What is this? What have you done?"

"He was unworthy. Mere flesh for the feast."

"No, you have betrayed us." Jase threw his guitar aside and leapt onto the wall around the pit, one leg hanging down into it.

"Jase, no." Luke dropped his guitar and raised his hands in front but held back from moving any closer to the pit's edge.

"I'm going down, Luke, that was always the plan. I told Gubby we'd see this through together. I won't abandon him now."

"He's gone, man, it's over. This was always some sort of trick, wasn't it, Berbell?"

This time no voice was forthcoming. Jase smiled at Luke with glistening eyes, then swung his other leg over into the hole. He gripped the wall with both hands and lowered himself down until only his head and shoulders were visible. "Take the van and go, Luke," he said. "The keys are in the ignition. Gubby was always trusting like that."

"Come with me. Come on—"

All trace of an expression dropped from Jase's face as a small dark point emerged from his throat. It slowly grew bigger, like a large thorn being pushed through from the other side. His hands released their grip on the stone, and he was gone.

Luke turned and ran, clattering into a stacked pile of chairs that sent him spinning to the floor. He twisted his head to look over his shoulder and could see a great, dark shape rising out of the pit. A ragged, squirming outline illuminated by two glowing red lights.

"Do not mourn those foolish charlatans. You are our chosen one, our messenger on Earth. You shall be hell's bell ringer," said Berbell. "Fairchild shall ascend to the mortal plane, and together you shall reign in chaos from a throne of shattered souls."

Luke scrambled back to his feet and ran for the door. "Don't turn your back on me, boy," said Berbell.

The doorframe splintered and broken shards of wood sprayed across Luke's path as a pointed black projectile shot across the room and embedded itself there. He flung himself against the door and it crashed open, throwing him out onto the cold, moonlit concrete. "We have a hook in you, boy." He heard Berbell say. "We will meet again."

Sprinting up the steps, two at a time, Luke dared not look back. His feet skidded on the driveway, and he only just stayed upright as he lunged for the door of Gubby's van. He yanked it open and jumped into the driver's seat; sure enough, the keys were there. "God bless you, Gubby," he said.

Luke's heart was hammering in his chest as the engine coughed twice then kicked into life, and in a second, he was tearing out of the driveway, scattering gravel in his wake.

In the rear-view mirror, he watched the house, just as quiet and still as when he'd arrived, slip farther and farther into the distance. A few minutes later, he was pulling onto the highway. He finally felt able to settle back in his seat as he headed in the direction of home. Fingers drumming a marching rhythm on the wheel as he hummed to himself, a grinding, sludgy riff that snaked around and around.

BLACK HARE PRESS

ROBIN BRAID is a writer of stories of the mysterious and macabre. A resident of Fife, Scotland, he graduated from Dundee University with a degree in English Literature. When not working in his regular job he can often be found rambling over hills and glens in search of inspiration for further weird tales.

Bibliography
100 Word Bigger Zombie Bites, Reanimated Press Publishing, 2020
100 Word Horrors 3, KJK Publishing, 2019
100 Word Horrors 4, KJK Publishing, 2019
100 Word Zombie Bites, Reanimated Press Publishing, 2019
ANCIENTS, Black Hare Press, 2020
Forgotten Ones, Eerie River Publishing, 2020
HATE, Black Hare Press, 2020
LOVE, Black Hare Press, 2020
LUST, Black Hare Press, 2020
Mother Ghost Grimm Vol 1, NBH Publishing, 2019
OCEANS, Black Hare Press, 2020
Twenty Twenty, Black Hare Press, 2020

Connect
Twitter: @robinbraid

THE LAST DRINK

by Melinda Pouncey

Jimmy "The Demon" Quince ran offstage, the last chord of the last song still vibrating in his ears. Backstage was almost as riotous as the stadium audience still out there screaming for another encore. He pushed through the crowd with the help of security, his staff, entourage, and groupies all crowding and shouting. The claustrophobic cacophony swirled around him as he downed a bottle of water, scribbled autographs, gave the fans the occasional nod of acknowledgement, was towelled down by an assistant. The security detail ran interference for him and his bandmates, moving the crowd back a little to give the band some space. At last he reached his dressing room, crashing through the door and shoving it closed into the faces of at least a dozen people.

The relative silence of the room cleared his head a little. He grabbed an open bottle of whisky off the dressing table and slumped in the chair, taking a good hard swallow. He closed his eyes briefly. When he opened them, he caught a glimpse of himself in the mirror. The thick eyeshadow and lipstick were smeared, making his face look like a clown had exploded nearby. Red and black smudged together with white, not nearly as demonic as when he had taken the stage earlier. He snatched a handful of tissues and wiped the worst of it off. Jimmy did his best to avoid being photographed without his makeup. His baby-faced good looks were something straight out of *Tiger Beat*, hardly the hard rock persona he had cultivated into sold-out arenas and legions of screaming fans.

He sighed, running his hands through his hair then wiping them on his pants. He was so bored! Two weeks into the tour and still no girls worth giving a second look, no really good drug-fuelled parties, nothing new or different. Just the same as every other tour they'd done in the past four years. And he and his mates weren't getting along like they once did. The songs he wrote weren't as good or meaningful, they said. They wanted to update their sound and their image. The demon stuff didn't play as well these days; sales were down. It was all just blah blah blah to

Jimmy. He was the one who had started the band, wrote the songs, sang, and played lead guitar. They were turning into a bunch of hangers on, that's what, without a decent idea between them. Eager for the lifestyle but contributing nothing to maintain it. At least that's how he saw it. Sure, he shot down every idea and wouldn't consider any new songs they wrote, but they would all just be lame anyway. He wasn't going to let them hijack *his* band. Let them all go solo. He could get any studio band to back him up. The Demon was who they came to see.

A knock came at the door.

Jimmy threw a towel over his head. "Who is it?"

"Just me, Jimmy." It was his manager, Stephanie.

"Come in." He took the towel off and threw it on the table as Stephanie slipped in and quickly closed the door before anyone could get a look inside.

"The limo is almost ready. Security will collect you in a few minutes."

"Great. That will give me time to reapply."

She came over and smoothed the damp hair from his eyes. "You don't have to bother with that, just use this." She handed him a bandanna he could wear over his nose and mouth that bore a silkscreen of a monstrous slavering maw, teeth dripping with blood, much like the teeth he painted over his own mouth before every show.

"Hey, this is pretty cool. Where did you find this?"

"One of your many admirers gave it to me, actually. Don't worry, I ran it through security," she said in reply to his frown. "It's not covered in chloroform or arsenic or anything."

Jimmy took and tried it on. It gave him a demonic look similar to his makeup. It was not sheer so it wouldn't go see-through with a camera flash. He squinted his blue eyes into slits. The effect was pretty creepy. "This'll do," he said, turning his head this way and that to see how it looked from different angles.

"Would you like to meet her? She's right outside. I told her to wait just in case."

"What's she look like?"

"Petite, cute, between sixteen and nineteen, I'd guess. Hard to tell, but she's young. Dark hair, brown eyes. Bites her lip when she's nervous."

Jimmy definitely had a type, and this girl was it. He liked them young and a bit naive. It was fun to corrupt them and easier to bully them into keeping their mouths shut if it came to that.

"Yeah, I'll see her."

He tried to keep the excitement out of his voice, but Stephanie raised a knowing eyebrow. Still, she managed to refrain from making the obvious reply.

A few seconds later, the door opened, and the girl came in. She was a little punk baby doll with her Hot Topic ripped crop shirt revealing a delightful bit of tanned midriff with just a hint of baby fat. The shirt sported his demon persona on a black background, the painted on teeth bared in a snarl. Her hair had a streak of tomato red on one side and chartreuse on the other and was pulled up into a ponytail on top of her head, tiny white girl dreadlocks sprouting from it like weeds from a sidewalk. Her makeup was as thick and garish as his own—bright red lips, magenta glitter eyeshadow with heavy black eyeliner. Low-cut black jeans and motorcycle boots with a silver chain completed the picture. Unfortunately for her, it was the picture of a child trying too hard to pull off a look of badass maturity.

He found himself wanting to get her in a shower and wash the rock chick persona away, bask in her obvious youth and innocence.

He stood, towering over her, and offered his hand. "Thanks for coming to the show, Miss…"

"Sarah. Sarah Bruce."

And he thought James Kristandunder was bad. She needed a stage name as badly as he did.

"Nice to meet you, Sarah. Thanks for the bandanna, too. Would you like a drink?"

"I'll go check on your limo," Stephanie said, taking the

hint. Behind Sarah's back, she held up a hand, fingers spread, and mouthed, "Five minutes."

Jimmy ignored her. "So, what do you say?"

She bit her lip. "Uh, I guess so."

Jimmy turned away and poured her a drink, shifting his hips to accommodate his sudden arousal. He handed her the drink.

She accepted the glass and took an uncertain sip, grimacing as she swallowed.

"Are you old enough to drink?" he asked with an amused grin beneath his mask.

"Of course I am!" She was even cuter when she tried to look indignant.

He held up his hands. "All right, all right. Just checking. I have to be careful, I don't want the press to call me a paedophile."

"Oh, I'm sorry," she said. "I would never put you in a position like that, Jimmy. Can I call you Jimmy? You must think I'm some kind of crazy fan, but I'm not. It's your music that speaks to me." After her rush of words, she took a more confident swallow of her drink, causing her to choke and cough.

He put his hand on her shoulder and patted her back. "Easy there. It's so refreshing to meet someone who is all about the music. I don't suppose you'd like to come to my

hotel? We could talk for a while. I like to wind down after a show."

Her eyes widened in surprise. "I can come with you? Really? Oh, Jimmy! That would be so awesome! I can't even!"

Jimmy couldn't believe his luck. With a little finessing, this might prove to be the highlight of the tour.

All during the ride to the hotel, she talked about his musical style, the instruments he played, how she had followed his career since she was a little girl. She was more passionate about his music than he'd been in many years. It would have made him feel nostalgic if he hadn't spent the ride looking down her shirt, thinking lascivious thoughts.

When they got to the hotel room, the driver parked in the back and the two of them slipped through the rear entrance and took a lift to the VIP suite. Sarah goggled at the opulence of her surroundings and the view of the city lights spread out before her from the glass wall at the end of the room. Jimmy smiled at her wonderment. There was something about seeing the reaction of these little girls to lavish hotel suites that never got old. He doubted many of them would ever get the opportunity to see such a sight again. He invited her to sit on a long couch upholstered in gold velvet and poured them both another drink.

"Do you have a cell phone?" he asked.

"Yes, Jimmy. I guess you wouldn't want to pose for a selfie with me." She blushed a little.

"Sure, darlin', with your present on, of course." He lifted the end of the bandanna slightly.

She beamed him a grateful smile. "Really? Oh, thank you!"

He positioned them with a white pillar as a backdrop. It could have been taken anywhere. With the bandanna on, there was no proof it was even him.

She snapped a smiling picture of herself with a demon leering over her shoulder, eyes squinched into slits. *"Wait till the kids on Instagram get a load of that,"* he thought.

"Now why don't you turn that off and put it in that desk over there. I don't want to take any chances of you getting a candid shot."

"I would never do that!" she said, aghast at the idea. She dutifully turned off the phone and stored it in the drawer. "It's done." She turned back to him. "Does that mean you're going to take it off so I can see your face?"

"Maybe later. First, tell me what were you saying about my last album?"

"Only that it's the most transcendent thing I've ever heard! I could feel your emotion through your vocals. It really spoke to me."

"What's your favourite song off that one?" he said,

amused by her enthusiasm.

"'Ravage My Soul.' You know, the one that goes, *Ravage my soul, take me to the gates of Hell and beyond, I want to feel the burn, feel the rage take its toll as you ravage my, ravage my, ravage my soul!*" She tried to mimic his throaty growl as she sang and almost pulled it off. He was impressed to hear such a strong voice in such a small package.

"Well, that's real nice." He downed his drink and poured another. "Here I am on number two and you haven't even touched yours," he said, indicating her full glass. "Is alcohol not your thing? Do you prefer weed, maybe some cocaine?"

"No thanks, Jimmy, I'm fine. I don't do drugs."

Now he was annoyed. How was he going to get into those luscious little black jeans if she didn't drink or do drugs? "Haven't you ever tried any of that stuff?"

"Well, my dad gave me a beer at my graduation party, but I didn't really like it."

Holy shit! Her graduation party? Her daddy? This was too good to be true.

"How do you know you won't like drugs if you've never tried them? Come on, you like to party, don't you?" He made it sound like a challenge.

She didn't take the bait. "Yes, my friends come over

and we play your albums and dance."

"Your friends come over… Don't you work up a thirst dancing?"

"Sometimes. When I do, I have a soda or a wine cooler."

"Wine cooler, now you're talkin'." He went into the bar area and took a wine cooler out of the fridge, uncapping it and sneaking in a little hyoscine. *"This should hit her drug-deprived little nervous system like a freight train."*

He took it over and handed it to her, then sat down and picked up his drink. "Here's to rock-and-roll," he said, clinking his glass with her bottle.

"To rock-and-roll," she agreed and drank.

"And to daddy's beer," he said with a laugh.

She hesitated. "Say, Jimmy," she began, biting her lip. "Would you take your bandanna off now, so I can see your face? I promise I won't tell anyone."

"Sure, darlin', why not? We're friends now. Just make sure you don't say anything. I don't want word getting out what a pushover I am." He removed the bandanna and beamed her his most charming smile.

Her eyes lit up with delight when she saw his face. "Oh, Jimmy, you're more beautiful than I ever imagined!"

He didn't know how imaginative she might be, but he doubted that. His face still had streaks of black and red makeup, and, despite his youthful looks, there were lines around his eyes and mouth that hadn't been there a few short years ago. Still, he found her adoration to be both touching and…stimulating.

"Thanks for the compliment, sweetheart, but I really need to wash up. Why don't you just sip on your drink while I put on some music? I'll be back in a minute." His departure had a dual purpose. It would give him time to clean the gunk off his face, which was starting to get uncomfortable, and would give the drug time to work.

He hit the button on the stereo and popped into the bathroom while "Ravage My Soul" thundered through the speakers. "To the gates of Hell and beyond," he whispered into the mirror, "I want to feel the burn…"

When he returned to the room, the sight that met him was just what he'd hoped. Sarah was slumped on the couch, her eyes closed, arms loose at her sides, one ankle twisted outward, the other foot flat on the floor. Her pouty red lips offered an irresistible invitation.

Jimmy went over and chugged straight from the whisky bottle, then laid out a few lines of cocaine on the table, snorting them one after the other until he felt that heart-racing kick he craved. This was going to be so good.

He lifted an arm, released it. It fell, limp, back onto the couch cushion. Jimmy leaned over and captured her lips with his, tasting a combination of lipstick and strawberry wine cooler. He put his hand at her back and pulled her up a little for better access. Her eyelids fluttered.

"What's happening?" she slurred. "Where…? Ji…"

He kissed and bit at her neck. Her eyes opened a little, her hand twitching like she meant to raise it but was unable.

"It's all right, darlin'. It's just a party. You just relax now."

"N-no…"

"Shh," he crooned, slipping his hand up her shirt.

The cocaine urged him to go faster, to take his pleasure now, but the whisky softened that edge, gave him another idea. He let her go and picked up the bandanna, imagining what she'd think if she opened her eyes and saw her favourite demon doing her. Would she think it was a hallucination? What if he had Billy drive her back to the arena after and dump her? She might not even remember coming up here, and he'd be free and clear. Oh, yes, what an amazing idea. Even if she squawked later, she'd have no proof. Hell, he might even let her have her cell phone back, make things a little more interesting.

Jimmy tied the bandanna back on and took a moment to admire his reflection in the mirror hanging over the desk. A demon from the pit, inflicting delicious torment on his victim like a figure from his favourite Hieronymus Bosch painting. He imagined himself with bat-like wings, flying over the flames with little Sarah in his talons. The image in his mind made him bark a big, husky laugh.

Then, a strange feeling took hold of him. Something he had never felt before. The bandanna clung to his sweaty face like a second skin, hugging…no, more than that. It was melting into his face, transforming into flesh, the razor-sharp teeth melding with his own, growing, sliding into tapered white points. At the same time, his head and jaws expanded to accommodate the change. He watched in horror as his head widened, his forehead receding as his muzzle formed into a canid travesty of his face.

He tried to scream, but his voice came out as a howl of pain and rage. He fell to all fours, paws sprouting from the ends of his arms, from the ankles on his legs. As the hellish metamorphosis continued, Sarah rose from the couch completely awake and alert, her green eyes flashing red pupils that matched the colours streaking her hair.

"Easy there, Jimmy," she said with a demonic grin. "It's just a party. Relax now."

He opened his hideously fanged mouth to snap at her, but found himself unable to move.

"Oh, no. You can't do that, I'm afraid," Sarah said. "You need to save that energy for the gates. You see, we lost one of our hellhounds to an exorcism recently. Michael himself came and took the bitch's head off. I didn't know what to do, but then I started hearing your song, seeing it climb the charts, and it gave me an idea. Why not just make a new one? Now don't try to tell me it's not what you wanted. I could feel it when you sang, I felt all that raw emotion you pulled from your corruption of innocent flesh, what you've lived on, fed on for years. You want your soul ravaged, you want to feel the burn? Well, you will. Oh, you will."

With a wave of her hand, Sarah Bruce returned to Hell, taking her newly acquired pet with her, leaving only a faint scent of brimstone and strawberry wine behind.

MELINDA POUNCEY writes horror, fantasy, science fiction, and anything else that catches her interest.

She has authored numerous drabbles and short stories. Her shorter pieces, usually from her darker side, can be found in several Black Hare Press anthologies, Road Kill Volume 3: Texas Horror by Texas Writers published by Hellbound Books, and Fear and Fables published by Stormy Island Publishing.

Bibliography
APOCALYPSE, Black Hare Press, 2019
FEAR AND FABLES, Stormy Island Publishing 2019
HATE, Black Hare Press, 2020
LOVE, Black Hare Press, 2020
ROAD KILL VOLUME 3, Hellbound Books, 2018

Connect
Facebook: @Melinda.Pouncey

CROSS ROAD BLUES

by Raven Corinn Carluk

Desdemona strode through the stage door of Dante's Ballroom like she owned the place, the autumn breeze blowing leaves in with her. The demoness paused to let her eyes adjust from the sickly yellow light of the alley to the mix of work lamps and overhead fluorescents.

The walls thrummed with the bassline, hard and driving, and her heartbeat immediately fell into sync, driving her from stillness and towards her goal. Her PVC stiletto vamps carried her swiftly through the backstage and downstairs to the greenroom, rain dripping from her with every heavy stomp.

None of the staff stopped her to ask what she was doing here during the show. Some of the crew recognised her, though Lightbringer was the first band she'd booked at the Portland bar in years. Most simply observed that she was on a mission and left her alone.

Or they didn't want to fuck with the tiny angry woman in vinyl and spikes.

The music was even more muted downstairs in the greenroom, but she could make out the strains of the band's only original song. Desdemona towelled off her silky white hair with a smirk. If they stayed true, the young men would finish the song, then perform "Cross Road Blues" for their encore. No more than fifteen minutes until she could confront Lightbringer.

She snorted, tossing the towel to the floor. Lightbringer! What a ridiculous name, as pretentious as most humans. Desdemona had bargained with her share of silly humans, but these simply took the cake.

Desdemona chuckled at the ridiculous human phrase even as she thought it. As if there were cake in Hell.

How best to handle them? Her rage simmered just below the surface, begging for violence and retribution. Raw, cruel, and preferably bloody. The demoness had taken many souls during her time on Earth, but she'd never allowed any to attempt an escape without punishing them. She'd long ago learned that if one mortal was allowed to bend the rules, many others would try it.

But Lightbringer deserved something more than to simply be torn limb from limb. No, they needed something truly horrible to carry their souls down to eternal torment.

The music stopped. Desdemona waited for the encore, chewing her lower lip, letting her gaze rove the greenroom. So many items she could use to maim them, to remind them whom they were dealing with.

But she couldn't kill them here. Dante's was too popular a destination to be shut down while bodies were cleaned up. Were she to cause Crastix a problem at his bar, the other demon would never allow Desdemona to book another of her bands here. With his influence and connections, it wouldn't be unheard of for other demons to shun her as well.

Mack burst into the room, followed by the other two band members and their new manager. Laughter died when they saw her.

"Hello boys," she said, crossing her arms. A tiny muscle twitched along her jaw, then stilled. Even in her spike heels, she was a foot shorter than them, but none of them could maintain eye contact. Desdemona glared at each in turn, amazed by her own control.

The lead singer, Mack. Blond, slender, fond of tattoos and skulls, his good looks were balanced by his dim wits. He looked away first, ducking his head like he'd been caught lifting money from his mom's purse.

Wes played bass and lifted weights. His crewcut gave him a military look, but his penchant for petty crimes and casual drug use made him unfit for taking orders. He swore and flopped onto the couch.

Stefan held her glare the longest. The drummer had written the summoning song. He was the poster child for misfit outcast, turning to heavy metal and occult lore as solace in an uncaring world. When he finally lowered his eyes, he took a step closer to the demoness.

The manager cleared his throat. "Are we going to do this here?"

Desdemona arched one snowy brow, locking eyes with him. "Yes, Valrax, I think we are." The scent of sulphur filled the air as the two demons stared at each other.

The moment dragged out, the distant murmur of the crowd the only noise. Mack coughed, shifting uncomfortably.

"Why didn't you play the encore?" she finally snapped, continuing to stare at Valrax. He looked like a caricature of a sleazeball music producer; his smoked glasses were too big and gaudy, his shirt open too far with too many gold chains and chest hairs. She wondered that normal humans hadn't realised something was wrong with him.

"The crowd wasn't really feeling it tonight," Stefan mumbled. "They didn't seem—"

"Bullshit!" She unfolded her arms to plant hands on her hips. "Who the fuck told you to skip that song?" When no one spoke, she turned her glare on each of them again.

"Just fucking tell her," Wes snapped from the couch after another uncomfortable silence. He fumbled for a pack of cigarettes and a lighter, taking a huge drag while markedly not looking at her.

"Oh, yes, *do* tell me." Desdemona stared at Mack, slinking closer, hands remaining on her slender hips. "Is there some pertinent piece of information that I, your manager and producer, should know?"

Mack shifted, staring at his feet, his voice too soft for mortal ears to catch his whisper. "We have a new manager."

She moved to within an arm's length from the singer and cocked her head. "I'm sorry. Could you repeat that? Because I couldn't possibly have heard you correctly."

His head snapped up, and he loomed over the demoness. "I said we have a new manager. So just piss off." Mack stomped towards the greenroom bar, only able to stand up to her for that brief moment. The air reeked of his fear.

Desdemona threw her head back and laughed. Her cackle went on and on until she felt the young men shifting uncomfortably. When she stopped, she shook her head. "Do you fools really think that's how this works?"

"Val said he'd buy out the contract." Wes finally looked

at her. "You're gonna get compensated."

She narrowed her eyes. "Do I look like I care about compensation?" Her rage shifted against her control, and she felt some of her human disguise slip.

Mack downed a shot of whiskey, poured himself another, and drank it as quickly. "Yeah, well, what about us?"

"What about you?" She turned to him, jaw set.

The blond singer helped himself to a third shot, then slammed the glass on the bar top. "We asked you for fame and everything else that goes with it. Where's the money, and the bitches, and the awesome gigs?"

Desdemona's brow arched farther. "Oh, you expected all of that right away?"

Stefan shuffled away and sat, head down. Wes chortled, taking another heavy drag of his cigarette. Mack held her gaze, the liquid courage giving him the strength to do so. "Yeah, you dumb bitch. You were supposed to give us all that."

Desdemona counted to five, jaw clenched, wondering what he'd sound like if she ripped the tongue from his arrogant little head. Only after the surge of anger passed did she speak. "Haven't I given you the album and the venues? Haven't I given you the chance to earn your way?"

"An album of cover songs." Mack clenched his fists,

pulling his shoulders back. "Singing *other* people's songs about the Devil at crummy dive bars with skanky groupies. I mean, Dante's? For fuck's sake, were you trying for the ironic crowd?"

"You're unhappy with our arrangement?" His obvious stupidity quelled her rage. Would he even understand whatever punishment she doled out?

Mack sputtered and stared, face flushing with suppressed emotion. Stefan ducked his head, trying to remain unseen. Valrax stifled a laugh, stalking around behind her.

Wes leaned forward and stabbed at her with his cigarette. "What do you think? Why else would we bring Val in?"

She turned her ire on him, eyes hard, hands becoming fists on her hips. "Seems I'm just a stupid bitch who doesn't know how to manage a band, so why don't you explain it to me?"

Remarkably, he held her gaze, though he couldn't speak right away. Desdemona stared back, eyes wide, and tipped her head while waiting.

Wes finally rose. "We gave you our souls so we could make it big. Instead of letting you keep dicking us around like this, we made a new contract." He crushed his cigarette out and lit another.

Desdemona's jaw tensed, anger spiking. So bold, so proud, flaunting their choice. They had no fear of repercussions. Almost no fear of Hell, like they didn't believe in its existence.

"Is it possible?" The three men offered her sharp frowns. "Do you really think this is like a normal record deal? Are there going to be lawyers and a judge and hearings, and we'll all just walk away with some settlement or something?"

Blank stares brought a smile to her face. Then laughter bubbled forth. "You really *are* the biggest bunch of jackasses I've ever met. Dumb, untalented, entitled, full of yourselves. And to think, I almost tore you all limb from limb." Anger dispersed, replaced by humour at the absurdity of it all. "This is certainly new for me."

Wes stormed around the coffee table to come to Mack's side, spluttering and swearing. He hit the singer as he turned his attention to Valrax. "You got anything to say about this?"

The other demon chuckled. "Like what?"

"I dunno." Mack gestured sharply. "You're our new manager, so how 'bout you fucking manage this."

Desdemona smirked, glancing over her shoulder at Valrax. The other demon fiddled with one of his large gold rings before licking his lips and giving a toothy grin that showed off his veneers. "This came to a boil a whole lot faster than I expected."

Wes and Mack stared in silence, confusion playing across their faces as they shifted their gazes between Val and Desdemona. Wes tried to say something, but his mouth merely opened and closed. Just like a dumb fish gawping at its own reflection, she thought.

Stefan laughed. Just a snort at first, then a broken chuckle. When mad cackles started, everyone turned their attention to him. "I told you this would happen, you stupid fucks."

Mack snapped at him, "You said it wouldn't work, but Val said he'd take care of us."

"Actually," Valrax drawled, regaining the group's attention. "Maybe you should remember the words I really used."

Wes exchanged another look with Mack. "I don't remember."

"Me either."

Stefan rose slowly, face drawn. "He said we'd get what we deserved. We just *wanted* that to mean fame and fortune." He made eye contact with Desdemona. "He meant something bad, didn't he?"

"Of course he did."

Mack hadn't accepted it yet. "No. We negotiated a new deal. A new demon, with new terms."

"So dumb and pretty." Desdemona sighed and began stalking around the room. "If you'd have just done what I said, the money and women would have come, and maybe even a second record."

"But it needed to be done with care. A spell that powerful gets noticed if it shows up all at once, on *all* the stations, getting covered by all the popular bands. We're connected enough to do it, but we're also smart enough not to."

"Spell?" Wes sputtered.

The demoness sighed, rolling her eyes. Stefan spoke before she spat sharp words at the bassist. "Our song. The one I wrote that we played, that summoned *her*." Stefan dared glance at the demoness even as he shrank in on himself.

"It's a spell. So fucking what?" Mack glared at her, fists on his hips. "We need to get things straightened out, right fucking now!" Wes and Stefan had the wits to pull back, though only the drummer looked contrite.

Desdemona locked gazes with Valrax. "Do you want to be the one to tell them?" She licked her lips as anticipation built.

The other demon smirked. Then smiled broadly, showing off jagged fangs. "Oh, no, Dezzie, you get all the honours." He laughed and flopped into a chair.

Mack closed the distance and grabbed her arms, yanking her around to face him again. "What. The. *Fuck!*"

She hissed, grabbed one of his thumbs, and twisted. Mack was nearly twice her size, but he cried out and collapsed to his knees. Desdemona kept her grip on him as she glared down into his contorted face, letting some of her demonic nature loose.

"Listen here, you pathetic mortal shit," she snarled. Wes took a step closer, and she speared him with a glance. "*All* of you, fucking *listen.*"

"You act like hot shit, but you are pretty far from it. Even with my powers, your mediocre band is barely passable. I only agreed to take you on because that spell has more power than anyone expected. We want it, and we'll put up with a lot, but this is too far."

Mack whimpered, and Wes shook his head. "What's going to happen to us?"

She pulled Mack to his feet and shoved him back towards the others. "Well, I still need Lightbringer and 'The Crossroad', so let's just have a little audition."

"A what?" Stefan asked. His voice trembled, and he hid behind his bandmates.

Desdemona gestured at the greenroom around them. "I only need one of you. Some tragic accident will kill most of you, but the survivor will bravely continue on to honour his closest friends. Maybe some charity concert or memorial tour up the coast. I suppose it all depends on how very much one of you wants this."

They stared blankly, letting the words sink in. Maybe just unable to comprehend them. She wasn't sure which, though she leaned towards the latter as time continued to pass.

"Fuck it," Valrax said with an exasperated sigh. "I'll kill these little punks."

Desdemona held up a forestalling hand. "If we're going to owe Crastix for having to delay the next show while we clean up the aftermath, then it might as well be entertaining." She tipped her head and made eye contact with each of them. "Either *one* of you gets out of here or *none* of you do." The demoness flexed her hand, revealing razor-sharp claws.

Wes struck first, punching Mack in the back of the head. The singer stumbled forward a step, then spun on his bandmate. Mack swore and lunged, barrelling into the bassist, the pair of them crashing over the coffee table and to the floor, shattering it in the process. They bashed at each other, grunting and swearing.

Stefan watched from the side, avoiding flailing limbs. A handful of furtive glances were tossed towards Desdemona, but he said nothing. He made no move to flee, nor did he try to break up the fight.

Mack grabbed Wes by the throat, held him down with one hand, and punched him repeatedly in the face. Blood splattered and bone crunched, and the singer's voice rose in a guttural howl.

Wes stopped trying to pry the hand away from his throat and began clawing at Mack's face. His struggles weakened, but a finger found an eye, causing Mack to pull back, loosening his grip. Wes drew a deep breath and threw the other man off him.

Desdemona smirked, eyes hooded, feeding upon their violence. They were base and brutal, exhibiting no finesse, no strategy, no real drive to kill the other yet. Entertaining for the moment, but she was quickly growing bored.

Mack kicked and flailed at Wes, rubbing his eye, but couldn't stop Wes from pummelling him, kicking him. He wheezed when the bassist kicked him in the gut.

Wes didn't stop there, fell upon Mack with a furious growl, landing numerous blows upon the singer's head, breaking through meagre defences. He continued to growl between ragged breaths, spittle flying from bared teeth as Wes locked hands around Mack's throat.

He lifted Mack's head to pound it against the floor with a meaty thunk. Blood hung in strings from Wes's broken nose, dotting the singer's face as he gasped for air.

Mack blindly reached for the other man's face,

attempting his own escape. Wes was taller, stronger, and used that to his advantage. He kept his face away from Mack's questing fingers, and he slammed Mack's head into the ground again.

And again. Again and again, until Mack ceased to struggle and a puddle of blood spread from the back of his skull.

Wes turned mad eyes towards Desdemona, one of them already swelling shut. "Now it's your turn, you fucking bitch." He rose with clenched fists, intent only upon the demoness.

Stefan bashed him in the head with the leg of the coffee table.

The bassist collapsed back to his knees, though for only a moment. He rounded on Stefan and swore through a split lip, but the drummer gave Wes no time to attack. He swung the table leg like a bat, crunching bone with wood. A second swing tumbled Wes back, and Stefan followed, looming over the beaten man. Shrieking, he drove the broken end of the table leg through Wes's eye socket.

As the man twitched, Stefan locked gazes with Desdemona. He panted, blood and tears mingling on his cheeks, a new strength radiating from him.

Desdemona resumed her human hands as she cautiously approached the man. He was in a delicate place, and might break completely. "Beautifully done," she praised, reaching for him.

Stefan relaxed, laid his cheek in her hand. He said nothing, but she watched the tension ease from him, replaced by triumph.

"You did very well," she said softly. "After the appropriate mourning period, we'll get you some new bandmates."

He stared at her, face neutral, a final tear sliding down his cheek and across her fingers. "Better ones?" Stefan finally asked, voice level and calm.

She smirked and drew him to her for a hug. *He* was the one she'd rooted for, though she'd told herself it didn't matter. Desdemona ached to harness his power, to use his skill to ensnare more souls. Mortals who could craft a summoning spell like his were rare, often shackled by the mundane, held back by the less talented.

And now he was free of the other two, baptised in blood, reborn of death. "Oh, yes, my dearest Stefan. Much better ones."

BLACK HARE PRESS

RAVEN CORINN CARLUK writes dark fantasy, paranormal romance, and anything else that catches her interest.
She has authored and self-published five novels and one novella, where she explores themes of love and acceptance. She has also self-published two collections of short stories, ranging from the lustful to the horrific, the darkly humorous to the tragic. Her shorter pieces, usually from her darker side, can be found in several Black Hare Press anthologies, at Detritus Online, with Fantasia Divinity, and through Alban Lake Publishers.

Bibliography
All Hallows Blood,2011
ANGELS, Black Hare Press, 2019
BEYOND, Black Hare Press, 2019
Deep Space, Black Hare Press, 2019
Martyrs (The Birdman Project), 2019
Midsummer's Unveiling, RCC Tales, 2012
MONSTERS, Black Hare Press, 2019
Nomycha, RCC Tales, 2018
Saint Valentine's Clash, RCC Tales, 2011
stories with bite o,.,o, 2010
The Birdman Project, Forever Morris Publishing, 2019
WORLDS, Black Hare Press, 2019

Connect
Website: RavenCorinnCarluk.Blogspot.Com
Amazon: amazon.com/author/ravencorinncarluk
Smashwords: smashwords.com/profile/view/RavenCorinnCarluk
Twitter: @ravencorinn
Facebook: @RavenCorinnCarluk

FRACTURED FAIRYTALE

by Alanna Robertson-Webb

Elise let out a frustrated wail, and if the teen had been using her powers, then the agitated pixie in front of her would have been bleeding from her ears.

"Dammit, Courtney, you come in during the *second* verse, not the first! Get your act together, or I'll replace you with that zombie Maryjane Symmons. She's been dying to be in my band, and you aren't the only overgrown moth in this Podunk town who can strum. Fractured Fairytale will perform live in exactly a month, with or without your bumbling ass."

The pixie fluttered her wings, tiny patches of scales

moulting as the dominant siren glared at her. Normally siren magic was no match for that of pixie trickery, but Courtney was unusually passive for a fae. She played the role of doormat for Elise, even to the point where she ran errands after school for the diva siren. No one else wanted to be her friend, not when her family was in disgrace, so the pixie took whatever companionship she could grasp.

As if reading her mind, Elise let out a slimy, sinister chuckle.

"Don't even think about saying no, or you really won't have anyone. You know that your dad was supposed to have stopped the Midtown Murderer, not let them escape."

Courtney choked back a sob, her glittering tears staining the midnight duvet. The tambourine fell listlessly against the satin pillows, and with what little dignity she had, she stood, her back nearly ramrod-straight. Her voice came out in a breathy whisper, but the sharp-eared siren heard the pixie well enough.

"Shut up."

"What did you just say, you insect? You might want to think carefully about your next words."

"I said *shut up*."

The unexpected slap took Courtney's breath away. Elise had never struck her before, nor had anyone else, and the fae was momentarily stunned. Before she could blink,

Elise was cradling her cheek, her clawed fingers digging cruelly into the red-tinted alabaster skin.

"Now, be a good girl and go get me a soda, yeah? We'll take five, then rehearse it from the top. You know we have our very first show soon, so by my ancestors you'd better be ready because we aren't going to botch up my chance at stardom. In case you have second thoughts, remember this: All it takes is one very convincing word from me, the mayor's daughter, and the whole town will know that your dad is way worse than just some shitty, half-baked policeman."

Courtney nodded mutely, her wings folding about her shoulders in a pitiful attempt at self-soothing.

"Say 'Yes Elise, you're the best' or I'll make your punishment worse."

"Yes, Elis…"

Elise quickly wrapped her hand around the pixie's delicate neck, shoving the girl back against the wall until she heard a satisfying crunch from her minion's wings. Courtney cried out in pain, her back spasming as her wings tried to stretch out, so Elise put more pressure onto the fae's neck.

"Get my drink, now."

She let Courtney drop to the floor, the pixie worth a little more than garbage to her.

After a few minutes, Courtney wordlessly fetched Elise a drink, her hands shaking so badly that she nearly sloshed the soda down Elise's expensive, studded crop top. She managed to make it through the rest of rehearsal without further upsetting the siren, and as the pixie escaped the opulent mansion, her heartbeat finally returned to normal. She hated Courtney, and she wanted to wrap her green-thumbed hands around the cerulean-eyed girl's scaly neck, but she knew that she couldn't.

She would never risk her family like that.

As Courtney made her way home, the fae's stilettos clicking rhythmically against the concrete, she began to hum the first few strands of a new song that had been weaving in the back of her mind for the last few days. Her steps matched the beat, and soon she was dancing through the dark like a spiralling star. After a few minutes, the crescendo of concrete gave way to the soft thudding of heels on dirt, the howl of the night wind no less melodic. The young pixie made her way through a field, then onto the wooded path that she had taken dozens of times.

Her pointed ears led the way, her willowy body bending in time with the trees that swayed in the gentle summer breeze. That was when she heard something that sent an instant shiver racing down her spine, her already large eyes widening to doll-like portions.

Silence.

The forest should never be so quiet, and the fae was instantly on high alert. As she made her way cautiously to the halfway point of the trail, she heard a snap behind her, the sound too loud to have been made by an errant deer or rabbit. She tried to shrug it off, but a few heartbeats later, the sound came again. It was bipedal, the successive *crunch-crunch* sounds too close together to be a four-legged animal.

"H-hello?"

No response.

"Elis-se, is that-t y-you?"

A deep rumble, not unlike thunder, spread outward from the darkness of the forest. Those with fairy blood could see as well as a cat in the dark, their eyes saucer-shaped in order to allow extra light to filter in. Even so, Courtney couldn't make out any distinctive shapes, and that unnerved her nearly as much as the silence.

"Hi?"

The voice was coming from the trees off to her left, and it sounded just like the prima donna siren. Courtney let out a furious huff, her heartbeat attempting to return to a normal rate once she realised who it was.

"Elise! What in the Underworld!? You scared me half to the morgue."

"Help?"

The pixie paused, a semi-scorching rebuke halting on the tip of her pointed tongue. Elise had never asked for help before, she always demanded assistance, so something was wrong.

"Help you with what? Are you okay?"

"Please…"

Elise's normally smooth voice came out in a choppy scratch, and Courtney wondered if the siren had hurt herself. It sounded like she was moving deeper into the forest, and without thinking, the pixie began following her bandmate.

"Elise? You've gotta stay still, or I won't be able to find you. What do you need help with? It's dark, and I really just want to get home."

Finally she caught a glimpse of the siren, her silhouette a few metres ahead. The girl was crouched down; her webbed hands pressed against the soil. She looked like she was heaving, and her normally neatly braided hair was a wild mess around her heart-shaped face.

"Leave…"

"What?"

"Leave meeeeee!"

The thing, for Elise definitely couldn't spring to her feet like that, charged at Courtney. The fae squealed, turning on her heels and sprinting back towards the path. For a moment, she heard the whooshing of footfalls behind her, but then they were coming towards her instead. Courtney twisted about frantically, the steps beginning to encircle her, and as her unseen tormentor moved closer, the pixie realised that the rumbling she had heard before was a growl.

"No bad experiments."

The voice was so close that Courtney jumped, her tiny wings barely grown enough to allow her to hover above the ground, but she still couldn't see the long-haired creature.

"W-who's there!? Show yourself! I know you aren't Elise!"

Just as she finished another fruitless circle, a set of claws pierced her chest, the tips burying themselves a millimetre from her heart. Everything was frozen, and Courtney felt that if she so much as breathed, she would die. The creature, now visible, gazed curiously at her—its milky, moss-hued eyes seeming to almost glow in the darkness. Its head was cocked like a puppy, and it was examining the young pixie carefully. It wiggled its claws the tiniest bit, causing the fae to inhale sharply at the alien sensation.

With its free hand, it inspected Courtney's clothing, its fingers running slowly across the tulle of her pink skirt.

"No doctor. No badge. Good…friend?"

It slowly retracted its claws, leaving a dripping trail of blood between their bodies. Courtney collapsed to the forest floor; the fae's body wracked with violent shivers. The creature squatted in front of her, its webbed hands resting on its knees as it observed her. The pain subsided after a few minutes, and Courtney was relieved that her wound wasn't worse. Once the pixie had regained some semblance of normalcy and was able to stand, the thing repeated its request.

"Friend?"

Courtney was too terrified to run, or to speak, so she merely nodded. Child-like joy flared across the creature's face, a grin filled with needle-like teeth stretching from cheek to lopsided cheek. Courtney's mind raced, and the only thing that she could think to do was play along. If she kept the thing happy, then it wouldn't hurt her, hopefully. It didn't seem to like doctors, so the pixie took that route.

"I'm not a doctor. Doctors are bad. I'm just a high school kid."

"Kid?"

"Yeah. Like I go to school, and I sing backup in a band."

Courtney had been slowly backing away, trying to keep some distance between herself and the thing. It didn't seem like she was in immediate danger, but she wasn't willing to take any gamble.

"So, um, what kind of person are you?"

Courtney's hesitant whisper was met with a blank stare, as though the creature didn't understand the question. The fae slowly pointed to herself, gesturing cautiously to her wings and ears.

"Pixie, *pix-ee*. I'm a pixie, a type of lesser fairy. What are you?"

She spoke slowly, as though talking to a young child, but it didn't garner any reaction. Thankfully, the creature wasn't making any move to attack her, but its unwavering gaze was beginning to unnerve the fae almost as much as the claws in her chest had. After a moment, she pulled out her purple, bedazzled wallet and removed a picture of her and Elise. Extending the photo, she pointed to herself, then to the merfolk.

"Pixie, siren."

The fae gestured to the creature's webbing and then to Elise. The creature cocked its head, trying to use body language to convey her meaning.

"Siren?"

The monster manoeuvred itself, leaning forward to get a better look at the photo. It flexed its webbing, and then the membranes began to retract into the skin. Within seconds, the thing was sprouting a pair of pixie wings instead, and Courtney felt cool air across her teeth as she gasped.

"What the Tartarus!?"

The creature's eyes widened at Courtney's shout and it flinched, freezing mid-transformation. The thing had halted somewhere between pixie and siren, an amalgamation of both species that made it appear misshapen and grotesque. A forked tongue slithered anxiously over cracked lips, and for a moment, Courtney felt a pang of guilt. The thing was strange, sure, but the longer she spent around the creature, the more it seemed like a lost kid.

It didn't appear to be the savage, bloodthirsty monster she had first feared it was.

She stared at the creature, contemplating what to do about it, when it began to speak. It pointed to itself, a raspy, guttural pair of syllables spewing forth.

"Roo-sahhh."

"Um, what?"

"Meeee!"

It was grinning, obviously very proud of the communication achievement it had made.

"Me, Rosa."

It patted its head, humming a disjointed tune that

sounded vaguely like a music box. It spun in a small circle, limbs flailing wildly in a poor mimicry of the dance that Courtney had been doing. A sudden cracking of twigs caught the fae's attention, her eyes flicking back towards the path.

"What in the actual fuck!?"

The siren stood just inside the treeline, a now-forgotten flashlight landing with a dull thud at her feet. Elise's too-familiar shriek caused Courtney to flinch, her hands covering her pointed ears as best as she could. Elise was staring at them, her face rapidly switching from shock to disgust. The flashlight illuminated her in a mockery of a stage light, almost as though it had anticipated her dramatic reaction.

"Ewww, what kind of costume is that? Is this some sort of sick joke?"

"It's not a costume. She's…"

"*She?* Ugh, is that one of those weird theatre geeks or something? You moron! Get away from it now, before it turns you into a nerd and drops my popularity by association!"

Elise let out a glass-cracking laugh, and for just a moment Courtney thought she had missed some sort of actual joke. When it was clear that no punchline was coming, a hot wave of anger surged down her spine, her wings fluttering disconcertedly as she stopped herself from making too sharp of a retort.

"No, Elise, just listen. This is my friend, Rosa, and she has a really cool abil—"

"Riiiiiight, as if! You don't have any friends, at least not any other than me."

"N-no, I, I do…"

Elise stalked closer to Courtney until they were face to face, her voice taking on a commanding, melodic tone. The diva stopped a mere inch from the pixie, her pupils dilating in the dim light as her magic began to surge forth.

"Whatever, just get her and that *hideous* ensemble off of my property. Nerds are, like, so gross!"

Each syllable was a sing-song spike of cruelty, a jab at a creature that Elise already viewed as inferior even though she had no basis for her attitude. No one deserved to be treated that way, and Courtney felt her tiny fists clenching, a burst of magic racing along her fingers as though the old gods had bestowed their lightning upon her. Sparks began to spurt from her fingertips, the little bolts crackling and fizzing sporadically.

"Stop being so mean. Rosa is nice!"

"Look, you moron; I call the shots, and I say she needs to get lost. If you don't get rid of her, I'm going to tell Daddy the truth about your dad. I know what he did to

your mo—"

That was it.

Elise's words were the final nail in the coffin that housed Courtney's patience, and the pixie couldn't take it any longer. Without thinking, she shoved her hands outwards, an electric pop breaking the air as her palms collided with Elise. The siren let out a pain-filled wail, her hair standing on end as the silver-tinged electric magic shot through her. Her body convulsed, the volts digging into every pore and ventricle as a blast of pure fae magic followed the electricity. Flowers began to grow from Elise's orifices, rapidly spreading tendrils of perennial sweet peas crisscrossing the teen's lightly scaled body as their roots burst apart her organs. Within moments, they had covered her from head to feet, their delicate fragrance a sharp contrast to the coppery, storm-like scent tainting the air.

The siren's flesh had roasted, the black, crumbled scales dropping into the forest soil. Courtney stared in disbelief at the flower-covered mound that had just been a living, breathing person. She had thought her magic was dormant, or even that it had completely skipped her generation, but she had never heard of another pixie having this ability.

Maybe the rumours of her father not being her

biological parent were true.

"Shit…"

The pixie's wings gave out, dropping her to her knees in the blood-stained dirt. She heard Rosa move towards her, and a timid, comforting hand came to rest on a winged shoulder. Courtney couldn't react; she couldn't do anything but stare. Rosa hunkered down beside her, neither of them paying attention to the pool of siren viscera that they were seated in. Blank eyes alighted on shadow-dusted sweet pea petals, tears trickling their way down Courtney's gore-spattered cheeks.

"Soorry. Accidennnnt?"

Courtney tried to respond, but a hysterical hiccup was catching in her throat. She tried to draw in air but ended up choke-sobbing instead. All she could do was nod, and Rosa slowly mimicked the bobbing of her head.

Elise had known the truth: Courtney's dad had killed her mom in a fit of rage, blaming his action on a serial killer, and now she was following in his footsteps.

"I'm, I'm…I caused that… Did I…she's…?"

A sob punctuated some of her words; the trembling of her body was so intense that her teeth clacked like ice cubes in a glass. She had begun rubbing her arms in a poor attempt to calm herself, and she took as deep of breaths as possible.

"It okay, her baddddd. Mean! Better like now."

Rosa was pointing to Elise's corpse, a crooked, needle-toothed grin plastered across her asymmetrical features.

"I be better her?"

"What?"

"Rosa be new her? More nice."

"No, Rosa, you're you. You need to be yourself…"

"No help, friend. You good, nice, no get in trouble! Teaching a me?"

Courtney was floored by the offer. She hadn't had time to process what she had done, much less the consequences of her magic-infused outburst, but it looked like the Three Fates were smiling upon her.

"You'd do that for me? Why?"

"Rosa need home, pixie need friend."

The simple answer brought a fresh wave of tears to Courtney's eyes, and she threw her arms around Rosa in an awkwardly angled hug.

"Thank you."

***

"Give it up for Fractured Fairytale!"

The crowd roared; their fanatical screams and excited

sign-waving filling up the town's auditorium. The stage lights were sweltering, and Courtney felt beads of perspiration trickling between her wing folds. She glanced at the siren next to her, the other teen's webbed fingers plucking expertly at the guitar strings. She was completely unfazed, as though she had been born to perform on stage in front of thousands of people.

No one could tell that the siren had only learned how to speak a month ago, much less sing and play an instrument.

Her hair gleamed under the spotlights, the long, violet curls cascading down her back in a way that fooled even Elise's parents. If Courtney looked closely, the teen's eyes were just a little too bright to be cerulean, and her nails were just a bit too dull for a siren's. Everyone at school had been gossiping about how nice Elise had turned in the last few weeks, and how happy they were that her bullying had seemed to vanish overnight.

Their classmates praised Courtney for being such a good friend, since she had continually supported Elise while the siren regained proper speech after a bad concussion. The official story was that Elise had snuck into the woods to meet a boy and had tripped in the dark and smashed her head off a boulder. She was diagnosed with retrograde amnesia, but otherwise had a clean bill of

health and was cleared to still play in the show.

Courtney and Rosa had never been happier.

BLACK HARE PRESS

ALANNA ROBERTSON-WEBB is a writer and lover of dark fantasy, horror, and high fantasy. She has been featured in over fifty-five different collections, and even co-wrote a sci-fi novella. As of the time of this publication, Alanna has edited eleven different books, and she adores her side job as the chief editor of Eerie River Publishing. Her day job is a receptionist at a veterinarian clinic, which means she gets to spend her days around two of her favourite things: books, and adorable animals.

Bibliography
Afromyth Volume 2, Afrocentric Books, 2020
Angels, Black Hare Press, 2019
Castles and Kimonos, BWWP Publishing, 2020
Clockwork Dragons, Zombie Pirate Publishing, 2019
Daughters of Darkness, Black Widow Press, 2018
Death and Butterflies, Nocturnal Sirens Publishing, 2019
Infected, Blair Daniels, 2018
It Calls from the Forest (volumes 1 and 2), Eerie River Publishing, 2020
Sirens at Midnight, NBH Publishing, 2019
The Trees Have Eyes, Haunted House Publishing, 2018
What Monsters Do for Love, Soteira Press, 2019

Connect
Website: arwauthor.wixsite.com/arwauthor
Amazon:amazon.com/Alanna-Robertson-Webb/e/B07LFYJYS5
Twitter: @HorrorMythology
Facebook: @MythologyLovesHorror

WAITING FOR THE BEGINNING

by Steven Streeter

"Okay, what the fuck is wrong with you this time?"

Johnny X stared at Miriam Sunderland and simply scowled, although without real malice, then turned his attention back to the electronic tablet in his grip, scrolling through comments that were being written even as he watched.

Miriam decided to continue, however. "Look, over the past year, you've grown insufferable. You've been moody and distant. It's getting worse. And now…" Her voice trailed off.

"Now?" Johnny gazed at her with undisguised

contempt.

She shook her head and turned to walk away. "Press are waiting," she stated over her shoulder. "You said you'd talk to them tonight."

"Yep." He barely acknowledged her any longer as he returned his attention to the small screen.

She slammed the door, and he finally set the device aside. He wasn't stupid; he knew what his manager's unfinished "Now" statement meant. "Now" he'd performed three shows in a row that could, at best, be described as "crap." Unfortunately, they were the first three shows of his current world tour, and they had not gone down well with the public or critics alike. The online comments, even from the most ardent, zealous fans, were not what he was used to reading. Over twelve years of success was coming crashing down very suddenly.

Yes, more than twelve years. He'd once worked out that that would be his finite time, so he'd known the fall was coming. Now…was it here? "Insufferable," Miriam had said. But that was because he knew what was coming. Still, she'd been his manager for six years, since his first manager, her husband, had killed himself. Theirs was what could politely be called a professional relationship nowadays; the thought that the discovery of their external escapades had been what had driven Malcolm to commit suicide had driven a wedge between them personally.

He should have fired her years ago, but he couldn't be bothered. Almost thirteen years after he had achieved his gift, it had to go. That was what he had been expecting. He knew the nature of the beast. But he had been prepared. He'd squirrelled away a lot of money, so he could afford to simply disappear, and that would be that. Friends were not what he cared about. He'd had his fame, he would let it fade, and so now he would enjoy his fortune.

Were these shitty shows an indication the end was starting, or were they symptomatic of his fear of what was to come? He should have kept better records, because then he'd have an exact date for when it would all fail. But it had to be getting damned close.

The door opened and Miriam poked her head in. "Five minutes, your majesty," she stated coldly.

"Yep," he returned. She waited for something else that never came, then shook her head, and deliberately slammed the door behind her harder than before. He wanted to laugh at her, but it didn't come out. Was her issue just the fact he'd had a terrible tour thus far, and that his last album—*Take an E*—was not as well received as the previous seven, no matter how well it was selling? Or was his own attitude truly that awful? Or was it even that they hadn't slept together since Malcolm's death, and just lately he'd made no secret of sleeping with an endless parade of nameless faces? He did laugh now, though at himself; he decided it was most likely an unhealthy mix of all of that and maybe more.

He stood slowly, walked across to the door and locked it, then leant against it. He was not in the mood to face a hostile press. Crap shows, mediocre album, and standing them up twice so far would only add to their negativity. So being late—or maybe not turning up again—would hardly make things worse. Although it could well affect Miriam's standing. That would anger her even more; it was almost worth that to stay right here.

He went to the ice bucket and pulled out the bottle of Jamieson's Scotch Whiskey. He cracked the seal and slowly unscrewed it, inhaling deeply as he did so.

He almost gagged.

The odour that struck him briefly yet intensely was foul, assailing his nostrils until the scotch managed to dominate. He didn't bother to search for a glass, he simply downed a mouthful, enjoying the slight burn as it slipped down his throat. That was better. Maybe after he finished the bottle, he'd go and face the media after all—a bunch of bloggers, some TV people, a magazine or two, online reporters; some media!—and let the old cliché *in vino veritas* come to the fore.

That strange, putrid aroma though…

It was definitely an "off" smell, almost mouldy. Great, they'd given him a dressing room with a fungus problem. Maybe he shouldn't have referred to the place as a "toilet" on Twitter last week. Oh well, it was one night only. Who cared? Again, he tittered a little. A year ago, he would undoubtedly have got into a screaming match with Miriam or the auditorium manager. Now…he knew it simply did not matter.

But the memory that came with the odour was sudden and stark. Why should that hit him? No, that was a stupid question. He had already been thinking about it too much lately. From the time he had found that book in that musty, old shop near Cambridge, going to that hidden cemetery near that small village outside Albi in Southern France, and then…

Shit. That whole ridiculous ritual. At least, that was what he had thought at first. But he was desperate. He had wanted to be a singer, a front man, a heartthrob so bad since he was a child but could barely hold a tune and had zero charisma. And so, he'd resorted to arcane hokum. He had initially wanted to utilise Jim Morrison, but the *Père Lachaise Cimetière* was too well protected, too full of security, too popular, so that idea was quickly discarded. Then he discovered that a nineteenth-century opera singer,

Antoinette something, was buried in that out of the way town near Albi, in a tiny graveyard behind a small Catholic church that was shielded from all onlookers by trees and hedgerow fences. He'd since learnt a little about her—that she was said to be the most beautiful woman of her age, chased unsuccessfully by Toulouse-Lautrec amongst others, and that her voice was said to be able to stop birds in mid-flight. Oh, and she'd died at the age of twenty-seven in 1892, at the peak of her too-short career.

What better subject for his own future success could he have selected?

The tome was written in what he always considered "Ye Olde English," and it had taken him a while to get the full meaning of the words. It said that if he wanted to be a writer, then the hand of a writer must be taken and treated as per the instructions. He had extrapolated that and taken what he thought he should from the body he had chosen. A shovel, digging, black candles, a desecrating ritual, a sacrifice of the dead, a fire, a week of intense pain, and then he would have glory for six centuries of Sundays plus a further threescore and six. Then after that time, it would be all taken from him. He knew the deal.

Yes, he was perfectly willing to have what amounted to a short career. It was worth it just to have the career he had had. And then he would retire to the country with the memories and the money. He might even finally find a nice girl and settle down. A quiet life beckoned. Peaceful. Free from stress. He was going to have the best of all worlds.

He lifted his tablet and stared at the screen. The negative comments were accumulating, an avalanche of derision. His few defenders—clearly ardent, blind fans— were being rapidly drowned out in a sea of abuse.

The show had not been good, granted, but had it really been bad enough for one commentator to wish "it had been a lip-synch show like Britney Spears instead of what we got"? That was harsh. If Miriam had been here, he would have ranted at her about it, taking it all out on her. But without anyone here, what came out was a giggle, which turned into a self-deprecating laugh.

He could not take himself seriously. He knew what ridiculousness he'd done to get here. Was that why he resented those who were so earnest about his career? Everyone he knew—even his family—seemed to treat him like something beyond human, fawning over him, acting like he was stupid. Miriam was the worst, but her whole job did depend on him being a "superstar." Yet there were others. The members of X-taz-E, his backing band, were almost sycophantic, but he was fully aware they were planning on leaving him at the end of this tour to go at it alone. The media used to treat him well, but that relationship had been deteriorating for some time, and he knew he was to blame for that. To his face, everything he did was worshipped; behind his back, they treated him like shit.

The problem—if, in fact, it was a problem—was that he no longer cared. He knew the end was nigh, and he really did not give a fuck. When it all vanished, he would be ostracised by them all, shunned, ignored. Why should he care when they would not? Insufferable, Miriam had called him; setting himself up for a future life away from this unreality was how he saw it. No ties that would be broken when he lost the cash cow that was his voice; no emotional bonds with people he knew would just abandon him anyway. Over a decade in this industry had taught him that yesterdays mean nothing; it's all a case of "What have you done for me lately?"

He wasn't being a bastard; he was making the end easier for everyone.

He swallowed another mouthful of scotch and scrolled once more through the lengthening list of comments filling his Twitter feed. The positives had all but stopped. Now it was only abuse. He shook his head and dropped the tablet on a low table, then turned reluctantly, trying to decide whether to leave and face the press or…

The whole room came to a complete standstill.

She smiled at him, leaning against the door. Her face was perfectly structured, with a gently rounded chin, lips that were not too full but not too thin, a nose that was in perfect proportion, ever so slightly upturned at the end, and the most amazing blue eyes, the blue of a Jamaican sea or an Australian sky. A deep blue, full of life and vitality. She was wearing what appeared to be an elaborate evening gown and a lace bonnet, both pale green. "I hope you do not mind me," she said. Her voice held a strong European accent, one he could not easily place, yet it was still a sing-song sound.

"No, not at all," he replied with a grin. "I didn't hear you come in, uhh…"

"I am Mademoiselle LeCroix," she cooed, stepping forward, letting her headwear fall to the floor. Her black hair was cut to one length, trailing down her back, smooth and silky. It added to the perfection of her form. Somehow, this was turning into a positive evening after all.

He wanted to laugh at that thought, but her mere presence stopped him. It was such a childish cliché, but she really had taken his breath away.

She approached him slowly, languidly, her full buxom figure obvious even beneath the large dress. Johnny's eyes darted behind her; the door was locked. Excellent. She'd had the foresight to… Hang on. Hadn't he locked that same door behind Miriam? So how…? "Should I leave?" this woman whispered with mock disappointment as she stood before him, breaking into his thoughts.

"That depends on what you're here for," he replied casually. When it came to women, he had casual down to a fine art, and he knew it.

Her grin was lupine as she lifted the bottom of her skirts and settled onto his lap comfortably and confidently.

He ran his hand up her leg and started. She was wearing nothing underneath.

Johnny stared at her a little too long, then grabbed her roughly and crushed his mouth against hers. She responded in kind, forcing her tongue into his mouth like a darting viper. He slid his hands up her legs and down again as she worked his sweat-covered top over his head. He'd kept his body in reasonable shape, but he was always pumped after a two-hour show and his physique reflected that, which gave him even more confidence.

Their kissing resumed with a passion that Johnny had not felt in too long. Her hands ran over his body in simple yet effective patterns as he settled on squeezing her buttocks like he was kneading dough. Her fingers gradually slid down the front of his jeans. His physical response was instant and she took a firm hold of him and slowly pulled him back and forth. He let one of his hands drift around to her front where his fingers forced themselves inside her. Her other hand undid his pants in one fluid motion, giving her room to increase her fervour. He also lifted his tempo and their groans rose like an operatic duet into the air.

She stopped quite suddenly; he felt compelled to do the same. She smiled at him broadly. He returned it, feeling like a teenager on the verge of sexual awakening. She stroked his cheek and ran her fingers over his jawline. Finally, she stood and took him by the hand, leading him to a couch where a gentle shove forced him to sit heavily.

"So, just who are you?" he found himself asking.

"An old friend," she whispered seductively. "Very old."

He shook his head. "Are you sure?" he asked. "I'm sure I would have remembered someone like you." His smile was, he hoped, enticing.

"Oh, *oui*, but you do know me already," she sang, forcefully and slowly pushing him to his back. "You yourself came to me. We were very close." Her accent was as alluring as the melodious tone of her voice, bringing to mind the French countryside. "Surely you remember."

"I…where…where…oh God…" She removed his pants smoothly and sat astride him.

"You do not remember little me?" she cooed sweetly.

He shook his head. "I'm pretty sure I would have."

She looked momentarily thoughtful. "Mayhaps not," she murmured. "I did look a little, uhh, different when last we met."

"Oh?" He felt a strange sensation in the back of his head.

"*Oui*," she whispered. "So, now 'tis time I took back what you took from me."

He was suddenly confused. "Took from you? But I…"

"Twelve years and almost nine months ago," she interrupted. He fell silent. She grasped his cheeks with her hand. "You, Xavier Johnson, disrupted my eternal rest. You took my jaw to steal my talent and then burnt it. I demand something in return."

Johnny's eyes widened. "Aren't you supposed to take my talent away, leave me what I was?" he squeaked.

She looked at him as if he was a child. "That is hardly a fair deal," she giggled insanely.

"But, but, but I, I didn't…" Johnny stuttered. He understood sort of where this was heading, and terror was rapidly overwhelming him. "I, I, I thought…"

"You must accept this." Her voice became harsh and guttural, the accent more pronounced, and the hands on his cheeks strengthened their grip with a power that he could barely withstand.

"Please," he managed to say as tears welled in his eye.

"Please…"

"Oh, but *mon ami*," she breathed, once more virtually singing, "you know the truth. You have no choice."

"Take my voice," he hissed. "Just do it—take my voice."

"You have not understood," she sighed. "I shall indeed take your voice, but also what you have taken from poor Antoinette LeCroix, from me."

His eyes widened in a wild panic, and he tried to speak again, to beg, but her fingers tightened agonisingly, digging into his flesh like thin, blunt daggers. She stared into his eyes with cold fury. And then, without warning, she whipped her whole arm sideways. In a spray of blood that exploded like an erupting volcano, his entire jawbone was removed. His body spasmed and gasped, his eyes bulging out ludicrously. His arms flailed uselessly, his strength waning, his head swimming. He struggled to get any air into his liquid-filled lungs. No sound came out except a pathetic gurgle. Then his every muscle heaved and jerked by a jolt of electricity, and he fell still.

Antoinette dropped the lower half of Johnny's face onto the floor and stood slowly and carefully, the man's blood covering her clothing and face like fresh war paint.

She smoothed her gown and smirked at him. His eyes somehow followed her. "'Tis never as easy as you assume, *non*?" she whispered to his inert form. "The conditions have been met now. I do hope you had *joie de vivre* while it lasted." She gazed at the door. "And now I must leave you." His vision faded, his eyes clouding over, and the last thing to register in his mind was an image of absolute beauty.

"Johnny?" yelled Miriam's voice from outside, her anger unconcealed, and this was followed by furious pounding on the door.

No response came. There was no one to respond, just a jaw lying by a body, separated from everything, appearing as half a grin, holding half a voice, poised as if waiting, waiting for one more song, waiting for the end.

STEVEN STREETER writes predominantly horror, fantasy, science fiction, and humour, as well as too much poetry.

He has had over 70 short stories published in anthologies and magazines, as well as a number of novellas, all through a number of publishers, with more to come.

WHILE MY GUITAR GENTLY WEEPS

by Holley Cornetto

Tucked away on the back roads between Birmingham and Gadsden, Mudder's Hole had built a business catering to local alcoholics. It was a place to drink oneself to death, a Coors Light at a time—or fuel-grade whiskey, for those in a rush.

At first, Kelly thought it was a practical joke. She hadn't heard of the place before and couldn't imagine why Jason's contact would want to meet in this desolate shithole. But tonight, the place was packed. Peanut shells and brown wads of tobacco spit littered the floor. A purple miasma hung in the air, blanketing the room with the sharp stench of body odour and stale cigarettes.

Kelly waved at the bartender, but it would be a miracle if he could see her through the haze. She yelled at Jason as he elbowed his way through the crowd. "Damn, man. Your dude wasn't lyin'. This place is packed. Shit's for real."

Jason grinned. With his long dark hair to his shoulders, he brought to mind a young Gavin Rossdale. "Told ya. Guy's a fuckin' miracle worker. Like Helen Keller or some shit."

Kelly rolled her eyes. "Anne."

"Huh?" He tilted his head, brow furrowed. He wore that cocker spaniel expression often enough, and Kelly always found it endearing.

"Anne Sullivan, the teacher. She was the miracle worker, not… You know what? Never mind."

Taking notice of her, the bartender wandered over. He was the same guy in every crap bar in the USA. Muscle under a thick layer of fat, ex-military, rode a Harley if he could afford it.

"Can I get two Bud Lights?"

He nodded and pulled two bottles from under the bar.

"Tap?" Kelly asked.

He shrugged. "Tap's broke."

"Hey, is it always this crowded here?"

The bottles stuck to the caked-on grime coating the

bar. "Only when the Freedom Riders are playin'. Place fills up every time. People come from damn near ever'where." He nodded to a group of men across the bar. "Hell, I heard one of them fellas say he's from Chicago."

"Chicago? Man, that's a long ride. Can't they just listen to that shit on YouTube or somethin'?"

The bartender shook his head. "Nope. The Riders ain't never cut no record. Ain't never been played on the radio, and don't let nobody record them on their phones, neither."

Jason took a swig from his bottle. "How do people in Chicago hear about a band in bumfuck-nowhere Alabama?"

The bartender shrugged. "Word of mouth, I reckon."

"That's a big fuckin' mouth, man."

Kelly snorted. The carbonation from the beer tickled her nose.

"How'd ya'll hear about it?" the bartender asked.

Kelly placed her elbow on the bar and a gummy black wad of something she didn't care to identify stuck to her. "Do you know Jackson Tate?"

The barkeep frowned, glancing around the room. "Sure 'nough. I know Mister Tate."

"He invited us. See, we have a band, too. We're looking to do some business with him, maybe sign some contracts."

"Y'all be careful. Mister Tate ain't nobody to mess

around with."

Jason winked. "Don't worry about us, grandpa."

Kelly frowned at Jason, then turned back to the bartender. "What have you heard?"

Before the bartender could answer, the lights dimmed, and the raucous shouts of the drunken crowd died down. A spotlight flickered and drifted across the sea of heads, coming to rest on the stage announcer. "Ladies and gentleman, it's my pleasure to introduce the Freedom Riders!"

The crowd broke out in whoops and cheers and stomps.

Jason leaned in and bumped Kelly's shoulder. "Hear that? They could be cheerin' for us."

Kelly looked around, trying to see through the thick layer of smoke. The people here weren't the usual for this type of bar. Must be one hell of a band to draw such an eclectic crowd, she thought.

To her right was a smarmy looking man in a business suit out slumming it for the evening. He'd had a few too many and was already staggering around, a little too close. She shoved her elbow into his back. She wasn't about to let this fucker block her view.

Jason stepped from behind her and shouldered the guy. "Move it, jackass."

The man staggered away, joining a woman in a designer suit, who looked equally out of place.

"My hero."

Jason shrugged but looked pleased. He was humming with excitement. He loved discovering new music. Hell, the only job he ever held on to for more than a few months was the gig at the record store. Tonight was a big deal for him. His excitement was palpable.

The stage lights dimmed to crimson. She nudged Jason and nodded towards the stage.

There was an audible sigh from the stage, then the first few chords of the guitar permeated the room. Kelly froze, transfixed by the sound. It was blues and rock and soul. It was familiar and yet like nothing she'd ever heard before.

The singer sat on a stool, grey beard cascading down his chest. He wore a black cowboy hat and matching leather vest. He cradled the guitar in his arms with the tenderness of a father. The sound of his voice put a name to a pain she had never felt, but could imagine all too well. It was the sound of someone not knocking on Heaven's door, but trying to beat that fucker down. The desperate wail of someone who knew they couldn't get in.

She looked past him to the band. The drummer stared blankly forward, looking at something only he seemed to see. The keyboardist twitched his head so unnaturally to the melody that Kelly was surprised he kept tune. The only one onstage who looked even remotely aware of what he was doing was the singer. *Don't do drugs, kids.*

The crowd clapped and stomped as the melody changed, evolving into something new. It was country and gospel and bluegrass—all and none of them.

She jumped from the icy touch of a hand on her shoulder.

"Are you enjoying the show, young lady?"

The sharp-dressed man wore a silk suit and black tie. He was handsome, in an old-fashioned way. Around him hung a cloud of sweet cigar smoke, barely masking the stench of rotten eggs.

"You must be Tate?"

He nodded. "Pleased to meet you."

She tapped Jason's shoulder, but he stood, mesmerised, watching the band.

Tate cleared his throat. "Don't worry about him. He's enjoying the show. I'm here to speak with you."

She poked Jason hard in the shoulder. He didn't even flinch. "What the actual fuck, man?" She took hold of his shoulders and shook him. "Jason! Wake the fuck up!"

Tate shrugged. "It's the song that makes him that way, you see. The best song in the world." He winked at her. "That was what you wanted, right? An *epic fuckin' song*?"

He twisted his features into a snarl as he spat the words back at her.

"I might've said something like that, yeah." She motioned towards Jason frantically. "But that doesn't explain what's wrong with him. He's fuckin' catatonic. Do something!"

"Catatonic? Such a big word."

"I'm not stupid, asshole. I got a—"

"Fifteen hundred on your SATs?"

Kelly went cold as goose bumps kissed up her neck. He couldn't have known that. She'd only told her parents about her score, and the scholarship from the University of Alabama that she'd turned down. Of course, she'd applied to college *before* she met Jason. With his closet full of band t-shirts and greasy hair, she'd been drawn into his magnet tarpit trap—love at first sight. "How did—"

"I know about your test scores?"

"Stop butting in while I'm tryin' to talk, asshole."

He lifted his hands, palms towards her, and took a step back. "My apologies."

She rolled her eyes. "Okay, go ahead."

"To save time, assume I know everything about you. To save even more time, assume that if there is, in fact, something I don't know about you, I could find out without so much as lifting my little finger."

"Who are you really?" Kelly asked. She'd heard rumours about Jackson Tate and the weirdness that stuck to him like a shadow. She had never really believed the stories, but she could see what the song was doing to Jason. That was some fucked up shit.

"I'm the guy who is going to give you what you asked for." He nodded towards the band. "Do you hear that? That's the sound of a platinum album. The sound of sold-out venues and Pandora station seeds."

"It's rad, sure. But these guys ain't just gonna give us their song."

He winked at her. "They will. They just need the appropriate motivation."

"Don't wink at me. It's fuckin' creepy."

"See? There you go again, hiding behind vulgarity. These things should be handled with a sense of poise and rationality. I thought you were a smart girl, Kelly."

"Smart enough to know not to trust you. You give me the song, then what? What's in it for you? Are we talkin' a cut of the profits? You wanna be our manager or something?"

He threw back his head and laughed. As Kelly flinched from the sharp, cruel sound, the stage caught her eye.

The song had changed again. It was metal and rock and grunge, echoing back to her years of anger and the futility of her rage.

A minute passed before she realised Tate was still there, still smirking. "Don't be ridiculous," he said. "I couldn't care less about your money or fame, or whatever it is you teenage dirtbags want."

She felt her temper flare. "Then what?" she snapped before turning to Jason. He was slack-jawed with cataract eyes. *It's just the song, Kelly. Chill the fuck out.*

Tate shrugged. "The usual. Your soul."

"Haha," she said, crossing her arms over her chest. "But really, what do you want?"

He swept his hand in front of her, motioning around the crowded bar. "Do you see how these people don't notice us?" He snapped his fingers inches from Jason's face. "See? Nothing. Or, I can make it all stop, if you'd prefer?" He lifted his hand and everyone in the room, even the band, froze. The last note lingered like the chime of a church bell.

She took a few steps backwards. "How the hell did you…? What even is this?" She glanced around the room, part of her hoping it was all some joke everyone else was in on, but no one moved. The lingering note of the song died, leaving the room in a veil of silence. She looked back at Tate, swallowing a lump in her throat.

"It's getting late. Let's not talk falsely now, Kelly. You know exactly what I am. You knew when Jason set up the meeting. He was terrible at guitar until a few months ago. You didn't imagine he just got better, did you?"

"He took lessons. You arranged it."

He smirked. "He told you himself that he sold his soul."

"I thought he meant figuratively."

Tate crossed his arms over his chest. "Let me level with you, sweetheart. The Freedom Riders have turned out to be rather a disappointment, and I *hate* to be disappointed. This song deserves to be played in *stadiums*. It deserves more of an audience than…" He waved his hand at the room as if shaking off a bug. The song started back up in response. "This."

This ain't happening. It can't be happening. Shit like this *doesn't* happen. The devil didn't just come down to Alabama, no matter what Charlie Daniels fuckin' said. She realised with horror that Tate was right, Jason *had* told her that he'd sold his soul, and he wasn't happy with what he'd got in return. He hadn't remembered the little details, the fine print.

If Jason literally sold his soul, that made Tate what? A demon? The devil? Her hands trembled, and her heart felt like it would tear a hole in her chest. *I can't sell my fuckin' soul.* But Jason had, hadn't he? It wasn't like she was using her soul anyway, and at least she wouldn't be lonely in Hell with Jason there to keep her company.

She straightened her spine. "My soul is worth more than one song. Even if it is 'an epic fuckin song'. Let's deal."

The song played on, soaring and frantic now. Kelly could feel the blood pulsing through her veins. A bottle smashed into the wall, exploding into glittery green shards. Shouting became shoving, shoving became punching, and a brawl engulfed the room.

***

Kelly sat on a ratty couch in an improvised waiting room backstage. She wondered how many drunks had slept it off on that very couch, and if she was sitting in a dried-up lake of vomit. She shuddered at the thought.

"Dude, they never grant meetings. How'd you get 'em to agree?" Jason asked, inhaling deeply. The entire room reeked of bad weed.

"Tate set it up."

Jason coughed. "I told you not to talk to him alone." He offered her the joint.

She pushed his hand away and wrinkled her nose. "I'm a big girl, Jace. I can do what I want to do."

"Yeah, well, what you wanna fuckin' do is gonna get

us *all* in trouble. Speakin' of trouble, did you see that big fuckin' brawl? The bartender had one dude in a headlock."

She stood up, catching the scent of something sour. Something the funk of Jason's weed, and decades of stale cigarette smoke, couldn't cover.

Jason sat up, watching her. "Kel, are you nervous?"

"It's a big fuckin' deal, Jason. He could make us famous."

"Well, he's still a douchebag. And he's all tricky and shit. You gotta watch what you say 'cause he'll hocus pocus your words around. You gotta think. Gotta be smart about it."

She bit her lip to suppress a smile. She damn sure hadn't fallen for him because of his brain. He cared, but he didn't know the half of it.

The door cracked open, and the band members ambled into the room, followed by Tate.

"Now that we're all here, we can get to business," Tate announced.

For the most part, the band was a bunch of washouts. Kelly looked at Tate. "What the fuck are they on, man? They ain't just dancing with Mary Jane. That's some hardcore shit."

Tate shrugged. "I'm not responsible for their recreational activities."

"How are they gonna teach us the song when they can't see two feet in front of their faces?"

"Teach them the song?" The one she recognised as the lead singer turned to Tate. "What's she talkin' about?"

Tate sighed, running a hand through his slicked back hair. "I've decided to release you from your contract." He smiled like a predator, flashing his teeth like a shark in a fuckin' suit. "But first, you will teach these two the song. Once you've passed the song to them, your work is done. You will be free from further obligation."

The singer cleared his throat. "Okay, Tate. Okay." He turned his attention to Kelly. "I'm Lester." He motioned to the drummer. "This is DuBob. Seth here plays guitar, and that's Boogie on the keyboard."

Kelly nodded to them. "I'm Kelly. This is Jason. He plays lead guitar. I do vocals and bass."

"You got a drummer?" Lester asked.

She nodded. "Back home."

"Where's home?"

"Birmingham."

He expelled a stream of brown spit that narrowly missed Tate's shoe.

"Why are you willing to just give over the song? You saw how packed that bar was. Don't you want to be famous?"

Lester smirked and shook his head. "I'm old enough that my wants won't hurt me. An' you oughta be careful what you wish for, youn'un."

She cast a meaningful glance at Jason. "No kidding."

Tate stepped forward. "Loathe as I am to break up this happy meeting, I think we all have places to be. At least, *I* have places to be. We'll start work next week." He turned his icy gaze on Kelly. "What do you call yourselves?"

Jason broke in. "Megapocolypse!"

Tate raised a finger to his lips. "Be quiet, son. The adults are speaking."

Kelly's face flushed with anger. "Don't talk to him like that, it's his fuckin' band."

"Nevertheless, that name won't do." Tate pursed his lips. "Per our arrangement, you're the star. He's the accompaniment. How about…Black Betty?" He reached out and caressed a strand of her jet hair. Kelly flinched. She hadn't realised how close he'd been standing.

Jason's jaw dropped, and Kelly held a hand up to silence his protest.

"Fine."

***

Kelly spent the following weeks organising rehearsals,

tuning instruments, and scrounging up enough money to repair or replace broken equipment. True to his word, Tate attended every single rehearsal. She wondered if he was actually invested in their success, or if he simply wanted to make sure Lester and the others kept up their end of the bargain.

Lester turned out to be a pretty cool old fucker. He'd lived a lot of life, and he knew more shit about music than she'd thought possible. He loved it, and it showed. Sometimes, she tried asking about the song again, but he'd grow quiet or change the subject.

The other band members were less talkative, content to let Lester be their spokesman—in fact, she couldn't be sure DuBob spoke at all. The drummer spent all his time high, staring into space like a fuckin' rocket man or some shit.

Kelly nodded towards DuBob. "Is he ever not stoned out of his gourd?" she asked Lester.

Lester shrugged. "It gets to you, after a while. You play the song at a few shows, then a few more, and a few more. You get stuck in a loop."

"Why don't you play other stuff? Even covers? You must know a shit-ton of songs."

Lester's expression grew dark.

"My dudes!" Jason sprang up from his chair, his can

of Coors splashing out onto the rug. "Kelly's right. We've been playin' this song for weeks. Why don't we have a jam session?" He sat the beer can on top of the amp and picked up his guitar. He struck the first chord, and his face twisted in confusion.

Jason looked at his guitar as if it had betrayed him. He strummed again, the same chord, and pushed the instrument away in disgust.

'Kelly smirked. "I thought you wanted to play somethin' else."

"I did." He stared at the guitar, his face a mask of confusion.

"It's okay, Jace. You're tired. We've been at this for hours. It's probably just muscle memory or some shit."

"Some shit is right." He looked at Tate. "I know I was playin' *Sweet fuckin' Emotion*. What the hell?"

Tate shrugged. "I can't have you playing inferior music. From now on, you play my song. It's the only song you need."

"Bullshit!" Jason wheeled on Lester and shook his fist, as if ready to strike him. "Did you know? You fuckin' knew, didn't you?" The words came out as a half sob.

Lester winced and glanced at Tate, but it was DuBob who answered. "Yeah, we fuckin' knew. But we're sick as shit of playin' the same goddamn song all the time. And now, it ain't our problem no more."

Kelly turned on Tate. "What the fuck is this, man?" She felt a burning sensation below her ear and grabbed her neck. "Ow. What the…" The pain intensified, like flesh being scratched by tiny needles.

Tate crossed the room and pushed her hair back. She slapped away his hand. Ignoring it, he smiled. "It's done."

"What's done? What did you do to me?"

Tate drew from his pocket a small, silver-cased mirror. He flipped it open and handed it to her. When she glimpsed her reflection, the devil's mark glared red and angry across the milk white skin of her neck.

"What the fuck?" she asked. "Is that a tattoo?"

Tate shrugged. "A reminder."

Lester made a choking sound and grabbed his own neck. "Let me see that mirror!"

Tate tossed the mirror to Lester.

Lester inspected his reflection. "Hot damn!" He jumped out of his chair. "Boys, we've done it!"

"Not so fast," Tate interrupted.

Lester's eyes narrowed. "You said if we passed the song on, we'd be free."

Tate nodded. "And so, you are." He snapped his fingers, and as one, Lester, DuBob, Seth, and Boogie hit the floor writhing.

Kelly knelt beside Lester. "Oh, God! What's wrong with him? What did you do?"

"What I promised. I freed them from their obligation. Debt paid, bargain over, so on and so forth." He waved a dismissive hand.

Lester twitched. White foam spewed from his mouth.

"No," Kelly gasped. She grabbed a sweatshirt and stuffed it under the man's head to prop him up. It didn't help.

Lester was dying, really dying—the whole band was—while that asshole, Tate, just watched and smiled. "Jason, don't stand there like an idiot. Call 911! They must have OD'd on something!"

Tate chuckled and shook his head. "It isn't an OD. It's just designed to look like one. There's nothing you can do."

Kelly's chest heaved as she breathed in sobs.

Tate knelt beside her. "It was never about them, nor is it about you. It's about the song."

Jason backed himself into the corner and stood staring in disbelief. "This is a bad fuckin' dream, man. Wake up, wake up, wake up…"

"But…why kill them?" Kelly asked.

"They tried to cheat me. They didn't play the song anywhere except a crap-hole bar in the middle of nowhere. It needs bigger venues, real crowds. Stadium crowds. It deserves to be *heard*." He scowled at Lester's body. "And that's where you rock stars come in. We're going to get your picture on the cover of the *Rolling Stone*."

"Asshole. If it's such a big deal, why not just play it yourself?"

He shrugged. "I can't. Music never was my talent. Besides, it isn't your place to question me."

Jason stepped forward. "We can record it. Then you have your song, and you can spread it. Radio, YouTube, Spotify, whatever. Then we can play other stuff." Kelly had never seen him look so desperate. "Please? I can't play just one song for the rest of my life."

Tate shook his head. "Maybe *heard* isn't the right word. The song needs to be *experienced*. You will play this song, and only this song. You will play it live. That is your end of the bargain."

"But, won't people notice if we only ever play one song?"

Tate smiled, flashing his shiny white shark teeth. "Sweetheart, they won't care."

***

Black Betty cycled through four drummers in as many months. For whatever reason, the first three couldn't get their heads around the song, couldn't play it the way it *ought* to be played. But Laine, she *got* it. She wasn't the best drummer, at least technically, but the song clicked for her like she was born to play it.

Laine was a wild one, with a bleached-blonde mohawk and leather wrist straps. She beat the drums as if the sound took up space, and she wanted to fill the world with it. With Laine filling out the line-up, the band started gigging local venues that they sold out with ease.

Every time they played a show, Kelly looked out to the sea of faces in the crowd, and they were all as they had been the night the Freedom Riders played in Mudder's Hole. Eyes glazed over, no idea what was going on. When the song ended, they went back to normal, as if nothing had happened. She wasn't sure what it meant.

Since the deal with Tate, Jason drifted further from her every day, fading to black, to the ghost of a shadow. Unable to play anything but the song, he lost his joy, his love for music. It was part of what had made her love him in the first place.

Jason staggered into the next show, tripping hard. Kelly sat him in a suede chair in the corner. "You've gotta knock this shit off before you kill yourself. You're like the second coming of Scott Weiland."

He smirked. "It ain't my fault if the drugs like me,

man."

"You can't go onstage like this."

"You put a guitar in my hand, and I can play that shit in my sleep." His eyes were vacant, mind gone on some magic carpet ride while his body went through the motions.

She frowned. He was right. He could play it in his sleep. They all could.

"Here," Laine said. "Drink." She pressed a Styrofoam cup of dirt-black coffee into his hand. As he sipped it, she turned to Kelly. "You know Tate ain't gonna like this."

"You called?"

Kelly jumped as Tate seemed to materialise out of thin air. "Where did you come from?"

He looked past her, at Jason, ignoring the question. "What's he on?"

"I'm not sure," she admitted.

Tate threw his hands up. "You get him under control or I'll replace him. I need you at your best. I had enough of this crap with the Freedom Riders."

"You did this to him, Tate. Music was the one thing he loved, and you took it. You saw what it did to the others, I mean, how did you think it was going to go?"

Jason retched, covering his shoes with coffee vomit. When he straightened, Kelly put an arm under him, helping him from the chair.

"I'm going to get him cleaned up. We'll cancel the show."

Laine scowled. "Like Hell we will."

"He can't go out there like this. He's gonna black out on stage."

"I don't care. It's his dumb ass that took shit before the show. I need to go out there, you get it? I need to play the fucking song."

Kelly looked at Laine's hands and realised they were shaking. "Laine?"

"What?"

"Are you okay?" Kelly nodded towards her trembling hands.

"I'll be fine. I'm always like this before a show. It goes away after we play."

Kelly shook her head. "It's bad enough that Jason is cooked out of his mind. You can't keep shit from me, too. Tell me what the fuck it is. A medical condition? Drugs? Stage fright?"

"No," Laine sighed. "No, not like that. It's like…if I go too long without playing the song, I start to feel like…like I'm going to burst or something."

"How often does this happen?" She kept a wary eye on Tate as she spoke.

"Every time."

"That's it." She adjusted Jason's weight on her shoulder. "This is too fucked up. We ain't playin'. We're packin' up. From now on, we go our own way."

Tate disapproved, "Tsk, tsk, tsk. So ungrateful. I've given all three of you everything you asked for."

Kelly turned to Laine, shifting Jason's weight again. "You've got to be fucking kidding me. You, too?"

Laine glared at Tate.

"No, don't fucking look at him. You talk to me. What did you ask for?"

Laine sighed, "Money… I didn't give a fuck about the song. You want to know what I *do* give a fuck about? A new car, a big house, closets full of outfits I'll only ever wear once."

Tate flashed his sinister grin. "You see, I own all three of you. And if I say you play, then you *will* play."

"No," Kelly said, almost to herself. "No. This song is killin' us. We ain't gonna fuckin' play." She half-dragged, half-carried Jason out of the room, with Laine trailing behind her.

***

It had been eight and a half weeks since they'd last played the song, at least in public. Every once in a while,

Laine would pick up her drumsticks and pound away to fight off the shakes. Each time, Kelly noticed, the fits returned sooner than the last.

Jason sat on the faded burgundy sofa, hugging his guitar to his chest. He talked to it constantly, asking it questions like a magic eight ball. Like some holy diver, he'd started wearing a crucifix, and even took up praying. Sometimes to God, sometimes to Dio.

The tattoo on Kelly's neck burned and itched like an angry rash, no matter how many creams or ointments she tried.

"K…Kelly?"

Kelly jumped. "What?" she snapped, too on edge to be polite. Her nerves were as raw as her tattoo.

Behind her, Laine stood twitching, drumsticks in hand. "You…uh, you're do…do…doing it again, man." She nodded towards Kelly's arm.

"Shit!" Kelly dropped the safety pin she hadn't even noticed she'd been holding. Words covered her arms in angry red scratches. Lyrics. Unable to sing the song, she'd carved it into her flesh.

"M…Maybe…you know, maybe we should play it a…again."

Kelly sighed and reached for her guitar. It wouldn't help, and she knew it wouldn't help, but it was all she could do. "Okay, sure."

"No, I mean like, y…y…you know, a concert."

She glanced at Jason, who was frantically shaking his guitar and shouting, "Play the best song in the world, or I'll eat your soul!"

Kelly rubbed her swollen arm and turned back to Laine. "Hear me out, okay? This song, there's somethin' fucked up about it. About the fact that it's all we can play, about the fact that Tate said he needed us to play it, but didn't say why. Playin' it was drivin' us crazy."

Laine twitched. "*Not* playing it is making us c…c…crazy. Hell, just look at Ja…Jason."

He had gathered the guitar back into his arms. "I look at you all," he cooed, "see the love there that's sleeping."

They had lost, and she knew it. "We need Tate."

***

Kelly sat in the lounge, waiting for the interview to begin. She tugged her sleeves down to cover the scabs of lyrics scratched into her skin, into the very fabric of her being. She couldn't exist without the song. The evidence was carved up and down her arms.

Tate had been gleeful when she called to admit defeat. After their first gig back, Laine's stutter vanished, and

Jason stopped talking to his guitar. Kelly's tattoo had stopped burning. She wanted their return to feel like a victory, but it was hollow. They'd simply exchanged one prison for another.

The reporter, a woman in her late twenties, turned to Kelly. "I'm Lizzie McDonald, from IROC radio, with an exclusive from Black Betty, who just played live to a sold-out crowd at the Colosseum. I'm here with band members Kelly Palmer, Laine Stiles, and Jason Hopper." She smiled at Kelly. "That was an amazing show."

"Thanks, Lizzie."

"Why don't you tell us about your set? It was amazing."

Kelly smiled nervously. "Well, the song, you know, has been very well received since we started playing it. I think we owe a lot of our success to that."

"And which song is that?" Lizzie asked, tilting her head.

Kelly furrowed her brow. "Uhm, that is, the song we just performed."

Lizzie looked at Kelly with a vacant expression. "That was an amazing show. Why don't you tell us about your set?"

Kelly froze. It was as if the woman had reset. She'd repeated the exact same questions and didn't seem to realise it.

"I'm sorry?" Kelly asked.

"That was an amazing show. Why don't you tell us about your set? It was amazing," she repeated.

Tate stepped forward. "Lizzie. May I call you Lizzie?"

The woman nodded.

"These guys are exhausted. It's been quite a night for them, as you can imagine. We just wanted to announce the new tour dates."

Kelly looked at Laine, who shrugged.

Tate spoke briefly to the woman, who seemed unable to ask any questions other than the same one she'd already repeated. She had a glazed-over expression and nodded stupidly at Tate. Satisfied, the radio crew packed up their equipment and left.

It was Laine who finally broke the silence. "Was that fuckin' weird, or what?"

"It was like she didn't even remember the song," Jason said.

Kelly looked at Tate. "Did you do somethin' to that woman to make her forget?"

"Me?" Tate asked, feigning ignorance. "Oh, *I* didn't do a thing to her."

***

Kelly sat on an amp beside Laine, surrounded by a swarm of scurrying roadies.

She rubbed her arm absently. "Did you notice the review in the *New York Times* didn't mention the name of the song, or lyrics, or anything? They just talked about how great it was. No details, though."

Laine shrugged. "Maybe they aren't musicians? You said you tried to teach it to other drummers before me, but they had trouble with it?"

"There was a mass stabbing at a QuickChek in Newark, the same night we played there."

"Yeah, but that's *Newark*…"

"What about the nursing home fire, a few blocks from our gig in Phoenix? They're calling it arson. Or the mall shooting in St Louis?"

Laine shrugged. "Coincidence, I guess. I mean, the world is full of bad shit. What's it got to do with us?"

Kelly watched Jason chat up one of the roadies. He put on a good front for other people, but when it was just the three of them, the facade dropped. He was withdrawn, depressed. Still, it was better than batshit crazy.

"Maybe," Kelly said.

"But, between that, and people not remembering the song…I don't know, shit seems fucked up."

Laine slid off the amp.

"Let's see, then." She waved over one of the roadies. "How long have you been with us? How many shows?"

He shrugged and rubbed his stubbled chin. "Six or eight, I guess."

Curious, Kelly hopped down and joined them. "You've heard us perform?"

The man nodded. "Of course."

She nodded. "Okay, how about you sing us a few lines of our song? Any part you like."

He shifted uncomfortably. "I've been having trouble remembering things lately. I took a hard hit to the back of the head at one of the shows. The road crew got into a brawl."

"After they heard us play?" Laine asked.

He nodded.

"It's alright. Thanks for tryin' anyway."

He walked away, muttering under his breath.

Kelly turned to Laine. "Told you shit was fucked up."

***

For the next few weeks, Kelly and Laine fought nonstop.

"Laine, somethin' is wrong. The song is makin' people do fucked up things. Every fuckin' time we play somewhere, the place goes fuckin' nuts. People get killed; shit gets destroyed. *We're* making people do this."

"The fuck do you care? What, did you suddenly realise the world wasn't some brotherhood of man? We all ain't gonna hold hands and sing Kum-ba-fuckin'-ya? What have any of those fuckers ever done for you?"

Jason was listening to the two argue. "Bad things happen all the time. We didn't do shit, man."

Kelly sighed and picked up the *Daily Record*, waving it at them. "This is more than the usual bad shit. I mean, we're talking mass fuckin' murder."

Laine crossed the room and spread out over the couch. "I don't care, okay? I don't care what people do. That shit ain't on me, Kel. It ain't on you, either. Just take the fuckin' money and run."

"It's a song," Jason said. "I mean, what are you even trying to say? A song can't hurt people."

Kelly ran a hand through her hair. "It ain't just a song. It's Tate's fuckin' song. If we don't try and stop this shit… then we might as well be the ones doin' it."

"No." Jason frowned. "You're imagining things."

Kelly slung the newspaper onto the floor. "We can't just pretend this isn't happening!"

Laine threw her hands up. "Well, what do you suggest, Kel? We tried to stop playing, remember? We can't. The sooner you accept that and move on, the better off we'll all be. We're fuckin' out of here. C'mon, Jace." Laine left, with Jason trailing behind.

Kelly kicked the newspaper. "Goddammit!"

After the show, Tate showed up backstage, arms extended. "Do you hear them sing? Bloodthirsty again." He flashed his shark-tooth grin.

The tattoo on Kelly's neck burned.

***

Madison Square Garden was sold out. There wasn't an empty seat in the house; all those people had come to see Black Betty.

Kelly smiled. The attention was flattering, but she knew from experience the havoc the show would wreak on New York City. All according to Tate's plan.

Jason took the stage first. His ripped jeans and white t-shirt looked exactly like the thrift store clothes he used to wear, even though they cost ten times as much. He looked empty, like a shell waving to the crowd. He didn't talk to the guitar anymore, but he didn't talk to her anymore either. There was no point, she knew. His pain was beyond words, something he could only channel through his guitar, making it gently weep with every chord he played.

Now more than ever, she wished for the old days. Before she'd made the bargain with Tate. Before they'd learned the song.

Laine crossed the stage, waving her drumsticks to the fans. Watching her, Kelly felt a pang of regret. She wished they were on better terms. Laine had made her deal for money, but it hadn't been for her. Laine's mom was dying of cancer. Not that Laine told her that. She never asked for help, not with anything. She'd stopped playing the first time Kelly asked, but after that, she refused. After it drove them all crazy. "It's us or them," Laine had told her, "and I know which side I'm on."

Kelly felt herself tremble. If Nirvana had taught her anything, it was where bad folks went when they died. She had no illusions about what she had to do, or about what the cost would be.

Kelly crossed the stage to the deafening cheers of the crowd. Ten steps. Twenty. She squinted against the brightness of the lights. They'd once seemed warm and welcoming, but now they glared down on her accusingly. The song had cast a spell on them. It drove people mad—the band if they didn't play it, everyone else if they did.

Kelly took her cue and reached in her pocket.

The cold steel felt good in her hand. For the first time in a long time, she was exhilarated to be on stage. No one noticed as she drew the gun and levelled it at Laine.

The boom was louder than Kelly had imagined. The muzzle flashed, and Laine dropped to the floor with a muffled groan, a dark pool growing beneath her, staining her bleached-blonde hair.

Kelly turned to Jason and whispered, "I'm sorry." She was surprised at how easy it was, only the smallest amount of pressure against the trigger was required to end a life. Security rushed the stage. The lights blurred.

"One last time," she muttered under her breath as she turned the weapon on herself.

***

Security cleared the building while the NYPD took witness statements from the crowd.

Samuel Jones left Madison Square Garden that evening with a song in his head and a burning, scratching sensation on his neck. He climbed into his car and fastened his seatbelt. He adjusted the rear-view mirror and noticed a mark just below his ear. Funny, he thought, it kind of looked like a tattoo.

BLACK HARE PRESS

HOLLEY CORNETTO is a writer of horror, dark fantasy, and weird fiction.

Holley was born and raised in Alabama, but now lives in New Jersey. She enjoys creating stories set in the American South, with characters that remind her of her youth. To indulge her love of books and stories, she became a librarian. She is also a writer, because the only thing better than being surrounded by stories is to create them herself. She has stories forthcoming in Daily Science Fiction, Sonorous Silence (Pavor Press), Scare Me (Esskaye Books), and The Half That You See: Nightmares, Deliriums, and Illusions (AM Ink Press).

Bibliography
A-Z Of Horror: B Is For Beasts, Red Cape Publishing, 2020
Harvest, Blood Song Books, 2020
It Calls from The Forest, Eerie River Publishing, 2020

Connect
Twitter: @HLCornetto

ANGIE BABY

by Kimberly Rei

The small bar was packed. It always was when Angel Yuki-Onna played. The push for her to play larger venues was relentless. Every interview, every fan meeting, every email asked the same question: "When are you going to go break out? When are you going to go big?"

The answer was always the same—a quiet, enigmatic smile that gave no answer at all. When pressured, she would offer a demurral. She could never fill a larger venue, her music wouldn't carry well, she enjoyed the intimacy of dark spaces.

Everyone knew it was a lie, but few called her on it. Instead, she was painted as an eccentric artist and the waitlist for her shows grew. She worked two, sometimes three, shows a night, six nights a week. Her dedication to her craft bordered on obsessive. She became the subject of every weekend celebrity update show, every news show psychologist's analysis.

The further they dug, the more reclusive Angel became.

***

I was twelve when Oliver disappeared.

The nine years between us had never really mattered. I worshipped my older brother, and he was delighted to have a sister so devoted.

When I turned ten, I was devastated. Oliver was away at college and double-digit years seemed such big deal to me. Mom threw a party, and I had made up my mind to enjoy it, no matter what. While I was making the rounds, greeting my friends and pretending to be overwhelmed by it all, a droll voice drifted from Dad's chair in the corner.

"No hugs for your brother? I'm crushed."

Mom's laughter was a distant sound as the world became a tunnel, and all I could see was Oliver. I hurled myself at him, giggling and crying all at once. He missed two days of classes and an important soccer game. For me.

Two years later, on that same day, Oliver went missing. It would be another four days before my parents were called, but I knew something was wrong when I went to bed that night. If he wasn't there for it, Oliver always called me on my birthday, an hour past my bedtime. He wanted his wish for me to be the last thing I heard before sleeping.

He didn't call that night. Or the next. Or the next. My parents were impatient with my fretting. "He's in college, Jenny. He's got responsibilities."

I remember howling something about my name being Pixie and flouncing off to my room. The next day, my parents called the cops and filed a report. Posters went up, rewards were set, final steps were retraced. The river near his university was dredged for his body.

***

"Where to next, Ang?" The woman, idly tuning a koto, brushed hair out of her face and leaned over the instrument. Her voice barely carried to her bandmate, currently muttering as she dug through a closet.

"How the fuck does Musume find anything in here? Ya know, when she said not to worry about finding an apartment, that we could stay with her, I bloody well thought she had the room for us!"

Onago laughed. "How long have you known us? Musu's heart is bigger than her…"

Angel cut her off, "Closet? Or brain? Aha!"

She victoriously pulled out a long velvet skirt, oxblood red with a slit nearly to the hip. "Found it! Uhm. Toledo, I think."

Onago stared for a long moment, koto forgotten. "I'm sorry, did you say Toledo?"

Angel moved to stand in front of a full-length mirror, holding the skirt up. "Mmmm. We haven't been there in a while. It'll be good for us."

"Toledo. Ohio."

"Hai."

***

By the time they gave up the search, Pixie was the only name I would respond to. Jenny was buried. I locked her in a box and vowed that only Oliver would touch the key. Blonde hair became lavender or pink or a combination. I was the sparkliest goth in my school and the most gossiped about. No one dared say anything to my face. If I didn't launch into a damaging rage, I ignored them entirely. Without Oliver, without knowing where he was or even if he was, I didn't care what people said. I hid behind my masks and spent every ounce of free time searching for him.

My parents weren't wealthy. We never needed for

anything vital, but there wasn't a lot of room for extras. As the years passed, they stopped hiring private investigators and started attempting family vacations. No one actually moved on, but they couldn't live in constant worry and fear forever.

To keep my parents happy, I went to college. They thought I'd got over Oliver. Without him, they'd poured everything into me, and while there was no pressure to be a doctor or a lawyer, there was an expectation that I would hold my life as precious and do *something* with it.

Music had kept me sane, so I went to school for business management with a hard lean on the entertainment industry. The parents were happy, and it turned out I had a knack for management.

That's when I met Musume.

***

The youngest member, by about three minutes according to the twins' birth certificates, of Yuwaku rifled through the thrift shop racks with a growing sense of dread. To be sure, Musume, her sister, and their talented lead angel could afford to shop in any store their hearts desired. Designers would trip over each other and likely draw blood for the chance to dress the trio. But Musu had a reputation.

She had a style one couldn't simply slip into, and haute couture killed her creativity. And her hunger. She craved new outfits like other women craved chocolate. Today, the buffet was terrible.

She was about to give up on the entire adventure and head to the mall—to pick pockets, not shop—it was good to keep skills honed. Waves of lavender hair caught her eye and strummed a chord deep in her chest. Slinking into a deceitfully lazy stroll, she made her way towards the owner. Her hands trailed across hanging dresses and out of season sweaters. Casual. Calm.

Predatory.

The lavender-tressed woman was flipping through a meagre offering of jackets. There was only one good item on the entire rack. Musu knew. She had seen it. A true Papineau was almost impossible to come by. Musu leaned against an end cap and waited. The slender hand reached out and stroked the butter-soft leather. One finger, the nail a shimmering indigo, trailed across the tiny logo embroidered into the shoulder. Too many knockoffs forgot the butterfly. This beauty was authentic. The woman lifted the price tag and shuddered as she dropped it and physically stepped back. Someone at the thrift shop knew what they had, and they weren't about to let it go for too much of a bargain.

"You should treat yourself. It would look stunning on

you."

The woman looked up, startled. Musu trapped a gasp in her throat before it could reach the air. She'd expected blue eyes. Or maybe green. Something to clash with that hair and make a statement. Instead, she found herself tumbling into a darkness too deep to crawl out of. One could get lost in those eyes. She dropped her own lashes and laughed, low and sensual.

"I'm sorry. It's none of my business. But I hate the thought of that jacket on some idiot teenager."

The voice matched the eyes. Cold, with a promise of warmth if one were found deserving. "Then why don't you get it?"

Musu shrugged one shoulder. "I have three."

Dark eyes turned to saucers as a riot of thoughts ricocheted. "Oh, holy shit, I thought you looked familiar. You're Musume!"

Laughter as Musu stepped forward and held out a hand. More than anything, she wanted to touch this woman. A shock raced up her arm, through her chest, and downward. She covered it with an exaggerated, courtly bow. "'Tis a pleasure, m'lady. And you are…?"

Cool fingers wrapped around hers, and her knees threatened to buckle.

"Pixie."

"Pixie! I love it. Come on, Yosei, you've gotta meet my friends." Musu tightened her grip on the handshake and snapped the jacket off the hanger, dragging both to the register.

***

Turned out Yosei is Japanese for fairy. In the space of about two minutes, Musume had decided she was keeping me. There was a terrifying ride in her tiny little expensive-something-exotic car, a sweep into the most unexpectedly small apartment, and introductions to Onago and Angel herself.

I owned every album Yuwaku released. I'd seen the few shows they allowed to be recorded. Seen them more than once. Never in all that time had I realised Musume and Onago were twins. You had to look past the surface to find it. One was classic, with long waves of ebon silk and delicate hands that could stroke a koto to a most exquisite life. The other was a mash of old school punk and future cyberpunk. One side of her hair fell in an asymmetrical cut to her shoulder, the other side halted just above half a dozen ear piercings. What she could do with a guitar was unfathomable. Coupling the two of them with Angel's voice was quite simply unfair.

And there I was, standing in the middle of a living room decorated in Modern Closet, every surface covered in a splash of cloth. Angel looked around and snorted.

"That's it. First, dinner. Then I'm setting fire to this place. Pixie, that jacket is fantastic! A Papineau, isn't it? Good taste!"

It was over tacos at a trashy little place off Sherman Street that my life entirely changed entirely. We talked about childhoods. The more Musu and Ona talked, the more alike they seemed. And less. They had a language all their own that Angel could clearly understand, but not speak. When I looked too confused, she would explain a phrase. I told them about Oliver, which was odd because I never discussed him. Not to anyone at college, not to any co-workers at the barely sustainable record shop I worked at part time. Nowhere. To no one. Oliver was mine.

But as we sipped Mexican beer and nibbled chips long after we all declared we couldn't swallow another bite, I told them what happened. How much I missed him, still. How every new experience was bittersweet because I couldn't share it with him.

They expressed deep sympathy, though none had ever suffered such a loss. Ona wiped tears until Musu shoved a handful of napkins into her hand and pretended she was unaffected.

Angel's smooth voice cut through the tragedy, "What are you in school for?"

I took another sip of my beer and muttered something about business management. As all three cringed, I was quick to clarify, "I want to be a music manager!"

They stopped nibbling and stared.

"Ona. Musu."

"Yes."

"Hai, exactly."

Angel looked at me over the rim of her beer bottle. "So, Yosei. Want a job?"

None of them would ever again call me by my name. I was Yosei. I was theirs.

***

Toledo was a mess. Oh, no one at any of the shows could see it, but the girls knew. They were starting to snap at each other. Onago was going for long walks at night, often not coming back to the hotel until the sun was up, and Angel's temper was starting to fray. When Musu knocked over Ona's cup of cheap coffee, Angel had to physically step between them.

"Get your shit together. We've got five more shows here and then you can relax. Understand? We do these towns so we can do the others. Now get the fuck out, both of you. I'm taking a nap."

The tension lingered for half a heartbeat. Neither dared push her any further. The twins waited until they were out of the room, in the elevator, out of the elevator, and down the hall before hissing at each other. Angel had remarkable hearing.

They parted ways, returning in time for that night's performance.

The next few days saw no more than two of them in the executive suite at one time. When Ona tried to lighten the mood by suggesting the suite was larger than Musume's entire apartment, Musu threw her sister's suitcase out of the twenty-sixth-floor window. The fact that the windows couldn't be opened that high up didn't bother Musu at all. The fact that the window wasn't broken didn't surprise any of them.

The man on his cell phone who nearly got plastered by a suitcase was most surprised.

***

They didn't wait for me to graduate before putting me to work. But as an apology, they did offer to play a show at a graduation party. It was the largest venue in their history and they didn't linger. I would have been the hero of the night saving two events.

The first was known immediately and stole the evening. Frat boys, drunk and high on finally being let loose on the world, crashed a brand new Lambo into the University President's house. It wouldn't have been such a big deal if Frat Boy #1 hadn't spilled his 40 and Frat Boy #2 hadn't dropped his joint. Like love at first sight, the flames took over. Wispy, useless curtains hung in tatters across the backseat of the car. They caught. The more serious curtains caught. The ceiling caught. It all caught fire. Years later, the amount of money Frat Fathers had to "donate" to the University to protect their boys would stagger the minds. But that night, there were no tell-all books. Just flames and gossip.

The second event took a little longer to surface. Quiet inquiries became silent investigations became the evening news. Alan Waters, valedictorian and the guy on campus who managed to get along with everyone, had disappeared. He was at the graduation, but it got fuzzy after that. He'd been at the concert. No, he was drinking with the frat boys and ran off after the accident. No, everyone gossiping was stupid. He was off on a world tour on his father's yacht.

The investigation turned up nothing. Not a single clue. Because Yuwaku didn't allow recording, there were no videos to examine. The frat boys hadn't seen Alan in weeks, and the yacht was in dry dock.

The night I saw Alan's face on the news, with "MISSING" in garish red across his handsome face, I threw up. I couldn't seem to turn off the news. When anchors are given big news to run with, but no information, they tend to repeat a lot. I spent hours huddled on the couch, clutching a blanket and trying to stop the relentless heaving.

Oliver.

Oliver.

Oliver.

The phone rang.

"Yosei, my heart, are you well?"

Angel. The concern in her voice was enough to undo me entirely. I tried to say that yes, I was fine, but a choked sob spilled free instead.

"Oh, my darling. Tell me what you need. Bring you booze or fuck off?"

***

I was tired. Graduation was barely a month behind me, and the girls had been unforgiving with their needs. Their definition of business manager didn't quite line up with mine. We were on the road all the time, so I found local dry cleaners and researched the best take-out. I sewed torn costumes, shopped for new shoes, replaced lost mascara. All while booking venues and fielding calls from fans and reporters. I loved it, but I didn't have nearly the energy I used to. Did becoming an adult wear you out that fast?

But, as the saying far more tired than I went, the show must go on.

The set was wrapping up when the world tipped. One man near the back of the bar caught my attention. He was handsome, in that careless way that melts hearts and knees. There didn't seem to be any arrogance in him. Just a deep joy of the music. He swayed slightly, lost in the sounds. And then he grabbed the wall. His head shot up, and he caught my gaze. His eyes grew wide, knuckles white as he dug fingernails into the wall. I started pushing my way through the crowd to get to him. It was the last song, and everyone was on their feet. I kept losing sight of him.

Each time I caught a glimpse of him, he seemed a little farther away. A little less there. He stumbled back, clearly seeking the exit, but afraid to turn away from me. Except it wasn't me he was looking at. He was looking to the left and right of me. Above me. Terrified. By that time, I was starting to see through him. The glowing door sign. The posters of other bands. Hell, a waitress walked behind him, and I could read her name tag.

And then he was just gone. His eyes had been filled with terror in that last moment. I shook my head, clearing my perception a bit, looking around. He had to be there. I'd been peeking at him all night.

The girls were done. The crowd was pushing past me, laughing and humming bits of their favourite song. I couldn't move. I wanted to throw up. I wanted to call the police. I wanted to call my mother.

Ona found me gripping the back of a chair, paler than usual. She ruffled my hair, then turned to call out to the stage, "Angel! We broke Yosei again! I'm taking her to the room."

On the way, I tried to tell her about the man. She smiled, hooking my arm through hers and gently patting my hand.

"You're just tired, honey. We're off tomorrow night and you're going to sleep, understand? I'll give you a pill tonight."

I protested on both counts, but she overrode me. People didn't just vanish like that. I was projecting. I was exhausted. A good twelve hours' sleep would set me right. By the time she had me undressed, drugged, and into bed, I had stopped arguing. Sleep. That was all I needed.

***

The dream rose from a fog, obscuring everything else.

There was no ground, no hotel bed, no walls. Just a misty world that held a flavour of fear. I turned and turned, and turned again. Something was there with me.

Angel stepped out of the fog, that enigmatic smile of hers telling me it was alright. Her mouth moved, but I couldn't hear her. Ona stood next to her, nuzzling Angel's shoulder and nodding. Musume slipped up from the side and flashed her hands at me in a silent sort of "Boo!" motion. I shuddered, wanting to pull back from them. They were my family now. My sisters, my life. Never had I so desperately wanted to get away from them.

They moved as one, drawing closer, then spreading out to surround me. Angel shifted first, but the other two were so close behind her it almost didn't matter. Long black hair became pure white, tumbling farther down her back than it did in the waking world. Her eyes slid the same, dark to utter white in a blink. I glanced at Ona and Musu. Their faces had morphed into Angel's. All three looked exactly the same as they reached for me with fingers gone knotty and clawed. Razor sharp talons extended, growing as I began to panic.

The mist thickened, and now I could hear them, sibilant and speaking as one, each identical in tone and cadence.

"So sweet."

"Such a delightful treat."

"We treasure you, Yosei."

Their gazes turned feral, and they smiled; their mouths full of sharp, dripping fangs.

***

I woke screaming and kicking at the bedsheets. I had a fleeting thought that if I kept showing myself to be emotional and hysterical, they'd fire me and then what? The fog was still with me though, and I was more frightened than I could remember ever being.

I wrapped myself in a blanket and stumbled out to the shared sitting room. All three were still up, sipping wine.

"Bad dream, Yosei? Here, come sit with me. Those pills can be a bitch if you're not used to them."

I snuggled in next to Ona, waiting for the panic to ease. It didn't. The primal creature that lived at the base of my brain was screeching at me. But I was so tired. I laid my head on her shoulder and an image flashed. Ona's head on Angel's shoulder. Clawed hands. My heart raced.

Musu leaned over me and when she smiled, her mouth was full of sharp, dripping fangs, "Relax, Yosei. We don't take much. Just a little taste to refresh."

Ona's arm tightened around me, holding me in place as Angel rose from a couch and floated… Tiny gods, she was floating!…to me.

I pushed at Ona, tried to kick at Musu. I could feel the tears and snot running down my face.

Angel got closer.

I started babbling, "Wake up, wake up, wake up, please wake up!"

Angel laughed and the sound scratched my soul. "Oliver thought he was dreaming, too."

I tried to shove them away again, before Angel got to me. But I was so tired. My limbs were weighted down. My head hurt and I couldn't figure out what was real. Oliver? What did he have to do with this nightmare?

Angel leaned over me, eyes completely white, and kissed my forehead. "Your brother was a delicious feast, over far too soon. We'll be keeping you. Our own little snack to keep us topped off between shows. Unless you'd rather we visit your parents?"

I went down screaming yet again as the fog closed in around me.

***

"Where to next, Yosei?"

I stretched and took the extra-large coffee from Musu with gratitude. Every week, I told them where we were headed. Every week, they pretended to forget.

"Nope. Not telling. Just bring your sweaters."

Damn, I was tired.

"Ona, I don't think your pills worked."

KIMBERLY REI does her best work in the places that can't exist…
the in-between places where imagination defies reality.

With a penchant for creepy shadows and hooks that leave you guessing, she can be found in anthologies from Black Hare Press, Eerie River Publishing, and Iron Faerie Publishing as well as behind the scenes of various collections editing, beta reading, marketing, and encouraging fellow authors.

Bibliography

ANCIENTS, Black Hare Press, 2020
APOCALYPSE, Black Hare Press, 2019
Darkness Reclaimed, Eerie River Publishing, 2020
Forgotten Ones, Eerie River Publishing, 2020
HATE, Black Hare Press, 2020
It Calls From the Forest, Volume 2, Eerie River Publishing, 2020
LOVE, Black Hare Press, 2020
OCEANS, Black Hare Press, 2020
Quietus 13, Black Hare Press, 2020
The Best of Iron Faerie Publishing 2019, Iron Faerie Publishing, 2020

Connect
Website: Tales.studiorei.org
Amazon: amazon.com/Askani-Aichi
Twitter: @SeersDaughter
Facebook: @ReiTales

SEX TYPE THING

by S.O. Green

It was like the start of a joke. A stout and stocky Marshall amp and a skinny-necked Fender Telecaster walked into a dressing room.

"I can't believe you're going to open for Sin," the Marshall said.

The Fender grinned so broadly, the top of her head almost popped off. "Yeah, gurl. This is what it's all about. I'm so hard right now I could fuck a hole in the world."

Marshall laughed. "You're silly."

"I'm not silly, baby. I'm a rock star."

Laura set the stack down in the corner while Jules marvelled, guitar in hand. A tourist at her own personal Notre Dame, she breathed deep from the rock-and-roll sacristy. What an ambience! Stale sweat and old booze. Someone had left a pair of leather pants hanging on one of the coat hooks, and now they were just part of the décor. The wall-length mirror was swarmed. Old makeup, eyeliner, hairspray. Like cockroaches that hadn't scuttled away when they'd flicked the lights on.

Jules was wearing her paint already. Black lipstick and rainbow fingernails. Might have been the only walk of life where the men were expected to wear more.

Through a door, there was a porcelain throne where heavy metal gods had snorted mythological amounts of ambrosia off the cistern and said things like "Let's rock and roll."

It felt like they'd finally made it. No more playing in bars, hoping the folks would buy them a beer after the set. This was once in a lifetime.

And all because Jezebel was a diva.

She said she never wanted to play with the same band twice. Sin toured alone. Legend had it, their manager once tried to book two shows with one act. Jezebel had unplugged them halfway through their first song, pulled a couple of folks out of the audience to play in their place. By all accounts, not the craziest thing she'd ever done.

"This is the shit," Jules breathed, hands spreading to encompass all that everything.

Jules, whose only prejudice was whether something was punk rock or not. Jules, who'd learned to swing her guitar around her neck before she'd learned to play a single chord. Jules, who had sex and drugs in abundance and only needed rock'n'roll to complete her bingo card. Jules, who'd been in a band for a year, but who'd been a rock star her entire life.

And Laura, her roadie. Her girlfriend. Toting an amp as big as she was. Thicc and fire-haired. A woman born out of her century, because a Norse myth somewhere was missing a Valkyrie. A short, chubby Valkyrie. Jeans with chains, military boots, and a black tee stretched over bulky arms and a considerable bosom, a size too small because that's how Jules liked it.

Band slogan. Juliette & the Romeos. A woman with half her head shaved, movie kissing a skull. Suspicious resemblance to Jules herself.

"Hey, you know how they say never meet your heroes?" Jules asked.

Laura looked over, wondering if the nerves were finally starting to catch up to her. "Yeah?"

"It's bullshit. Let's go meet Jezebel."

***

Jezebel was lounging on the tour bus. Something about the way she watched all the traffic around her, limbs curled and head upright, reminded Laura of a panther sprawled on a rock. Watching antelope, tail flicking.

Her pelt was crimson silk and black leather. High collar and high heels. They called her a lesbian. She insisted she wasn't that particular.

Someone had once told Laura that Jezebel's makeup was tattooed on. It didn't look like a tattoo. It didn't look like makeup either. Lips bloodstained. Eyelashes that caused hurricanes in China with every coquettish batting. Brows arched, suggestively suggesting *something*. Something that made Laura blush.

They stepped onto the bus in the middle of an argument. Jezebel and Sin's manager, Norman, whose name alone meant he could never be a rock star. He tried, bless him. Kept his blond hair lank and greasy, wore denim and leather, but he just looked like someone's uncle having a midlife crisis.

Jezebel argued like she kissed. Half-committed. Eyes roving, searching for something more interesting.

She settled on Jules and Laura as they climbed aboard. Norman didn't approve.

"This venue isn't sufficient," he insisted, fighting to win back her attention.

"Don't you think it has character?" Jezebel asked. Her tone was like a yawn.

"It doesn't have *enough* characters. We've got two hundred people here, standing room only. That's not good enough."

Jules and Laura exchanged a look. Two hundred people was one hundred and ninety *more* people than Juliette & the Romeos had ever played to. It was *better* than good enough.

"I enjoy these smaller shows." Jezebel, unaware that small was a matter of perspective. "They're more…intimate."

"The point of being a celebrity is to be intimate with as many people as possible, Jezebel. It's how we make money. We *need* money."

"My fans adore me and adoration is all I need."

The argument was over. Norman didn't get the memo. "Maybe they do adore you, but they're not buying tickets. They're not buying merchandise or albums. They're too busy killing themselves to prove they love you."

Jezebel reclined and sighed wistfully. "Yes. It has a certain tragic beauty to it, doesn't it?"

"Dead people don't buy things."

She scowled at him. She was good at scowling. It didn't just convey displeasure. It conveyed misfortune.

"Their lives matter to *me*," she said, like hers was the *only* opinion that mattered. "Two hundred will be enough."

He scoffed. "It's never enough for you."

"For either of us," she reminded him.

Laura cringed. It was never pleasant, watching other people air their dirty laundry. Jules seemed impressed, like someone watching a cheetah run down a gazelle and wishing they had spots.

"Maybe we should come back later," Laura muttered.

Sin's drummer, Spike, shrugged. He and Laura might have been distantly related, because they had matching arms, except his were sleeved with tattoos. He was lounging across two empty seats, toking.

"They're always arguing. If I didn't know better, I'd say they were doing it. Money and fame, money and fame. In circles."

"Aren't you in the band?" Jules asked.

"Yeah. I guess I am."

Jezebel summoned them forth with a wave. "Is this my supporting band for tonight?"

"Yes, ma'am," Laura said. This was her chance to make a good impression, for Jules's sake. "This is Juliette of Juliette & the Romeos."

"And you are?"

"I'm just here to help."

Jules squeezed her shoulders. "My girlfriend."

Jezebel arched one of those suggestive eyebrows. "An uncommon breed of woman. But then, we could say the same about you, couldn't we, Juliette? I have seen you perform. I think we will fit together like a hand in a glove."

Laura balked. "You've *seen* her?"

"Yes, of course. You just didn't see me."

"How? No offence, but…you stand out."

Jezebel laughed. Unsurprisingly, it was musical. "Would we be in rock-and-roll if we didn't *love* to be seen?"

There was a crash from outside. The beginnings of an argument. Jezebel smiled. It was like standing in the warming light of the noon sun.

"Perhaps you should go and see to your Romeos, Juliette. If they keep fighting like that, there won't be a band left to play your slot."

Jules nodded and ran off the bus. There wasn't even a thought that she might disobey.

Jezebel smiled at Laura. She patted the seat beside her. "Come sit by me, dear."

"Maybe I should go too. She might need help."

"And you like to be helpful, don't you? Tell me, what is it that you do? Offer emotional support?"

"I lift heavy things, too."

"Yes, you seem strong. I admire that in a woman. Though strength of will is my drug of choice. Is your will strong?"

"I smoke, so probably not."

Another musical laugh. Followed by another crash from outside. Laura hesitated, one foot turning to the door and Jules. Jezebel fixed her with a look, her mood turning like a coin in the air, about to land.

"It sounds as though your girlfriend could use some of that emotional support. Or perhaps she needs you to lift something heavy."

Laura realised she'd been dismissed and hurried away. Spike leaned in as she passed and whispered, "Careful. She bites."

Jezebel, inevitably, overheard. "Yes, but where is the pleasure without a little pain?"

***

Jules vomited twice before their set started. She hadn't eaten anything, so she splashed the drug throne with whiskey and whimpering. Laura held her hair and wiped her eyes while the others headbutted walls and slapped their cheeks and shadow-boxed their instruments.

The space filled up above them. Two hundred

stomping pairs of feet, two hundred chattering mouths, two hundred heads nodding to old classics. "Two Minutes to Midnight". "Reign of Blood". "For Whom the Bell Tolls".

Then Jules was ready. She wiped the bile off her lips and cracked that lopsided smile that earned her the nickname "Crazy Jules", no matter how much Laura didn't like it. She high-fived her Romeos. She kissed Laura and opened her guitar case.

"Where's the photograph?"

Laura noticed it was missing before Jules did. There should have been a photo of them taped to the inside of the case. Laura's favourite, because they both looked so normal and happy and it was the closest Jules ever got to a real smile in any of their pictures together. Soft flannel and bed hair. Hands in pockets and heads nuzzling at one another. The least punk rock thing there ever could be.

"Must have slipped out."

"You mean, you didn't notice?"

"Relax, babe. I'll find it. After the show. Alright? I love you."

Another kiss. Hot and drunk. Then she marched onto the stage, dragging her axe behind her like she was going to war, throwing horns and snarling.

Laura followed them to the wings, but those shadows were the closest she ever wanted to get to the limelight.

Their set was short and brutal. A skirmish before the war began. Juliette strangled melodies out of her Fender, while the Romeos ground bass, smashed drums, and slashed the songs apart with samples and old movie quotes. Their audience didn't wake up until the set was half done. They'd been waiting for a bus. Then the conversations stopped and the nodding and the toe tapping and the singing along with the chorus started. Pretty soon, the few folks in the crowd who'd heard of them were hollering requests and Jules obliged with a maniacal grin on her face. This was the closest she'd ever been to being who she wanted to be. To being Jezebel.

At the top of the setlist, she played the opening chords to "Laura's Lips"—her magnum opus. She screamed the chorus and there was a bridge you could punch people to. Down below, it was moshing room only.

Made Laura blush every time. Parental guidance: explicit lyrics. And, yeah, maybe oversharing a little with two hundred people, but Jules always said, "I want them all to know."

She wasn't shy. Wasn't ashamed. She could bare all. Strip down, naked, if it brought her that adoration Jezebel had talked about on the bus. She was thirsty for it. Ravenous. Lustful. She shredded her fingers apart on her strings and bled punk rock on the edge of the stage. Like her music, they lapped it up.

Laura wondered if they'd ever be the same again.

She wished she could be happier. This was what Jules wanted, but all she felt were doubts. She wondered why she couldn't live in the moment like the girl on stage, bleeding and screaming and soaking in adrenaline and loving every single fucking minute of it.

Jules took her bow. Her fucked up fingers precluded an encore. She was sweating, and her eyes were glazed. She fell into Laura's arms and bled on her tee. She looked like she was going to puke again.

Instead, she giggled, hiccupped, and asked, "How did I do?"

"I thought you did magnificently."

It was the compliment Laura wanted to pay, but she wasn't the one with the currency. Jezebel was there, ready to take the spotlight. Laura had thought she looked vampish before. Now she had a cravat knotted at her neck, and she was perched on precarious heels like a bird of prey. Her band lurked behind her like pack betas, like they might try for alpha if they didn't think she'd keep her lips red with their insides.

She prowled closer, cupped Jules's sticky face like she was going to drink from her mouth. She said, "You got them warm for me. I'll give them the climax."

She shot Laura a look that was *more* than suggestive. Then she marched onto the stage.

The band hovered, keeping to the shadows until the crowd had eaten their fill of Jezebel in all her gothic magnificence and she was done bathing in their idolatry. A transaction that needed no third parties.

Laura felt like she should take Jules back to the dressing room. The rest of the band were already gone, punching each other and grinning like it was prom night all over again. But Jules found her feet and stared, wide-eyed, as Jezebel took the two-hundred-strong crowd her band had only just managed to entertain, gathered up their misspent love in the palm of her taloned hand and stuffed it greedily into her mouth.

She had one hand on the microphone. The other bestowed blessings, pointing out individuals, singling out hearts and minds and souls.

They wanted her. They wanted to be wanted *by* her. She could pick and choose, so she did. She stirred emotions and libidos. She breathed heat into them until they frothed over.

Laura had read an interview with her once. She'd said she hated the word "fan." Hated the way people used it so loosely. Wasn't it supposed to be short for fanatic?

"That kind of word implies religious devotion," she'd

said. "Loyalty. Extremism."

"It implies that I'm a god," she'd said. "And I like the sound of that."

Jezebel strutted back and forth across her own altar. That chapel was for the deification of her. She was the preacher and the power. She was the idol and the graven image. She was everything the crowd wanted her to be, and Laura couldn't tell what had come first. Jezebel or the empty spaces she filled.

Laura had been to ten Sin concerts. Every single time, she'd gone with Jules. They'd gyrated in the front row, rapturous and hedonistic. Music too loud, alcohol too much, desire too difficult to ignore. They'd made out on the bus home, even though they knew everyone was watching, and spent the night in Jules's garage, entangled behind the drum kit.

In her mind, Jezebel had towered over her for a week afterwards.

The drums kicked. They started to play the band's only cover—"Sex Type Thing." It had earned them a lot of headlines when the single came out. A female rock star, singing about sexual aggression. About *being* the sexual aggressor. Was she promoting it? Endorsing it?

They'd asked her if she thought those lyrics, entirely unchanged from the original, were appropriate. She'd asked, "Why? Are you afraid I might do something to you?"

It had made Laura afraid somehow, but she was probably the only one.

It wasn't a song about sex. It was a song about her drug of choice. She was offering up her will and her fans tapped veins to mainline on it. Anything not to think for themselves. They wanted what was on her mind. They *liked* what was on her mind.

By the time she reached the bridge, chanting, "Here I come, I come, I come, I come," most of the audience seemed to agree with her. They played that song at every show. Laura had heard it tenfold. She still wasn't used to the way it made her feel. Jules squirmed in her arms. Her girlfriend breathed on her neck and Laura was struck by the sudden realisation that no one could see them in the darkness off stage.

Except Jezebel, who turned and looked right at them. Just for a heartbeat and at that very moment.

"Baltimore, tell me you love me!"

The venue came alive. An outpouring of desire. The audience shrieked themselves hoarse, trying to be heard. They hadn't sung that loud. They'd been saving themselves for that moment. That chance to catch her eye by screaming just the right thing.

"Tonight's a special night, isn't it?" The venue fell

silent. The preacher was preaching. "You're all so special to me. Each and every one of you. I don't think I've ever loved an audience as much as I love you. You feel it, don't you?"

They wouldn't tell her no. They poured from themselves, and they'd keep pouring until they were empty. What Jezebel planned to do with it all was anyone's guess. But she never seemed quenched.

"I know a way that we can make this a night to remember. You want to make this a night to remember, don't you? You want me to remember you."

The answer was yes. They were climbing the walls to tell her. They wanted to be remembered. They'd do anything to prove it.

Literally anything.

Jezebel smiled.

She pulled a lighter from leather pants so tight Laura could see the outline of it in her pocket. She held it up, clicked the flint. She'd done something to the lighter fluid, or maybe it was just the house lights, because the flame looked the same deep red as her blouse and lips.

"You all have lighters, don't you?"

They did. There was a staccato crackle of metal lids and snapped flints, and then the air above the audience was filled with tiny flames. And everyone was wondering what was going on, because lighters were for ballads. Sin didn't play ballads. They didn't stroke their fingers through the audience's hair and sway with them gently. They grabbed them by the throat and forced their tongue into their mouth because Jezebel was that kind of woman.

Laura was the only one who looked at the rest of the band and saw they were just as confused, but just as curious, as everyone else.

"Does anyone know what my favourite sin is?"

She waited for an answer. Everyone knew, but the implication made everyone dizzy and dry in the mouth.

Jezebel licked her lips. The answer was no longer in doubt. "Desire. Like a flame that burns you up from the inside. I want to know how strong your passion is. How much do you really feel for me? Show me you're telling me the truth."

Everyone held their breath, waiting. Tell us, Jezebel. Tell us what we can do to prove it.

"I want you to burn this place down. Light it up. Light each other up. Do this for me and I promise I will remember you. I will sing about you. I will tell everyone that it was *you* I loved the most. Do this for me and I'll be yours for eternity. Each and every one of you."

The notion wasn't as absurd as the fact that everyone started to do *exactly as she fucking said*!

Down below, they were setting fire to curtains and posters and each other's clothing, and no one—absolutely no one—was doing anything about it.

Sin gaped down into the crowd, clutching their instruments like crucifixes. Jules hung off Laura's arm, transfixed by Jezebel, who was watching the lambs beneath her with the fire reflecting in her eyes.

Laura was the only one that moved. She shrugged Jules off, marched onto the stage, and kicked over Spike's drum kit. The cymbals clattered like an alarm clock ringing. *Wake up!* She grabbed a guitar that cost more than anything she'd ever owned and smashed it against the stage. *Wake up!* She kicked over an amp, snatched Jezebel's microphone, and banged it off the floor at her feet. *Wake up!* The sudden screech of feedback sliced through the haze.

There was an alarmed patting out of clothes, and one of the building's custodians came around with a fire extinguisher. Everyone glared at everyone else, and there was an unspoken agreement that no one would ever speak of this ever again.

Instead, they all started asking: Who is that girl? Why did that roadie just smash all of Sin's instruments? Is the show over then? Do we get a refund for this?

Jezebel's temple emptied out. Everyone was feverish

and foggy-headed. They were heading out into the cold to try to find the pieces of themselves they'd lost. Norman had his fist in his mouth as he tabulated the cost of all-new instruments and two hundred partial refunds.

The band marched off stage, stoop-shouldered and empty-handed, like men waiting at the gallows.

Jezebel looked at Laura. And smiled.

"A pleasure to have met you, Laura."

She left her alone in the emptiness. Jules was there, but Laura didn't know what to say to her.

Other than "I want to go home."

***

Sin and a small cadre of diehard groupies climbed aboard the tour bus. Their driver pumped the pedals and grunted.

"Need to take her in at the next stop. Brakes are feeling spongy."

"Wonderful," Norman snarled. "More cash flow problems."

Jezebel glided through it all, heading for the seat at the back. She didn't have an admirer with her, and all the girls who'd climbed aboard were wondering why. Instead, all she was holding was a photograph.

"What gives, Jezebel?" Norman demanded. "You said we'd be rich and famous until the day we died."

"And so you shall, my dear. Have no fear."

And that was it. The conversation was over. Jezebel had hung a tie on the door handle. Do not disturb. Bass and keyboard were churlish, agitated. Not even temporary intimacy could kiss away their unease.

Spike sat down close to Jezebel. She eyed him. Partly a threat and partly curious. Would one of them finally be man enough?

"What you did back there... Lisa-Marie wouldn't have..."

"Don't say her name." It was not a suggestion. "It makes her cringe to hear it from your mouth. She's still with me, you know? In the cage you built for her. My little songbird. My muse. Mine."

Spike nodded. Because that was the deal they'd made. Jezebel unknotted her cravat and popped buttons, and Spike stared at the body he'd wanted back when it had a different name.

"You've followed me this far, Spike. Don't second-guess me now."

Spike heaved a sigh and wanted to say, "If not now, then when?" But he didn't.

Instead, he asked, "What is that?"

Jezebel looked at him over the top of the photograph. A photograph of two girls standing together, arms wrapped around each other, smiling with their bed hair and flannel.

She said, "Never you mind."

She stared at the picture as they started to drive. Her seat in the back was the perfect place to hear the brakes hissing as they struggled to keep hold of the wheels.

Maybe Sin had already had its day in the sun. Maybe it was time to find a more comfortable outfit.

Something with an…interesting accessory.

S.O. GREEN is a science-fiction, fantasy and horror writer living in the Kingdom of Fife with husband, John.

Their work has appeared and will appear in publications by Dragon Soul Press, Otter Libris, Rogue Blades, Storgy Magazine, L Ellington Ashton, Iron Faerie, Eerie River and Black Hare Press. They also won 3rd Place in the British Fantasy Society's Short Story Contest 2018 for the feminist post-Apocalypse piece, 'Travesty'. Writer, vegan, martial artist, gamer, occasionally a terrible person (but only to fictional people). They thrive on the unusual, which might explain why there are so many cats.

Bibliography
BFS Horizons, British Fantasy Society, 2018
Eerie River Patreon, Eerie River Publishing, 2020
Full Metal Horror 3: The Unknown, Zombie Pirate Publishing, 2020
Lethal Impact, Dragon Soul Press, 2020
MCSI, Otter Libris, 2018
Reign of Queens, Dragon Soul Press, 2020

Connect
Website: thebasementoflove.blogspot.com
Amazon: amazon.co.uk/-/e/B0876CYBJJ
Twitter: @SOGreenWriter
Facebook: @TheBasementOfLove

JUST A SINGER IN A ROCK N ROLL BAND

by Gregg Cunningham

CHAPTER 1

The thought of leaving Wantham City was still fresh in Dmitri Timbrado's mind. Why wouldn't it be? If he stayed where he was, frying burgers inside his food truck, Dmitri figured he was surely going to end up in a world of pain. Or worse—wrapped up inside a bloody sheet and entombed under twenty tonnes of concrete poured into some cookie-cutter shopping mall construction site.

If he thought Dmitri had squealed to police, Vanivich would order his men to torch Dmitri's *Geisenburger* food truck—with Dmitri gagged and tied to the gas bottles underneath the grill plate—without a second thought.

Any information leaked about the supply arrangement and the lost bag of produce Dmitri was supposed to distribute for Vanivich would surely cause a problem for the mob once the word was out. The fact that somebody had jumped one of the mob's debt collectors the other night and set about his bald head with a brick, before robbing him of almost fifty grand's worth of Dexi pills, was just be the tip of the iceberg. The two junkie fucks who had murdered the courier had been so distracted by the huge stash of Dexi pills, that they left almost twenty grand in the poor bastard's pocket. When Dimitri came across the money meant for Vanivich, he pocketed the bundle and blamed the kids—thus becoming suspect number one in Detective Deeds's eyes.

Luckily for Dmitri, Detective Harry Deeds was also working for Vanivich, applying similar rules to Dmitri—get away with what you can to survive the streets. Deeds was as corrupt as they come.

The only option left for Dmitri was to run, get as far away from Wantham as possible. But if Dmitri did run, well, that would only prove his guilt and surely get him an escorted visit to Vanivich. He would probably have every one of his teeth pulled out until he eventually talked, even though he had nothing to do with the robbery or the hit on

Vanivich's drop-off man. He'd just seen an opportunity and taken it.

Damn those fucking junkie kids. He knew the kids were playing him, even when he was pounding the cute one behind his food truck. He later realised she was just fucking him as a cover for them casing his place for the robbery they were planning.

The ultimate *fuck you,* though, was when Barry, one of the junkie kids from the ghetto, showed up stoned off his face at his food truck last night with some of the stolen gear, hoping to sell it back to Vanivich for a price to suit both parties. The kid had no idea the world of hurt he was about to find himself in, but Dmitri doubted he would even realise Vanivich was feeding him his balls when the time came because he was so stoned out of his head. For that reason, Dmitri had called Detective Deeds.

Dimitri would have to wait out the madness and see which side would come out on top, then see if there was any way to make a getaway after the dust had settled. Perhaps Deeds would arrest Vanivich and things would be quiet for a week or two, maybe then he could take a run down to the coast and find a club where he and his brother could lie low, get lucky, and make a few bucks on the side playing guitar for the punters for a few beers. Dmitri had enough money stashed away to disappear; all he needed was some wheels and he could leave this fucked up city for good. But chances were the cartel had bugged his car, any Uber trip he made would be tracked for sure.

The truth was, though, he didn't expect either Deeds or Vanivich to show up with smiles on their faces when they came to confront him—both would want answers, and Dmitri was going to have to talk sooner or later. Willingly or unwillingly. Teeth or no teeth. Deeds would probably just punch them all out for the hell of it, then take back the money Dmitri had stolen for himself.

"Oscar, hey buddy, it's Dmitri. You busy?" He scratched nervously at his wrist, looking around for an empty bench to sit on as he removed his greasy apron and stuffed it into the empty cardboard box by the door of his food truck.

"Hey, bro. Whoa! Long time, no hear. You okay?" Oscar seemed happy to hear from him as he shouted down the phone. "Me? Yeah, I got a gig tonight down at Moody's. Say, why don't you come? I could do with a sideman, they're getting harder to come by these days. Even the fat balding ones."

Dmitri ignored the jab. "Yeah, I don't know. I'm kinda busy tonight. Look, truth is, I was hoping I could shout you up for a favour?" Dmitri was tired, and his eyes darted between the trees and the *Geisenburger* fast-food sign as he locked the padlock to the truck and descended the three metal stairs to the wet grass. "I was hoping I could use your van for a couple of days; I'm thinking of taking a trip down south!"

"The Timbrado tour bus? You want the *Magic Bus* for a few days? Shit, bro, what am I going to do with all my sound gear?" Dmitri paused for a moment, hiding in the shadows of the gas bottles behind the truck to watch a black SUV as it rolled into the car park down by the lake. "Come with me, Oscar. Stretch your legs. We can go take a drive down to the cabin, it's been too long." Dmitri hesitated as he watched the car swing into a parking bay. "Yeah… Maybe catch up, smoke a few roaches."

Oscar sensed his unease. "Are you okay, bro? Somebody giving you hassle?"

Dmitri laughed, trying to cover up his paranoia as the driver got out of the car with her dog on a long leash and walked the other way. He sat on one of his worn customer benches, wiping the discarded tomato sauce sachets to the ground. "Yeah, I'm good, mate. Just need to get clear of the kitchen for a couple of days, y'know. Close the shop." He hoped that would be enough for Oscar to understand.

"Oh, right? Getting too hot in there to cook?"

"Something like that. So, what do you think?" Dimitri's sneakers were bouncing on the slab beneath the bench as he nervously watched the people in the park go about their daily distancing measures.

Oscar knew the score; he had helped his brother out on more than one occasion—making the odd drop off around the city for Dimitri when he was stuck, even doing the odd pick up. So, when Dmitri dropped the old "closing the kitchen" line, he knew something was up. Oscar had warned him about getting involved with Vanivich.

"This got anything to do with that mob guy getting Wylie Coyoted with a brick down your joint the other night? I heard Mal Bicho is on the warpath." Oscar liked to call Vanivich Mal Bicho—the bad man image was quite appropriate for the Russian mobster.

"Yeah, well, I don't know nothing 'bout that, Oscar," Dmitri lied. "I just need to get away from here for a while, thought you might like to too. You know it's five years since Dad passed?"

"Five years? Shit! That long? I guess we should get together a bit more often, eh?"

"We sure do... So, you gonna lend me the *Magic bus,* or what?"

The *Magic bus* was just a poorly spray-painted black 1983 GMC Vandura cargo van, complete with a small red rear spoiler fitted to the roof and matching red swoosh lines across the body art work. The band's logo was airbrushed along the side panelling in sweeping Gothic calligraphy, spelling out the band name: Timbrado.

Oscar always considered himself the "Face" of the Latino band, and while they toured the bars, he thought the retro eighties cargo van was the best way to travel.

"Look, I need the bus tonight, bro. It's already packed for the gig, but how about you meet me down Moody's at eight and help me unload? Then we can ditch the gear after the show and take that road trip together before they close the borders up?"

"Sure, sounds good." Dmitri nodded, looking at his watch. "That gives me a couple of hours to grab a bag and head on over. Okay, Oscar. Thanks, brother. Catch up later."

"No probs, bro. See you there… Oh, and bring some Dexi, you sound like you need a hit." Dimitri hung up and pocketed his phone, pulling out his vape pen, which was already loaded with one of Vanivich's dodgy Dexiflex cartridges, and switched it on. Oscar was right. He did need a hit, and at this point, he didn't care who saw him light up—he was already up to his neck in the brown stuff. Maybe getting locked up in Wantham's cells for the night would be a godsend. That way, he wouldn't have to worry about his teeth being pulled by some dodgy Russian backstreet dentist with a bag full of Jack the Ripper props to play with.

Dmitri sat back and inhaled the narcotic vapour, holding the vape juice in his lungs for a moment, almost feeling the dopamine being released as the buzz of the nicotine hit his brain, calming his shaking legs that bounced on the concrete beneath him until the pistons eased to a halt.

Fuck Mal Bicho.

CHAPTER 2

Moody's nightclub was a large dingy back-alley drinking den over by the Wantham docklands. Notoriously a place for bikers and Latino rock chicks to gather without the threat of the cops interfering in their social gatherings. The club always drew big crowds because of the cheap drinks and loud live music. Word was, they were going to close all the bars in the city soon. If they did, then Moody's would be the last to close, and only after one hell of a street fight resulting in several arrests. It was that kind of shit kickers underworld joint: *You can take my beer from my cold dead hands.*

Oscar's cover band played there most Friday nights; just him and Fritz with their guitars, Ken on brass, and the drummer, Sergio. They had played together for more than twenty years—along with Dimitri—scraping together enough money to get them by each week. It paid for the essentials like gas, jewellery, weed, Cheetos, and liquor. To be honest, they were pretty good in their heyday. Dmitri made for a half decent front man when they'd toured the college campuses and nightclubs. They called themselves Los Fabulosos Timbrado Trio back then—a tribute band—until Dmitri packed up a few years back after an offer to make more cash distributing for Vanivich. Oscar decided to drop the Trio name and just go with the Timbrado family name logo. It seemed more in line with the alternate Latino rock they were starting to play. Folks liked their sound, but Timbrado never made it bigger than the club scene after Dmitri left. He was the one with the looks and the voice, but looking at him now, you'd never have guessed with his beer gut and his sweaty brow.

Oscar was unpacking instruments from the *Magic Bus,* but stopped when he saw Dimitri. "Amigo!" he said, his arms outstretched. "What the hell happened to your hair?" His multitude of silver and leather bracelets jangled on his tanned forearm as Dmitri approached. "And your belly…? You got fat, bro!" His gleaming white teeth beamed with humour as he hugged his big brother tightly. "You were right, you do need to get away from that greasy spoon trailer, my friend!"

Dmitri shrugged, and slid his hand across his forehead to flick away his thinning, sweaty fringe. He dropped his heavy backpack with a smirk as the dull sound of a drum being played echoed from inside Moody's nightclub and a trumpet blurted out a few random Mariachi high notes.

"You still blow drying that wig then?" Dmitri replied, pointing at Oscar's wavy locks. Oscar was standing there like a poor man's Steven Tyler—the ageing rocker was complete with bandannas around his wrists, the worn leather waistcoat he'd been wearing since the band's college days, silver-tipped cowboy boots, and his skinny legs barely filling his skinny jeans.

"And I see the lips are getting bigger too, Captain Jack!" Dmitri pointed. "Gloss?"

"Fuck you, man. These teeth cost me six months' worth of gig receipts." Oscar winced in jest. "Hey, gotta give the fans what they crave." He smiled again, and the club lighting showed his leathery gaunt face, pulled back to reveal his recently polished, implanted teeth. He put his thumbs up in a cheesy Fonzie pose.

"Hey, I got you something from my garage. Check it out." Oscar reached into the tour bus and pulled out the old guitar delicately.

"My Rickenbacker! Sweet..." Dmitri took the instrument and held it out to inspect. "Wow, it's been a long time since I played this." His smile widened. "Is it tuned?"

"Is it tuned? Christ, Dmitri, you think I'd bring an

untuned guitar to a gig?" Oscar frowned in disgust. "Course, it's tuned, bro!" He lifted Dmitri's bag from the ground and went to place it in the van, but Dmitri grabbed his wrist. "Whoa, buddy. I'm just sticking it inside the cab for safe keeping, dude. If you take it inside, it's sure to go missing." Dmitri let go and nodded. "Sure, just watch it. It's just got a few things I need inside."

A few things…like twenty thousand of Vanivich's greenbacks.

"Okay, quit bitching and give me a hand with the gear. Sergio is inside setting up with Ken." Oscar slapped Dmitri on his back, leaned inside the tour bus, and threw the rucksack behind the seat.

"Hey, it's real good to see you again, Dmitri."

They walked under the club's torn canvas sail shade as it flapped above them. "What about Fritz? Where's he at then?" Dmitri asked, as he inspected his old Rickenbacker guitar with wonder, before sliding the sling over his shoulder.

"He's been gone a couple of weeks, bro, I was serious on the phone," Oscar said, handing him a box of CDs. "Space is vacant, want to try out?"

"Are you shitting me, Oscar? I haven't played for years," Dmitri replied, taking the weight.

"Hey, why not? Just follow my lead, play some rifts

from the back. It will do you good, loosen you up…we'll do some old shit!" Oscar smiled. "Come on, bring that box of promo CDs. The audience is arriving, so let's get this shit inside. We can discuss contracts over a cold one." He pointed to the group of Latino ladies strutting the catwalk towards them in their tight figure-hugging skirts and high-heeled boots. He opened the club door and handed the large bouncer the keys to the tour bus.

"Concierge, I'd like the full wash service, please."

The bouncer sighed at the weekly regurgitated joke and took the keys from Oscar. "I'll have to park her round the back tonight, we're expecting a full house."

"Sure thing, Phil. I'll get Sergio to grab the keys from the bar later." Oscar beamed as the young ladies half his age, and then some, walked up to the open doorway and lined up by the kiosk. "*Hola senoras bonitas!*"

"*Hola Papa!*" they replied, giving him the eye and smiling as they handed over their IDs. Oscar clutched his chest and staggered back a few steps, and they laughed.

"*Quizas mas tarde.*" The tall dark-haired girl at the back of the group winked and Oscar winked back, before turning to Dmitri, who was now getting the point of his brother's "beauty" ensemble.

"Later, yeah? You're on!" Oscar smiled at the girls, then turned to Dmitri. "You coming?" Oscar motioned to the sign on the kiosk wall—Ladies' Night Free Entrance Every Friday—and beckoned Dmitri through the club door, struggling with the band merchandise.

Dmitri smiled and sucked in his belly—he felt like a Mariachi again. He followed his brother inside Moody's nightclub and forgot for a moment about Vanivich and Wantham City.

Maybe playing some of their old music was what he needed.

CHAPTER 3

The crowd inside the club was jumping by the time Oscar introduced Timbrado's third song. Dmitri was actually starting to play some cool solo rifts, stepping up every now and then to join his brother at the front of the stage. The music was fine, and the mood was good. Dimitri was beginning to wonder why he ever quit the band for the pursuit of quick money in the first place. This was his true passion. Not flipping burgers in that shitty old *Geisenburger* food truck of his, down some grotty public park filled with junkies and skanky whores.

No, this was far more fun. With the promise of some action at the end of the night too, instead of picking up those old fifty-something drunk girls ordering up late-night Uber rides to take them back to their seedy motels.

The Dexi vape hit Dmitri had taken before they got on stage had loosened him up enough to be able to recall most of the old cover songs Oscar prompted him with. The ones he didn't know, he just played along with until he found the rhythm with the drums. Folks were too busy dancing to notice his mistakes.

"You want to take one?" Oscar asked, leaning back from the microphone as Ken played out the trumpet fade to the applause and cheers of the audience.

"Sure, what you thinking?" Dmitri shrugged.

Oscar held his cupped hands to his ears as the audience began chanting for the next song. People were shouting and clapping, the bar was cheering. Everyone was shouting out for their favourite cover song, and not one of them was participating in the social distancing measures the city had implemented.

"Mal Bicho… Mal Bicho!" they all chanted in unison. Oscar clapped, throwing his head back and laughing at the irony. "Mal Bicho… Mal…Bicho."

"Mal Bicho?" Oscar shouted back and the floor erupted.

"Mal Bicho!"

Oscar nodded. "Okay, bro. The stage is all yours." He bent down, picked up his beer, and turned as Ken shook the spit from his trumpet.

Dmitri smirked and shook his head. "Mal Bicho? For real, bro?" They both laughed.

"Mambo!" the crowd hollered.

Sergio raised his sticks and began the drum intro as Dmitri slung his Rickenbacker guitar around his back, grabbed the microphone from the stand, and took a deep breath.

"Mambo!" Dmitri shouted back with his hands in the air. The crowd cheered again, their bottles raised. The drums began the quickfire beat as Ken swayed from left to right, his trumpet blurting out the short sharp notes of the ska tune. Dmitri's gritty voice spat out the Latino rap lyrics like he had never left the ghetto.

"Vos que andas diciendo que hay mejores y peores..."

The crowd went wild, jumping up and down as Dmitri swaggered around the stage, bouncing and gesturing to the beat. The folk down at the front in the mosh pit body slammed, and frothy beer sloshed into the air, as the angry Latino rap beat pounded the walls. The cheap spot lights whirled around the stage, and lit up the faces of the audience as the trumpet tempo raised. Oscar joined in the onstage pogo routine as both he and Dmitri slung arms around each other's shoulders and belted out the chorus together.

In a booth at the back of the room, Vanivich sat

motionless upon the red leather seating, nestled between two young ladies as they swayed to the beat. He quietly watched the brothers as he sipped his black Russian cocktail and stroked the ladies' bare thighs. His nod was slight, hardly discernible, but his bodyguard, Boris, acknowledged it and left the booth.

Boris called over three other burly bouncers from the door and they quickly followed his whispered instructions."Clear the cellar."

The curtain was about to come down on the Timbrado reunion tour and there would be no reunion this time.

CHAPTER 4

"I'm going to ask you one more time." Vanivich stood in the dimly lit cellar with the bouncers blocking the doorway. "Who da fuck stole my merchandise?"

Dimitri watched the snarl of Vanivich's lips curl under his nose and realised he was in trouble. To his left, he heard Oscar wriggling and grunting against the binds holding him to the chair. On the floor, lying in a pool of his own blood, was Ken and his trumpet. Dmitri had watched on in horror earlier as each of Ken's fingers had been bent back until they'd popped and snapped like the legs of a Sunday roast chicken being pulled from their greasy sockets. There was no sign of Sergio—he had fled before the bouncer could lay a hand on him. What was left of the band was now on the run.

"I…I told you, Vani. The junkie kids jumped your man and stole what he had. I swear that's all I know."

Vanivich nodded, biting his bottom lip as he walked to the beer kegs at the far side of the room, processing the information. Oscar was gagged and bleeding from a deep gash on his forehead, but remained silent as his brother sweated on the seat next to him.

"You're telling me dat a skinny junkie bitch with blue hair, jumped my man, Igor, brained him, and ran off with her boyfriend into the night with my merchandise and my cash?"

"Yes, I swear on my life, Vani!" Dmitri begged, watching Boris crunch his knuckles as Vanivich nodded. He watched as the Russian picked up one of the Timbrado's CDs from the promo box and began reading the tracks to himself.

"This is your brother, no?" he asked, pointing at Oscar with the CD. "Oscar Timbrado. He's Italiano, no?" He waited for a reply. "You swear on this brother's life, too?"

Oh shit, now Dmitri was in trouble.

"What, no! He's Spanish, Vani."

"I don't care if he's a fucking Cossack! I said do you

swear on your brother's life, too?" He turned to Boris and clicked his fingers. Boris responded automatically, punching the singer in the face twice with his big meaty fist, one to the left, one to the right.

"Stop! Stop… My brother has fuck all to do with this. He's just a singer, Vani…he just sings!"

"Uh huh, and when he sings…" Vanivich looked down the list of cover songs on the CD like he was buying a Christmas gift for his wife. "When he sings…Mal Bicho? What does he mean?" He looked up.

Dmitri felt the colour drain from his face as the Russian boss stood waiting impatiently for an answer.

"I…I'm not sure. It doesn't mean anything… I guess. It's just a phrase for…a bad person."

"No more lies, Dmitri. You think I'm a Mal Bicho… You think I am a bad person, no?"

Dmitri said nothing.

Vanivich sighed, then dropped the CD to the floor, crunching the plastic sleeve under his Cuban heel. "Okay, Boris, make these two Spanish canaries sing. I don't have time for this nonsense. Find out where my money is. Fast!"

Boris smiled and began pounding his fist against Oscar's flopping face. Dmitri watched as broken teeth were spat onto the floor in bloody wads of mucus.

"You see, tonight, I received a call from Detective

Deeds who says you *do* know where my money is, Dmitri. So, you better start chirping like a good canary, or your brother here won't be able to whistle a tune, let alone karaoke his way through a set anymore." Vanivich knelt down beside Dmitri, kicked aside a crate of empty beer bottles, and grabbed Dmitri's greasy hair.

"Tell me now, or I burn dat food truck of yours to the ground, and pull every one of your teeth from your mouth with a set of rusty pliers and make a necklace for my wife with them."

"Where is my fuckin' money?"

Dmitri turned and watched the blood slowly trickle from Oscar's pulped face and down the binds that secured him to the chair. He realised that no matter what he said now, they weren't getting out of the cellar alive.

"Let him go, Vani, he's just a singer, man. Just let him go and I'll get you your money!"

Vanivich stood up, his eyes opening wide in anger as he picked up Dmitri's discarded guitar propped by the door.

"A very nice musical instrument indeed, Dmitri." He nodded impressed with the Rickenbacker guitar. "Do you know who else plays a guitar like this?" Vanivich plucked at the strings clumsily. Dmitri said nothing, accepting defeat.

"Any guesses?" Vanivich began swinging his hips left

and right, mimicking playing the guitar.

"I'll get you your money, Vani," Dmitri pleaded.

"Oh, you better. You better…" Vanivich mocked. "One guess. Go on…" He was now swaying and bending his knees to a silent beat.

"I…I don't know, man. I have no idea. Please, just let Oscar go." Dmitri sighed.

"No idea? Dat saddens me, Dmitri. Here's another clue. You ever heard of Pete Townsend?" Vanivich stopped swaying, grabbed the neck of the guitar with both hands, and swung the Rickenbacker high in the air like a baseball bat. He swung the resin base, bring it down heavily on Oscar's face. Oscar's head flew back with the impact on his nose, and the splinters of bone fragments driven deep into his skull. The guitar twanged as the neck snapped in two and fell to the floor. Vanivich spun around as Dmitri screamed out in shock.

"You tell me where my money is or you'll die down here with your music. Man!"

Boris leaned in and grabbed Dmitri by the hair, yanking his face up to his boss. "You listen to Mr Vanivich, or you die…fly!" Boris had him in a headlock, clenched tight underneath his chin, and was squeezing the life out of him, making Dmitri choke on the bodyguard's tattooed hairy forearm.

"Fuck you… I won't do what you tell me!" he choked, feeling his eyes bulge from their sockets.

But then Dmitri's song was over.

"It's…in the…van!" he quacked between his squeezed cheeks and crunching teeth as his corneas ruptured and bled out.

Vanivich smiled and walked from the cellar, satisfied. Soon he would have his merchandise back.

Dmitri couldn't move. He was paralysed by fear, caught like a fly in Boris's web. The more he struggled, the tighter his assailant's chokehold squeezed around his windpipe.

And as he struggled to gulp his last breath in the cellar of Moody's nightclub, surrounded by the toppled kegs, his nostrils filled with cigarette smoke and stale alcohol, mingled with the stench of bleach, Dmitri's final thought was this is it, this is the end.

Hello, darkness, my old friend.

Then he faded away.

GREGG CUNNINGHAM, 48, is a short story writer from Western Australia who has contributed to various genre anthology books published by 559 Publishing 13 Bites volume 3,4,5, Plan 559 from Outer space volume 2 and 3, Other Realms, Heard It on The Radio, 559 Ways to Die.

He has had several short stories publishing by Zombie Pirate Publishing in anthology books such as Relationship add Vice, Full Metal Horror, Phuket Tattoo, World War four and Flash Fiction Addiction, with their Grievous Bodily Harm thriller due later in the year.

He hopes to one day dust down and edit the huge manuscript under his bed and get it out to the Sci-Fi community.

Bibliography
ANGELS, Black Hare Press, 2019
BEYOND, Black Hare Press, 2019
Deep Space, Black Hare Press, 2019
MONSTERS, Black Hare Press, 2019
Storming Area 51, Black Hare Press, 2019
WORLDS, Black Hare Press, 2019

Connect
Twitter: @GGGcunningham
Website: cortlandsdogs.wordpress.com
Amazon: amazon.com/-/e/B016OTHX0K

TEENAGERS

by Stephen Herczeg

"A Strathfield grandmother was, today, arrested for shoplifting from a local grocery store" typed Jennifer. She stopped and read the sentence again. A sigh of exasperation left her lips.

Has it really come to this?

When she'd moved to the crime desk, two years previously, Jennifer dreamed that her reporting life would be thrills, spills, and criminals. The reality was far different. In between the interesting stories, there were nothing but boring petty crimes to report on. The more senior journalists received the juicy assignments. Jennifer still had to earn respect and precedence amongst them.

She stabbed at the save icon and sat back for a moment,

gathering her thoughts and working up enough enthusiasm to finish the article. Jennifer stared at the screen and failed to motivate herself, instead she switched across to her email.

Her eyes lit up when she found a new message in her inbox. She smiled as she read the sender's name.

"Superintendent C. Dupris, Australian Federal Police," it said.

Claire.

Jennifer's mind ran off several images of her and Claire in better times. Just reminding herself of Claire's face made her tingle inside.

Theirs had been a wild, tempestuous relationship, full of passion and excess, but had crumbled when Claire's career took priority. It was because of Claire that Jennifer had requested a move to the crime desk, but then Claire had broken Jennifer's heart. Her lover had been given a promotion within the ranks of the Australian Federal Police, but it had required a move from Sydney to Canberra. Only three hundred kilometres away, but within a few weeks, it may have well been three thousand. Their jobs kept them busy at the best of times but trying to keep a relationship going as well proved too difficult. The strain became evident from the outset, and once Claire found a new love in the nation's capital, their romance ended.

Jennifer shook her mind back to the content of the

email.

Hey Jennifer, check out these names, locations, and dates.

Ruby Dawes (15), Newcastle, 10th February;

Natalie Haskins (16), Gosford, 11th February;

Emily Veerkins (16), Enmore, 13th February;

Belinda Smith (15), Wollongong, 15th February.

Each girl disappeared. No trace at this stage. Too much of a coincidence for me.

I can't move on it until they've been gone for at least two weeks, and at this stage, it's only New South Wales. AFP won't do anything until it goes across borders.

Claire

Jennifer read the email again, trying to work out a pattern to the disappearances or any obvious reason to pursue it further.

Claire's not the sort to jump to conclusions.

To satisfy her curiosity, Jennifer brought up the New South Wales Police missing person's website. She entered the cities and spread the search across the entire set of dates. Several people popped up. She recognised the names from the email and realised that of those listed as missing; the girls were the only ones of that age. The others were mostly elderly people or men. She clicked on the entries for the four girls and downloaded the extra details, plus the photographs provided.

Do I go talk to the families? The local police?

Jennifer moved the mouse pointer around the screen while she gathered her thoughts. She unconsciously clicked on the tab for her social media account. It popped up and refreshed with a series of notifications and posts. Her eyes were drawn to the exploits of her friends and associates, and she scrolled down to live through their lives for a while.

A small window popped up on the right of her feed, and the screaming tones of a death metal band blasted out of her desk speakers. She dragged the pointer across to mute the sound, but only managed to expand the popup until it displayed across her entire desktop. Finally, she cut the music, hiding from the annoyed stares of her colleagues. Jennifer shrugged in apology to those around her, before her eyes rested back on her screen.

The popup was for Hard Road Tours, a local music promotion company, and advertised the tour of an international death metal band called Eve of Destruction, with a banner splashed across the video announcing their next show in Canberra on the 18th of February.

Saturday. I wonder if Claire wants to go. Could be worth a trip, for old time's sake.

The style of music wasn't really Jennifer's cup of tea, but thoughts of Claire made her wish things had turned out differently. Her eyes dropped to the bottom of the screen, then grew wide in shock.

What the—?

The previous tour dates were displayed in smaller writing beneath a video of the band in full flight. Jennifer read the dates, flicked back to the Claire's email, then back to the popup. Each date and location matched. The band had performed four dates in New South Wales finishing up with a final performance in Canberra in two days' time. Jennifer clicked on the video and began to watch as the five-piece band played one of their most famous songs "Teenagers."

Appropriate.

Jennifer's eyes were drawn to the lead singer known simply as Eve—a tall, statuesque woman, with a huge shock of blonde hair, teased up into a mohawk. She wore heavy makeup, but Jennifer felt she didn't need any. The photos showed a thin and athletic body, encased in black leather, but with curves in all the right places. A tingle ran through Jennifer as she imagined what the leather hid from view.

The band itself was something else entirely. Each member dressed similarly to Eve but wore thick rubber masks with all manner of protrusions. The drummer pounded away relentlessly behind a face full of metal tubes that extended in all directions.

She must be bathed in sweat in that getup.

The twin guitarists and bass player were the same. Pipes, tubes, spikes, all jutted out of their masks, making it impossible to even tell the shape of their heads. The musicians followed along with Eve, bouncing and writhing their way through the song.

As the video stopped, Jennifer brought up the band's website and read their biography. The bandmates were simply known by their aliases. Jennifer supposed it kept the continuity going, in case one of them left the group or, given the chaotic nature of the lives of musicians, left the world permanently.

Eve's story surprised Jennifer the most. Her biography had no date of birth listed, but said that the band formed at the height of the punk culture movement. Jennifer ran some calculations.

Even if she'd only been fifteen, she'd be almost sixty years old now.

She flipped back to the video and stared at the gorgeous creature in black.

No, way. I've got to find out her secret.

Jennifer closed down the popup advertisement and stared at the email again.

Emily Veerkins?

***

"This is what I've had to compete with," Emma Veerkins said.

Jennifer's eyes followed the forty-something woman's hand as she swept it around the room. Eve of Destruction posters peppered every wall. Most depicted the titular lead singer, her youthful appearance striking deep into Jennifer's mind given her knowledge of Eve's assumed age.

"The only thing she ever talked about was Eve this, Eve that," she said, "I don't even think Emily was gay, but she was fixated on that woman." Emma stood and stared at one of the posters that angled up Eve's legs for a few moments before continuing, "Though I sometimes do understand the appeal." She smiled at Jennifer and nudged her. "Hell, I'd turn for that woman."

Claire had sent a follow up email giving Emma's details to Jennifer. Claire wrote that she'd known Emma since high school, and from Jennifer's reading, almost implored her to take up the case. Leaving her heartbreak aside, Jennifer had no hesitation in tracking Emma down and making contact.

Jennifer found Emma a little standoffish to begin with, but once she mentioned her past with Claire and expressed a shared concern over Emily's whereabouts, the despondent mother opened up. Emma mentioned that the police had been useless so far, though she did admit Claire had acted differently to the regular Sydney cops. When Jennifer mentioned she would be writing up a piece for the daily paper and would be happy to mention the hairdressing salon that Emma worked for, the woman brightened and began to open up. Jennifer often found that everyone had their price.

"She went to the Enmore concert then?" Jennifer asked.

"Well, yeah, Emily had front row tickets, bought them within seconds of them appearing on the Hard Road Tours site," she said. "She went with a couple of girlfriends."

"She actually attended the concert?"

"Well, yes," said Emma, surprised at the question.

"Sorry, I just presumed she never made it," Jennifer said.

"Oh, no, she certainly made it," Emma said, pulling a phone out of her pocket. She gazed down at the screen for a moment and flicked through a series of social media posts, before showing Jennifer the screen. "She was pulled up on stage by Eve."

Jennifer watched a video probably taken on one of Emily's friends' phones. It showed the leather-clad lead singer holding out a hand and beckoning to Emily. A security guard helped Emily over the barrier and led her up to the stage. Eve and Emily then sang parts of the next song before a roadie led Emily off to the side and supposedly

backstage.

"Do you know where she went?"

Emma flipped to her messages. A short, one-sided conversation followed with a series of messages from Emily's phone. They stated that she met Eve and had a great time. The final message arrived at about one o'clock in the morning: "Heading home. See you soon."

A small tear formed at the corner of Emma's eye. Jennifer saw her resolve finally evaporate.

"That was the last thing I got from her. The police have been useless. They said she's a teenager and it's only been a few days. I just don't know. She's never done anything like this before."

Jennifer's heart went out to the woman; she gently placed an arm around her. Emma put her head on her shoulder and burst into tears. Jennifer placed her other hand on Emma's back and let her get it out of her system.

"I'm hoping I can dig up what's going on," she said in a soothing voice. Inside, thoughts of dead teenage girls ran riot across her mind.

***

Once they found out about Jennifer's job, the other parents acted the opposite to Emma. Two simply hung up;

the third suggested that Jennifer should go forth and multiply, though in not so many words.

Disappointed, Jennifer needed to find more evidence.

Phil won't be convinced by one girl's disappearance.

She considered what she knew so far.

Is it all just a coincidence? Are the girls off partying on their own somewhere? Is it something to do with the band? Is someone following the band around and preying on the girls?

Jennifer fired up her laptop and started searching social media posts for the other girls. Their individual feeds were all dormant, with nothing more than photos from their final moments at the concerts, though that gave Jennifer hope. Each one had actually attended the gigs.

She searched further and found several videos from the Eve of Destruction concerts. After viewing them, her mouth dropped open in shock. Played out before her, in several different angles on phone videos, she saw Emily called up by Eve, singing along then going backstage. Each of the three other girls had been in the front row of their respective concerts, and each had been invited up on stage to sing with Eve before disappearing off to the side, supposedly to the backstage area.

Eve is possibly the last person to have seen each girl.

Jennifer viewed each girls' friends list and cross-checked their personal feeds. She considered it a long shot but left personal messages for several of them in the hope they'd respond. Finally, she took a deep breath, stared at her own feed for a moment, and thought about her next steps.

A message popped up. She quickly clicked on the link. Verity, one of Natalie's friends, had written back.

"Last saw Natalie on stage at Eve show. Got a text an hour later. Since then, nothing. Never done anything like that before. Am scared for her."

Jennifer wrote back: "Thx. Do you have her number? I can try to track her phone."

Verity wrote back with a mobile phone number straight away. Jennifer sent her a polite thank you.

She brought up the *Find my phone* website and typed in the number. It scanned across the country and finally zeroed in on an area just south of Gosford. The date of the last access said 1:30 AM, 12th February. Verity had said Natalie sent a message around 1:00 AM.

Damn, similar to Emily's phone. There's something in all of these.

Jennifer wanted to go to write it up, then go to the police, but with no bodies and no solid evidence, they would treat it like any other missing persons case. Claire knew something, or was at least worried, either because of her friendship with Emma or the frustration that more wasn't being done.

I need to go to the Canberra concert.

***

"Are you sure there's something here?" asked Phil Smart, the crime editor and Jennifer's boss. "Teenagers. They just go missing all the time. They turn up usually when their money runs out, or they get beaten up by their boyfriend or girlfriend. That's why the cops don't care. No body. No case."

"Each one went to an Eve of Destruction concert in a different city. Each one disappeared. I've got two who then sent text messages an hour later, only to have their phones turn up abandoned nearby."

"My teenage daughter loses her phone all the time, drives me nuts."

"Yes, but each one of these girls was last seen in the same place, on stage after being brought up by the lead singer. Each one was in the front row. Each one was picked by Eve, then headed backstage. Only to disappear."

"I still say coincidence. It's only four."

"Four out of four."

"Any others?"

"No, they started in New South Wales; they'll be in Canberra on Saturday, then Victoria next week."

"I'm assuming you want to go to Canberra. Wouldn't have anything to do with a particular policewoman?" Phil knew all about Jennifer's relationship with Claire.

"Claire was the one who put me onto this. I'd like to meet up and discuss my findings; she might even have more info by now."

Phil smiled. "Right."

"What? Claire knew one of the mothers, that's why she reached out. She couldn't do anything from Canberra, and the local cops are treating this as a simple set of missing persons."

Phil crossed his arms, leaned back on his desk and looked at Jennifer with a fatherly level of scepticism. Eventually he shrugged. "Okay, I'll organise tickets. I assume you'll need two?"

Jennifer nodded.

Phil stood up and pointed at her. "But you drive down to Canberra. You can expense the miles, but I'm not flying you there. And get the entertainment reporters to set up an interview or something."

Jennifer smiled. "I'm happy with that."

***

Jennifer stood amongst the sweaty crowd of black-clad teenagers and twenty somethings, anxiously waiting for the headline act to grace the stage. She looked around the room. A typical Canberra club, tiny by Sydney standards, but with an eager crowd that dragged her expectations higher with their enthusiasm.

A figure pushed into her. Jennifer turned and looked into the expecting eyes of her ex-lover and smiled.

The vision of Claire, a messy spectre of a woman, wrapped in a towel and drying her hair with another, as she opened her front door the previous evening still circulated around Jennifer's head.

To answer Claire's question of "What the hell you doing here?", Jennifer had simply held up two concert tickets and replied, "What are you doing tomorrow night?"

Claire's apartment had room for one more, as did Claire's bedroom, so they spent the intervening time catching up. Some of it discussing the missing girls, most engaging in other things. Claire handed Jennifer a drink and they toasted the moment, lost in their own circle while the maelstrom of sweaty bodies revolved around them.

As the lights dimmed, they quickly downed their drinks and, failing to find somewhere close by to place the cups, simply dropped them to the floor to join the growing pile of discarded plastic.

Jennifer turned and grabbed hold of the barrier. She and Claire were at the very front of the audience with the best view in the house, a benefit that her press pass accorded her.

Four figures shuffled onto the stage, taking up positions around the central microphone stand. Single spotlights blazed on each one. The lead guitarist moved, and the room split open with power chords. Drums pounded a driving beat. The bass joined in, pulsating in time.

Finally, the blonde-haired figure, clad in black leather and studs, strolled onto the stage and stood before the mike stand. As her hand reached out, the lights blared, and the show was on.

The band executed the deep, thrumming rhythm and screeching guitars riffs of a dozen songs, with Eve strutting around, growling, screaming, and playing with the emotions of the rapt audience.

Jennifer's attention stayed on the lead singer, watching her every move and formulating the questions she would ask this incredibly powerful woman when they meet after the show.

Suddenly, the lights dropped, and silence descended on the room. A dozen fans sighed in horror, expecting the show to finish; the disappointment turned to cheers when the familiar bass line of Eve's biggest song, "Teenagers," thundered across the crowd.

The lights blazed again as the guitars and drums joined in. Eve prowled the front of stage, searching for the lucky one that would be coaxed into joining her on stage. Her eyes met Jennifer's. A faint trace of recognition floated between them. Jennifer assumed that Eve had researched her in preparation for their interview. Then Eve pointed, but not at Jennifer, at the figure beside her: Claire.

The policewoman fell into the moment. A joyous grin spread across her face as security helped her over the barrier and led her up to the stage. Eve hugged Claire, then hand in hand brought her to the microphone where the two of them belted out the rest of the song. Jennifer cringed on a few of Claire's missed notes, but rode along with the audience until the song concluded. At the end, Claire disappeared behind the rear curtain and the lights dropped to full black. A cheer went up from the crowd, complete with chanting for another song. When finally, the house lights came on, signalling the end of the performance; a collective sigh ran through the audience and they began the difficult act of leaving.

Jennifer pushed her way through the crowd and stepped up to the burly bouncer guarding the flimsy black curtains that protected the venue's green room where the bands would chill out before and after their gigs. She pulled out her press pass and showed it to him.

"I'm Jennifer Danes, from the Sydney Mail. I have an interview scheduled with Eve," she said.

The bouncer looked down at the pass and read her name; he tapped his ear, spoke, then listened for a moment. He focused back on Jennifer and handed back her press pass. After a quick look to make sure no one would try to shadow her through, he finally drew back the curtain.

Jennifer stepped through into another crush of bodies. A sea of sweaty, black-clad people stood about talking to each other at an audible tone, rather than fighting to drown out the thumping death metal previously heard. She saw the tall, imposing figure of Eve talking to several people and pushed her way through the crowd towards her. As Jennifer approached, a tall, black bodyguard stepped in front of her. She pulled her press pass and thrust it up towards his face, stating her name and intention. He peered at the pass, then back at Jennifer before stepping aside and leading her towards Eve.

The bodyguard sidled up to Eve, leaned in, and spoke. Eve eyed Jennifer and smiled. She held out a hand to introduce herself, then suggested they speak somewhere quieter. The proposal took Jennifer completely by surprise; she hadn't expected a formal interview, rather a roughly put-together chat that fought for dominance over a background of noise.

As Eve led her by the hand towards a door at the rear of the room, she caught a glimpse of Claire, sitting with the other members of Eve's band. All five looked out of it. Before Jennifer could catch Claire's attention, they reached the door.

Inside, the area had been set up as a private sanctum especially for Eve. She sat on the edge of a low couch and unlaced her knee-high leather boots.

"So, what is it that the Sydney Mail wants to know about me?" she said, patting the couch. Jennifer sat down and pulled out her phone. She started the voice recorder and placed it on a nearby coffee table.

"The public doesn't know much about you. You were on the punk scene in the late seventies, but before that nothing. I'd like to delve into your past."

Eve smiled and fixed Jennifer with her deep-coloured eyes. The reporter's mind wandered and sank into those eyes.

"My life is a long story, one that has stretched across the ages of time," Eve said, reaching forward and tracing a finger along Jennifer's jawline. She shivered with the touch. An ice-cold blast ran through her system. "But that is not the real reason you are here, is it, Miss Reporter? I believe you are seeking someone, or someones to be more

correct. Four missing teenage girls. Am I correct?"

Jennifer's face dropped in shock.

"How?"

Eve smiled and leaned in closer, her breath mingling with Jennifer's own. "I have my ways," she said just as the door opened and the four band members, leading a dazed Claire, entered the room and sat around the coffee table.

Eve drew back slightly and clicked her fingers. The four band members reached up and slid the rubber masks from their heads. The sweaty and red faces of the four missing teenagers were revealed.

Jennifer stood in shock. Her eyes darted to each of the girls in turn, settling on Emily's face. Finally, Jennifer took in the changes the girls had undergone. They were older, years older. Behind the sweat and exhaustion, each appeared to be well into their fifties. Deep lines ran across their brows, under their eyes, and down their cheeks. Their skin sagged as gravity took hold.

A breath on the back of Jennifer's neck snapped her attention back.

"These teenage girls. So full of life. Life that I have more need of than them."

Jennifer tried to move, but her feet felt welded to the floor, resisting her commands.

Eve stepped around Jennifer and leaned in close again.

She inhaled Jennifer's breath and threw her head back in delight.

"Oh, you are so full of life. I long to taste you deeper."

She stepped behind Natalie and bent down towards the girl. She peered up at Eve with glazed eyes and a loving grin. Jennifer gasped as Eve opened her mouth, revealing a pair of long fangs. The singer bent down, nuzzled the girl's neck, then gently stabbed the points deep into her throat.

After a few moments, Eve stood up. Blood dripped from her fangs and ran down the front of her shirt. The lines deepened on Natalie's face. To Jennifer, she now looked well into her nineties. Jennifer tried to cry out as the girl's eyes rolled back into her head and her body caved in on itself.

"Their life essence is all too fleeting." Eve smiled at the crumbled body, then peered at the blood running down her shirt. She slowly undid the buttons and let it slide down her arms to the ground.

Jennifer stared at Eve's chest. The full breasts she expected to see were slowly shrinking, sinking into a series of wide banded segments, like the underbelly of a snake that ran down her entire body.

Eve stepped out of her trousers. Her long, luscious legs began to change, merging and joining together, almost immediately, until they became a single, powerful tail. The reporter's eyes were drawn towards the woman's head. Gone was the blonde hair. Instead, a giant snake's head rested atop a long and slender scaled body. It stared at Jennifer and smiled.

"You wanted to know my past? I am the Eve of legend. The early chroniclers had it wrong. The serpent didn't tempt me. I was and I still am that serpent. I took Abel, the child of Lilith and Adam, for my own; his blood kept me young. And it still does, but I need a constant supply of young bodies full of the youthfulness of teenagers." The snake's smile stretched across its entire face. The tongue flicked out, testing the air, tasting the new life on offer. "That is why I chose this life. There is always another city. There are always more young ones to consume."

The snake slithered across to Jennifer, curled around her until their mouths almost touched again. Jennifer tried to pull away in disgust, but her body would not obey.

"We have a problem. There are those that wish to find me. I cannot let that happen. Anybody that discovers my secret must be eliminated, or better yet, join with me. You will join me. Forever." It was not a suggestion.

The snake's mouth opened wide. The blood-flecked fangs stood inches away from the reporter's eyes.

Jennifer tried to scream, but her mouth was no longer her own.

BLACK HARE PRESS

STEPHEN HERCZEG is an IT Geek, writer, actor, film maker and Taekwondo Black Belt based in Canberra Australia. He has been writing for over twenty years and has completed a couple of dodgy novels, sixteen screenplays and dozens of short stories and scripts. He has had over fifty short stories and seventy drabbles accepted for publication.

Bibliography
Sproutlings, Hunter Anthologies
Hells Bells, Australasian Horror Writers Association
Anemone Enemy; Petrified Punks and The Body Horror book, Oscillate Wildly Press
Below the Stairs; Behind the Mask; Beyond the Infinite; Beside the Seaside; Tricksters Treats #1, #2 & #3; Shades of Santa; Guilty Pleasures and other Dark Delights, Things In the Well
Beginnings; Journeys; Capricorn; Aquarius; Pisces; Aries; Taurus; Gemini, Dead Set Press
Sea of Secrets; Coffins and Dragons; Organic Ink Vol 2, Dragon Soul Press
Demonic Carnival, Battle Goddess Productions
Deep Space; What If?; Eerie Christmas; Pride; Lust; Jibbernocky; Bad Romance; Storming Area 51; Worlds; Angels; Monsters; Beyond; Unravel; Apocalypse; Hate; Love; Oceans; Year One, Black Hare Press
Curses and Cauldrons; Forest of Fear, Blood Song Books
Sherlock Holmes through Belanger Books and MX Publishing:
In the Realms of H.G. Wells; Beyond the Canon; In the Realms of Steampunk; The Early Adventures; The Great Detectives; The MX Book of New Stories - Vol XI; XIV; XVII, XIX and XX; The new adventures of Solar Pons; The Necronomicon of Solar Pons; A Tribute to H.G. Wells.

Connect
Amazon: amazon.com/-/e/B07916SQQS
Goodreads: goodreads.com/author/show/17100782.Stephen_Herczeg
Facebook: @StephenHerczegAuthor

by Stacey Jaine McIntosh

I stand before the microphone, blinking into the spotlight, momentarily blinded by the light. With my glamour up, all evidence of the executioner's work has vanished. The remains of my wings and bloodied t-shirt? All but washed away—made invisible to the humans, and the rare few faeries that frequent the nightclub, those who can't see through glamour.

To the casual observer, it seems as if nothing is amiss. *Except something is.*

The Winter Queen is out for blood. *My blood.* And I'm not altogether sure why.

Once I finish this last set, however, I plan on finding out.

And then I will make the executioner pay…

A plan takes root even while I push all thought of payment, and revenge, from my mind, to focus on the music. The nightclub, although not at capacity, is brimming. The smoke machine simply adds an ethereal quality to our surroundings.

A stale undercurrent of sweat lingers in the air as the humans dance, swaying to the music, unknowingly captivated by the faerie magick that swirls about unseen by those it would affect. Each human caught in the sticky web of our magick reacts differently, as each faerie's magick has a different signature.

Music is a powerful tool when used correctly, and while I am certainly no siren, the magick I possess is such that I can easily be mistaken for one.

I am a mimic. Gifted with the ability to mimic the talents of others, but with no real talent of my own. The art of song has served me well so far, until today. The talent I have is not meant to harm anyone, nor bring harm to me, and yet it has. Which means I have only one choice. It is time to give it up and find a new talent. I only hope Atticus and Wesley are able to forgive me for breaking up the band.

When the final strand of guitar music fades, and the spotlight dims to the point that it is no longer blinding, I move away from the microphone.

"Great set, eh?" Atticus asks.

I half-smile. "I suppose."

"It's not like you to be so glum, Frey. What's wrong?"

"I need to…"

Leave.

But the word sticks like glue in my mouth. It feels like betrayal. I can't do it, and in the end, I don't need to. Wesley has me figured out before I can even spit the final word out, anyway.

"You're leaving the band, aren't you?" he asks.

"Yeah," I say, thinking of the Queen's executioner, Tiernan, as I speak. "There's something I need to take care of."

"Would you consider coming back?" Atticus asks.

There is hurt in his voice. I understand why. For a band that does pokey little bars and shady nightclubs in the worst parts of Ireland, we are well received nonetheless and get paid pretty decently, too. Not that I want for money. But it isn't that straightforward for the guys. With me gone, they'd have to find a replacement lead singer or find other means of employment.

"I don't know." It is as honest an answer as I can give right now.

A frown creeps over his face. "It won't be the same without you."

Tears well in my eyes despite my not wanting to get emotional.

"I know," I say. "I'm sorry."

"Don't be, Frey," Wesley says. "It's not like it's goodbye. We'll see each other again. I'd put money on it."

I nod. "Sure, we will."

But I am not convinced we will. The Winter Queen has a temper, and for all I know, sending the executioner to sever my wings was just a preview of the main event…one which may culminate in my death.

"I'll help you get the gear packed up and into the van."

"Now you're just prolonging the inevitable. Go," Atticus says, "with our blessing. Before we change our minds and force you to stay."

I shiver at the thought. Not that I don't love them both dearly, but I am a liability to them if I stay.

"Alright already," I say. "Consider me gone."

And with those final words, I walk out of the club and don't look back.

***

I find two old and gnarled yew trees in the local cemetery; their branches entwined like lovers to form a natural archway. It is this archway that signals the entrance—one of many—into Faerie. Stepping across the threshold, I feel suddenly trepidatious. I have no idea what I am walking into, and it has been years since I last set foot in Faerie.

When my feet touch down on the other side, I don't expect to be greeted by Grimalkin. *Is the Winter Queen anticipating my moves before I have even made them?* I am only marginally surprised. She has a gift for this sort of thing, and Grim is a favourite of hers.

"I did hope Tiernan's work would lure you back." The cait sith's tone is sardonic with something of an icy edge to it.

"What is it I'm accused of?" I ask.

"You did the crime so you ought to know."

"I haven't set foot in Faerie since I ran from here, having been made a laughingstock in front of the entire Court, when I failed to exhibit a talent of my own. You were there. The Queen said herself that mimics are of no use at Court. So, I left before she could exile me…or worse, kill me."

"So, you didn't steal the Queen's favourite horse?" Grim asks. "Witnesses report a girl who looked remarkably like you riding off into the forest on Limerick."

I wince, remembering the pain of Tiernan's knife as it sliced off my wings.

All this for a horse?

"No!"

"Well, if it wasn't you, then who was it?"

"You say witnesses saw a girl that looked like me?" I ask.

"Yes."

"Then it has to be Isley," I state. "She was always getting me in trouble with our parents when we were children. I guess age hasn't mellowed her."

"Your sister?"

I nod. "My *twin* sister. Find Isley and I guarantee you'll find the Queen's prized mare."

"The Queen's Guard have combed the woods and haven't seen hide nor hair of her. Any chance you might know where to look next?"

"Before I say 'yes', what's going to happen to her once she's in the Queen's custody?"

"She'll be punished." Grim's eyes drift to my torn and bloodied shirt. "In the same manner as you were, and then she'll be housed with all the other miscreants."

"So, she'll lose her wings then?"

"The Queen doesn't suffer criminals," Grim says.

"Shame she's an act-first-ask-questions-later kind of Queen. There's no magick throughout all of Faerie that can restore my wings to me."

"No," Grim agrees. "But not all fae possess wings, as not all fae possess magick."

I frown. "No, but at least what I lack in magick I could make up for by having wings. Now—without either—I'm no better than a human."

"Mimics aren't without power. I thought you would have learnt that by now."

"The Queen doesn't think so," I mutter.

"The Queen does not speak for all of Faerie, Ferelith," Grim says, turning on his heels. "Now, come! Were you to find your sister and the Queen's prized mare, I suspect the Queen might favour you with a position at Court should you desire it."

I sigh, downhearted. Isley has once again cost me something precious I have no means of ever recovering.

"Cheer up, Frey."

I look up. If I didn't know better, I'd almost say that voice belongs to Atticus.

I blink in disbelief at what I am seeing. Atticus stands before me, dressed in jeans and a black t-shirt. A guitar slung over one shoulder, his knapsack over the other. Despite being our band's drummer, he's dabbled a little in guitar and is getting pretty good at it. Wesley stands next to him, a guitar also slung over one shoulder.

"We know who stole the Winter Queen's horse,"

Atticus says.

"You do?" I exclaim. "How? And how are you—both of you—here? Only fae, or humans that know the way, get into Faerie."

Atticus laughs and Wesley joins him. Their human guises fade before my eyes.

"You're—"

"—fae?" Atticus asks, mischief shining in his blue eyes. He suddenly looks younger than his thirty mortal years. "Yes, though only on my mother's side. Swore I'd never set foot in Faerie again, but when you said you were leaving, it didn't seem right letting you go off alone, so we followed you."

I smile, warmth emanating from my chest. "That answers one of my questions, but not the other."

"My sister, Scarlett, is the former Summer Queen. Her daughter, Mercedes, now sits on the Summer throne. It is through them that I heard that the Winter Queen's horse was missing. The horse and rider were last seen in Herne's Grove."

"Any chance the Wild Hunt won't be passing through?"

"Knowing Herne, it's unlikely."

"We best be off then, before your sister decides to move on."

"So, Frey, why did you choose to leave all this behind?" Wesley asks.

"Being fae isn't all it's cracked up to be," I answer.

"I'll take your word for it."

***

Darkness replaces daylight by the time we hit the edge of the forest that surrounds the area known as Herne's Grove.

The trees rustle in the wind that has been non-existent up until now, and from a tree branch above me, an owl hoots. I shriek in surprise.

"Next you'll be jumping at the sight of your own shadow," Atticus chuckles.

"Can't say I'm a fan of this place," I mutter. I have never had the honour of seeing the Wild Hunt up close before, despite all my years in Faerie, and yet—truth be told—I hope to avoid it this time around…but it isn't to be."

"Watch your step. The Wild Hunt isn't always as it appears," Grim says.

In the darkness, all that I can see of him is the yellow glow of his eyes, giving him a distinct, otherworldly quality.

From out of his knapsack, Atticus passes both Wes and

I a flashlight. I take it, grateful for his forethought, and switch it on. The beam of artificial light illuminates the path in front of me. The tall oak trees cast shadows that make me think of long, skinny fingers; fingers that might snatch me up and carry me away some place far worse than the forest we were currently standing in.

I shiver at the thought of the trees coming to life and walking off with me. Many a rumour circulates about this forest. Some say it is haunted by the souls of the dead that Arawn himself has harvested. Others say the trees have voices and speak of things unknown to even Herne himself.

I have never bought into the rumours before today. I've never had reason to believe any of it is true, but the rustling of leaves does almost sound like whispers, which makes me wonder if there is some truth to it after all.

"Frey! Watch out!"

The thunderous sound of horses' hooves advances towards me at an alarming rate. I'm going to be trampled— I realise in horror until a hand grips the yoke of my shirt and tugs me out of the way.

I scream, half falling, half stumbling, bumping into something hard, but soft. Atticus grips my wrist tightly, as if he thinks I will go and step back into harm's way.

"You should be more careful," he says, blue eyes boring into mine. "I might not be around to save you next time.”

"Yeah," I whisper. With a shaky breath, I straighten. "Sorry." Embarrassment stains my cheeks a shade of red, but Atticus still holds my wrist and it doesn't appear that he has any intention of letting go. I glance up and find his face inches from mine, his eyes shining brightly in the darkness. "You can let go now," I murmur.

His lips curl up into a semblance of a smile. "I think it'd be better if you stay close."

Footsteps sound, growing closer, and Atticus moves away, dropping my wrist suddenly. He crosses his arms, leaning against a nearby tree trunk as Wesley appears. Grimalkin circles in between my legs in typical cat fashion. I take a deep fortifying breath and hope my burning face is lost to the shadows that surround us. Wes shoots Atticus a suspicious glance, before focusing his all too intense gaze on me. An impish grin splits his serious demeanour.

"Are you all right, Frey?" he asks. "We heard what sounded like horses, followed by a scream."

"I'm fine," I tell him, rolling my eyes. "We should keep going."

"Agreed," Atticus says. "We've wasted enough time as it is."

***

Walking along a leaf-strewn path, I find myself reminiscing back to when my sister and I were young. We'd often play in this forest as children, never venturing too far in case we were to get lost. It had been summer then, and wildflowers were sprinkled every which way. There are no wildflowers now, but I spot several white moonflowers on display.

Atticus and Wesley don't say a word to each other as we continue on our way, which is probably a good thing considering I am not sure what to say to either of them.

From time to time, Grimalkin vanishes, bounding off into the trees, only to reappear with no explanation of where he has been. I'd have thought it strange, had he not been a cat—albeit a faerie cat.

"We're being watched," Grimalkin says, jumping down out of the trees. "You might want to pick up the pace a little."

"Watched?" I ask, spinning in a circle. "Watched by who?"

"Could be one of Herne's people, or it could be one of the Queen's," Grimalkin replies. "Do you really want to stick around to find out? The Queen thinks you stole her horse—not your sister—you. There's no wonder she's got people out searching."

"Stop!" a deep voice shouts. "On order of the Queen

of the Winter Court, I command you!"

"Told you," Grimalkin murmurs before disappearing up into the trees.

"Grim!" I hiss.

"I think we're on our own, Frey," Atticus says. "Just my luck to run into one of the Winter Queen's henchmen without anything to use as a weapon."

"What do you mean you don't have a weapon?" Wesley asks, dodging the intruding faerie's blows. "What about your drumsticks?"

"What good are…ooh!"

"Might be a good time for you to run, don't you think?" Grimalkin suggests from the treetops.

Running means leaving the band behind, and I am not sure if I can do that. I look behind me and watch as Atticus stabs the Queen's henchman in the eye, while Wesley strangles him with a guitar string. They seem to have it all under control, so I run, only to run headlong into something. I look up into the eyes of a stranger and scream.

"Where's the Queen's horse, thief?"

I shake my head, trembling like a leaf.

"You know what they do to people who steal, don't you?"

I shake my head again.

"Well you're about to find out," he says smiling

ruefully. "Tiernan!"

The executioner appears, and I feel my eyes grow wide with terror. He carries a wooden block, and a silver blade is sheathed at his side. Before I can resist, iron cuffs encircle my wrists with a resounding click, and I am forced onto my knees; my arms made to rest across the block.

"Don't worry, love. He'll only take one," says the stranger.

I scream as Tiernan raises the blade above my head and brings it down upon my left wrist, severing it from my arm, somehow missing my right hand completely. Blood rushes from the open wound, the pain registers in seconds, and I let out a piercing wail of anguish.

"My job here is done," I think I hear Tiernan say, before I fall to the ground and there is nothing but darkness.

***

Regaining consciousness, I find that I am lying on a cot near a small fire; a thick bandage wrapped around the stump of my left arm.

Atticus has a chair pulled close and is holding my good hand in his own, the pad of his thumb making small idle circles over my skin.

"Easy," Atticus says softly. "You lost a fair amount of

blood. You might be dizzy for a while."

"Where's Isley?"

"Your sister?" Atticus asks.

I nod.

"Herne's out looking for her now. If he finds her, he'll hand him over to Tiernan himself."

"No! I want to be the one to do it," I say, swallowing hard. "I want to be there when her head is set upon the butcher's block, and his blade cleaves her head from her shoulders!"

"That paints a very vivid picture, Frey," Atticus says. "Are you sure that's the path you want to take? There's no going back if you do."

"I'm sure," I say—resolute. "It's because of her that I've lost my wings and my hand. It's only fair that she pay with her life!"

"Then I guess tonight is your lucky night," says an unfamiliar male voice.

Standing just a few feet away is Isley. She wears cuffs similar to the ones I've been subjected to twice already. A faerie with dirty blonde hair, and wearing nothing more than brown leather pants, grips her tightly by one elbow.

"I've sent for Tiernan. He'll return shortly," he says. "You must be Ferelith. I'm Herne. I can see why the two of you caused such a fuss. You really are identical, aren't you?"

"You'll regret this," Isley shrieks, tears running down both cheeks. "You won't be able to live with yourself!"

"Oh, I think I'll live with myself just fine, Iz," I retort.

"I am crippled because of you!"

"There's nothing worse than a drawn-out execution," Tiernan interrupts, appearing suddenly. "If you don't mind?"

"You'll pay for this," Isley hisses at me as Herne pushes her to her knees and forces her head down upon the block.

"I already have."

The blade swings up towards the sky and then down, tearing through the flesh and muscle that holds my sister's head to her shoulders. When it is done, her head falls with a soft *thud* from the block to the ground below.

"The horse?" Tiernan inquires.

"In the stable with the others," Herne answers.

"I'll retrieve the animal and be off then."

I watch as he wipes my sister's blood from the blade on a white cloth before sheathing it once again.

"What's to be done with her?" I ask.

"We'll burn her remains," Herne replies. "Don't worry, she won't be left to rot."

"That's not why I ask," I reply as I am hit by an

unexpected pang of guilt. My sister is dead, and I was the one who gave the order. It takes all I have to remind myself of all that she has cost me. First my wings, then my hand, and now, my own sister. All this trouble for the Winter Queen's horse? What was she was thinking? What was she getting out of it? I cannot fathom her reasoning, and now she is gone… and as I stand here, painted in her blood, I realise that I will never know.

There's nothing left to do but search Faerie for Atticus and Wesley—and reunite the band. Justice has been done.

STACEY JAINE MCINTOSH writes Celtic, medieval, gothic and fairytale inspired dark fantasy and paranormal romance with heavy doses of fey and other pagan influences littered throughout. She lives in Perth, Western Australia with her husband, their four children and two cats. Although her first love has always been writing, she once toyed with being a Cartographer and subsequently holds a Diploma in Spatial Information Services.

She is the author of Morrighan, Le Fay and the third and final instalment of the Camelot Series, Pendragon. She has also self-published one novella, Solstice, as well as a collection of short stories entitled Lost. A second collection is in the works.

Her shorter works and poetry can be found through Iron Faerie Publishing, Black Hare Press, Blood Song Books and Fantasia Divinity.

When not with her family or writing she enjoys reading, genealogy, history and witchcraft.

Bibliography
A Rueful Equinox, Falling for Shifters, 2020
Charmed, Winter Tails, 2021
In My Blood, Midsummer Night Shifters, 2020
Stolen, Of Fables and Fae, 2020

Connect
Website: staceyjainemcintosh.com
Twitter: @StaceyJMcIntosh
Instagram: @morrighanfae
Facebook: @StaceyJaineMcIntosh

ACKNOWLEDGEMENTS

When we embarked on our Black Hare Press journey back in late 2018, we never envisioned the huge support we'd get from the writing community. We have been truly humbled by the number of submissions we've received (around 3,000 over our first eight publications!) and have loved reading every single one.

So, thank you to everyone who crafted tales just for us—from the tiny tales in our Dark Drabbles series to these rock star infused tales of horror you have read here in Banned—we thank you from the bottom of our hearts.

To our families and friends, collaborators, random strangers who took pity on us, and everyone who has helped us on the way: we couldn't have done it without you.

And to you, our discerning reader, we and these talented writers did it all for you. We hope you enjoyed these tales, and if you did, don't forget to leave a review.

Thank you all—see you next time.

Love & kisses
Ben & Dean

www.blackharepress.com

BANNED PUBLICATIONS

466

BANNED

BANNED

BANNED

BANNED

BANNED

BANNED